CURSE
OF THE
GODS

BLURB

After the death of my boyfriend, I left my family's motorcycle club behind, choosing to save lives instead of take them.

Seven years later, my brother orders me to infiltrate our rival club and avenge our father's death. I'm the only one who can get close without being recognized.

Destroying my enemies from within won't be the hard part. Hiding my identity will be. And it won't be long until the Jackals discover my secret, and I end up like my dad.

Once I'm in their club, I discover the Jackals and I are bound as fucking fated mates. I'd rather die than lie with a Jackal.

Hearts won't be the only thing I'm breaking when my enemies declare me theirs... if I live long enough to extinguish my enemy.

Curse of the Gods is book 1 in the Jackals Wrath MC series (Operation Isis) featuring a stubborn, yet strong heroine and four badass, haunted bikers. If you love shifters, Egyptian mythology, urban fantasy and romantic suspense, this is the series for you! This book contains dark elements with trigger warnings, suitable for 18+ readers. BEWARE it has daddy kink and gun sex.

Curse of the Gods (Operation Isis #1) © Copyright 2021 Skyler Andra.
Cover art by Dark Imaginarium Art & Design.
Chapter vector art by Eerilyfair Design.

All rights reserved under the International and Pan-American Copyright Conventions. No part of this book may be reproduced or transmitted in any form or by any means, electronic or mechanical, including photocopying, recording, or by any information storage and retrieval system, without permission in writing from the publisher/author.

This is a work of fiction. Names, places, characters and incidents are either the product of the author's imagination or are used fictitiously, and any resemblance to any actual persons, living or dead, organizations, events or locales is entirely coincidental.

Warning: the unauthorized reproduction or distribution of this copyrighted work is illegal. Criminal copyright infringement, including infringement without monetary gain, is investigated by the FBI and is punishable by up to 5 years in prison and a fine of $250,000.

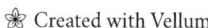 Created with Vellum

OPERATION SERIES UNIVERSE

Welcome to my "Operation" series, featuring a world of godly avatars. **What's an avatar?** They're humans embodied with the power and characteristics of their patron god i.e. Ares is a hot-head ex army soldier, Hermes is a slippery and fun ex-thief, Eros is a former Phone Sex Worker who runs from love, Hades is lonely, cold and hard until he meets Persephone in the bubbly and warm Autumn. So if you're expecting a re-telling of the gods' story, then this isn't for you. This is my unique spin on the mythology.

OPERATION CUPID (completed reverse harem mythology romance)

1. Battlefield Love
2. Quicksilver Love
3. Awakened Love
3.5 Stupid Cupid - a Valentine's short story

OPERATION HADES (completed fated mates romance):

1. Lady of the Underworld
2. Lord of the Underworld
3. Rulers of the Underworld
4. Return to the Underworld

OPERATION ISIS - Jackal's Wrath MC (reverse harem paranormal motorcycle club romance with shifter gods)

0.5 Prophecy of the Gods - prequel exclusive to newsletter subscribers
1. Curse of the Gods
2. Captive of the Gods
3. Legacy of the Gods - coming 2022

BLOOD DEBT MAFIA (Operation Anubis) (paranormal mafia arranged marriage romance)

1. Married to the Mafia - coming 2022

REFERENCES

Below is a list of names used throughout this series.

Aaliyah Heller - Avatar of Isis.

Alaric Hawke - Jackal's Wrath MC Road Captain & Avatar of Horus.

Avatar - a human embodied with the power and characteristics of their patron god i.e. Set is the devil of the Egyptian pantheon and his avatar Slade is made of sin.

Bagman - a person who receives payoffs.

Castor Redding - Jackal's Wrath MC Enforcer & Avatar of Thoth.

Church - Official MC meeting.

Cut - MC member's vest.

REFERENCES

Horus - hawk-headed god of the Sky. God to Alaric.

Isis - Goddess of Healing, Fertility and Magic and consort to Osiris (wife). Goddess to Aaliyah.

Little snack - pay off or bribe.

Osiris - God of the Underworld and consort (husband) of Isis. Zethan's God.

Patch - Club logo emblem worn on an MC cut.

Pharaoh - drug made exclusively by Jackals' Wrath MC.

Set - Jackal-headed god of Chaos, Destruction, the Dessert. Slade's God.

Slade Vincent - Jackal's Wrath Vice President & Avatar of of Set.

Stunt man - fall guy set up to pin petty crime on to divert police attention when conveying a shipment.

Thoth - Ibis-headed god of Writing, Science & Magic. Castor's god.

Zethan Stone - Jackal's Wrath MC Vice President & Avatar of Osiris.

AUTHOR'S NOTES

Just a heads up:
1. This book contains alternating points of views between the heroine and her four men.
2. Contains daddy kink and gun sex.
3. This book contains dark themes with **4 x trigger warnings**:

Chapter 7 - beating of the FMC (not by her harem)

Chapter 10 - beating of culprit from 7

Chapter 16 - one of harem accidentally hurts the FMC (sorry, it's part of their journey)

Chapter 28 - dangerous sex scene that might distress some readers

4. Oh, and heads up, this ends on a MAJOR cliffhanger. Like, I'm talking HATE MAIL cliffy. Be warned... #skyleryoucruelwench #loveyou
    #nowhinyreviews

GRAB A FREE BOOK

One last thing before you jump into the book. Sign up to my newsletter here to grab an exclusive *reader's only* ebook copy of the prequel, **Prophecy of the Gods**.

https://dl.bookfunnel.com/1hwipcn67p

CHAPTER 1

<u>Authors Note:</u> Please see warnings on Author's Notes tab before reading.

Aaliyah - Avatar of Isis

Gray storm clouds hang heavily in the sky, a premonition of the war brewing. Fat raindrops dripped off my umbrella, a precursor of the bloodshed about to be unleashed on the Jackals by Savage Wolves MC.

Rain muddied the grass of the cemetery, and my heels sank into the waterlogged ground. Drenched and chilled to the bone, I used a large oak as cover from the wind, but it did nothing to deter the angrily blowing downpour from hitting my body.

My chest ached, my eyes burned, and I couldn't breathe. I tapped the keyring my father had given me four years ago when I graduated from college. Heartbroken, I watched the ceremony from a hundred feet away, squeezing the umbrella's handle as if it were the only thing keeping me from blowing away. Droplets of rain washed away the salty tracks of tears from my cheeks.

Guests huddled underneath the white canopy, better suited for a wedding than my father's funeral. It was a mixture of friends, business associates, and club members, the last of whom I once considered family. Trousers, suits, shirts, and ties drowned out the twenty or so Wolves dressed in their standard leather, denim, and cuts. Hair combed back and gelled, beards trimmed and brushed, they all looked sharp for the funeral. Not a dirty nail in sight. They scrubbed up good. All to pay their respects for their fallen comrade and president.

Rev, a biker turned pastor, stood at the small podium at the head of my father's grave, concluding the service. Groundskeepers waited in the wings, their excavators rumbling, drowning him out. They were ready to push a mound of freshly turned earth over the casket and usher away friends and family. The world never stopped spinning – not even for Alexander Heller.

Men from the funeral home lowered the cherry wood coffin into the grave, signaling for the guests to depart for the wake. A parade of bikers in black leathers made their way back to the vehicles and bikes. Dozens of motorcycles rumbled with straight pipe modified exhausts that shook the ground as they rode off, flying the red and black of the Wolves' colors.

My brother remained, clutching my sobbing mother, letting her toss a white rose onto my dad's coffin.

The groundskeepers didn't care or respect the grieving, swooping in, pushing my family away from the casket.

I couldn't join them. Couldn't say goodbye. I'd left that world— that life— behind seven years ago after my boyfriend, Jimmy, died in a fight trying to protect me. Some dick at one of our bars grabbed my ass, and Jimmy went nuts, laying into him. One nasty blow from behind was all it took, and he went down, smacking his head on the bar. Severe brain injury left him in a vegetative state, and the family ordered the doctor to switch off his life support. That was the day I turned my back on bikers and the Wolves.

Golden Hills Memorial Garden's brochure showed a variety of inclement weather options in appropriate shades of black, but the thunderstorm came as much a surprise as my father's death. Mom told me my brother called in some favors to get us a slot with the overbooked funeral company and the cemetery. The slapped-together service was nothing like my father deserved or my mother wanted, and every bit what I came to expect from the men of the motorcycle club he rode with.

Amid the sea of bikes, four men leaned against another oak, watching the ceremony. Canopy from the overhanging tree and the parked vehicles had hidden them from the mourners. The gold and black of their patched cuts stood out. *Jackals.* Our rivals. Murderers of my father. My throat clogged.

Metal from my keyring bit into my palm as I squeezed it. "Son of a bitch."

What the hell were those bastards doing here? My heels slogged through the wet grass as I marched over to them to force them to leave. Unsteady on my feet, I wobbled, struggling with the height when I normally wore sneakers or flats.

Danny's temper ran hot enough to vaporize the rain, and if my brother caught the Jackals at my father's funeral mocking us, he'd start a damn bloodbath. The last thing my grieving mother needed was a graveside outburst from him in full view of two or more local reporters.

The Jackals retreated before I reached them, treading through the cemetery to wherever they'd parked their rides.

Only then did I cross back to the Corvette my brother had driven my mother in. Two seats, not enough to fit me, but that was fine, I'd driven my Ford Fiesta. A nurse's wage didn't pay for large, expensive cars, and I hadn't taken a damn dime from my dad, despite his insistence. I didn't want blood money on my hands or conscience. The only thing I'd accepted from him was the keyring I now clutched in my hand, cutting off the circulation.

Bloodshot eyes, sunken skin beneath them, and dark spots like a Dalmatian gave my mom the zombie look. Dazed, confused, and crying, she shuffled down the path led by Danny, who helped her into the car, buckling her in and shutting the door. Hair frizzed from all the rain, she sobbed into a handful of chipped or missing fake, red nails. Mom never stepped out of the house with a broken nail or hair out of place. I'd never seen her like this. Once dad was shot, she lost it and didn't know what to do with herself.

I wanted to be there for her but could only manage a four-day break from Royal North Shore Hospital where I worked.

Danny came around the driver's side to address me, dark, straight hair and beard slicked neater than I'd ever seen them. "They're gonna pay for smokin' Dad."

I wasn't sure if he'd seen the Jackals too, but I kept quiet. No point in poking the dragon. Blood had already been spilled, and I didn't care to send another member of my family to the grave.

Unaccustomed to wearing collared shirts, my brother undid the top button, and exhaled. "Tell me you hate them as much as I do for what they did to Dad." His shoulders snapped back, crunching the leather of his cut as he backed me up against the side of the car.

"I don't plan on making friends with any of them." I wedged my arms between us and pushed him back.

CURSE OF THE GODS

While I was neatly pressed, with our mother's cheekbones, caramel complexion, and pin-straight ebony locks, Danny was distressed denim, grease-under-the-fingernails, and the spitting image of our father.

As much as I resembled my mother, we had our differences. She was the stand-by-your-man type of woman, sticking through thick and thin, even cheating. While I couldn't wait to get away. Even as a child, I felt out of step with my family. At seventeen, I went off to college and earned a nursing degree to put my unique healing skills to better use than a triage nurse for the Wolves.

Hard and fast as I ran away from the reckless life of typical MC members, Danny ran toward it. Graduating from the University of Life, he gathered a rap sheet thicker than my transcripts. While I spent countless hours with my nose buried in a book, studying for grades worthy of a scholarship to boarding school, he studied mechanics and how to strip down a car and sell it for spare parts. We were two sides of the same coin. Except Danny thought himself badass, earning his place as dad's second in command by being the first to take the fall for him. Life in and out of the penal system had its perks.

The Wolves built an intricate network of dirty cops and prison guards. Recognizing a few of their faces among the crowd of mourners, I couldn't help but wonder if they wept for the loss of my father or a lost bonus. My money was on the latter.

Still, if not for the police on the Wolves' payroll, we never would have learned the truth about how my father died—shot by one of the members of the Wolves' rival club. A tight-lipped gang unit played their cards close to the vest but not so close we didn't notice the surveillance unit parked four cars behind the hearse that had carried my father's coffin.

Cheeks reddening, but not from the cold, Danny waved

in the direction of the plot where our father was being buried. "A pile of dirt is being pushed over our father's casket, and you make a joke?"

"Dad was never going to go peacefully in his sleep," I threw back at him. "The same way it will end for you if you keep going down this path. And what will happen to Mom, huh?"

"We know you won't be moving back home to take care of her. You'll just cut and run like you always do." Trust Danny to throw that up in my face every chance he got.

Tempers flared as we fed off each other's pain and picked at the scars from past slights. Nothing ripped open old wounds like time with the family.

"I didn't abandon the family, Danny." My reminder always fell on deaf ears. "I went away to school, earned a degree and work in a hospital."

"So, you love to remind us." Danny's hands clenched into fists, but they remained at his side. "Saint Aaliyah, savior of the sick and the helpless when she should have been home helping her family."

I ignored the fact that he called me a saint and chose to address the rest of the accusations he slung my way. My hot-headed brother drove me crazy, and knew better than anyone how to push my buttons.

He got in first, as he always did, refusing to be swayed to any point of view than his own. "They killed him, Aaliyah. Put him down like an animal." The darkness in his eyes frightened me, and for a moment, I feared he'd start some shit and suffer the same fate as our father.

My mother wouldn't survive it.

"You know who did it, and so do the police." God, what I wouldn't do for a cigarette. In times of stress, I needed one to calm my nerves. "Let them do the job you're paying them to do and just be there for Mom." I left off the *for once*, but it hung heavy in the silence between us.

"Enough!" My mother cracked the window enough to yell at us from inside the Corvette. "We were supposed to be at the clubhouse ten minutes ago."

"I'm sorry, Mom." I pressed my palm against the glass. Some of the tension drained from my body when she mirrored my hand with hers on the opposite side of the window.

"Get your ass there and do your duty," Danny said as he flung himself into the driver's side.

CHAPTER 2

aliyah

AT THE WAKE, I avoided the mourners, the apologies and condolences, my mother's devastated sobs, and the raucous laughter from the Wolves at the good old times with my pop. All of it was too much, and I needed to escape to find some peace and quiet. A space to catch my breath. Low blood sugar from not eating the last two days had left me weak, my fingers numb and tingly. The smell of food nauseated me, and I couldn't look at it without retching.

Squeezing my mom's crystal champagne flute, I wandered along the parqueted wooden-floored hall and entered my father's office. The smell of his aftershave, a warm, spicy cologne my mom insisted he wear, mingled with the thick, heavy smell of his cigars. Papers littered his heavy, oak desk. By the look of it, mom had been in here trying to sort them out into piles and take care of them. Bills for the club, house, bank statements, his Will and death certificate, all of them in neat stacks, unlike my dad's mess and disorder.

Nostalgic, I moved to my dad's cabinet, proudly displaying trophies won from the vintage cars he refurbished, raced, or sold off. Photo frames covered one of the walnut-paneled walls with pictures of club members, anniversaries, famous people he'd met, prize vehicles, and all the family's pets. He loved to capture everything in a photo. I used to hate it, but admiring them now, I was glad he'd done it. This wall summarized his life and all his achievements.

My dad had worked hard as the president of the Wolves MC, building the club up from its humble beginnings fifty years ago to one of the leading clubs in New South Wales and the tenth club in Australia. Our trade extended across the whole country, dealing in illegal cigars, tobacco, weapons, and hard drugs. Things were about to change now that my brother had taken over, and that would piss off the senior members of the Wolves.

My father earned the moniker Hell Hound from his fellow club members. At eighteen, he worked his way up from pledge to president the hard way and dragged his family along for the ride. At least one of us went kicking and screaming. Over the years, I overlooked the laundry list of felonies my father and his cohorts committed on a regular basis. With family, he tried to be a regular dad when he was at home – *when* being the key word.

Behind every good man was an even better woman. My mom stood by her man and raised his children without complaint. Bailed him out and visited him in prison every single time he was locked up. Did her best to fill the void left behind with a felon for a husband. Shame she hadn't deterred Danny from joining the Wolves. I knew better.

Missing my father, I stroked one of his many photos, feeling closer to him. Mohammed Ali, from a fight in Vegas, one of his all-time heroes. Dad loved boxing and horse racing. Anything he could gamble on and have a beer down the clubhouse or pub with his mates.

Someone opened the door and slid into the room behind me.

"Brought you some sandwiches," Danny said, his voice choked and hoarse.

"Put them on the desk," I replied. "I'll eat them later." A total lie.

Danny sidled up to me, examining the photographs with me. "Remember this?"

He took down a picture from the middle row and clutched it to his chest, the image facing me. Taken in 1996, I was four years old. My dad and his best friend, Jerry, went on a ride along the south and west coasts of Australia. The photo celebrated one thousand miles into the trip.

"Yeah." I smiled. "Dad used to go on about it all the time."

On retirement, he planned to go on more rides around Australia, taking different routes, seeing other parts of the country. For his sixtieth birthday, I'd saved up enough leave and had planned a surprise six-week ride up the east coast. A ride we'd never get to share now. A dream neither of us would ever fulfil.

"Guess you'll have to cancel your ride in April, huh?" Danny replaced the picture on the wall.

My chest ached harder than it ever had. I'd been looking forward to the trip so much. Dad would have been thrilled to go.

"I'll still go," I got out, all choked up and broken. "To honor Dad."

Danny sat on the edge of my father's desk, shoulders weighed down, and not just by death. "The cops have a suspect. They found a cigarette at the scene." He paused to rub his wrist. "They pulled DNA off it and got a match."

Heart crushed all over again, I leaned against him and the desk, resting my head on his shoulder. He had a smoky scent, formed by cigarettes and bikes. A big guy, stocky too, tattoos covered most of his visible skin. Mom hated them and said they looked cheap and nasty. A classy, well-dressed woman, my mom went off her rocker when dad snuck in a tattoo. She chewed dad a new asshole for months until he caved and promised he wouldn't get another. Mom ruled the roost in the home, while dad led the club.

Normally, the Wolves tried to handle these sorts of matters internally, extracting justice for injustices like this. But the cops had stuck their noses in, and there were too many eyes on the Wolves. Too much heat while the detectives conducted their murder investigation.

My blood iced over as I studied Danny's piercing, light blue eyes, waiting to hear the name of the man who destroyed my world. "Who?"

Danny's jaw twitched as he struggled to contain his rage. "Slade fucking Vincent."

President of the Jackals, the most notorious club in Australia, and the Wolves rival for the last five years. All the clubs feared him. No one dared touch the Jackals, they were too damn formidable, and anyone who tried, ended up dead. The Wolves had a falling out with them a few weeks before dad's death, which the police believe motivated the murder.

"Two witnesses from the factory identified him too." Danny cracked his knuckles and rolled his neck.

I knew that look. Eyes dark and mouth set in a furious scowl. Danny would never let this slide and seeking revenge for the murder would be a priority. Once, a man at a bar hit Melissa, his girlfriend at the time, now his wife, and Danny almost beat him to death. If it wasn't for his best friend, Bud, the guy would have been dead.

"We can't let this go, Aaliyah. Dad wouldn't have." Danny

grabbed our father's bike keys from the desk and crushed them in his hand.

Slade fucking Vincent was not someone the Wolves or Danny wanted to screw with. Whispers spoke of the Jackals possessing strange, deadly powers that enemies rarely escaped. The power of the elements. Fire, lightning, storms, and hail, coming out of nowhere. Winds that cut down bullets or knives aimed at the members. Absolute chaos and destruction. A hawk that pecked out eyes, and a wolf that tore out people's throats. Enemies having their breath stolen from them, a heart attack brought on and dropping dead. Darth Vader shit right there. The Jackals were not a club to mess with, and no one ever got close enough to get vengeance.

I reiterated the words I'd given Danny earlier. The smart choice. "Yes, we can. We can let the police do their jobs."

Blood dripped down the sides of Danny's hand. "This is a family matter, and the Wolves will handle it." He gritted his teeth. "We could use your help. Can I count on you, Aaliyah?"

"What for?" I folded the handkerchief I'd been clutching in my hand until I was left with a clean square of linen and wiped the blood from where the keys Danny gripped had pierced his palm. The cut was small, a waste of energy, but I tapped into the healing magic within me to close the wound.

"No one knows where their club is." The full weight of his stare landed on me. "We can't get near the bastards. We need someone to infiltrate them and take em' down from the inside."

That someone being me. Seven years away from the club and I'd be the least recognizable to the Jackals. No way. They could have seen me at the funeral and recognized me. Infiltrating our enemies put me in a pit full of vipers. My heart thudded just thinking about their fearsome reputation.

Danny had lost the plot. That kind of task would take

years. Clubs were very particular about who they took on as members. They put prospects through hell for at least two years to test their loyalty, secrecy, and resilience before considering giving them a patch. Prospects were never assigned critical tasks due to their rank and were never privy to church events and decisions. Many clubs didn't accept female members, and I wasn't sure what the Jackal's position was on that. If the Jackals were anything like the Wolves, they'd guard their secrets close to their chest. What he asked of me could get me killed.

"I'll never make it out alive." My magical power finished clotting the vein and sealed the wound. "Besides, I have a job, and I can't just pause my life for you."

For the last two years, I'd worked my way up to head ER nurse. Taking months off to spy on the Jackals would be frowned upon. A two-year break to prospect for the Jackals, career suicide. No thanks. I barely got the six weeks leave approved to go on the ride with my father.

"So quit. Family's more important," Danny said as if I hadn't just worked my ass off for the last nine years to get to where I was. "You can get a job anywhere."

I don't think my brother understood the importance of my work. Who I was. What I was. My calling.

"I'll think about it." It wasn't a yes, but it wasn't a no, either. It was the best I could do, and it seemed to pacify my brother. For now. He'd not stop until he got the answer he wanted.

Without a word, I left the room, grabbed my handbag and keys, and climbed into the driver's seat of my Fiesta.

War was coming whether I liked it or not. I had two choices; get caught in the crossfire or fight. Born a Heller, I'd pledged my allegiance to the Wolves the day I was born.

CHAPTER 3

Slade - Jackal's Wrath MC President & Avatar of Set

Six months later

The call came in around nine. Seamus "The Mick" O'Malley's name voiced from my Blackberry's speakers. Long-term Jackal's ally, Mick, was a good scout to keep on the payroll with his bar along William Street. Less liked for deals in dark alleys out of the back of his beat-up Chevy van. What The Mick lacked in scruples, he more than made up for in distributing our inventory. Total pain in the ass. But, a reliable and loyal pain in the ass I couldn't afford to lose. Not with the tension choking my club and territory.

"Yeah?" I answered his call, leaning back in my well-worn, brown leather chair, throwing my feet up onto my messy desk.

"Got word that the Savages crossed into your territory last week." Mick's gruff Irish accent came down the line.

My pulse throttled as I picked up the silver Jackal paperweight on my desk, running it over in my hand. Squeezing it helped me work out my stress. I had other ways to work out stress, but I reserved them for special occasions.

"Moved Frosty," Mick added using our code for Ice. "Some punks selling it at the Ox."

We always used code when speaking with contacts to avoid being deciphered by the feds. A little help from a certain god of writing also helped us remain untraceable even if they looked into us.

Leather on my cut creaked as I leaned forward, elbows on my desk. Those fucks were not cutting in on our territory. Ice had been banned from our region after my friend Mac died of heart arrythmia on the shit. The Jackals only sold coke, weed, and party drugs after that. We'd kept a good handle on it, too, until now.

The Oxford, or Ox as locals knew it, was a bar popular with the university crew. Sold fifty grand a month of our special blend there. "Pharaoh" pills sold for a twenty, and we couldn't keep up with the demand. Orders had come in from all over the country once users heard about the good times they could have with no side effects. Thank you, Castor, for that little recipe.

Knowing The Mick, he probably scored a deal with a few college kids hopped up on Mt. Dew, looking to role-play their GTA fantasies. Better nip it in the bud before they ruined our customer base.

I scratched at my beard. "Gimme the names of the dealers."

Paper crinkled down the line as Mick read from it. "Darren Treadwell and Gavin Hessian."

"I'll look into it." The line went dead as I hung up.

Pulse running wild, I removed a Ranch rolling paper from my pocket. I packed it with tobacco, added a filter, licked the paper's edge and sealed it. A flame sparked on my fingertip, and I lit the cigarette. My neck twitched as I drew in a deep inhale. Hot smoke filled my lungs, soothing the thump in my pulse.

Lines were not to be crossed. Yet the Savage Wolves MC kept pushing and pushing. Old Hell Hound respected boundaries. Rest in Peace, brother. His son, Danny, was another kettle of fish. Punk wanted a piece of our pie. Fuck that. I'd teach him and his club a lesson for crossing the line.

I shoved my cell into my jeans pocket, and drew in another sweet lungful of smoky air as I climbed to my feet. My boots thumped on the wooden floorboards of the clubhouse as I crossed through the recreation room. Zethan and Alaric played pool while Benny and Brix competed at darts. The shots lined up on the bar would have to wait. I had business to discuss.

Three doors down the hallway, I came to Castor's office. I didn't knock as I entered. Didn't have to. As usual, I found my Enforcer hunched over one of his damn books, scribbling something from the hieroglyphs in his notebook. Magick, history, mysteries of the fucking universe, and other books lined his bookshelves. Voodoo shit to me. I wouldn't expect anything less from the avatar of Thoth, God of Writing, Science, and Dark Magick.

Castor pressed his wrist into the spine of the book, closing his fingers, highlighting the three symbols tattooed on his fingers. Something about law or some shit. Not that I could read a word when letters blurred, appeared out of order, or damn well changed into fucking hieroglyphics. A shitty gift from the God of Chaos I served. At least I could blow shit up.

"Yes, President?" He set his honey-brown eyes on me.

I snatched the book away from him, demanding his attention. "Get your mind off that shit and talk to me, Bird Boy."

His body was born to devour knowledge. He didn't just need his eyes to read. Any contact with a book and he'd consume the whole damn thing, word for fucking word. Prick had a photographic memory. The reason he was such a hot-shot prosecutor in his day. The only thing I had to give him shit about was his Ibis-headed god. Hence the Bird Boy.

"What can I say, Prez?" He leaned back in his chair, smirking, threading his hands behind his head. "I'm a multi-tasker."

I tossed the book and it thud on his table. Multi-tasker, my ass. I could do that too. This fucker was just quicker at his job. The fastest of anyone I'd ever met. Earned him a lot of spare time to read from his god's tomes.

I coiled my forefinger into the loop on my jeans. "You secure that shipment of rifles?"

"Ordered and tracked to ship in three days." Lines formed in the corner of Castor's eyes when he smiled. The women went wild for it. That and his Arabian prince good looks.

"Smoke bombs?"

"On top of it, Prez." Fuck he was good. Too good. I was lucky to land him when I met him in my bar. The gods were smiling on me that day.

"Good I've got another job for you." I exhaled a long stream of smoke and flicked ash from my butt. "Need you to get me addresses on these two assholes." I gave him the two names supplied to me.

"On it, prez." Castor's eyes glazed over as he scanned the information highway his god granted him access to.

Two more of my men performed the bidding of other Egyptian gods, and we kept it a secret from the rest of the club. Couldn't be too careful when people would use that shit against us. The gods had chosen us based on characteristics that matched theirs. Set, my patron, was a fiery, chaotic fuck who liked to destroy his enemies, just like me. Castor's god, Thoth, was a geek who knew shit about practically every topic. And if he didn't know, he'd find out through his channels, searching through books, the internet, phone calls, emails, texts, databases, you fucking name it. Came in handy when we needed to track some dirty fucker down.

Castor's eyes brightened as he returned from his investigation. "Found them in the Roads and Maritime Services directory."

Licenses, addresses, and vehicle plates. Just what I wanted.

"Come with me." I jerked my head.

Castor joined me as we strode down the hallway.

As club President, I gave the orders, and my men carried them out. I never asked anything of them that I wouldn't do myself – until I became the prime suspect in a murder investigation. Alexander Heller, the Savage Wolves' president, turned up dead. Five bullets to the back.

Two sworn statements and one cigarette placed me at the crime. But the witnesses were sketchy on details, and a cigarette butt was my smoking gun. While the cops built their case on circumstantial evidence, I had a rock-solid alibi courtesy of my crew, and my cell's last ping was on a tower clear across town at the time of the murder. According to my mole in the department, the Crown Prosecutor's office wanted more evidence before they sought to charge me. For now, I remained a person of interest.

In the recreation room, I grabbed my bike keys from the hook by the entry and called out, "Alaric, get your ass over here."

My Road Captain set his pool cue down and approached me, standing to attention as he always did. "President."

An Air Force man of ten years, he never lost the habit, not

even when he joined us. Distant, bloodshot eyes reflected back at me. His mind, his gaze, were always another world away, never the same again.

One of the radios on his belt crackled with a message. Some truck driver talking smack on the Bathurst channel.

Waiting for it to end, I twisted the Jackal-headed ring on my finger until one ear hit the opposite finger and I couldn't move further. Pointy and deadly. Just the way I liked it. "You look like shit. You sleeping?"

"No, sir." Alaric rubbed his eyes with the heel of his palm. "The drugs Doc gave me aren't working."

Alaric had nightmares and woke in a panic, smashing shit, or people, if they happened to get in his way. The last time he got out of control, he hurt someone I loved. I'd not let that happen again.

"I'll get him back here tomorrow after he's done at the shelter." I clapped my Road Captain on the side of his arm.

"What do you need, President?" Mismatched eyes landed on me, one gray, one golden, the combination strangely hypnotic.

The Jackal's ear from my ring dug into my finger. "Word on the street is Wolves are selling meth in town."

Castor shrugged on his riding jacket over his cut. "They're punching low since Heller died."

Steel bit into my palm, bringing on blood. "Fucking Danny Heller's sending that club straight to hell faster than they can work up a thousand miles on their bikes." I crunched my hand into a fist to stop it from dripping. My shifter healing would fix this up in a day.

My Road Captain ran a hand through his crew cut.

"Alaric, I need you to decoy for me," I ordered. "Take my bike and get the cops off my tail."

He needed the structure and order of command that he'd been raised with in his family and through the ranks in the

Air Force. Fit in perfect here, obeyed every command, no bitching and asking for another assignment. Made my life easier and my blood pressure lower. And God knew what happened when that spiked.

"Sure thing, President." We swapped cuts to complete the look. "Want my radios?"

Alaric always carried three to four of them. One to keep track of the happenings in town. Two for contact with the clubhouse and a private one for when we traveled in remote areas. Carrying them eased his mind, and made him feel safe.

"Fuck no!" They were his thing, not mine. "We'll be gone an hour. I want you ready for when I get back. We need to find their shipment line and crew and take 'em out."

"Yes, President." Gold flashed in Alaric's right eye. The power of his god.

I nodded in dismissal, letting him enter the garage, warm up my bike and leave. Cops would take the bait and tail him, leaving us alone to investigate this lead.

Zethan, my Vice President, came over to get the low down and I filled him in before leaving. Asshole was good with numbers and kept our books cooking. That was all the Jackals needed. And Blackberries. Couldn't forget them. Hack-proof and untraceable.

In the garage, Castor and I threw on our helmets and cranked the engines to life. Alaric's bike purred between my legs, the vibrations traveling through my body. This was better than anything, even pussy. Except the pussy of my old lady. But I didn't want to think about what happened to her.

I took the lead for the short ride, headed for the first address Reg had given me. I parked a quarter of a mile away. Didn't want to warn the worm of our arrival. Helmets buckled to our handlebars, we walked the rest of the way.

Castor took off his riding gloves and shoved them in his jacket. "Who do we need to sort out?"

As both club Enforcer and Sergeant at Arms, he took care of matters like this. He made sure rules were followed inside and outside of the club, and enforced justice where necessary. He replaced those gloves with a different pair for trips like this.

"One of the fucks The Mick said was dealing meth." I paused by a tree to scope out the house. Thanks to the godly power flowing through my veins, I could hone in on shit like that. Get a bird's eye view. Not as good a view as Alaric's, though.

Paint peeled from the house's timber boards, eaves, and windows. Just about every surface. Rust ate away at the aged roof and gutters. Flyscreens hung loose on the windows and doors. Shit hole. A dirty old brown van was parked in the driveway. The TV blared from inside. Smoke curled from out of the chimney.

"I want the name and location of the distributor," I told my Enforcer. "Then we pay him a visit too."

Castor locked the last button of his gloves. "No problem, Prez." He removed a silver necklace with a pendant and kissed it. Claimed the black tourmaline and obsidian protected him from magic. I didn't believe in that fairy crystal shit.

I wasn't sending him in alone. Laying low wasn't my style. Cooped up in the clubhouse for days, I was itching for a fight. Under normal circumstances, this would be just the thing to scratch it, but I couldn't afford to get picked up on assault charges while the cops built their bullshit murder case against me. I had to be careful how I dealt with this, not bring too much attention to myself. That went completely against my nature when chaos raged in my veins, shouting at me to take this fucker down in style.

No one came into my territory unless they wanted to end up dead or with their nose sliced off. Leads went cold real fast when you couldn't chase them down beyond your own front yard. Mouths talked when you put the fear of God into them. Literally.

We marched right up to the door. Dark tentacles of magick swirled around Castor's hands and he flung them at the door. Both the security screen and dead-bolted door tore off their hinges with a crack. They clattered on the shitty old couch on the porch as he tossed them aside.

When the Jackals came to visit, we did it in style. Castor reined in the magick for now. Didn't need the people of Bathurst to know about our little secret. We'd have every MC coming at us, wanting to take us out.

"What the fuck?" the startled occupant shouted, thumping to his feet, probably off his scratched, faded recliner.

Fucker marched right out of his family room in his pajama pants and wife beater. Thick, dark hair covered his head. A five o'clock shadow darkened his jaw. Tanned skin despite the winter of Bathurst. Smelled like smoke from the fireplace, sweat, and beer. Animal. At least he wasn't high on his own stash.

"You Darren Treadwell?" Castor's refined voice came out gruff, disguising his university education by talking like a gang member.

"Who wants to know?" His dark brown eyes squared on us.

Castor plucked his gloves to highlight them. "Heard you've been trading in some illegal methamphetamines."

Darren's eyes zeroed in on the gloves. His pupils dilated with realization of what was about to go down. "Got bills to pay. My mom's got cancer."

"This is our town, and we don't do that shit here." Castor layered on the threat as he examined a framed family snapshot hanging on the wall behind Darren. "If it happens again, this pretty little family of yours will go bye-bye."

"No, please." Darren tried to back away but hit the wall.

Castor flicked his raised fingers. "Gimme the packages."

Darren raised two palms as if we were gonna arrest him. "Just don't hurt my mom, okay." Castor let him scurry away to retrieve his stash.

Pleading gestures wouldn't work on me. Seen 'em one too many times. This prick needed to be taught a lesson. We owned this fucking town and the Central West region around it. This was ours to trade in.

"Here." Darren held the three bags of Ice. "Promise me you won't hurt my mom? She had no part in this. It was all me."

The Jackals respected and valued family. But if one of ours was harmed, we didn't hesitate to retaliate. This fool's mother could rest easy. Couldn't say the same for her son.

"I won't hurt your mother." Castor took the bags and handed them to me. He was a man of his word. A man of law and order. Former solicitor and man of the law. "You, on the other hand ..."

I let him do his job as I took the bags into the adjoining kitchen. Dishes were piled up on the sink. Empty beer cans covered the counter. Old pizza boxes piled up on top of each other. Filthy pigs.

Fists thumped into flesh. "Let's start with where you got the Ice?"

"Got it from my supplier," Darren groaned as Castor laid another one into him. "Was told to sell it within the month."

"Imma need more than that." Bones cracked as they snapped. Screams accompanied each break. "Who gave it to you? Where'd you pick it up?"

I drowned out the pained groans and Darren's responses by switching on the faucet. Water flushed the sink as I emptied the bags' contents down the basin. I could have burned the shit in his fireplace, but I would have smoked out the place, and gotten us high as the mad fucking hatter with it.

When I was done, I lit up a cigarette, enjoying it.

Five minutes later, Castor stuck his head through the doorway. "Done."

"Good." I moved through the hallway, kicking the bloody fuckwit on my way past. "If I get word that you're selling drugs in my town again, you're a fucking dead man." I put out my cigarette on his arm, and he screamed.

Business finished, I moved into the family room, flicking my cigarette into the fireplace. I watched until it had all but burned. Destruction and disorder thrummed in my veins, ready to be unleashed and devastate. To teach Darren a little lesson for messing with my club, I hijacked his fire, and let that baby free. Flames crawled over his rug and caught on his sofa and curtains. My god relished that shit and so did I.

"Fuck, fire!" Darren screamed, and I smiled, the darkness inside me delighting in the disarray.

Castor waited behind me with one of his classic smirks. "Darren didn't tread well, did he?" he joked, mocking the fucker's last name.

I barked out a laugh and jerked my head, indicating we were splitting. "Fucker stepped out of line." We descended the steps to the path leading to the driveway. Out of earshot, I asked, "What'd he say?"

Castor wiped the blood from his gloves. "Their supplier's a trucking company in Orange."

The Savage Wolves had invaded our territory. It was time to send them a message. Stick to their lane and not cross it again. I'd make sure of it.

CHAPTER 4

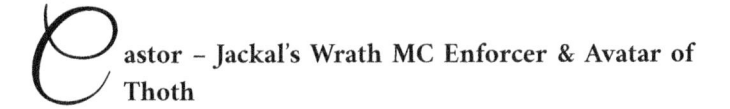

*C*astor – Jackal's Wrath MC Enforcer & Avatar of Thoth

ALARIC GAVE the signal up ahead. Stop and scan our target before investigating it. That meant shifting into his hawk and hiding it from the rest of the club.

Our Road Captain knew the streets like the back of his hand and could outride any beat cop, but those weren't his only skills. We needed a vantage point before we barged in and surprised our rivals. Club rules; conduct reconnaissance every time, without fail. It assured our longevity and kept our losses to a minimum. Additionally, we had some special patrons backing us.

Slade dropped his bike's pace, pulling over on the roadside, waiting for the rest of us to follow suit. Ten club members formed a line behind him in order of rank. Jackal's President, Vice President, me as the Enforcer, and patched members. Men I trusted with my life. Lights on the bikes were killed, drowning us in shadow, the quarter moon now our only source of illumination.

Road Captain responsibility dictated that Alaric rode up front, protecting the club, scanning for danger. However, our Road Captain had a distinct advantage over other clubs, with him possessing the gifts of Horus, the sky God.

Slade took off his helmet and set it on his bike, giving Alaric the space to survey the warehouse address we were about to investigate for any danger. Half a mile ahead of us and out of sight of other club members.

Alaric knew the drill, and would be stripping off his radios, boots, socks, leathers, and underwear, storing them in the saddle bag. Neat and folded like a good little soldier. Bones, muscles, and tendons would crack as they shortened, twisted, transforming him into a small bird of prey.

Boots crunched on the gravel as Slade approached me. Sheathed knives on his belt slapped his thighs with each step. Weapons weren't necessary with the powers we all possessed, but our president preferred precautions. He lit up a rolled cigarette and smoked it. A cant of his head signaled for me to go with him, protect him as my duty as Enforcer.

I cast off my helmet, shaking out my shoulder-length hair, resting it on my second seat. Night traffic from the Great Western Highway droned in the background. Trucks mostly, with a few cars and law enforcement vehicles in the mix. We took the less-traveled route to avoid getting pulled over by them.

I grabbed my saddlebags from the back of my Royal Enfield Classic 350, then caught up to him.

The rest of the club would hang back with their VP until we returned with further instruction.

"Where the fuck are your weapons?" Benefit of being the god of Chaos and Disorder, he could tell when someone was packing.

I tapped my head. "Right here." Guns and knives were messy. Accessories I didn't need with my talents. Autopsies were blind to fatality by magic or Zethan's death breath.

"Take them in with you, or you're riding home in your boxers." Slade left me to think about the repercussions on a nearly zero-degree night.

I rolled up and tucked the map away, slinging my holsters on underneath my worn leather jacket. The Jackal's president preferred precautions and backup plans, thoroughly covering all bases. In this climate, where our club teetered on the brink of war with another, we couldn't take chances.

"Smoking will kill you, Prez." I ran a hand through my flattened hair as we walked along the road. Lung cancer, heart disease, stroke, erectile dysfunction. Take his pick of diseases. I didn't go near that shit. Too many people died of smoking-related-illnesses, and I wouldn't be one of them.

Pressure from the murder investigation and the death of a rival club's president sent Slade spiraling back into hard liquor and tobacco after two years of being clean.

The red tip of his cigarette cast an eerie glow over his face, shadows highlighting the sharp jaw, angular features, and hard scowl. "I'm gonna die young anyway, Bird Boy."

Slade lived the hard life. His motto: party hard, sleep when he was dead. Lately, it had turned him into a moody prick.

"Bird Boy?" I smirked. "That's all the insult you got, Fox Boy?"

Fuckers harassed me because of the god I represented ... and not in a legal sense, like my former life. Thoth, the Ibis-headed Egyptian god of Writing and Magick. I wasn't getting my dick out of joint because I couldn't soar as high as Alaric and my bird sight wasn't as sharp. Nevertheless, we each had our role, and I knew mine. Talons or a beak weren't necessary to carve out an enemy's eyes when I controlled the dark forces.

"Fuck off." Slade flicked his worn cigarette past me. "I'm more wolf, and you know it, book brains." Insults were on a roll today.

"Whatever you say, Prez." I fished out my map and unraveled it, my ibis night vision assisting me to study the route Alaric had planned. Two escape paths and one back road route if we needed it.

Slade moved on to his second smoke as we arrived at Alaric's bike and waited for him.

A bird's squawk warned us of his return, and I outstretched my arm, letting him land, claws extended. Deep scratches in the leather showed the many times his talons had dug into me. He blinked three times, our signal to proceed as planned. I ran my hands along his soft feathers. Scars marred his frame, leaving part of his body absent of plumage. My brother in arms had been through a lot, the marks a reminder of his nightly terrors. With a leap off my arm, he made a quick transformation back into his human skin, dressing back in his gear.

Slade took a long pull of his cigarette. "What have we got, Hawk Man?" Fucking Hawk Man. He blew out a long plume of smoke that curled into the shapes of guns and bullets. That shit would never get old.

"We've got a problem." Dehydrated from the shift, Alaric grabbed his water bottle from his bike, draining it in two gulps. "They weren't Wolves. I didn't recognize their colors. Out of staters, perhaps?"

Slade's brows slammed down hard. "A new crew?"

Criminal investigation into old Heller's murder. Heat from the Wolves invading our territory. We didn't need another opening for a rival club with all eyes on the Jackals.

Rocks skittered as Slade kicked them. "Better not be The

Mick wanting to level up his gun-running career, upping his game from back-alley deals to an actual warehouse."

"I highly doubt it." I voiced my opinion. "The Mick's been a valuable ally, and we're good with the other clubs. They have no reason to stab us in the back."

Promises were sacred to the Jackals. Slade was a ruthless motherfucker who would extract deadly retribution in a heartbeat if he was crossed. In my four years with the club, I'd witnessed him burn down a clubhouse and bar in a matter of minutes. But he had no reason to arbitrarily move in on the Wolves' territory or put a hit on their family. The Jackals were in the top five clubs of Australia and didn't want the Wolves' shitty business.

Yes, I was a skeptical asshole. Record keeping for the god of Writing and Messages, I filtered all the stories, scanned all their messages, email, text, phone, fax, all possible forms of communication. Not many decent people existed today. Those poor suckers that believed in the law and justice and blew the whistle on corruption were threatened into silence and sometimes even murdered. Exactly the reason I quit the law. When I say I knew everything, I meant it. This brain inside my skull was bursting with information on everyone in this city and beyond.

Looking troubled, Slade scrubbed at his light beard, mulling over the next step. "Let's get back to the others."

Back at our bikes, Zethan, our VP, came over to join us, his ear-length blonde hair reflecting the moonlight. Leather from his shoulder holster was visible beneath his cut. The guy never took his weapon off, and he sure as hell never let his guard down. Never stopped assessing threats, a habit ingrained from his days as a beat cop.

After Slade filled him in, Zethan set a calming hand on our president's shoulders, which could go either way. Best friends since middle school, these two either got along like a house on fire or were at each other's throats. Rivalries between their gods playing out in real life. Brothers Osiris and Set competed for the throne of Egypt, and we all know how that played out, with Osiris ending up cut into fourteen pieces.

"I know you want to burn these assholes to the ground. But let's check it out first." Zethan's hand tightened on his friend's shoulder, easing the tight muscles in Slade's neck. "Whoever they are, they're fucking with the wrong club, transporting their shit through our territory."

Clubs had to give permission for that, and we didn't provide it to bastards who tried to undercut us or attempt covert transport through our territory under our noses.

Slade nodded, inhaling deeply on the last of his cigarette and flicking the butt into the dead of night. "Head out."

Tank, our mechanic, had fitted our bikes with larger exhaust pipes to maximize their noise. Before we set out, I cast a spell over the riders, enclosing the sound of our bikes within a magical bubble. We stuck to the back roads and killed the engines once our destination came into view. Rides concealed along the roadside, I set an invisible illusion over them as we moved in.

Red parking lights and headlights illuminated the old, condemned warehouse halfway between Bathurst and Orange. It had seen better days, abandoned for at least five years, the roller doors rusted, the rusty metal gutters hanging off the roof. Two trucks were parked back to back, their cargo doors wide open. Two men in cuts unloaded from the left truck and stocked the right one. Similar scenes described over and over at trials I prosecuted.

Slade paused on the edge of an old van chassis. "Zethan, take Hawk and Bird Boy with you for a closer look."

Precaution normally prevented the President and Vice President from being in the same spot simultaneously. If one perished, the other could assume leadership. Slade had broken the rule tonight because he was pissed and wanted to be present. Usually, he only attended higher-level meetings, like suppliers, distributors, and buyers.

Zethan moved out, flanked by Alaric and me. While Alaric kept vigil, I set up a magical trap, locking the fuckers inside the confines of the parking lot. The two men packing the trucks didn't see us coming until we were on them. They clutched a box of yogurt tubs tighter as if that would protect them from bullets. Another guy paced the lot on his cell, and a third patrolled the perimeter with a rifle. Imbecile won scout of the fucking year. He wouldn't last a day in the Jackals. Slade would have roasted him for letting anybody through.

Their rockers read Red Coast Vultures MC. Never heard of that club.

Utilizing my godly analysis abilities, I filtered through thousands of records, locating a police report mentioning the arrest of two Vulture members for theft. Another hit came back for the Red Coast Vultures MC located in the Sunshine Coast, Queensland. Few clubs other than the five largest, including the Jackals, conducted interstate business. These fuckers were out of their element and had ventured too far south.

"Mind if I take a look at those packages?" Zethan gestured to the tubs of yogurt the men hefted onto the second truck.

"You the cops or something?" The hand of the furthest man reached for the gun he concealed beneath his cut.

"I'm your worst fucking nightmare." Zethan's control over death was lethal, but he only reserved it for complicated situations.

"Get the fuck outta here." The asshole with the gun came over, waving it in our face. "This is private property." His shout encouraged the approach of the guy on the cell, who hung up and dialed another number.

Shadows bunched around Zethan as he stepped forward. Death was knocking tonight! "This is our territory, pal. The Vultures aren't welcome."

The ejector on the rifle failed. Cell reception went dead for the guy on the phone, and he repeated his warning to whomever he tried to contact. Everything went dead.

Something didn't sit right with me. Call it a hunch. God's intuition. It prompted me to conduct another scan of these fuckers. In the directory of the guy with the phone, I found a number with no name. Curious, I searched for data on its owner, tracing cell tower locations, pinging the recipient at the Wolves' clubhouse.

I removed my gun and marched up to one of the idiots, relying on theatrics to make them spill. "They're in bed with the Wolves."

Relations between the Jackals and Wolves had been strained since old Heller took five bullets to the back. Those assholes tried cutting in on our territory and selling meth. They swayed dealers to their side with bribes and threats of death. Treacherous bastards.

No one had a bone of loyalty in their body these days. Everyone was out to make a quick buck, and they'd screw over their grandmother to do it. One of the main reasons I left law. Rife with corruption and treachery. The innocent being tread on by the rich and powerful.

Motives rang with absolute clarity in this case. The Wolves wanted to expand and were willing to start a turf war with the most powerful club in the state. Slade Vincent wouldn't stand for it. Blood would spill.

"Who?" The guy clutching the box of yogurt continued to play dumb.

"Don't play games with me, asshole." I pressed the gun harder to his temple. "Who do you work for?"

The guy started to tremble. "They told us to wear these vests when we made the delivery."

I flicked off the safety of my gun. "Who?"

"Shut your fucking face, Don," the guy with the cell barked.

"Trev, what the fuck's going on?" Don dropped his box, and it clattered on the ground.

That distraction was all the one with the cell needed to make a run for it. A howl cut the night. Slade's call sign. He'd shifted and would chase the fucker down. He moved faster in his Jackal form.

The trigger clicked as the idiot carrying the gun attempted to shoot us, prompting a laugh from Zethan.

The Vice Prez strode over, ripped it from his grasp, slamming the butt into the guy's forehead, knocking him out. "Alaric, tie these fucks up inside the warehouse."

Alaric acted without question, grabbing Don and slamming his head into the truck door, causing him to slump to the ground. The second guy tried to run, but Alaric was faster and fitter, catching him, sending him crashing with an elbow to the jaw.

Zethan's piercing green eyes shot to me, communicating the next step.

By the time I'd swapped my riding gloves for my Enforcer gloves, Zethan had retrieved rope from the back of the truck. I dragged old Don into the warehouse, securing him to a post opposite the second box packer. Light from the vans extended a few feet inside.

A little spell to replicate smelling salts roused Don and his buddy as I crouched beside them. "You're going to tell us everything you know, or I'm going to beat it out of you."

Don scraped his boots against the concrete. "We don't

know anything. The guy with the phone organized everything."

The guy Slade hunted.

Right on cue, a pained howl broke through the silent night. Slade was hurt.

"Stay there." Zethan's steps thumped on the concrete.

A few precisely placed punches yielded a little more information. Delivery locations, times, dates ... five spread out across our territory.

"Castor, over here." Zethan dragged a naked Slade into the warehouse. Blood dripped down his torso and legs. A knife jutted from his abdomen. "Slade can hardly breathe. I think the wound is penetrating his lung."

Hell, I was no medic. Bandaged wounds like a biker would make a cake. Messy and rough. But with all the knowledge banked in my head, I was the closest thing to a doctor. I inspected his seeping wound, pulled out a bandana from my back pocket, and handed it to him. "Fuck, Prez, you need to get checked out by a doctor."

"I'm fine," Slade wheezed, getting paler by the second.

Zethan dialed Doc Shriver, the club's backyard surgeon for instances like this, and had a brief conversation with him. "Doc Shriver is tied up and can't make it. Take him to the hospital to get patched up."

"I don't do hospitals," Slade's growl shifted into an urgent rasp. "My shifter healing will take care of it." He pushed me away and tried to sit up, gasping, clutching his torso.

"Your choice," I said. "But your lung could collapse before your healing kicks in."

He speared me with a glare. "Fuck. Fine. Take me."

CHAPTER 5

Aaliyah

"Are you sure you want to jump back in with triage?" Barbara pushed a vitals cart into the small examination room. "I can put you somewhere else. I'm sure someone from peds will switch."

First day back from the two-week ride dad and I were supposed to take for his sixtieth, and my boss tread carefully. No matter how many times I promised I was fine, she didn't believe me. The trip was my way to say goodbye to my dad. I cried plenty of tears, ate way too much junk food, and took a ton of photos for his wall. Lamented how much I missed him. Dry-eyed and carrying an extra two pounds, I was ready for work, and didn't need to be babied.

"Barb, it's the ER." I took the cart's handle from her. "It doesn't matter where you put me."

Before she could argue, I wheeled it away.

Barb chased after me. "You need to charge that."

"Dammit." I moved over to the outlet for charging and plugged the cart in.

Day shift never plugged the damn things in when they were done. Made us night-shifters look incompetent when we wheeled up to a patient with an inoperable machine.

Barbara sidled up to me, leaning against the wall, clutching a clipboard, brown eyes dark with concern. "Aaliyah, tell me if things get too much, okay?"

I gave her my best *I'm fine* smile. "If you're really worried about my *fragile* state, would moving me to the children's department where they're sick or in pain be the smartest move?"

Peds wasn't for every nurse, and it could be hard seeing the children suffering. That aside, I loved working there. Healing kids, easing their pain, bringing a smile to their cute faces felt like the best use of my gifts.

I'd be damned if I got special treatment because my father died. Whispers and accusations already chased me because I was best friends with the Director of Nursing. Sue me, assholes. I never took advantage of it.

"The adults are bigger babies than the kids." Barbara offered a warm smile. "You sure?"

"It's Wednesday." I busied myself with taking inventory of the supply cabinet. "Should be a slow night. Broken bones, chest pains that turned out to be acid reflux and a laceration that requires stitches for a little excitement."

Barbara chuckled darkly. "You know better than to wager on the incoming. It's bad luck. If the shift goes south, I'm holding you responsible."

"Margaritas at El Matador's on me if I'm wrong." Bets were our thing. It was how we initially became friends. Friday night drinks at El Matador's built our relationship.

"You're on, but let's up the ante." Barbara grinned. "Margaritas and a chicken quesadilla." She leaned closer, squinting at the name tag I'd borrowed because I forgot my own. "Nurse Alexa."

"You're on." My friend took the hint when I moved from counting boxes of gauze to rapid strep test kits and made her way back to the nurses' station.

Barbara disappeared behind a stack of charts piled high on top of the semi-circular desk in the center of the ER.

The night passed at a snail's pace. Happy hour on Barbara's dime was assured. Salt tasted on my tongue as I imagined the rim of my margarita glass and the sweet burn of the extra spicy salsa. My stomach growled its displeasure at having to wait forty-eight hours to collect. Taking advantage of the lull, I snuck off to the vending machine to grab a snack. Replenish the old blood sugar.

I should have known better than to tempt fate. Less than five minutes later, all hell broke loose, the waiting room packed to standing room only. Across the sea of people, Barbara wagged her eyebrows at me. Based on her little charades, she was as excited to collect on our bet as I'd been moments before. My friend was going to want a steak burrito after tonight.

I tossed the half-eaten candy bar into the wastebasket and called in the first patient. The shift flew by in a blur of temperature checks, blood pressures, and pulse ox. One after one, I escorted patients into my room to review their symptoms and determine the order of priority for the doctors to examine further.

"They should have installed a revolving door," I grumbled after instructing the last person to return to his seat in the waiting room.

The monitor on the wall taunted me with blue flashing names and wait times. Another just came in and it was a priority.

"Vincent," I read from the patient's file.

The name triggered a warning bell in my mind. *Slade Vincent.* President of the Jackal's Wrath Motorcycle Club. Prime suspect in my father's murder case. No. I was being paranoid. North Shore hospital was well out of the Jackal's territory. Unless they had a tussle with another club. *Don't be silly, Aaliyah.* Hundreds of people had that surname in Sydney. Million to one odds.

Still, my legs weakened as I crossed to the waiting room. "Mr. Vincent?"

Please let it be an old person with chest pains.

Fuck me, I should have played the lottery. A rugged man eased up from his chair with the help of a friend with shoulder-length wavy hair. Bundled fabric covered in blood pressed against his side, immediately pushing him up the urgent queue. It wasn't the severity of his wound that sent my pulse racing. The black leather vest with the gold and black Jackal on it soured my stomach and brought all my repressed emotion to the surface.

The one and only Slade Vincent stood a few feet away, surprisingly handsome for a sturdy, hard man. Blond hair cut Mohican style, shaved at the sides, long on top. Short, rough beard, hiding a sharp jaw. Indigo eyes with honey rings around the middle. Broad, bulky, like a damn bear. Body built for sin. The devil in leather and denim.

Of all the hospitals in the city Slade had to walk into, he walked into mine. North Shore Hospital. Bleary-eyed and swaying on his feet, he'd lost a lot of blood and needed immediate attention. Why was he here when clubs had medics and doctors on their payrolls?

My heart thumped in my chest, frightened that he'd recognize and hurt me. I hadn't had any involvement with my father's club for over seven years. Rival clubs always knew the family of their adversaries. Call it a safeguard.

I swallowed hard at the words plugged in my throat.

Murderer. Bastard. I will kill you for what you did. I couldn't treat the man who killed my father.

Shit. I couldn't leave him there, either. Four years ago, I'd sworn a Hippocratic oath to protect my patients and serve them no harm. All my training, every oath I took, was about to be put to the test.

I struggled to keep my voice neutral and calm as it had done so many times before. "This way, Mr. Vincent."

I held my breath as his fellow Jackal carried him into the exam room and lifted him onto a gurney. Not just any club member. Enforcer by the name stitched onto his cut.

My heartbeat went wild. If they recognized me, they'd shoot me in the head. I needed to get the Enforcer out of the room, treat Slade and get out of here as fast as possible.

Lifting my gaze, I addressed the second Jackal. "I'll have to ask you to wait outside, please, sir."

The brown-haired guy didn't leave. His eyes narrowed, he tilted his head, staring at my right eye. President's orders. Protect their leader.

"Afraid I'll have to stay, Nurse." Lord. That voice. Deep, sexy, mysterious.

Equally as handsome as Slade, more polished and put together, the other Jackal wore a Rolex and smelled spicy like cologne, rather than the typical smoke and whisky of a biker. For a few moments, I got lost in his maple-colored eyes, at how beautiful they were, framed by thick, dark lashes. He was like a dashing Disney prince with an edge of darkness and mystery.

Lust, fear, and confusion wreaked havoc on me as I stumbled into the bed, withdrawing to grab the materials I needed to treat him.

Slade's indigo eyes flicked to my ID badge. "What's your name?" The shallow rasp told me he barely got enough air into his lungs because of the wound in his chest.

"Alexa. Like the badge says." I skirted the question with a partial truth.

Power flared to life within me. Magick I might need to cut off his air supply before he put me six feet under.

"What's your surname?" *Shit.* He knew who I was. Recognized me.

Distraction time. "Can you remove your shirt Mr. Vincent, or do you need me to cut it off?" My hands trembled as I filled a stainless-steel roller tray with gauze, alcohol, and steri-strips.

Sweat broke out on my forehead from the fear of him seeing through my fake badge and discovering my identity. Oh, and maybe a little because he was packing a gorgeous body beneath his shirt and leather.

Thoughts of ending his life shot bolts of adrenaline through me. Killing him went against everything I stood for as a healer, but if I had to choose between a bullet in the head and survival, I'd defend myself from danger. Odds I wasn't sure I'd win with his Enforcer by his side to protect him.

Slade grimaced as he set the blood-soaked wadded-up t-shirt on the tray I rolled next to the gurney. "If I knew the nurses here were as beautiful as you, Nurse. Alexa." Peeling off his cut and shirt exposed the pistol beneath his leather. My heartbeat went wild. "I wouldn't have waited so long to step inside a hospital."

Bastard toyed with me. Enjoyed playing with his prey. The reason he had such a fierce reputation. One hand remained on the weapon he'd removed.

He swung his legs up onto the gurney and stretched out. Legs so long they dangled off the bed. Lord he was tall. Did I mention ruggedly handsome?

"You've got more curves than a mile of mountain road, Nurse. A."

I couldn't tell if he flirted or messed with me. Whatever it was, I had to keep my head in the game, not let his or his Enforcer's good looks distract me.

"Just as deadly if you aren't careful." I aimed for a politely veiled threat, removing a scalpel and setting it in the tray at my disposal. Safety precaution in case that gun turned on me or I had to slice his friend up.

"I think I know where I've seen you before." Slade laced his fingers together and placed them behind his head. That must have hurt like hell. Hoped it did for what he did to my father.

For the first time since inheriting my healing power, I contemplated not using it, letting my brother have his revenge.

Shit. You can do this, Aaliyah. You have to.

"Are you sure you didn't injure your head? You're babbling incoherently. I recommend an MRI, just to be safe." After grabbing a wound flush kit, I stopped to make a note about a scan on the computer.

The second Jackal smirked behind the hand he lifted to his mouth.

Slade smiled at my attempt to shut him up. He did whatever he wanted, when he wanted. "Scan me all you like, Nurse Alexa. I'll stay here for hours if I get to look at you."

Oh, God. That voice. Gruff and sexy.

Snap out of it, Aaliyah! You are not attracted to your father's killer.

Either he had no clue who I was, or he fucked with me. My bets were on the latter. Surely the president of my father's rival club knew who I was.

CHAPTER 6

Aaliyah

"Scrubs are a hot look for you. I especially like the owls." Slade reached for the stethoscope wrapped around my neck, and my breath hitched at having him so close. "Listen to my heartbeat. It's going boom, boom, boom."

So was mine, and not just out of fear. He made my heartbeat erratic when he leaned into me.

"Mr. Vincent, I'm not worried about your pulse." I removed the squeeze bottle from the sterile packaging and set it on the tray.

Come to think of it, a lack of pulse might be an improvement. The man was a murderer. Even experienced nurses questioned their oath and themselves when known violent criminals came in for treatment. Except, in this case, the victim was my father. Gods knew how badly I wanted to let him bleed out. Blame it on the delay in treatment. But Slade Vincent wasn't worth the paperwork involved when a patient died. After my first night back, I just wanted to go home and kick back with a beer. Or ten, after treating the Jackal's president.

You will save him, came the voice of my patron, wise and ancient. *He is not bound for the Underworld.*

Fuck. When *she* spoke, I obeyed. That was how my gift worked. If I disobeyed, she could easily take it from me and choose another.

"This may sting." I cleaned the excess blood and dirt from Slade's side and tossed the used wipes into the hazard waste bin.

One two hundred and fifty milliliter bottle of saline solution later, the wound was clean. Slade's almond complexion paled to the color of the fitted sheet covering the gurney when I slipped two fingers into the puncture. A spark of white light shot through me at touching him, and I had to bite back the urge to moan at the sweet pleasure drifting within me.

Fuck, Aaliyah. You're tending to a patient. A murderer. You're sticking your damn finger in his chest. What the fuck is wrong with you?

Lightheaded and confused, I was tempted to pull out, call another nurse to tend to him. I pushed on, eager to get rid of him as soon as possible.

"Are you experiencing any tightness in your chest or difficulty breathing, Mr. Vincent?" I panted from what he did to me. Panted, for God's sake! Shit, I had to keep it together.

The cut was deeper than I expected, and he had blood in the pleural space, his lung on the verge of collapse. I had to get a doctor down here and get him into surgery.

I carefully removed my finger. "Whoever stabbed you nicked your lung."

Sweat beaded along his brow. "I'm a first name during

penetration kind of guy. You can call me Slade and I never said someone did this to me."

Kill and don't tell kinda guy. Known plenty of those. Smarter to hide their crimes than admit to them.

"You didn't have to, Mr. Vincent. You're not my first—"

"I'm already wounded, Nurse. A. There's no need to break my heart too." Slade managed a wink and flirty smile combo that would knock a normal woman off her feet. Pity I wasn't normal. I had immunity to arrogant, cocky men like him. No amount of mystery, muscle or a well-defined jaw would make me forget what he did or was capable of doing.

"Stab wound, Mr. Vincent," I corrected. "You're not my first stab wound. A stiletto, if I had to guess. Jealous ex-girlfriend, perhaps?"

I bet he had plenty. A man like him probably used his woman like nurses and doctors disposed of their coffee cups.

He issued a gruff laugh that stoked my insides.

"It's procedure to notify the police, but something tells me you won't be pressing charges." Which was fine with me. I wanted him out of my triage room, and that wouldn't happen if the police showed up.

"I'm impressed. You know your knives, but don't worry your pretty little head about it." Slade's tone matched his patronizing smile.

My fingers curled into a fist, itching to slug him. "You know, I'm really starting to empathize with your assailant."

As much as I wanted him to suffer the way my father had, it was time for the leader of the Jackal's Wrath MC to get the hell out of my hospital. But he was on the verge of pneumothorax and a lung collapse, so I had to do something. Summoning a doctor to take him into surgery would mean he and his buddy would stick around. The whole club might even visit. Something I couldn't let happen.

"You're not like other people, are you?" The Jackal's president stared at my right eye the same way his subordinate had. Like they recognized something. Recognized me.

I recorded notes on my findings. "What the hell's that supposed to mean?"

"You don't need to summon a doctor, do you?" He cast his indigo eyes all over my body, leaving a burning trail of fire. "You possess certain gifts."

Shit. Slade Vincent knew who I was, and to make matters worse, I suspected he knew what I was. But that wasn't possible. Was it? He couldn't know about my avatar. Unless … unless he was an avatar as well.

"Don't you, Isis?" Slade caught my hand, clasping it tight, running his thumb over the top of it. The act shot sparks all over my body.

Fuck. Cat was out of the bag. I fell into the fighting stance my father drilled into me when I was a little girl. *You need to know how to defend yourself, baby girl. I won't always be around to protect you.* The memory of his words came back to haunt me. Countless afternoons working the bag after school and the swell of pride in his eyes when I mastered my jab. I took Wolves' protection for granted—took him for granted because despite what he said, he had always been there.

Right then, the gods chose to show me the kohl symbol like eyeliner over his right eye, marking the eye of Horus. I gasped and glanced at the second Jackal. He had one too. The gods must be crazy. The first person to know what I am was the same person who destroyed my family. We were all avatars. Servants of the Egyptian gods. Powers like mine would be useful to a man like Slade Vincent. Deadly in the wrong hands.

As if sensing my thoughts, his grip clamped harder. "How about you do your little trick and get me out of here before anyone asks questions?"

If it would get him out of here and out of my life, I'd do it.

Against my better judgment and conscience, I tapped into the power granted to me by my goddess Isis. Magic thrummed through my fingertips into Slade's body. Warmth spread from the center of the wound, the same way an infection might, but I regenerated it instead of destroying tissue. I worked on the damage to his lung first, moving to muscle and nerve only after the burden of breathing shifted from his diaphragm back to his lungs. I pumped more magic into his wound, edging back as the tissue knitted itself together. Not my best work. My heart wasn't in it, and I wanted him gone, pronto. Still, it wasn't the worst repair job I'd ever done. Slade Vincent was alive and well. As well as a murderer could be, anyway.

The Jackal's president stared at my right eye the same way his subordinate had. Like they recognized something. Recognized me.

"What's your name?" A simple question, but something in Slade's voice commanded the more complex answer. In a quick movement, he grabbed my hand and forced it back down over the fresh scar just below his ribcage.

"Alexa. Like the badge says." I skirted the question with a partial truth.

"I can read a name tag. I didn't ask for your given name." His dark brown eyes flicked to my ID badge.

Shit. Slade Vincent knew who I was, and to make matters worse, I suspected he knew what I was. But that wasn't possible. Was it? He couldn't know about my avatar. Unless … unless he was an avatar as well.

Right then, the gods chose to show me the kohl symbol like eyeliner over his right eye, marking the eye of Horus. I gasped and glanced at the second Jackal. He had one too. The gods must be crazy. The first person to know what I am was the same person who destroyed my family.

. . .

Cheeks flushed with anger, I tugged until my hand was free and Slade was left clutching a latex glove. "You're free to go, Mr. Vincent."

"It's been a pleasure." Slade rose from the gurney and onto his feet in a fluid movement that should have been impossible for someone recovering from his injuries. Magically or otherwise.

I mended bones, knitted tendons, and tissue back together, but plasma and platelets proved to be a problem. More than a pint of blood, and my powers were limited. Slade lost a lot of blood. He should have been lightheaded, not light on his feet.

I wanted to know what he knew but never had the chance to ask since Slade and his buddy cleared out faster than a biker chased by a cop.

"I'll be seeing you again, Nurse. A." Slade's warning chilled me to the bone as he and his companion disappeared into the crowded waiting area.

Patients stared at the burly man wearing only a vest on his upper half. An older woman gave him a saucy wink, and I cringed. If only she knew.

My heart thudded in my chest, and I needed a moment. I leaned against the wall, rubbing my forehead, feeling faint. The button for security lingered a foot away. I should call them and get them down here. Call the fucking cops to tell them my father's murderer came in here to harass and threaten me.

Except a new threat loomed just down the hall from the triage room. The familiar squeak of the uneven wheel on the portable registration cart grew louder as one of the girls from up the front came to finish Slade's paperwork. How I managed to keep my cool around a cold-blooded killer, I'll never know, but the possibility of losing my job fried my last nerve.

Panic set in as I scrambled to clean the blood and hide any evidence of the severity of Slade's wounds. I couldn't explain away the blood or the shiny pink scar tissue where a gaping stab wound had been. Not without exposing my magic. I would be fired, or worse: sent to the fifth floor for a psych eval. As I went to throw out Slade's shirt, I paused, running the bloodied pale blue cotton between my fingers. An ancient urge welled in me, prompting me to draw the shirt to my nose for a quick sniff. Gods, he smelled crisp, smoky like whisky and sharp like cloves. Everything a flirty, sexy, gruff leader should smell like.

Bloodied like a murderer. That reminder snapped me out of my daze, and I gasped at what I'd done. What the fuck had come over me? Sniffing his shirt. Really? Disgusted, I tossed the garment into the disposal bin, burying it at the bottom, so no one questioned it.

There was a knock from the other side of the door to the ER, and I jumped.

"Admin," Jenny's voice called out. "I'm here to finish your insurance information."

"Hi, Jenny." I ripped the bloodied sheet from the gurney, bundled it up, and buried it with Slade's shirt a split second before she stepped into the room. That was close. Too close.

"Hey, Aaliyah. I thought you had a stab wound?" Jenny looked around the room for the missing patient.

"He split as soon as I mentioned we notified the police for stab wounds." I rested my hands on my hips and shook my head, feigning disgust. "I had just sterilized the room too."

"Do you think he'll be okay?" Jenny worried about everyone as if they were her own family.

I was concerned whether she'd make it working in the ER.

"I'm sure he'll be fine," I reassured her. "It didn't look serious."

"I hope so." Jenny backed her computer cart out of the room. "Oh, hey. Barb asked if you could stay over. Damon called off sick, and we're drowning."

"Yeah, of course." I held the door so it wouldn't close until she was clear. "Tell Barb she doesn't have to lay it on so thick. I already know I'm buying and that she wants a burrito to boot."

I took some time out to breathe and ground myself before calling the next patient. Everything looked in order. Slade Vincent took off after I healed him, but no one needed to know that part. Especially Danny.

When my brother asked for my help, I'm pretty sure aiding and abetting our enemy wasn't what he had in mind. But one thing from my run-in with Slade Vincent was abundantly clear. The Heller family would be another one short now that Slade knew about me.

CHAPTER 7

*Z*ethan – Jackal's Wrath MC Vice President & Avatar of Osiris

HEADLIGHTS ILLUMINATED the front of the clubhouse. After the night we had, the Jackals were on high alert. Rivals moving into our territory and trying to frame another club. Slade getting stabbed. The juicy morsels we got out of the captives.

On edge, I half expected an ambush, but only a solo bike rolled down the gravel drive of our clubhouse. Not letting my guard down, I spun a ball of death magic in my hands, ready to lob it. If my time with the New South Wales Police force taught me anything, it was to be prepared for anything. Familiar footsteps thumped on the porch outside, and I killed the ball I'd rolled around my palm.

"It's just Slade," I warned Alaric, Slim, and Robbie, and they fell away, shoving their guns in their holsters.

Slade threw the door open and entered, shirt missing and wearing just his cut. Dried blood tipped his blond hair and torso. Shock from blood loss had drained the color from his skin. Worn and tired, he moved to the bar with just a grunt of greeting, grabbing two beers, handing another to Castor, who trailed close behind. He didn't move like a stabbing victim. Last time I got cut up, I couldn't walk for a week, and moving hurt like a mother. They must have pumped him full of some serious pain meds.

Intrigued, I followed them over. "Expected you to be held overnight." At least that was how a run-of-the-mill stabbing went … longer even … but Slade wouldn't stick around a public hospital for too long with cops crawling around.

"Nah. Played doctor with a smoking hot nurse and then got the hell out of there." He took a long gulp of his cold beer.

I checked Slade for any sign he was flying high, but his pupils were normal, he wasn't slurring his words, and he walked in on his own without swaying. Through my tenure as a police officer, I'd seem the gambit of assholes high on drugs. "They pump you full of pain meds? You seem like you're feeling pretty good."

I asked because we needed an emergency church meeting to discuss what went down tonight, and it was critical for Slade to be coherent.

"Pain meds are for pussies." Slade chuckled.

"Well, you've been known to act like it around here," I said, half teasing.

Slade was great when he wanted to be. He could also be a royal pain in the ass. Emphasis on the royal. Slade thought of himself as a pharaoh and acted like one.

"You're a little pale, but for someone who had a knife buried hilt-deep in your side, you look good." In fact, he looked better than I expected.

"I feel good as new." Slade peeled back his cut to reveal a red, throbbing, raw scar that I peered at closer, tempted to run my fingers along. I'd never seen a wound like that heal so fast, not even with shifter healing. "We ought to give Doc Shriver a pay cut. This shit's a hella lot better!"

I glanced at Castor for answers to this riddle, but he only scratched beneath his right eye, prompting the dark Eye of Horus symbol to flash for a second before fading. Pupils dark, skin drawn under his eyes, he looked just as drained as Slade. It was 4AM, after all.

Our president circled his attention back to me. "More about my time with Nurse A. later." Who the fuck was that and why'd he keep mentioning her? He stood taller and threw his shoulders back. "Right now, I want to hear where we are with the Wolves. Call everyone and get 'em down here. Church is in fucking session!"

Slade came in like a bull in a china shop sometimes, but he was my best friend and worst fucking enemy at the same time.

"Castor, get me a shirt, would you?" Our president flicked his finger like Castor was his damn maid at his service to do whatever he desired. Slade might be our leader, but that was on matters related to the club. His legs weren't painted on, neither were his arms, so he could damn well get his own shit. We weren't his slaves, and as much as he liked to think it, he wasn't a god. Only the servant of one.

"Get it your fucking self, asshole." I was the only one who could get away with saying that to him. "He's not your bitch."

Slade snorted, shoving his drink at my chest. "Fuck you. You're all my bitches." He left to grab a fresh shirt, throwing it over his bare chest as he returned. *Fucking Slade.* Any chance to show off his body.

I ran my hands across my long-sleeved flannel shirt. Ridges underneath it whispered to the Frankenstein of scars below. Where I'd been cut up badly in a motorcycle accident that nearly killed me. Some asshole side-swiped me back in my days as a cop, knocked me off my bike, sent me careening across the pavement. Tore the shit out of me, left me looking like someone chopped up my body parts and sewed them back together.

Just like Osiris, my patron. His brother, Set, had cut him up and scattered pieces of his body around the fucking world. A story for another day that left me broken in more ways than one. Clutching my dick, I crossed to the bar, grabbing a whisky bottle and tumbler.

Alaric sat down at the bar. "Pour one for me too."

His patron god, Horus, gifted him a magical eye that enabled him to see much further than his hawk eyes, could pierce walls, peer into the past and determine a person's motives. What I wouldn't give to have an eye like that. To be able to detect an enemy just by peering into his eyes. They weren't lying when they said the eyes were the window to the soul.

Whisky sloshed as I poured us two fingers, sliding Alaric's across the wooden bar. It triggered us whenever someone got hurt, and we needed a stiff drink to take the edge off. Pussy, yeah. We shouldn't be in an MC if we couldn't handle it, right? Especially when we lived and breathed danger. Too many years spent in the force, attending murders, women cut to pieces, babies stabbed, some poor fucker beaten to death. That shit got to you after a while and hardened you. Dulled your fucking soul. I took a breath and dialed the onslaught back, all their faces, blue, bloodied, gone. Tonight, I'd need more than one drink to drown my demons.

Half an hour later, the club had assembled, and Slade thumped his gavel, calling the meeting to order.

"I think it's safe to say you all know why I called this meeting." He leaned back with his arms crossed over his broad chest. "The Savage Wolves have muscled in on our turf. We busted one deal, but how much of our business have they succeeded in siphoning off? That's what we need to find out."

Seated to Slade's right, at the head of the table, I took the lead on this one. "We took four captives and questioned them. They were smuggling meth, Ice, and fentanyl into our territory, setting up the Red Coast Vultures for the fall."

"Dirty fucks." Slade pulled out his papers and tobacco to roll himself a smoke. Back on the cigarettes again. "What beef have they got with the Vultures?" He licked his paper, sealing his stick, lighting it.

"Tell them what you heard, Alaric." I gestured at him.

"Made a few calls." Alaric twisted his fifth tumbler of whisky. "Got through to the Vulture's president, and found out the Wolves brown-nosed them. Agreed to supply them with fentanyl, then screwed them over and sold it in their territory. Two of their men went missing, and they suspected the Wolves but couldn't prove it."

Slade toyed with the end of his gavel. If he hated one thing, it was double-crossers. He might be pure chaos and destruction personified in a human body thanks to his god, Set, but he didn't cheat anyone, and he sure as shit didn't murder them unless they deserved it.

First lesson – economics. If the Wolves cut into their profit margin, the Jackals would be forced to cut down on our plans to expand Pharaoh and community services like the shelter we operated for battered women and children. We needed to crush the Wolves' expansion start-ups before they got off the ground. Danny Heller and his pack of rabid dogs needed to be taught a lesson, and I was more than happy to take them to school.

Castor had been sitting back throughout this whole exchange, rubbing his jaw, thinking. He always came at it from a legal perspective first. Dig up dirt, find out who owned what, who benefited from an operation, who just got a brand-new fucking BMW. With that knowledge in hand, we'd create havoc and tear them up from the inside. Slade and his god ate up that kinda shit. Chaos was their game. Destruction their name.

"Maybe we can flip someone from the Wolves," Castor threw in. "If I can get a line on a cell or an email, we can dig into Danny Heller's diversification plans now that he's running the show."

Most of the Jackals had no clue about the gods or our powers. Castor and I had to be careful with what we said. Every time we used our magic, Castor had to wipe their minds so they couldn't blab to anyone and get every other club breathing down our neck.

Castor snapped his fingers and sat up straight. "Hey, you remember hearing something a few months back about the Wolves strong-arming their way onto the fentanyl scene?"

Yeah, I'd heard whispers, but since they kept it on their side, we'd kept our noses out of it.

"I remember hearing something about it, but I'm pretty sure old man Heller found out and nipped it." Alaric played with his empty glass. "One of their low-level guys got picked up for trafficking out of the back of one of their nightclubs."

Enough said. He didn't need to elaborate on the type of trafficking. There was only one merchandise taboo enough not to be named. A lot of shady people did a lot of shady shit in this business: guns, drugs, prostitution, porn, and trafficking. We bought, sold, and bartered more than our fair share of the first two, but that particular product? That was a hard fucking no.

The Wolves weren't pushing their shit on our streets, and they sure as hell weren't poaching our people to fill orders.

"Castor, do some of your hacker shit." Slade slid a beer from the center of the table and downed a few gulps to stave off the nerves showing in his throbbing forehead vein. "I wanna know what the Wolves are up to, who they're paying, who else fucked us. Get on top of it. We'll be there to blow up their goddamn trucks next time."

"Of course, Prez." Castor leaned back and smiled.

Castor's magic came from Thoth, an Egyptian god who dabbled in writing, science, and all sorts of other weird shit. Light magic, black magic. It didn't matter to him. Thoth was as smart as he was dangerous. The powers related to the moon, scribes, and general wisdom manifested in interesting ways, like being connected to every type of message. Letter, email, report, text message, and all social media messaging platforms. His brain was connected to the damn internet. Hell, fucking Thoth invented it! This gave Castor insight into everything. We called him Hacker, 'cause he was our resident hacker. But unlike the neighborhood geek, Castor didn't need to design code for a program. He was the program.

If anyone could find out what was going on, it was him. In the past, he'd sifted through every and any legal document, even sealed ones, getting us access to confidential information that no one else could. It also helped that he had a legal mind behind it to explain what shit meant.

After spending three years at the academy to train and learn to be a policeman, I could do the same to an extent. Every law of the state of New South Wales was drilled into me. But I didn't understand so much the ways they could be twisted and manipulated by lawyers who charged two grand an hour, using precedent and other bullshit to get their dick clients off the hook.

"What do you want to do, Slade?" I refilled my empty glass with another round, offering him one, but he waved me away.

"President," Alaric reminded me. Old goody fucking two shoes. Worse than my miserable old third-grade teacher.

Fuck rules, fuck the law, fuck the justice system. Where

did it get my sister? Bruised, battered, multiple hospital visits, an Apprehended Violence Order for her cockhead of a husband to stay away. Did it work? Fuck, no. He respected the law as much as he respected her. Earned me a write-up and suspension when I visited the fucker off duty to deliver a warning. Three days later, my sister died as a result of a catastrophic brain injury.

"There's a good chance the Wolves will see this as a declaration of war." I upheld my obligation to the club and did my duty as Vice President, warning Slade about what could happen once we fucked with the Wolves.

We'd staved off war a couple of years back when a deal went bad with the Egyptian mafia. Colt Raine had exacted his revenge, and we lost our woman in the fallout. My chest tightened with the need to scream. I held it in, gripping the edges of the table. Slade shot me a look, and I calmed the hell down, releasing the wood. Another war could kill us. We had to avoid it at all costs.

"Oh, yeah? Well, Danny Heller fired the first shot." Slade's forefinger trailed along the wound site.

"Well, if you believe the cops and the evidence, it looks like you fired the first shot. Right into Alexander Heller's back." I shrugged. "Maybe Danny's just looking for retribution."

"Would it change your decision if he was?"

"No, it wouldn't change my decision at all."

Slade had that look in his eyes that said he was ready to stir shit up. I guess it came easy to him as the avatar for a god prone to disruption and destruction. Osiris and I had a different arrangement. I was judge, jury, and occasionally executioner. Where Slade could afford to be reckless and wild, I could not. My thoughts were linear, methodical, and it fell to me to weigh the pros versus cons of every decision we made, just like I judged the dead at night. Which meant I ran the scenarios and did the math. A war could cost us trade relationships. We could lose men. Good men. Brothers.

For the first time since I opened its doors, I worried my brothers-in-arms wouldn't put the needs of the shelter or our neighborhood before our own. Slade was salivating for revenge for the charges laid against him. Hell, the need to crush his enemies, the ones who wronged him, pumped in his blood. Set, his god, didn't take shit lying down, and neither did he. They made their enemies pay. I was lucky to still be alive around Slade. Osiris hadn't been so lucky with his brother and descended into the Underworld.

The Wolves were our rivals. We had run-ins with them in the past and chased them back to their home turf with their tails tucked between their legs. But this was different. This was war if the club voted on it.

"All those in favor of getting the Wolves out of our territory once and for all, raise your hands now." Slade watched as the hand of every single man seated at the table shot up. We appeared to have a unanimous decision. Slade still had a vote. As president, he could nix the whole thing, but I knew him almost as well as he knew himself. Slade wouldn't object. This plan was right out of his playbook. His hand casually went up too. "Let's do this then."

As Jackal's Wrath's Vice President, I bore the responsibility if something went wrong ... if someone died. Collateral damage was inevitable in conflict like this. Soldiers accepted that before going into battle.

Only we weren't soldiers. Slade, myself, Castor, and Alaric were avatars, and we worked our gods' will on Earth. If there was a side to choose, it was with the gods, because Osiris, Lord of the Underworld, gave us the edge we needed. Not many survived going up against the god of Death himself.

CHAPTER 8

Aaliyah

DANNY SHOWED up halfway through my second shift. Impatient bastard refused to wait for a lull in incoming patients, cornering me while I grabbed a snack from the vending machine.

"I'm working, Danny." I punched the number pad on the machine harder than necessary. "What do you want?" I didn't look up from the vending machine, staring at the metal coil, shoving my overpriced bag of trail mix off the shelf and into the catch below. He was the last person I wanted to deal with after a long, hard shift.

"You know what I want." Danny's boots squeaked on the linoleum floor as he moved closer and grabbed my arm, dragging me roughly away from the babble of the TV playing midday talk shows in the nearby waiting room. "I need an answer."

Thank God he hadn't been here last night when Slade Vincent dropped in. World War III would have broken out. Patients would have been caught in the crossfire. All-out chaos would have gone down.

Danny swayed on his feet, reeking of beer and cigarettes. I knew from experience that his blood alcohol was way over the limit. The idiot was lucky he hadn't been pulled over. Bloodshot eyes bored into mine. Sweaty hair stuck to his head from his long ride down to see me.

"Jesus, Danny, this isn't the time or place. I'm damn well working." I tried to yank my arm free, but he tightened his grip. "You're hurting me."

"You haven't taken my calls, Aaliyah." Danny clamped down harder, his fingernails digging into my skin. His abusiveness always grew with the amount of alcohol he'd consumed. My father would have him in a headlock if he were alive and caught him doing this. "You gave me no choice but to come here."

No choice? Asshole! "I'm not part of the club anymore. Haven't been in a long time." Seven years to be exact. He couldn't tell me to do jack shit.

That wouldn't stop him from trying. He needed me because of my distance from the club, since I was the least likely to be recognized by the Jackals if I infiltrated their club. Not happening. But Danny didn't care how I felt about the danger he put me in. Nothing but a yes would satisfy him. I couldn't give him one. I'd not throw myself into a den of jackals and end up like my father. Cold and dead, face down on the concrete in a warehouse.

"My answer is no, Danny." I held my ground and matched his glare with one of my own.

Cold winter air whooshed in the front door of the emergency department as patients—a mother and child—rolled in, following the red line to register at the admissions window to my right.

Danny didn't back down, his grip tightening to the point of bruising me. My brother and I never saw eye to eye on anything. We were too different to find common ground. Black and white. I knew what my brother was and accepted the fact that I couldn't change him long before he stepped out of our father's shadow. He lived by the club code and expected everyone else to do the same. In Danny's eyes, my show of defiance was the ultimate betrayal.

But I wasn't a Savage Wolf anymore. The death of my boyfriend, Jimmy, had seen to that. I didn't want anything more to do with bikers and had moved away for college, putting that life behind me.

More than anything, I wanted to confide in Danny, tell him what I *really was* and why I couldn't do what he asked of me. Unfortunately, we didn't have that kind of relationship. We were never close. While he wanted to kill, I wanted to save. I hadn't told a soul about my secret, and the weight of it was lonesome and heavy. If my brother knew what I was, knew the power I commanded, he'd send me straight into the Jackals, thinking me his damn secret weapon. My gifts were limited, though. Healing myself was much slower. And I hadn't exactly tested out resurrecting myself from a gunshot wound to the head.

Besides, it might all be for nothing. The mark of the Egyptian gods on Slade and his companion's eyes pointed to them being avatars too. It explained all the rumors swirling around their club. How Jackal's Wrath MC had gotten so powerful in a short amount of time. I'd be mad to walk into a club full of magicians who could kill me.

"No?" Danny caged me in with both fists pressed against the wall.

He'd been a ticking time bomb since our father's murder, and I just set him off. Nobody did a damn thing, some patients watching on with worried eyes from their plastic seats. Bunch of cowards. Like most people in this world.

My brother lowered his voice as an orderly rolled a patient out on a wheelchair. "Goddammit, Aaliyah. Why can't you ever do what's expected of you?"

I *was* doing what was expected of me. The goddess gave me her power for a reason. I belonged to her, not the Wolves.

Danny's muscles bunched tight the way they did before he took a swing. "I need you to infiltrate the Jackals, get intel for me, feed it back to me. That bastard Slade can't get away with this. Dad didn't do nothin' to the Jackals."

Dad had respected the territory and businesses of other clubs. That was his motto. He'd brought us up and burned it into the brains of his members that we respected other clubs and their families. We didn't do low-life shit like gunning a man down outside his home, in front of his wife or kids. We operated by a code. Facts about my father's murder never made sense, because my dad never broke it. He'd roll over in his grave if he knew Danny sent me into the Jackals. It was a death wish I didn't care to carry.

"I can't do it, Danny." My flight instincts kicked in, but at twice my size, there was no way I was going through him.

Danny's face flushed red as he pushed off the wall, hands still clenched into fists. "Then they'll come for you too, and you won't have the Wolves to watch your back."

He reeled back and punched the wall inches from my head. I flinched but didn't back down. My time in the club had taught me how to stand up for myself. How to not fear men twice as strong as me.

"Everything okay?" An orderly came around the corner pushing a mop and bucket, eyeing the hole in the wall. Not the first person to do damage in the ER. We'd had plenty of meth heads who wreaked havoc.

Danny glared at him as he stormed off.

"That guy threatening you?" The orderly gripped his mop tighter. "Want me to call security?"

"No, no. He didn't hurt me." The trick to a good lie was including enough truth that you could almost believe it yourself.

"You sure? You look pretty shaken up." He waited until he was certain I was steady on my feet before letting go of my hand.

I'd faced many drunken bikers before.

"He's my brother." I nodded in response to his look of surprise. "Our father just died, and he's not taking it well." The last part came out shaky.

"I'm sorry for your loss." The orderly went back to work.

I paused, collecting the breath that had been knocked out of me twice, once from my brother's appearance and again speaking about my father.

Thankfully, the rest of my shift passed without incident. Plenty of excitement for one day. Exhausted, I leaned over the nurse's desk.

"Happy Hour at El Matador's?" Barb suggested.

"Trying to collect on the margarita and quesadilla I owe you?" I teased.

Friday night out on the town was just what the doctor ordered. After my exchange with Danny, I wasn't sure there was enough chips, salsa, and tequila to drown my sorrows. But Aaliyah Heller never welched on a bet.

"You're on." Barb and I wrestled to swipe our ID badges on the time clock. "Meet you there?" My friend took her own car because she had to sneak away early to go home to her husband and kids.

"Sure." I smiled, leaving with her to take the elevator to the parking level.

"What floor?" A guy in a hoodie and sweatpants asked, finger hovering over the rows of buttons.

"Ground two, please," I said with an awkward laugh.

"Ground three, thanks," Barb added.

The buttons on the chrome panel clicked as he pressed them. Eyes closed, he leaned against the steel wall, arms folded over his chest. He kept fidgeting with his zipper. Rings under his eyes made him look as tired as I felt. The soothing elevator music probably rocked him to sleep, an idea the Director of Nursing had to have it playing. Soothe edgy patients and family members before their visit and after.

The three of us fell back into the silence expected of three strangers sharing an elevator. Barb and I knew better than to discuss plans in front of a stranger. Didn't want a stalker showing up.

The elevator dinged when we reached my floor and bobbed as the brake engaged. I gave Barb a smile as the doors parted. Fishing my keys out of my purse, I stepped out on the garage floor. The man from the elevator nodded as he passed me on his way down the aisle. An alarm went on in my brain, and I paused, recalling a button for a different floor had been lit when he pushed mine. My heart rate kicked up a notch.

Sometimes patients or family members stalked staff if they were aggrieved or upset. A few doctors and nurses had been assaulted for "failing to take proper care of the assailant's family member". We did all we could, but sometimes, we took the blame.

You're just being paranoid, Aaliyah.

This was one of Sydney's larger hospitals, the sheer size daunting, the parking garage even more of a maze with six levels and A to Z rows. The guy probably forgot where he parked. I'd done it a few times when I'd staggered out of my early shifts, exhausted from working a double.

My fight with Danny left me on edge, and I chalked it up to frayed nerves. I hit the unlock button on the fob and clutched the keyring in my palm. One key protruded through my index and middle finger as I moved down the green aisle of J, just in case.

The man came out from behind the pillar one car down from mine. The dark hoodie concealed his face, and he had his hands stuffed in his pockets. The guy from the elevator. "Gimme your bag, bitch."

Young, dumb, and one of few females in my father's club, I'd gotten into a lot of fights before I hit eighteen. Had to show those men I was just as tough as them. Whooped the ass of drunken bikers double my size or sleazy men who couldn't keep their hands to themselves. Bar fights with skank biker bitches. Dad always punished me, and by the time I had to apply for college, I stopped, conscious that my history might come back to bite my ass. Until Salina flirted up a storm with my boyfriend, Jimmy, rubbing her tits against him right in front of me. I showed her not to touch my man. Bitch needed two new teeth after I was done with her. Never laid her eyes on Jimmy again.

So, hell no, this dick wasn't getting my bag. I'd knock him out before he got close. While he was down and out for the count, I'd tie him up with the jumper cables in my trunk and then call the cops. Idiot tried anyway, rushing at me, all fists and no balance.

"Don't touch me!" I shoved the butt of my palm into his chin.

He grunted and stumbled backward, his hood peeling back to reveal his face. Blotchy, red skin, greasy hair, and dilated pupils. High as a kite. My money was definitely not contributing to his next purchase of drugs. Shit. Why hadn't I noticed this earlier?

He clutched his red jaw. "You bitch." He lunged at me, and I swung, hitting his shoulder. "Fuck!"

"Go home," I warned. "Sleep it off. Then check yourself into a rehab clinic." Hospital policy instructed us what to tell patients who were brought in from overdoses or drug-related injuries.

He pulled something out of his pocket, a long, thin metallic object. "Bitch wants to play dirty, huh?" The switchblade clicked as he flicked it open. Steel glinted in the dull overhead garage light.

Okay. Dealt with these too in bar fights. My dad taught me to fend off an attacker, get the weapon away, then drop them.

"You want my bag?" I dangled it out for him. The only way to get rid of him was to take him down with a punch to the chin.

The dickhead took the bait, pouncing. I swung my leg forward, but he jerked sideways, and I missed his balls by an inch.

Fuck.

This guy was fast, high on speed, or something else that gave him more agility. He backtracked before I could center myself, his punch sending me reeling. I tumbled to the ground, landing hard on my ass and pelvic bone. Pain shot down my left leg from the contact. My purse hit the ground, spilling its contents.

Before I could move out of the way, he kicked me in the face, I rolled over, and spat blood on the asphalt. Asshole gave me a busted lip. I crawled onto all fours, but his boot caught me in the ribcage. Blinding pain burned in my chest. I coughed, unable to move. This guy played dirty, getting me again in the stomach, and I groaned. Another blow struck me in the side, and I lost my breath. Every nerve in my chest blazed with a heated, furious ache. He brought his boot up into my chin, flinging me backward, and I hit with a thud. My head cracked on the pavement. Stars swirled in my vision.

The last thing I heard before I passed out was, "Fucking bitch."

CHAPTER 9

Alaric – Jackal's Wrath MC Road Captain & Avatar of Horus

"Get some sleep, you tired assholes!" Slade slammed the gavel, dismissing everyone. "We've got a big day tomorrow. I want everyone on their game."

Heavy-eyed, drowsy Jackals muttered as they piled out of the room we'd convened in for church. They should be used to it when Slade called an emergency church at all hours of the morning. Our job as Jackals spanned twenty-four seven.

Castor, Zethan, and I stayed put. The club's highest-ranking members and those backed by gods always stayed behind to talk pantheon business.

Deep lines swathed Castor's forehead. He got that look when something big was about to happen.

My two-way radio tuned into the local channel crackled with the voice of Brad from the State Emergency Services. A downed tree. I switched it off, along with the others. This was a conversation not to be broadcast if I accidentally pressed the PTT switch.

Slade refilled his tumbler with whisky then lifted the bottle, asking if we'd like a refill. I pushed my tumbler forward. Half a bottle before bed kept the nightmares at bay.

"You want me to kill the captives?" Zethan sipped at his whisky.

"Don't wanna talk about that now." Slade threw back his drink and poured another. His fist trembled the way it did when he prepared to raise hell. Revenge burned in his veins. He wanted to retaliate against the Wolves.

Zethan set a hand on our president's shoulder. "I know you want to kill the Wolves for what they've done, but you need to rein it in, and sit tight. The cops are watching us because of old Heller. We can't afford to give them anything else to add to the murder charge."

Flames tore across Slade's knuckles and hands. He closed his fist, killing them. I felt the power raging for release to create maximum havoc.

"Rein it in." Zethan hunched over with his elbows on the table as Slade's magic ebbed. "What else is on your mind, brother?"

I never took that liberty. Strict dad and all, a sergeant in the Air Force just like my grandfather, who fought in WWII. *No elbows on the table, boy. Eat with your proper fork. Sit with your back straight, or I'll whoop your ass.* Yes, sir. Discipline had been drilled into me pretty young, encouraging me to join the cadets at fourteen and the Air Force graduate police program at eighteen.

Slade's eyes flicked to Castor's, and they shared a thoughtful look before our president peeled back his cut and lifted his shirt to reveal a bumpy, red scar where he'd been stabbed. "She's back." He ran his finger along his scar. The air seemed sucked from the room as the weight of his words sank in.

Zethan didn't move as if every muscle were paralyzed. "You sure it's her? It wasn't an avatar from another pantheon?"

Slade scratched his right eye, encouraging the symbol of my god to flash over it. "She has the mark."

Isis had chosen her next avatar, the woman fated to be our mate, courtesy of the curse on all our gods. My chest stung that my beloved Liz, my first and only love, had been replaced. No one could take her place. I didn't want someone else. Didn't have the heart to go through it again. Whoever had cursed us intended for us to suffer losing our mate over and over again.

But the world didn't spin without Isis, goddess of medicine, motherhood, fertility, and magic. Gods were real. Very real. They influenced humanity and their world through avatars like me, who used their powers for the gods' will and our own.

Zethan snatched the bottle of whisky and poured himself a tall glass. Out of all of us, he had the right to be nervous at her return. He swallowed in three hurried gulps and slammed the tumbler on the table. Slade would turn into a protective Jackal and not leave them alone together. Ever.

"Take it easy." I slid the bottle away from him. With everything going on, we didn't need him to fall back into his blame and grief.

Slade's blue eyes lightened. "You should see her. She's beyond beautiful. Five feet six with curves like a coastal road. Dark hair halfway down her back. Lips like sugar. Cheekbones like apples. An ass meant for squeezing. Tits …" He curled his fingers and laid kisses in the air.

"Do you have to be so vulgar about our mate?" I wasn't a prude, but if this was our intended, I didn't appreciate the crude way he referred to her body. The men might view me as the one who followed orders, but I had no problem challenging authority when they were out of line.

My father raised me a gentleman. Kiss and don't tell. No sex on the first date. Woo her, wine her, get to know her, build a deeper connection. Opposite end of the spectrum from Slade, who jumped into bed straight away and built a heavy, addictive sexual connection. Deep as a puddle.

"Oh, I'm sorry, chap." Slade mimicked an English accent. "Didn't know I offended your gentlemanly sensibilities." He pretended to tip his top hat. "She is a fine woman. Educated, whip-smart, witty. Worthy of your adoration and romanticism."

"Fuck off, asshole." I swiped the bottle of whisky away, pouring myself another finger, ignoring topping off the other's glasses.

They always gave me shit because I treated our woman the way she deserved. With a lug like Slade objectifying her, dressing her in designer clothing, Zethan stealing her away for long weekends, and Castor teaching her magic, she needed someone to adore her.

"Zethan, Alaric, I need you to do a job for me." Slade leaned back in his chair with his fingers splayed and pressed together. "Go to North Shore Hospital and watch her. Make sure she's safe."

Overprotective, but Slade had reason to be. At six years old, he went on a picnic with his mom and dad, and a rival club mowed her down in front of him. After that, every woman he had, he never left alone and always had a man guard her if he couldn't.

Now he was paranoid about another club hurting our new mate after what happened with the Winter's Devils.

"I don't want any part in this," Zethan protested, body as tight as a tripwire. "Send someone else."

"You want us to stalk her?" I understood Slade's motives, but didn't know about this. Gentlemen didn't creep and certainly not on their mate. If she was bound for us, she'd come one way or another. Fate, and all that shit.

Slade aimed a cocked finger that resembled a gun at me. "Exactly."

"No." Zethan put his foot down, splaying his palms flat on the table.

The decision was made, and Slade rose from his chair. Our last mate was murdered, and he'd not leave this one to tempt the same fate. "Castor has a date with the captives, and I've got to make a few calls to the Vultures. That leaves you two, and I'd rather you than the others."

"We took care of the vultures." Zethan shot out of his chair.

Here we go. Another classic Zethan and Slade argument mimicking their gods Osiris and Set. Always at war with each other. Honestly, I didn't know why Slade chose to keep Zethan as his Vice President when they always bickered on decisions, especially those Slade made.

Slade jabbed a finger at Zethan's chest. "You're going, and that's final. Get your asses down to North Shore tomorrow for her shift. Talk to her if you can. I've waited for my mate too long. I won't wait any longer." And that was it. End of discussion. He swaggered out of the room, sliding his phone from his jeans pocket, preparing for his call.

I wasn't like my president and couldn't just move on a few months after Liz was killed, taking woman after woman into my bed. Fucking another hadn't even entered my thoughts. Hawks like those represented by my patron, Horus, mated for life, and so did I. The thought of another filling that void felt strange and unwelcome.

I shrugged my shoulders in a circle and said, "Meet you at the clubhouse tomorrow?"

"Fuck!" Zethan left me standing there, alone, longing for my lost mate.

I wasn't ready for a new mate. Didn't know whether I'd ever be when I'd had my one true love.

My gaze went to the shot of whisky left. Might as well drink it. Have a good night's rest before the ride down to Sydney.

***

Alexa was just as beautiful as Slade had promised. Everything faded away as I stared at her. Silky hair pulled back in a bun. Moist, pillowy crimson lips that I imagined crashing my mouth over. Eyes the color and depth of aquamarines. Full, dark brows that held an edge of stubbornness to them. Silky caramel skin with an inhuman glow to it. A body that would put the screen goddesses I watched as a child to shame. Move over, Marilyn Monroe.

My chest took a hit like I'd been struck with a round of mortar fire. Emotions I hadn't had in over two years. I fought them, feeling like I betrayed my mate in some way for also welcoming them.

The avatar examined an elderly woman, taking her vitals, handling the woman with the care I'd come to know from Isis. In this regard, she reminded me of Liz. Other than that, they were very different. Alexa carried herself with a natural assertiveness and toughness that warned people not to test her. Despite being a knockout, she didn't plaster herself with makeup or use her sexuality to get ahead with the male doctors.

Using the eye Horus had gifted me, I scanned her, searching through her past, trying to find out more about her. I got inky blackness back and a fraction of information. She had strength but also vulnerability, and she shielded that well behind an impenetrable wall. I'd never come across another I couldn't read, and that troubled me. It gave me the impression she had something to hide, and that always piqued my suspicions.

Normally, when I peered into someone's past, I saw their secrets, their deceit. Came in handy for the club, with taking on new prospects or questioning a traitor. People who hid things usually had ulterior motives. I wasn't good with strangers, and I didn't trust anyone who held secrets.

Planes were simple, and I knew the layout of every button, every function. Communication and navigation systems. Direction finder and altitude indicator. Radar and primary flight display. High-frequency radio communications. Nothing hidden, no mysteries, no deadly surprises. Nothing that could harm me.

I didn't like nasty surprises. I liked to know what I was up against. The fact I couldn't get a read on the nurse set me on edge and a wall went up between us. Trust was everything to me after what happened four years ago. And that didn't set a good precedent for our relationship.

"I can't read her," I told Zethan.

He stared at her too, swallowing hard, then sniffing and looking away. "I've got to get some air." He hurried out the sliding doors.

Fuck. Poor guy. He'd never forgive himself for that night. None of us forgot the night we lost our mate. The night everything changed. I'd give him some space and check on him in a minute.

Through the window at the registration desk, I caught Alexa clock out from her shift. Fuck. Time to go. I zipped up my jacket, stuffed my hands into my pockets, and went out the same door as Zethan. He leaned against the wall, sipping whisky from his flask.

I leaned my left side on the cold slip-formed concrete walls. "You remembering her?"

"Yeah. It's torture." Zethan finished the contents of his flask and tucked it into the pocket inside his cut.

I rolled onto my back and leaned my head against the wall. "Seeing our new mate triggered me too."

Shit had gone down when we lost her. We'd been busy recovering from a deal gone bad and gearing up for a war with the Egyptian mafia. Stress had been high. Morale within the club tested. Mac snorted ice, got high, pulled a gun on the Winter's Devil's member and shot him. Got us into a world of shit, and we had to put down another club. Not a good time. We paid the ultimate price in losing her.

I wanted to say more, but our nurse and a colleague wandered out the front door with her handbag over her shoulder. "We're up."

Zethan trailed behind me a few steps, keeping his distance, and for good reason too. Proximity between him and his mate presented an issue, and he'd not take the risk of hurting her again. Keeping our distance, we took the second lift down to her car in the garage.

This morning, Slade ordered us to make sure she got home okay and obtain her address. Stalkerish? Fuck, yeah. But if anyone found out what we were, what we could do, and our connection to the nurse, they'd use it against us, just like they'd done before. We had enough enemies and dogs biting at our heels and didn't need someone kidnapping her and using her as bait. Our mate bonds would kick in, and we'd be forced to defend her and protect her, leaving the club wide open.

So, we'd parked a couple of cars down from hers. We'd waited for an hour for her to arrive, watched where she parked, then Zethan had jumped when a nearby spot became free.

We got off the elevator, trailing her a hundred feet behind her. Before she got to her car, some dick jumped her. My mate fought back, but he was faster and stronger. Her cries burned into my heart as he knocked her to the ground and kicked her over and over. I'd never run so fast, my heartbeat thundering faster than my boots on the concrete.

When we reached her, Zethan went nuts, laying into the guy with fists, elbows, knees, anything he could. He had the guy on the ground in seconds, kicking him, ribs cracking loudly. More bones crunched as he stomped on his hands and kicked his face. Brutal. Punishing. Mechanical.

"Stop it." I grabbed Zethan beneath his arms, hooking him, dragging him back so he couldn't do further damage. He jerked against me like a wild beast. "You're gonna kill him."

Air heaved in and out of Zethan's mouth. "He fucking touched her."

The mate bond made us all go crazy when our woman was threatened. Logically, I knew she wasn't ours yet, and we didn't know her, but she would be ours soon. Regardless, we'd protect her as if she were one of our own.

"I know." I wrapped an arm around his neck and smoothed back his hair, letting him breathe it out. "I know."

Men who beat up women irked the hell out of him. If we were out at one of our bars or clubs and he caught a man threatening a woman, he was on it in seconds, and that man either left or learned the hard way.

"I'm letting you go now." I loosened my grip. "The nurse is hurt. We gotta get her to safety and take care of her. You promise to hold your shit?"

"I promise," he panted, eyes dark, almost black like a demon had possessed him.

I let him go and moved away, crouching beside the nurse. My hand shook with rage as I reached out to brush the hair from her badly bruised face.

Zethan stood a few feet back, fighting every instinct to take her in his arms and comfort her, something he couldn't do with the curse over his head. Just one more scourge for us to contend with.

"Put him in the back," I said to Zethan, warring with the part of me who rebelled at giving orders to my superior. Zethan outranked me, and I did what he or Slade said, but he wasn't in his right mind now. "We need him for answers."

My reminder prompted Zethan's hands to uncurl. He twitched, and I worried he might kill the guy before we could gather intel. Face burning red, he dragged the groaning fuckwit across the concrete and threw him into the back of the van.

The nurse's belongings were scattered around her purse. I packed them up and lifted her into my arms, carrying her to the back of the van.

Zethan hovered by the door.

"Zethan?" I nudged him with the nurse's leg.

"Yeah?"

"Answers, then you can kill him."

CHAPTER 10

*A*aliyah

THE NEXT THING I remember was the last thing I expected. I woke on a single bed with fresh sheets and a ridiculously soft pillow that sank under my weight. Dimmed lights made it difficult to see much detail of my surroundings. A long room like a scout hall or something. Other beds nearby with a few curled-up forms buried under blankets. Sniffling noises, snoring, and the drone of what sounded like a coffee pot. The smell of something sweet and spicy. Arnica, perhaps. Muffled voices came from the other side of the door thirty feet away. All of it a welcome relief to the pounding in my head.

The room spun out of control, and a violent wave of nausea hit as I sat up. Fuck. Mild concussion. Everything ached as I eased back down on the mattress. Where the hell was I? My heartbeat wanted to tear off like a bike at a traffic light, but I had to slow my breathing to ease the queasiness.

I tried to reconcile my memory. Leaving work and catching the elevator with Barb. Parking garage and the junkie who jumped me for my handbag. My face stung and burned. I lifted a hand to find my eye swollen and I whimpered.

Fuck. So much for kicking the hooded guy's ass. All talk and no swing.

I didn't know how I'd ended up here. My eyes adjusted to the dark room as I attempted to get my bearings. Wooden paneled walls, wide-planked floors, and wooden sash windows. Wherever I was, it was an old building. Not one car horn blasting, wailing car alarms, dogs barking and the countless other sounds that made up the city's symphony. Complete silence. We were somewhere secluded by the sound of it.

My head throbbed as I scanned the other beds. Women crying, some raised by pillows, others sitting on the edge of the mattresses talking to another female. Some asleep beneath their blankets. Some coughing woman, wheezing to breathe because her ribs were badly bruised. The woman seated on the edge of a mattress, talking to another woman, eyes darting about, clutching her coffee mug like her life depended on it. Hypervigilant and suffering from PTSD. Seen plenty of those women in the ER. I could heal them physically, but I couldn't take away the scars in their minds and hearts.

Fuck, I'd been taken, and so had they. By whom? My mind ran wild with different scenarios, all of which led to the same conclusion: that I was being held for ransom. The kidnappers didn't do their homework. If they had, they would have known my brother wouldn't pay. Not after the way we left things at the hospital. He made it crystal clear. I was on my own.

I glanced around the room. Five other beds. Women

hooked up to IV bags. Bandaged, bruised, beaten just like me. This abduction had all the makings of a human trafficking ring. The evening news ran a story about women forced into the sex trade and their babies into black market adoptions. I had to find a way out before I was drugged and sold to some scumbag pimp.

Once my stomach and the spinning sensation settled down, I tried sitting up again. *Easy, Aaliyah. Nice and easy.*

When my bare feet hit the floor, I had the presence of mind to pat myself down. I still wore the same green scrubs. The only items of clothing missing were my socks and shoes. After a more thorough check, I added a pair of amethyst stud earrings and a matching pendant to the list of items no longer in my possession. They let me keep my Fitbit and my ID, which dangled from the lanyard around my neck. At least I wouldn't have to file a report with hospital security for a missing badge on top of a police report.

If I wanted to file a police report, I needed to find a way to escape. First thing, check on the women, and do my duty as a nurse. The closest had the trademarks of a bad beating.

She whimpered as I examined her. "What happened?"

Her busted lip stopped her from getting out much. Overcome with emotion, she burst into tears and I stroked her face.

"It's okay, I'm going to get you out of here."

She clamped a hand down on my wrist. "No, it's not safe!"

I smiled, trying to inject some hope into it. "I'll be back."

I moved onto the next woman. My magic told me her ribs were broken, and the IV connected to her pumped her full of opioids for pain relief. Before I crossed to the third, more diagnoses hit me: swollen jaws from being hit, scratches, lacerations, torn frenulum from forced oral sex, rope burns, torn rectum, and tears in the posterior fourchette of the vagina. My eyes closed shut and I bit my lip. Oh, god, these poor women were victims of sexual and physical assault. I squeezed my thighs together and lowered my head.

When my grief and anger passed, I detected more magic inside the building. A power that heightened my own. Another fucking avatar. Fuck. Slade had told me he'd see me again. His men had kidnapped and brought me here. I was their prisoner. Completely out of my element. I healed, but I didn't cause injury, and if someone came at me, I didn't know how to protect myself or the women surrounding me.

Wary, I jumped to my feet. I had to get these women out of here. Next task, check the door and windows. I tested for creaks before I put my full weight on the floorboard. Then I took my steps one at a time.

"Where are you going?" someone whispered as I crept past her bed.

"Getting us out of here," I whisper yelled back.

"No, it's not safe." The bedframe creaked as she sat up, but I didn't look back.

To my surprise, the windows weren't locked, but I wasn't going out one. That left the front or back door. I scanned the place, finding a fire escape door, but I wasn't going near that as it was alarmed. A hallway dissected the room. My best bet was to try that. I pressed my ear against the raised wood panel and listened. The distant voices I heard earlier had stopped, so I decided to make a break for it.

Now or never, Aaliyah.

I kept moving, one foot in front of the other as I crept down the dark hall, passing two private rooms. Single beds with fresh linens folded and neatly stacked by the footboard, nightstand, and an armchair. The third and final room was the same, apart from one addition: a bassinet with a baby sleeping in it. Fuck, not children too. I swallowed back bile as I pushed on, finding a door at the furthest end of the hall.

The wooden floor croaked on contact and alerted anyone

within earshot of my escape attempt. Panicked, I turned the knob and inched the door open, completing my disastrous escape with a creak and groan. No one stood guard, encouraging me to tiptoe outside. Freezing fingers of cold air curled me into its grasp. Glued to the spot, I rubbed at my goosebumped arms.

Birds hooted in the distance, and animals scurried in the bushes. I squinted, trying to scan my surroundings. Shit, no cars or vans parked outside either. There was no way I could get five or more women out of here with me on foot. Two of them were out of it, probably drugged on pain meds or something else. I'd have to go alone, get to safety, find a police station and report this building.

"Where are you running off to?" a man called out to me, his sexy, stern voice, inviting me to spin around.

Light behind him gave him an angelic glow, but he was no angel. He was the devil. Jackal. Enemy. He clutched something under one arm, but I couldn't tell what it was.

"Get the fuck away from me, asshole." I backtracked a couple of steps, and my heel hooked on the edge of a paver or something, and I went down hard. I smacked my tailbone on the steps, landing in a crumpled heap. Intense pain flared deep in my muscles, and I wheezed for breath.

Hurried steps carried him to me, and I scampered backward. "Don't move, you've hurt yourself." He held one palm out in surrender as he set a metal bowl on the ground a few feet from me. "Carlie!" he shouted.

I scrambled for purchase, but my spinning head returned with a vengeance. Warm hands captured my upper arms, and I jolted. A different feeling replaced my lightheadedness. One of floating in a haze of pleasure. Electricity crackled all over my skin, snapping me out of it.

"Take it easy," the jackal warned, deep, steady, and

commanding, and a part of me fell under its spell, obeying. "I'm not going to hurt you."

The primal part of me reacted with survival instinct, and I thrust a fist out, hitting him in the cheek. "Like hell you aren't, you kidnapping scumbag!"

Startled, he cupped a hand to his cheek, then shook his head and snorted. "Fuck, Carlie, get your ass out here!" his louder shout had me trembling.

A woman dressed in jeans and a pullover sweater tumbled out the front door, looking left then right before landing on us.

"Shit, Castor, what happened?" She approached slow, cautious, the way one would if they approached a wounded animal. "Is she all right?"

"You traitorous bitch." I kicked, warning her to stay away. "How could you do that to your own sex? Kidnap these women like this?"

The woman chuckled nervously, a hand flying to her mouth. "Honey, trust me, I'm saving you from the kind of men who'd hurt or kidnap you."

What the fuck kind of answer was that? "Where the hell am I? Take me home."

Carlie crouched awkwardly like a waddling duck, and I got a better look at her. Blonde hair tied up in a ponytail, shirt sleeves bent back over her sweater, a pen hooked on the neck of her pullover. Pretty, in her late twenties to early thirties. Her swollen, pregnant belly, which she rubbed, explained her uncomfortable movement.

"You're in a women's shelter, honey." Carlie reached out for me, but I jerked backward. "We rescue abused women, victims of domestic violence. You were pretty beat up when my brother found you, and he brought you here."

Her words prompted flashes of memory again. Sodium lighting, concrete, pale green on pillars, lots of cars. The hospital parking garage. A hooded man attacked me. Two men fighting, one savage and viciously beating my mugger. Being lifted so gently and lovingly, carried into a van and tucked under blankets. Me falling unconscious. Waking, groaning, my whole body on fire. The same man, wearing a jackal cut, comforting me, holding me, whispering to me while he dabbed at my wounds. My angel. Where had he gone? Flickers of illumination from streetlights we passed. The whoosh of traffic and running engines and loud exhausts. Someone swearing and yelling from the front seat.

I touched my swollen eye, putting together the pieces. Someone had come to my rescue and driven me here. "Where's my attacker?" I looked to Carlie expectantly, then to the man collecting his bowl filled with bandages. He wasn't one of the two men who rescued me.

She smiled, a gesture that warmed me with trust and something strangely sisterly. "Don't worry about him. My brother's taken care of him. Everything's going to be all right. You're safe. You can trust them. Okay?"

"Them?" How could she mean the Jackals? My head hurt, and my brain only had enough juice to process survival thoughts and directed my body to heal from its injuries.

Carlie pointed a lazy finger at the man. "This is Castor. He's going to cleanse your wounds and bandage you up."

Unable to process what was happening and formulate a sentence at the same time, I nodded in response. I rolled over the name on my tongue. Castor. Unusual. Sexy. Mysterious. I drank him in for a moment. Tall. Really tall. Six feet something by my guess. Broad build. Wild, inky black hair brushed the tops of his shoulders, and my fingers twitched to reach out and brush the curls.

A lump swelled in my throat as it registered. This was the well-put together man who had carried Slade into my examination room at the hospital. The damn dark and sexy as sin one.

Fuck, Aaliyah. He's your enemy and not someone to admire.

My attention fell back to Carlie.

"Alaric's inside, doing a shitty job of keeping watch. And my brother, Zethan ..." She scratched her cheek and pressed her lower jaw forward. "He's hiding somewhere."

I detected a hidden meaning to her words. "By hiding, do you mean beating the shit out of the guy who attacked me?"

"Something like that." Castor chuckled, deep, throaty, panty-melting. "You catch on fast." He pushed his broad shoulders back.

Carlie left out the clue about the motorcycle club's involvement in the shelter and it set off my radar. Probably the reason Castor wasn't wearing his cut. Risk management. The jackals didn't want anyone to know the club was associated with a woman's shelter. Everyone with a bone to pick would target the helpless and defenseless women. Fuck, I had to get out of here.

"I ... I have to go." Somehow, I climbed to my feet. Not very steadily, though, and I wobbled.

Castor caught me by the arm and supported me. "You're not going anywhere."

My first instinct, the flight or fight one, wanted to give him a matching bruise on the other side of his face. Another instinct, one of safety and comfort, sank into his touch, the bright sparks chasing across my flesh from where he held me.

Oh, God. I was attracted to a Jackal. To my enemy. My stomach roiled. I must have taken some nasty hits to my head. Brain damage.

Looked like my brother had gotten his damn wish. I'd infiltrated the Jackals after all. Been thrown to the damn sharks. They were going to kill me if they found out who I was. Or worse ... hurt me, extract information from me, the way Zethan was probably doing to my attacker. Which I anticipated would be soon, once their gods whispered in their ear.

I had to get out of here without rousing the attention of the other women or the Jackals. For now, though, I'd gather intel on my enemies and find a way to feed it back to my brother. Find wherever they kept my phone and send him a message. If the Jackals didn't discover my identity before that. The thought made my stomach somersault, and I swallowed back bile.

Moments later, Carlie and Castor both had me inside and seated at my bed. Castor had stripped off his cut and tossed it in a nearby office off the hall. The woman gave me a gentle smile, leaving the Jackal to tend to me. He gently dabbed at my broken skin with steri wipes, and I winced. Finally, I was on the receiving end of this. Ironic.

"Alexa?" Lord, those maple eyes and rosy lips undid me, and some of the tension I carried in my back melted away. "It's Alexa, right?"

It took a few seconds for his question to register. He must have seen my name badge. Well, the name badge I'd borrowed again because I'd misplaced mine. Lost it in the wash or something, and had to order a new one.

I shifted on the mattress. "Yeah." The question made me more uncomfortable than the sting of the alcohol.

"Do you need anything for the pain?" Considerate. Hospitable. I didn't expect my captor and possible future torturer to hold those qualities.

He looked Middle Eastern, like a damn Arabian prince or something from a fairy tale. The kind of man a woman would admire, tongue hanging out, drool leaking. Not an attractive look.

I picked at invisible threads on my scrubs to avoid

looking into those deep, alluring eyes. "Just a Tylenol, please." It would take the edge off the pain. I probably should have asked for an anti-inflammatory too.

He made a call on his cell. "Carlie, can you bring me some water and a Tylenol?" He hung up without a thanks.

Arrogant. Abrupt. This was a man who gave orders that were obeyed. Not a president, but someone with a high rank in the club. Clean fingernails, his spicy cologne with a hint of cinnamon, and the Rolex on his wrist told me he took care of himself, took pride in his appearance. Designer jeans with slashes at the knees were another giveaway. Expensive taste.

I liked cleanliness in a man after being surrounded by grease monkeys in my father's club. Men who took care of their appearance and dressed well got ticks from me. Fuck, what was I even thinking of him like that for?

I stuffed that thought down and let him apply butterfly bandages to the cuts on my face. My thighs clenched when I remembered the bruises I'd find on my ribs from being kicked. Bruises I hadn't felt, thanks to the flood of adrenaline, but was bound to feel shortly, and I bit my lip, dreading it. That was the least of my worries. This sexy biker was not seeing me stripped down to my bra to treat my ribs. I'd attend to those wounds myself, thank you very much.

Castor ran his knuckle beneath my right eye, making it difficult to think straight. Uninvited. Presumptuous. I had a thousand other adjectives for this guy, gorgeous being on the top of the list.

"Zethan and Alaric were lucky to find you when they did." His low croon had me melting. Fucking melting! I was so screwed. Why did my enemy have to have the voice of the sexy, sophisticated guy in the *Mercedes* ads? The one that tricked you into buying one!

And while we were on that topic, why did he have to be so damned striking? It would have been a hell of a lot easier to despise him if he was missing a tooth, had tattoos all over his face, scruffy eyebrows, and nose hair. But everything about him was ... perfect.

I leaned away from the bandage he intended to stick to my forehead. "Please take me home."

"No can do." He cast his maple eyes over the sleeping and resting women, depriving me of their beauty. "President's orders are you're to stay here until we assess the threat to you."

My head throbbed as I scanned the other beds. Women crying, some raised by pillows, others sitting on the edge of the mattresses talking to another female. Some asleep beneath their blankets. Some coughing woman, wheezing to breathe because her ribs were badly bruised. The woman seated on the edge of a mattress, talking to another woman, eyes darting about, clutching her coffee mug like her life depended on it. Hypervigilant and suffering from PTSD. Seen plenty of those women in the ER. I could heal them physically, but I couldn't take away the scars in their minds and hearts.

CHAPTER 11

Zethan

TRIGGER WARNING: **mild torture ahead.**

"SHE'S HERE?" Slade speared a hand through his hair. "Fuck. That's not what I told you to do."

"What were we supposed to do?" I flung my arms wide. "Leave her bleeding and unconscious in the parking lot, for fuck's sake?"

My president closed his eyes and pinched them. "Fuck."

Carlie thumped me on the arm, then waved her fingers at me. "Pay up, both of you." She gestured down the hall to the women sleeping in beds in the shelter, and the one woman I wanted to go and see.

The mate bond called me to her. A damn happy song in my heart, like sunshine, rainbows, and fucking unicorns. It encouraged me to be by her side, hold her hand, pull her close to me. Longing tugged at my chest, irresistible, unbearable. But I couldn't go near her when I'd only hurt her. That would destroy me more than anything. I fought the pull and shoved it away.

I stuffed my hand in my pocket, fishing for a note, pulling out ten dollars and sliding it into Carlie's palm. "For the swear jar."

Money raised for the women we rescued and the shelter. The club funded most of it, but we had a few legit ways to earn an extra buck. Around the Jackal's Wrath MC, a swear jar earned a lot of cash.

Although, my sister had few rules, two were we weren't allowed to swear or get aggressive in front of the abused women. Certain words or behaviors triggered them, so we had to be on our best conduct. Alaric was a fucking natural at it. Mr. Gentleman. The chicks went wild over him, always asking about him. He wasn't interested, only had eyes for our lost mate.

Carlie thumped Slade. "You too, mister. I know you aren't short of cash."

"Jesus, this is extortion. Officer Stone, you should charge your sister with a felony." Slade's tone hinted at an edge of sarcasm. But he complied, sliding out his wallet, handing over fifty bucks, making my sister's damn day. Generous asshole. "For the next *nine* times I swear."

Yeah, he'd need it the way he talked. Luckily he was good with numbers too. He had to be with the cash we funneled through our clubs, bars and businesses.

"Extortion?" My sister tucked the money in her jeans pocket. "You're my biggest donor, buddy. Now keep your cussing to yourself while you're here."

Slade didn't often visit the shelter but made a trip when he found out we'd brought our new mate here.

I smirked at my sister. She'd been working with us for

five years and wasn't afraid of the Jackals. Far worse men existed out there. Men who hurt their women and treated them as their punching bags. Fuckers.

Slade's hard glare turned back to me, ready to tear me a new one for bringing her all this way. "Alexa's not ready for this. She wasn't exactly thrilled that I walked into her ER. Spoke like she'd dealt with bikers before…"

"She probably sees every kind of person in her profession. Junkie, gangster, biker, punk, average person." I hooked my fingers in my belt loops. "What's wrong with here? She'll be safe."

"She works in Sydney, asshole." He sighed. "Three hours from home."

"Ohhh! Lucky you paid up in advance." My sister removed the money from her pocket, licking her finger, pretending to count how much more Slade would add to her jar tonight.

"Carlie, be serious," Slade warned her, and she huffed, shoving the money back where it belonged. To me, he asked, "What makes you think she's not safe?"

I shrugged. "Gut feeling." Years on the force had honed my instincts. I could tell a mean motherfucker from an innocent one.

Slade glanced around the room. "Where's Alaric, Officer Stone?" He liked nicknames. Called me that because I used to be a police officer. Castor copped Bird Boy because he shifted into an ibis. And Hawk Boy for Alaric.

"With the asshole who did it." I fished out another note and pressed it to my sister's collarbone before she piped up. Tonight deserved all the colorful language.

"I'll deal with him." Slade pushed past me, fierce determination on his face.

I grabbed his arm before he could leave. We all knew his definition of *"handle someone"*. Torture and missing appendages. Lots of blood and screaming. Shit we didn't need at the shelter to set the women off. Besides, he needed his hands clean with the murder investigation ... not that they'd ever find the body once I was done with it.

"Leave it to me." I'd handle it clean and silent. None of Slade's brand of chaos. Normally enforcing and questioning captives was Castor's job, but I wasn't passing up this opportunity. No one hit my woman. No one.

She might not be mine yet, or ever, with the curse hanging over me like a noose over my throat. Castor and I were working on it, him more so than me. The shelter, club, and running the Underworld at night kept me pretty busy, with little spare time. But I clung to hope that I'd be able to hold her one day without hurting her.

I left by the back door, headed to the shed where Alaric had parked the van, and tied the asshole to a chair secured to a beam. Trees creaked in the wind. Bats screeched overhead as they made their way to a nearby fruit orchard for dinner. Light shining from my office was the only thing to guide me, not that I needed it. King of the Underworld and all that. These eyes could see in dark places that others couldn't. Shadows, darkness, and other dimensions where humans didn't dwell.

I threw open the door and entered the shed. The van's lights illuminated the space at the back where Alaric guarded our prisoner. A nod from me signaled for him to leave us alone. Beatings or torture triggered his PTSD, and he didn't stick around for it. I wouldn't put him through that shit again, either. The click of the door gave me my indication to proceed.

I hovered over the junkie. Blood crusted his hair and face. He glared up at me through one good eye. An eye I'd seal shut in a minute. He spat blood from a fresh punch to his mouth.

CURSE OF THE GODS

I cracked my knuckles, tender and bruised from smashing him in the parking garage. "Who the fuck are you?"

"None of your business, Jackal."

He knew who I belonged to. The prick was connected to our world somehow. Information to tease out of him. Much faster this way than the way I used to operate. *Police and all their rules.*

I smacked his jaw so hard his chair rocked back and forth, teetering on the edge of tipping over. "We can play this the easy or the hard way. Your choice, asshole."

One thing was certain. This guy wasn't leaving here. Once I got what I needed, we were taking a little trip.

He spat out a bloodied tooth at me. Dirty fuck.

"How many teeth would you like to lose?" I had my fist by my side, ready. "All of them? One by one?" I twisted my fist in my palm.

The guy lifted his head. Blood dripped down his chin. Sweaty hair clung to his forehead. "No more." Pussy. I'd never surrender.

I crouched in front of him. "Why'd you beat her?"

"Was paid to," he rasped, head lolling to the left.

I dragged my boot along the ground. "By who?"

"My dealer." The dick squinted against the light glaring in his face.

"What the fuck for?"

"Bitch slighted the wrong person."

Our nurse had connections? "Who?"

The guy flashed bloodied teeth as he smiled. "That's above my paygrade."

"How much did they pay you to beat the girl?"

"Couple of grams."

Lowlife scum beat a woman for a couple of hits. He'd never do that again. I'd not release him back into society. Creeps like this would do anything for drugs. Break into innocent folks' homes, beat up the elderly until they handed over their savings, steal a stereo system from a car and pawn it. Seen plenty of these types in my law enforcement career. A judge would lock them up in jail for a year, then they'd come back out and repeat offend. Next time he might go too far, seriously injure someone, or even kill them. Not on my watch.

I'd seen one too many women or children hurt by deadbeats like this or their partners. Men with too much power, anger burning in their blood, and one outlet to release it. My eldest sister lost her life to a jealous, insecure bastard who beat her every chance he got. The cops couldn't do a thing unless the women pressed charges, and half the time they didn't, claiming their man would change or their kids needed their daddy. Bullshit. No one needed toxic pricks like that in their life. Even if it did go to court, it didn't always amount to a conviction, the judge going soft on the guy. It left my colleagues and me helpless to do anything but watch, year after year, of battered faces, dead-eyed victims, or deceased bodies. Each time I lost a part of myself.

Until I had to quit and leave it behind. Had to take the law into my own hands. Now I was the lawmaker and lived by the club's rules. My own judge, jury, and executioner, and I preferred it that way.

"Were you paid to kill her?" I asked my final question.

"Nah." The guy chuckled. "Just scare her."

Even worse. I fucking hated men who abused their strength over women.

I rose to my feet, having everything I needed. Now I had to tie up loose ends. Hand lifted, I did my little Darth Vader move, cutting off his air, choking him. He rocked on his chair, fighting for freedom. Wouldn't do him any good. The human brain died after denial of air for six minutes or longer. My watch hand ticked his countdown. One. Two.

He gave a final gasp and shook his head as if that would help him get air. His body fell limp against the chair. Unconscious, but not dead. Three. Four. Five. Six. Seven. Keeping a hold of my magic trick, I moved to him, checking his pulse. No sign. Dead and gone. Good riddance.

Satisfied, I untied him, lifted him, and threw his body over my shoulder. No one would find his corpse where I'd bury him. A twist of my hand opened up the portal to the Underworld and I crossed through it, the gate slurping, sucking me through. Sand on the edge of a river kicked up as I dragged through it. Creatures surfaced in the river, yellow eyes trained on me. They knew when it was mealtime.

"Here you go, boys." I advanced to the edge of the water.

Crocodiles approached the banks, a replica of the Nile, paying homage to my ancestors. One of the larger beasts emerged from the water, growling deep within its throat. Water dripped off its brown scales and its claws trailed through the sand as it moved. Sharp teeth crunched as it snapped its jaw open and closed, inviting me to feed it.

"Hey, Croci." I tossed the body onto the banks. "Bon Appetit! I hear it tastes like chicken." I slurped, mimicking Hannibal Lector from the movie *Silence of the Lambs*.

The crocodile groaned its appreciation, then sunk its teeth into the guy's ankle, dragging him into the water. A fight ensued as the other crocs fought for a piece. Jaws clamped down on his arms and legs, and flesh tore as they snapped him apart, each swimming off with their prize.

"Vicious!" I clapped at them. My good little beasts.

They dealt with all the men the Jackals killed. No way to trace a thing to us. Search warrants didn't apply to the Underworld. Cops didn't have entry to my realm. They could get a one-way pass if they were dead, belonged to the Egyptian pantheon, and came to my kingdom to rest in fucking peace. Not much they could do then. Human law didn't apply to the dead. Only Osiris and I ruled here.

With that done, I returned to the Land of the Living, finding Alaric outside the shed, staring up at the stars. "All done?"

"Yep." I took the hand towel he offered me, wiping my bloodied fists clean.

His gaze lowered to me. "She's awake."

"She is?" The mate bond tugged at me again, summoning me to her side. Fuck, I wanted to go to her, make her mine, never let her go. Isis was Osiris' consort and wife, and her avatar my fated mate, but some sick fuck had played a cruel trick, cursing the three other gods, binding us all together. Now I had to share her with them.

I shrugged off my cut, leaving it in the van. No cuts worn inside. Then no one could ID the club and connect us to the shelter. Protect the women at all costs. Wearing just a navy t-shirt, I moved inside, catching Castor dabbing Arnica cream on Alexa's face to reduce the swelling of her bruises. Alaric stopped right beside Castor, while I kept my distance.

Her good eye, slightly bruised, roved over Alaric and me. Even with the temporary disfigurement of her face, her beauty shone through. Eyes as blue as the waters of The Maldives. Lips slightly paled from blood loss and the exertion of repairing itself. Delicate, yet strong hands. An air about her that told me she could hold her own.

"These two rescued you." Castor finished and packed up his stuff. Peroxide cleaner, bandages, creams.

"Thank you for saving me," she said. Christ, even her voice was heavenly. Feminine, yet firm. "Don't know what I would have done."

Appreciative. I liked that in a woman. Nothing worse than a female who wanted everything, demanded it, and kept taking. Slim's wife was like that, always expecting jewels and expensive gifts, growing bored the next month and on to the next thing. Entitled cow.

Words bubbled on my tongue. *Fuck, you're breathtaking, Alexa. Come here, baby, I've got you. You're mine, you're never leaving.* But all I got out was, "You can stay here a few days until you're feeling better."

Real charmer. What was I going to say to her that wouldn't scare her off? Something to encourage her to stay with us when she didn't know us? She had her own life and we couldn't keep her here. The woman would leave as soon as her body healed. Slade wouldn't let that happen, but I'd protest and stand up for her.

The Eye of Horus flashed on her good eye, confirming her identity. Yep, she was an avatar, all right. Not just any avatar. *The avatar.* The one destined to complete us. Or die trying.

I know what Slade would do when I told him that she'd pissed off the wrong person. Lockdown. He'd force her to stay, no ifs, ands or buts about it. Our mate was precious and to be protected at all costs. He'd chase her away faster than the confusion of the mate bond and all the emotions bombarding her. We had to find a way to make her stay with us. A way she'd agree to.

I couldn't go through that again. I wouldn't. Slade and the others never blamed me for what happened. They didn't have to. I did it for them. It was easy to chalk it up to some ancient curse and start the cycle over again when you weren't the reason someone was dead. There was only one murderer in the Jackals … and it wasn't Slade Vincent.

CHAPTER 12

*A*aliyah

I couldn't stop staring at the blond one. Guarded. Reserved. Lingering on the periphery of the three men. Hands jammed in his pockets, he flexed his massive forearms scored with tattoos, and my gaze went there. Bandages winding around his upper arms drew my gaze up to his ridiculous biceps. *Wow.* Someone liked to work out. Like bodybuilding work out. Or roids work out. Not an ounce of fat on him.

Gaze stuck to the floor, kicking at an invisible bit of dirt. The way he carried himself left no doubt he wasn't a shy one. He didn't look at me on purpose, and the goddess sighed within me. She missed her love, her soul mate. Something in me recognized him on a deeper level I didn't quite understand yet, but was beginning to suspect he belonged to Osiris, Isis' consort. It explained the bandages on his arms.

CURSE OF THE GODS

Osiris was portrayed with them all over his body in Egyptian art.

I snapped out of my daze, and everything came back into focus.

Surrounded by Jackals, the fight or flight response part of my brain reminded me. *Get out of there as soon as you can. Or you're dead.*

Four smoking hot bikers, my vagina added to the mix, not caring one iota about the danger we were in. Bitch loved the thrill of danger.

Bikers we're not going near, my brain concluded.

Men you are connected to, Isis threw in, dumping my simmering pussy in a bucket of ice-cold water, freezing that bitch.

I didn't want to be connected to these men. We were avatars, and that didn't mean we had to be friends, or work together, or even have to see each other. Once the three Jackals left, I'd contact my brother and get out of here. Danny would pick me up somewhere, and I'd hightail it back to Sydney.

Isis laughed in my head. An all-knowing laugh that came out condescending.

Suit yourself, she said. *But they can teach you things about your power.* With that, she receded into the depths of my brain and cut off our connection.

We weren't one and the same. Goddess to human, bound by a magical connection. The all-powerful celestial goddess dwelled in the stars. If she desired, she could manifest a human form to visit me, but she told me they weren't allowed to come to Earth, that the gods were banished a long time ago.

I thought for a moment about what she'd said, about the Jackals being able to teach me about my powers. Maybe I should stick around for a little longer and learn some new things. Most of what I knew I'd discovered through trial and error. Isis was a very secretive goddess and not forthcoming on that topic.

Goddess, listen to me make excuses.

These attractive and dangerous men were just a distraction from my mission. Divine providence placed me inside the enemy's camp, and I needed to stay focused on what I had to do to catch my father's murderer. Get more intel during my short stay. Short being the operative word.

My eyes locked with Castor's maple ones. Long, dark eyelashes framed his eyes. Sex on a damn stick. He knew who I was. Toyed with me. After the admission, he wasn't exactly forthcoming on his identity, so I'd clammed up. The words secretive and dark came to mind. A bit like my goddess. Something told me this one was even more precarious than the rest. Maybe it was the dark stones on his necklace that reflected his darkness.

I shifted my attention from his crouched position beside me to my lap.

"Alexa?" the one who'd introduced himself as Alaric spoke, calling me back from my thoughts.

"Huh?" I studied him for a moment.

Contrasting eyes sized me up. One golden, one gray. The pupil of his golden eye widened as if he studied me under a microscope. Strangest thing I'd ever seen. He gave off a military vibe with his buzz-cut, clean-shaven appearance, polished boots, and the scars along his arms. Four different radios were sitting on his belt. A cute quirk, maybe. Or he was someone high up in the Jackals. Sergeant at Arms was my guess, enforcing the rules and protecting the club. At well over six feet tall and probably two hundred pounds, he was an imposing figure. Handsome to top it all off, in a straight-laced way, very different from the rough, scraggy bikers I was used to.

Alaric repeated his question. "You want tea?"

Tea? Um. What time was it? It had to be late at night. Midnight, at least. The other women were under the blankets in their beds, most sleeping after Castor had tended to me.

"Got any herbal tea?" I wasn't sure what types the shelter had. Probably English Breakfast and instant coffee. These kinds of places didn't have the budget for an extensive range.

"Sure." He went off to get me one.

Huh. That was a first. Bikers didn't have manners. They expected the woman to do their bidding and get them beers or pizza.

My gaze dipped, appreciating his body ... the wide shoulders, tapered waist, and that button of an ass. Mmm. Damn, he was fine. An enemy, but fine. Nice to look at and admire while I was here. Nothing more.

To distract myself from the two other hunks, I grabbed my bag and riffled through it, removing my cell phone. I got as far as entering the pin code when the blond one snatched it, took out the sim card and snapped it.

I lunged to get it back but was stopped when everywhere ached. "What the hell?"

Fuck. He'd just destroyed my only means of contacting my brother and getting information to him. Getting help and getting out of here. Without it, I felt vulnerable and in more danger. I swallowed at the thickness settling into my throat. Oh, fuck, the gods had told him who I was.

"We regulate calls around here," the blond announced, and some of the tension coiling in me eased.

"Isn't that a bit controlling?" I scoffed, gesturing at the other women. "Considering what they've already been through, I would think you'd give them room to breathe."

"My shelter. My rules." The finality to his voice stopped

me from further questions. He didn't trust me. Didn't want me contacting anyone. The Jackals were holding me captive after all. He marched away, steps determined, before I could get my damn phone back. Asshole.

"It's nothing personal, Alexa. We had an incident." Castor's deep, resounding voice filled the space that the blond one left empty. "A husband tracked his wife using her cell phone."

Sensing a tragic ending coming, I dragged the blanket over my legs.

"Reported her kidnapped and then came out here before the cops showed up." Castor fixed the edge of the blanket, making sure it completely covered me. "Tried to kill her. Zethan too, but he grabbed his shotgun and fired. Hit the bastard damn near point-blank in the abdomen. It was a fucking mess. Literally and figuratively. You're a nurse, you know what I mean."

My fingers fisted the blanket. "Yeah, I can imagine." I was grateful he didn't go into detail. Saw enough trauma in the ER to make me a headcase. "No phone policy. Got it."

In the meantime, I'd have to find a way to get hold of a phone to contact my brother without one of the Jackals watching.

"It's safer for everyone." Castor set his hand atop of mine, chasing away the cold that had settled into me at his story. "We're more selective than we used to be. Carlie vets our cases now through her contact at the local women's shelter. Don't get me wrong, we're willing to help anyone, but they've got to want the help. Some people aren't ready, and that's okay. We'll be there when they are."

Smart. They had to protect the woman first and foremost. Over and over, I'd watched countless women walk out of the ER arm in arm with their abuser. Too afraid, too mentally beaten down after years of emotional abuse to remember they were worth saving.

"You can't force them." My voice came out a whisper. "No matter how much you want to."

I was taken aback that the Jackals cared about anyone other than themselves. This was at odds with the cold-blooded killers I thought them to be. But then again, I reminded myself, protecting the club was a whole other matter. Dirty tactics and disregard for treaties prevailed. My father had made a pact with the Jackals, and they left each other alone. Until the night they broke their vow and murdered him.

A raised voice stole my attention. "Just get here tomorrow." The blond one I felt drawn to. "I've got two new girls tonight who need your attention." His phone beeped as he hung up. He glanced over at me, glaring as he jammed his cell back in his jeans pocket. Something told me I was one of the two girls he mentioned.

Castor caught the conversation too, his gaze flicking between me and the blond one. "Just watch Zethan, okay, Alexa?"

"Why?" He wasn't getting away with a statement like that without an answer.

"He's dangerous."

I huffed out a laugh. "You're a member of a motorcycle club. You're not exactly a soft, cuddly puppy."

He laughed at my joke. Smooth. Buttery. Sexy. I bit my lip at the sound, the stab of pain reminding me of my split lip.

Castor's amber eyes pinned me. "I mean it. Stay away from him."

Okay. Message received loud and clear. My heart demanded answers. "I don't understand what makes him so dangerous when he runs an abused women's shelter. He obviously cares enough to remove them from the situation, protect them, and give them a space to heal from their physical and mental wounds."

Fuck. Listen to me. I was defending a damn Jackal. What was wrong with me? Was I sympathizing with them? Stockholm syndrome. My mind couldn't marry up the two extremes—murderers and saviors. Those kinds of men didn't exist in an MC. At least, not that I'd seen. Club members protected their club and family first and foremost. Anyone else was collateral damage.

Castor stood to leave, but I stopped him with a question. "Who are you? Which?" I mouthed the word *god*.

I couldn't place his god, but it was there under the surface, and I felt the pull of their magic. It called to me and my powers answered.

He smiled at me, secretive and mischievous. "Oh, I'm wary of telling you anything, Alexa."

"Why?" My heart thudded, and my mind went into overdrive with panic that he knew my identity. The damn gods had blabbed my real identity.

But his next sentence surprised me. "Your goddess encouraged a snake to bite the Sun God and poison him. Tricked him into divulging his real name. Inherited more power from that little ploy." He smiled again, this time more challenging. "I'll leave it up to you to guess my identity, treacherous goddess."

Just like that, he stepped away, traveling backwards, gaze on me, smirk widening into the sexiest thing I'd ever seen on a guy.

I'd be damned. I smiled back. Challenge accepted.

The further he retreated from me, the more the fog of lust dissipated, allowing my thoughts to return. Shit. I wasn't supposed to be getting friendly with the Jackals. Once they went back to their own business, I'd sneak out of my bed, find a phone and contact my brother.

Castor's nickname sank in, and I wondered if he intended it to have a double meaning. I'd been dropped into the Jackals' camp and intended to gather whatever intel I could get my hands on. And when I supplied that information to my brother, resulting in trouble for the Jackal's Wrath MC, I'd live up to that name.

CHAPTER 13

Castor

THREE YEARS. Three damn years I'd studied spells on how to reverse an ancient Egyptian curse with no answers. All I had to do was decipher centuries-old text that wasn't an exact match to the Rosetta stone and conjure a spell with ingredients that no longer existed. No pressure or anything.

Osiris, husband of Isis and Lord of the Underworld, had been cursed and because that wasn't bad enough, the priest who conjured up that nasty piece of black magic was murdered as well. The spell was tied to the priest and no easy thing to break. That kind of bad luck follows you, even through reincarnation. Which meant Zethan got hit with double the curses like his god. Disfigured, scarred, and with a certain appendage that went missing occasionally.

Slade, Alaric, Zethan, and I were cursed to live life on repeat until one of us broke the cycle. That monumental task fell to me. Enforcer and Sergeant at Arms by day, master of magic by night, I stocked us with guns and deployed spells to keep us safe from our enemies. If only that extended to our product and business. Working on it.

Being the avatar for Thoth came with one hell of a benefits package. Magic, both light and dark, was at my disposal and I had my very own signed copy of the Book of the Dead. I was a celestial badass trapped in human form. Did it help with Zethan's curse? Not yet.

Put me within a few hundred feet of a target and I could pull data from a hard drive down to the last megabyte and wipe the digital footprint before anyone knew what happened. I tapped phones, landlines or cells. All skills that upped my blackmail game.

While Slade and Zethan hammered out the details of rolling out a new price structure and what supplies would feel the pinch first, thanks to the interference of the Wolves. I wanted to spend a little time on my research before things with the Wolves heated up.

The answer to the curse was in the Book of the Dead. I sensed it hidden somewhere within its pages, but the book refused to give up its secrets. After being buried in a tomb for centuries, the magic scribed onto the grimoire's pages took on a life of its own, and it had a stubborn streak to boot. The Book of the Dead would reveal the cure when it was damned good and ready, and not a moment before.

Every night I read from the book, took notes or translated text, whatever it took to coax the answer hidden in one of the passages. I flipped to a section of particular interest that I bookmarked the night before and analyzed the text again. Index cards and sticky notes covered the corner wall of my office. Pieces of the puzzle that I knew fit, but not where. If I wasn't arming the club, protecting it, reinforcing it, enforcing the rules, and delivering punishments, I worked on the curse. There just weren't enough hours in the day. I burned the candle at both ends until the only thing left was a puddle of wax.

The moment Slade entered my study, I knew he had a job for me, and one that didn't involve magical spell books.

"Hitting the books?" My president hovered behind me, scanning the hieroglyphics, boring of it in seconds, and sitting on the edge of my desk, making himself welcome as he always did. More of a hands-on man, a man of action, he didn't read much.

Books were my friend, not his. Nomenclature my game. True epistemophile at heart, and I lived up to that reputation with an unquenchable thirst for knowledge.

"Don't listen to him. I'd never hit you," I whispered while stroking the grimoire's spine. "What have I told you about that, Prez? You're going to upset her. She's a vicious, wily witch to tame."

"So, the Book of the Dead is a *her*, now?" Slade sauntered the length of my bookshelves. Four in total, packed full of magical texts, encyclopedias, and other reference books. I didn't need copies when I memorized them, but I was a bit of a collector and an aficionado. "That's a little macabre, isn't it? I mean, Book of the Dead sounds ominous and masculine. But, that's just my opinion. What do I know?"

"Magical, powerful, dangerous, addictive." I ticked off some of the adjectives used to describe the book over the centuries. "What does that sound like to you?"

"A woman." Slade laughed, his shoulders rising and falling with the motion. "I can't argue with that logic."

It was nice to see him smile again. They were few and far between with all the shit that had gone down in the last six months. The strain showed on his face. More lines around his eyes and slashing through his forehead. Too many for a ruggedly handsome thirty-year-old man.

He parked himself back on the lip of my desk. "Speaking

CURSE OF THE GODS

of women, there's a beautiful one waiting for me at the shelter I have to visit."

Nurse Alexa. Captivating. Brave. Resolute. Just to name a few descriptions I'd ascertained from her yesterday. I popped a date in my mouth and chewed it, thinking about her. Something told me her kisses would be as rich and sweet as the ancient Egyptian fruit harvested from the Library of Thoth.

Slade would try and make the first move. Declare her his, and the first to have her. Same way it went down with Liz. That ruffled a few feathers with the rest of us, particularly Zethan. Again, the feud between their gods playing out.

I hated to share her with the others when I was a one-woman man. The curse had changed us all in that respect. When we laid eyes on Liz, we knew she'd be ours. None of us could withstand the allure of the mate bond. It held our hearts victim and captive. I couldn't stay away from my mate any more than I could stop myself from breathing. The more time I spent with her, I'd fallen for her utterly and completely, and not just because of the tether. To this day, she remained one of the classiest, most intelligent, sweetest, and most feminine ladies I'd ever met.

Thinking about her brought a smile to my face. She took a long time to win over. We were dirty bikers in her eyes, and she had to look beyond her prejudices to fall in love. Something not made easy with the connection binding us together.

Losing her had left a hole in all of our hearts. A hole that would be filled with the arrival of the mysterious, stunning nurse. I'd get my foot in there first. Friendly competition never hurt anyone. Slade liked a challenge, and so did I.

I swept my arms across my desk. "Don't let me get in your way."

"I won't." The glint in his eye told me he'd be onto her like a heat-seeking missile. He'd flirt, flash his dimples, flex his muscles, use his authority to get her to bend to his will. If Alexa was anything like her goddess, like Liz, she'd not fall for the cheap stunts. And that would only make him try harder. Entertainment to watch from the sidelines.

Throughout my time practicing law, I'd learned a lot about people by studying them, their body language, their reactions, what made them tick, especially when I picked them apart on the witness stand. The guilty always snapped when I backed them into a corner. The innocent broke down and shook, showing their compassion and remorse. With my gift, the guilty couldn't hide behind their lies. Just like Slade hid his darkness behind his charm.

I grabbed a piece of scrap paper, folding it into the spine for a makeshift bookmark so I didn't lose my place. "It's not like you to drop in for a chat while I'm studying. What's up?" My desk chair creaked as I leaned back in it.

Slade dragged a chair over and sat down. "Between being a murder suspect and the Wolves making moves on our territory, I haven't had a chance to check on our shipment upstate. Where are you with that?"

A topic that set me on edge. I hadn't heard from our delivery guy in two days. Working like a well-oiled bike, smooth-riding, no bumps, he delivered on time, pretty much every time. Delays in supply were sometimes inevitable, and when it occurred, he always communicated in advance.

Slade swung his leg, tapping the edge of his chair.

"I haven't heard from Joey, and I'm worried." I closed the Book of the Dead. "It's not like him to not check in with Alaric or me for an update."

Joey's silence made me nervous that the Wolves were scheming more trouble for us. The whole deal felt sinister, like they planned on exacting revenge for Heller's death. I didn't need the gift of foresight to see that one coming or know how it ended.

War seemed inevitable from the moment Slade's DNA turned up at that crime scene. The lawyer in me didn't like his chances of escaping jail. The cops had some pretty good evidence on him to tie him to the murder. Bullet casings discharged from the same make of weapon as his. Cigarette with his DNA on it. Multiple witnesses attesting to seeing him that night.

The friend and brother in me knew he was innocent. Hell, at least a dozen people saw him at the shelter when the murder occurred, except for a twenty-minute period nobody could account for. A few women offered to come forward, but Slade refused to jeopardize their safety and drag the club's shelter into the spotlight. I'd been away on avatar business and Zethan at the shelter for an emergency. That left Alaric as Slade's only club alibi.

The police didn't believe us, not that I blamed them. Known associates rarely made reliable witnesses in murder cases. Still, you'd think the cell records would have been enough to convince them. Slade's phone pinged the cell tower closest to the shelter, miles from the murder. Calls were made from that location. He couldn't have been there, and that should have been the end of it, unless someone else used his phone as a decoy.

The State Crime Command's Gang Squad were rabid to pin him for the murder and all too happy to let the bogus evidence do their work for them. Tied their investigation up with a nice little bow. A conviction as prominent as the notorious Slade Vincent would justify their future as a task force with the politicians who funded them.

We had a few cops on the take, but none worked the Heller investigation. That meant our information was on a drip-feed. I fed the dirty officers good money, and they fed us leads – which were few and far between.

Danny Heller wanted revenge and he didn't care how many people died for him to have it. Psychopath sure fit the profile. His actions were purposeful, designed to cause inconvenience and distract us. In my days as a prosecutor, I learned plenty about criminals and their enterprises. Biker gangs that wanted in on other's territory pulled the same stunts. Crossing territory lines, shipping drugs through other club's routes without permission, stealing shipments and selling them at discount rates. Even taking each other out using guns for hire and then asserting innocence.

"Get up there." Slade rubbed his tired eyes with the heel of his palm. "Check it out."

"I planned on riding up there tonight." I got up to pack a few supplies for the trip. A glance at my Rolex told me the time. 11AM. It was a long drive both ways, and I'd not be back till late. No Nurse Alexa for me today. Slade won this round. Clever asshole.

"Check in with me when you find Joey." Slade looked at the book on my desk and smiled. "Don't worry. I'll keep an eye on your *old lady* for you."

"You say that, and yet, I'm still worried." I said, only half-joking.

I trusted Slade with the book, but the State Crime Command's Gang Squad was gunning for him hard. A warrant wasn't out of the realm of possibility with the investigation looming. The book wasn't safe in the clubhouse for the first time since it came into my possession.

"I actually thought it might be better if I take the book with me." I wrapped the book in an old piece of velvet and shoved it in my pack. "We can't afford to lose it if the authorities come sniffing."

"Whatever you think is best." Slade thumped me on the

shoulder. "Those dirty fucks aren't taking our most valuable weapons."

My president wasn't a stupid man. He wouldn't have been president of the Jackals if he was. He knew what was up. The book went with me. If and when shit hit the fan, I'd send the book to the one place I knew they couldn't serve a warrant: Thoth's library in the dimension between this world and the god's.

"We probably should scatter our possessions," I suggested. "Just in case they raid the place."

"Yeah, been thinking about that." Slade brushed his beard with saw-like motions. "Dealing with the damn Wolves has been taking up all my spare time. I'll get on it right away."

He walked out of the room, and I finished packing up my gear, loading it in the saddlebag, ready to depart. Before I left for my ride upstate, I grabbed my sack with the book in it and opened the portal to Thoth's library, stepping through.

Flames danced on the sconces like belly dancing women enticing me with their curved shapes. Fluted columns ending in bundled reeds held the ceiling up. Hieroglyphs and paintings of men, women, workers, priests, and gods decorated every stone wall. Obelisks and statues of the gods rose every fifty or so feet to display the grandeur of ancient Egypt.

Scribes dressed in long aprons and shendyt skirts traversed the halls, removing scrolls, replacing them, transcribing them, or writing new ones.

I didn't intend to stay long. Just enough to hide the Book of the Dead.

The smell of ancient parchment and ink hit me as I moved through the aisles of books, scrolls, paintings, maps, and other important documents. Copies of everything ever written in ancient Egypt. Like nothing else ... except the sweet scent of my mate.

The reminder of Alexa brought up memories from our

short time together last night. However, it was enough to commit every detail about her to memory. I saw beyond her bruised face and busted lip to the beauty below. Her intoxicating vanilla and hazelnut scent that I couldn't get enough of. The softness of her skin as our fingers brushed and I set my hand over hers. Glossy hair that flowed down her back and over her shoulder, tempting me to reach out, curl it around my fingers, and draw her in for a steep kiss. My cock boxed my jeans thinking about her.

Not the time or place, man.

Not sure if getting aroused pissed off the old patron, and I wasn't going to risk it with all his knowledge and skills in magical practices.

A fern beneath a palm tree in the farthest aisle caught my eye. I decided to use this as my landmark for hiding the book and set the sack down. Conjuring up a spell, I concealed it, making it invisible to all eyes, even the scribes. Couldn't be too careful at the moment. I was not going to let the most powerful spellbook in all the world fall into the hands of another club or the police. So help me, God.

CHAPTER 14

Aaliyah

SHIT, I'd fallen asleep last night before I got the chance to sneak into Zethan's office to search for a phone or alternative sim card to plug into mine. Zethan had destroyed my sim card, but it didn't matter. Numbers were burned into my memory thanks to dad, who made us memorize everyone's numbers in case we ever lost our phones.

I didn't know how much time I had left here before the Jackals discovered my true identity and killed me. If I wanted to leave, it was now or never to sneak off. I crossed the hall, headed for the office out the back.

Alaric dropped his guard for five minutes to grab a morning coffee for himself and a tea for me. He'd been so attentive and sweet it made it difficult to dislike him. Already he'd layered my bed with extra blankets, got me another pillow, and made sure I was comfortable. He reminded me of a bird bringing its mate food and taking care of her.

Zethan hovered around the doctor while he treated the other woman who'd arrived last night too. She was in even worse shape than me. By the sound of it, she might have to go into his practice for an x-ray.

"Well, well, well." A voice made me jump and squeak. "If it isn't my favorite nurse."

Fuck. Slade.

I turned slowly to catch him crossing the hall carrying two mugs.

"Making a house call?" God, he was even more gorgeous tonight. Gray t-shirt over denim, and boots to top it off. Deadly as sin, wild and rough. In my way, as well.

"You wish." I rolled my eyes. Big flirt. My body reacted to him, leaning in, wanting more of his sensual eyes on me, drinking me in. We were both traitorous bitches!

He held out a mug for me. "Listen, I didn't get to thank you properly back at the hospital."

My face shifted from one of guilt to a blank canvas as I met his gaze and took the tea. "I don't recall you thanking me at all." I cupped my hand around the warm, steaming mug, needing the heat to stave off the fear that kept my body in a constant state of cold.

Where Castor's god was dark and mysterious, Slade's was different. Chaotic, dangerous, and unpredictable. Not a great combination when I intended to betray them for their kindness. I needed to be careful around him or risk him uncovering my real identity or plans now that I was here.

Slade plopped down on the bed next to me. Again, another Jackal uninvited but inserting himself into my personal space. My chest sizzled at the closeness between us. *Damn betraying bitch!*

"I'm grateful." He took a sip of coffee, and my eyes zoomed in on his upper lip wrapping over his mug. Thick, succulent, and rough. "You upheld your oath and healed me.

I don't know why you did that, but it says a lot about you as a person."

"I was just doing my job." I scooted to the edge of the mattress to put distance between us.

The way he stared at me like he wanted to devour me even though I was covered in bruises and swollen, had me boiling up inside. I must have looked a mess. Yet he looked at me as if I'd never been more beautiful. It was both comforting and disturbing at the same time. My mind spun in confusion over why I was attracted to someone who hurt my family.

"So, Nurse A., why do you need saving?" He inched over, closing the gap. "Why'd that guy ... hurt you?" He ground out the words like he wanted to kill the junkie.

I didn't know why he cared or what it meant to him when we were strangers. Unless he had some sort of vested interest in me. Like he too knew I was an avatar and wanted something from me. Or he suspected my involvement with the Wolves. A secret I couldn't keep forever with gods whispering in the Jackals' ears.

Slade reached over and cupped my jaw, turning my head until I met his gaze. "I'm a surprisingly good listener if you want to talk about it." Dimples formed in his right cheek when he smiled. Damn, I was a sucker for an adorable dimple.

My hormones betrayed me, but whenever those traitorous bitches started to act up around Slade, or any one of the Jackals for that matter, I thought of my father and the way he died. Worked better than a cold shower.

I slid out from his touch, resting one elbow on my knee and propping my head in my hand. My bruised chin protested. "He was just some junkie. Never met him before."

"Not in the ER?" Slade pressed, and I wondered what he fished for.

"Maybe." My tea had cooled down enough to sip. "I don't recall him. Thousands of people come through every year."

Slade twisted his mug back and forth. "He said he was paid to scare you. That you slighted the wrong person." His eyes drilled into me, and I shrank, frightened at the intensity that wanted answers to a situation that didn't add up to him. Hell, they didn't add up to me either now.

I cupped both hands over my mug, not sure what to say. Honest to God, I didn't know the guy who jumped me, and I had to make that clear to Slade and eliminate any suspicion my way.

The next part was critical in gaining the Jackals' President's trust. If I gave up too much too soon, I risked sounding suspicious or worse, being pumped for insider knowledge that I didn't have. I had to take it slowly and earn their trust, otherwise I'd never get the information my brother needed or escape alive. Emphasis on the alive.

"I was on my way to meet Barb at El Matador's." Another dramatic pause. *Really sell it, Aliyah.* "I owed her a pitcher of margaritas and a burrito from a bet I lost, thanks to you."

"Me? You bet on me?" Perfect white teeth flashed as he grinned and jabbed a thumb to his chest. Slade Vincent liked to play innocent when he was guilty as hell. Not in this specific case ... but others ...

"No, not you specifically." God, my nerves and the hormones were making me get this all wrong. "The rush in the ER after it started off dead."

He stretched out his arms, holding onto his mug as he encircled his knee. "You're saying a woman named Barb did that to your face because you lost a bet? And the payout was a burrito?"

I shook my head. This went way off course. "What? No! Barb might take her Mexican food seriously, but she's never assaulted anyone."

Slade stared at his mug, nodding.

"Well, there was this one time. But that was after several margaritas and it involved churros." I scrubbed at my face, regretting it the instant the pain hit me. Exhaustion made me forget all about my wounds. I sighed. "Barb's my best friend. She didn't do this to me." I ran my hands up and down my arms to chase away the goosebumps sparked by the memories of the attack flashing in my mind.

Slade rubbed my back in a soothing circular motion. Part of me wanted to recoil at his touch, the other leaned into the comfort he offered.

Play the part, Aliyah. Not that I needed much convincing. It would have been all too easy to answer the budding attraction between us ... or was it our avatars? To forget everything and lose myself in discovering the history between them. Slade was the triple d: dark, dangerous, and dreamy. With the right amount of muscles that made a woman feel secure rather than inferior. He was also the prime suspect in my father's murder.

"He won't hurt you anymore." Slade's voice deepened into a deadly warning. "We took care of it."

I groaned. "I don't want to know what you did to him."

His gaze snapped up to mine. Ice shards formed in my gut. Shit, I'd said the wrong thing and revealed too much. I had to play the part of an innocent, assaulted nurse, not someone familiar with bikers.

He tapped his right eye, provoking the dark flash of the Eye of Horus. "There's more to you than meets the eye, isn't there, Nurse. A.?"

Fuck. May as well give up the gambit. He knew who I was ... at least the magical part of me. Admitting it could build deeper trust on the celestial connection we shared.

Slade scrutinized the scrapes and bruises from my battle with the junkie. "You're lucky they found you in time." Something about the way his voice hitched spoke of a deeper meaning. Almost as if he feared the outcome if his men hadn't defended me and bought me back here.

I wanted to know what that meant and why. Other pressing questions nudged my mind for answers. "What were the odds, huh? How did your men find me?"

He smiled again, devilish and full of secrecy. "I ordered them to."

Ordered? They'd followed me. For how long? Was the stab wound a ruse to connect with me or get close to me? I squeezed my mug so tightly I was surprised it didn't break. His flirtations, piercing indigo eyes, and gorgeous smile wore me down and I had to put a stop to this before I lost my nerve and my edge.

"Cut the crap, Slade," I hissed, making my point. "You kidnapped me and brought me here."

"Rescued," he corrected me.

"Tell me who you are and what you want," I growled at him.

Slade cast a glance across the room full of sleeping women. Shadowy magic crackled around us as if sealing us in a cone of silence. "You can't tell who I am? Because I know who *you* are."

Fuck. Games. Secrecy. Exhausting. "I just want to sleep. My body needs to heal. If you're not going to answer me, then leave me alone, Mr. Vincent."

"We're back to that are we?" He grinned as if this amused him. Slade Vincent also liked to toy with his prey. Newsflash: I wasn't his next meal.

I set down my almost empty mug of tea and crawled into the bed, dragging the blanket with me. "Good night, Mr. Vincent."

Slade stiffened, swiveling to face me, all show of playfulness falling from his face. "You're the avatar of Isis." Finally, an answer.

"That didn't hurt, did it?" I wanted to sink underneath the sheets and woolen blanket, but Slade was in the way. Annoyed, I threw the blanket over my legs. "And? You're a Jackal."

Slade's eyebrows rose to his hairline. "Familiar with your clubs, are you?"

My mind whirred for an appropriate answer to eliminate suspicion. "I saw it on Alaric and Zethan's damn vests, and yeah, I've seen a few cuts in my time in the ER."

He answered with another question. "So, you can knit muscle and skin back together, but a black eye, bruises, and a split lip are too much for you?" Damn man was guarded and infuriating, never answering directly, lobbing questions back at me, keeping me running like a tennis player struggling to fight a stronger opponent.

"They're already healing on their own." I kicked at his back to try and get him off my bed. "I can't heal myself as well as I can with others."

"Yes, you can." He rubbed his hands, and the magic responded, crackling again. "You just don't know how."

"I haven't exactly had many tutorials from Isis. Everything I know I've discovered by sheer luck and practice." I was being somewhat of an open book. It was time for him to come to the party.

Slade lifted his hands as if praying, rubbing them up and down, and some deep part of me wished to be between his palms, having them glide over me. "You haven't asked the right questions."

I took that as a hint to dig deeper. "How many are there? Avatars, I mean." I knew there were others like me, but I'd never expected to be in the same place as one. Never mind four of them.

"Just in the Jackals? Or in the world?" Slade flashed a smile, complete with dimples. I needed sunglasses or complete blackout goggles, so I didn't have to melt under those damn dimples.

"Well, you and Castor are." I ticked off their names on my fingers. "So, it's safe to assume Zethan and Alaric are too?"

Slade filled in the blank. "Yes. Zethan runs this place. You know, blond and broody." Brutal also came to mind after witnessing flashes of what he did to the junkie in the parking garage. "Alaric, watchful, observant, killer instincts." The last part sparked a chill to run down my back.

I shrugged off the chill to focus. "How many more are there outside of the Jackals?"

"Well, there's you, and you're not a Jackal." Slade winked. "Yet."

Most clubs didn't let women in, but some made exceptions. When you came with the backing of the gods, it enticed membership.

I nudged him with my elbow. "Is this your thing? Flirting." Obvious attempt to bank any flames between us. I had to get a handle on this whole attraction thing when it dampened my ability to stay trained on my mission.

"Is it working?" he teased.

"No," I lied, because the truth made me uncomfortable.

There was more to Slade Vincent than a flirtatious nature and witty banter. It was all too easy to fall into a rhythm with him. All too easy to imagine my fingers curling around his beard, dragging him closer for a kiss.

"The truth? Fuck." He buried his head in his hands and scrubbed his whole face, his dark blond beard scratching as he moved. For a while he remained silent as if finding the words to break it to me. Finally, he came out with them. "We're fated mates. Your avatar and ours. Flirting takes …

the edge off." Slade looked at me with an intensity that pierced my soul.

"Fated mates?" I choked on the words and coughed, trying to clear my throat and the shock wedged in it. No. Wrong. I was not fated to anyone, much less my enemies. What kind of sick joke was that anyway?

Electricity sparked between Slade's palm and my skin as he lightly touched my upper arm. "I know you feel it—an attraction through our mate bond—and you've been questioning it since you laid eyes on me in the ER." His hold grew deeper, harder, more possessive by the second. "You're a fighter, Alexa. I can see that, but this is going to happen whether you or I want it to or not."

Hell, no. This was the last thing I wanted to hear. The last thing I wanted to admit to him. I sought out my goddess for confirmation.

It is true, my precious one, she replied from the depths of my soul. *The five of us were cursed long ago.* By five, I assumed she meant all the gods involved, which I still wasn't clear on. *We've searched millennia for avatars to break us free of these binds.*

Gods, no! We were not fated mates. End of story. My heart shattered into a million pieces, knowing I kidded myself. Shock stole the warmth from my body, and I hunched over despite the aching protest of my bruised lungs, gasping for air. Why me? Fuck. Of all the people to bring together. Enemies in arms. A real-life fricken' Romeo and Juliet. Sick! Bile launched up my throat, scalding me, and I swallowed it down.

Slade's firm circles commenced again on my back, freeing the block in my lungs, letting me breathe again.

When I pulled myself together enough, I looked up at him again. "Do you want it too?" My mouth went dry, and I licked my lips.

Slade's heated gaze flicked to my tongue before scorching a trail down the rest of my body. "Yeah." He swallowed hard. "I do."

No, he didn't. That was just the mate bond or whatever talking. He didn't know me, didn't love me. He was confused by the pull of magic between us.

Desperate to put space between us, I scrambled off the edge of the mattress, stumbling over my feet as I searched for a door, anything to get out of here, get some fresh air.

Alaric stopped me at the door like a damn security guard at a nightclub. "Where are you going?"

"I need air. And a cigarette." The stress of this news stirred cravings I put behind me years ago.

"Damn, Nurse. A." Slade belted out a laugh behind me. "You should know better than to smoke."

"A lot of nurses smoke. It's a dirty secret." I held up my hand, cutting off another pun before he had the chance to say it. "I quit in college and haven't craved one in forever. I guess everything's just catching up to me."

Alaric swung open the door for me, and I padded out into the early morning chill of winter. Condensation puffed out of my mouth. I rubbed at my goosebumped arms.

Slade came out with me, leaning on the cabin wall, kicking the toe of his boot on the wooden porch. "Need a minute?"

"Gimme a cigarette," I demanded, hand outstretched.

"As much as I hate to disappoint a beautiful woman, I quit a couple of years ago myself."

"Bullshit, I can smell it on you." Along with his intoxicating smoky whisky and clove smell.

"Things have been hectic lately. I picked it back up a month ago. Temporarily." He fished out his packet of tobacco, where he also kept his rolling papers and filters, offering them to me. "You keep them. I don't need 'em anymore."

My hands shook as I rolled one and lit it up, drawing down a big gulp of smoke, the heat warming my chest.

His demeanor changed from flirtatious to aloof, and the desire in his eyes cooled to suspicion. "I better head back to the clubhouse. Alaric will watch out for you. See you around, Nurse A." I stared after him as he bailed.

What did I say to run him off? I thought I made inroads in gaining his trust, but it felt like I hit a major setback. Slow on the uptake thanks to a concussion, it took a minute before I realized the trigger.

I glanced down at the burning stick between my fingers. The cigarette. The one piece of evidence tying Slade to my father's murder. Evidence I knew existed because my brother had cops on the payroll. I felt certain the Jackals had a few dirty cops of their own and that Slade must have assumed I mentioned a cigarette to trip him up. I crushed the packet in my hand, determined to hold onto this, get more DNA evidence to pin the murder on the treacherous president of the Jackals.

CHAPTER 15

*A*laric

NOTHING HAD MOVED while I completed my overhead scan of the factory. Lights out, no parked vehicles, all locked up. Complete opposite of the way Joey ran his shipping company. Radio blaring, every light in the place going, forklifts buzzing about the place moving crates of legit goods, and his side hustle of drugs and other illegal product shipments. A low swoop to investigate closer had come up short too. Dead silence and emptiness. Strange for a transport company that operated well into the night.

Cautious and on edge, Castor and I pulled our bikes into the empty parking lot on the edge of the warehouse. Clouds hid the sun and dimmed the afternoon sky.

The warehouse was on the opposite end of the manufacturing district, closer to the town of Bathurst and a couple of blocks from the freeway. Joey's Freight Transport was a reputable business that provided respectable jobs for the locals. Besides the illegal shipments, Joey was a stand-up guy, doing what he had to in order to make ends meet. Living the dream, even a mediocre one, costed money.

I shifted my ear into that of my hawk's, attuning my senses, listening. Mice moved inside, and my hawk squawked for a meal. Plenty of protein for my little bird form, but not my style. Someone heavier and larger shuffled about inside.

I'd rather be back at the shelter, watching over the women, admiring and getting to know my future mate. The company of a beautiful, smart woman beat that of Joey's, his beer gut, low-hanging jeans, ass crack, and food stains on his shirts. Night shift at the safe house was a welcome reprieve from the dredges of drug and gun running, turf wars, and dirty cops. I loved the action as much as the next guy, but I still needed downtime.

Being an avatar came with baggage, but I already had plenty of my own after years in military service. The women we rescued found peace inside these walls, and I made sure it stayed that way. It was a safe place for me. A way to disconnect from the darkness that haunted me every night.

But, as Road Captain, I drew the short straw. With Joey not responding to our calls, we had to do things the old-fashioned way, and by old-fashioned, that meant an in-person visit. By the look of it, Joey had ghosted us and run off with our one-million-dollar shipment of Pharaoh. If he had, Slade would kill him. Loyalty and commitment meant everything to him. Cross him, even once, and you were a dead man.

Concerned about the outcome, I performed another scan on the grounds. Doors were all padlocked. Lids to the dumpsters closed when they were normally open during operations and workers disposed of boxes and plastic. Trucks arriving from suppliers and leaving to transport products to buyers.

"Place is locked up tight," I told Castor.

"Let's check it out." Castor set his helmet on the back of his bike seat. When I did the same, he threw a spell over our bikes, protecting them from thieves. Handy to be the brother of the avatar of Thoth.

Together, we moved in, inspecting the front of the warehouse first, where the offices were located. They were locked up and dark, aside from the glow of the receptionist's phone and the flash of light from her sleeping computer screen. Castor thrust out a hand and shot off a blast of dark magick. The lock on the door clicked and gave. Inside smelled like a shitty excuse of an air freshener. Vanilla, my ass. Five percent vanilla scent with the rest of some bullshit chemical no one had ever heard of. We came to a row of offices, a conference room, bathroom, and a lunchroom.

Shadows stretched over Castor. "You know which one's Joey's office?"

In my role as Road Captain, I oversaw the transport of all our products, and any travel by the club. I frequently met with Joey to give him directions and organize new shipment routes. Castor always came with me as my backup.

I jerked my head. "Last one on the right."

"I'm getting something," Castor advised as we entered Joey's office, his screen still active, the blue glow providing a soft illumination behind the long desk. "A text message."

I nudged some papers on Joey's desk, scanning them for anything crucial. "What does it say?"

"Text to his wife." Castor's gaze was distant as he dug into the information highway that his god connected him to. "That he had to leave for a few days, lay low, for the wife to take the kids to their grandparents' place."

I flicked through the stack of paperwork, fuel bills, electricity bills, credit card statements, invoices for shipments. "Explains why Joey went silent."

Joey also shipped products for the Egyptian mafia. I

suspected a deal went south. Lost cargo, perhaps. I leaned toward retaliation from Colton Rain, but I couldn't rule out something from his personal life until I knew more.

"Anything else?" I moved behind the desk to his computer, which displayed the login screen. Locked screen. No problem. Castor could search for his password and get into it. "Money owed?"

Castor sat down at the desk chair, typing in characters, hacking into the computer. "All his bills were paid ahead of time. Plenty of money in the bank accounts. No threatening emails or letters. I don't get it."

The mystery deepened. Joey was in some sort of shit to disappear, not warn us and let us down for delivery.

I replaced the set of papers and flicked my nail on the desk's edge. "People don't just disappear if everything's great."

Castor nodded. "Someone's out back. We should check it out."

We cut through the back door into the loading bay, finding two tri-axle trucks parked inside, their rear doors left open. The motor of a forklift had started, puffing out diesel fumes, which choked the area.

"Fuck, something's gone down." Castor's tone made my nerves spark with full attention. My hawk sat beneath my skin, ready to shift at a moment's notice, to take to the air, scratch out anybody's eyes if they pulled out a gun.

A man unloaded boxes from a crate at the back of the truck, carrying them to a car at the back. Blood covered his protective coveralls and hat. He muttered to himself and moved in jittery motions as he dropped the box into his trunk. The moment he noticed us, he took off, racing down one of the nearby storage aisles piled with the latest deliveries to be shipped.

I pulled my Sig P226 from its holster. Guns drawn,

Castor and I went after him, splitting off at the fork in the aisle, me chasing him down it, and Castor heading for the opposite end to cut him off. As avatars, we were stronger and faster than the average human, and we trapped him at the end of the aisle.

He raised palms with dried blood on them. His name tag read Bill – Warehouse Manager. "I don't want no trouble. I just wanna get out of here."

Out of there with a truck full of illegal merchandise to sell from beneath Joey while he lay low somewhere. The evidence stacking up for Bill didn't bode well for him. Blood spatters on his clothes and hands hinted at foul play, but nothing about him struck me as dodgy.

Thinning brown hair, mustache, brown eyes, the guy came across as someone who quit school at sixteen, got a job with Joey's company, worked his way up to Warehouse Manager, and retired at age sixty-five. Your Average Joe Blow. Married, two kids, pets, a boat, and poker games on Friday night with the guys. The tremor in Bill's hands told me he'd never seen a gun, let alone shot one. More like he came across something that spooked him, and he'd acted on instinct to pack his trunk and hightail it before the cops investigated and he got questioned.

I flicked the butt of my gun to tell this guy to start talking. "We're looking for Joey. Where'd all that blood come from?"

"I … I." Bill's shoulders drooped. "I found the place empty after last night. Two shipments cleared out. Place all shot up. Twenty staff dead. Joey's in the …" Words caught in his throat as he swallowed thickly.

Fuck. My stomach sank with his hushed words, predicting the next shit storm to drop from his lips. Two shipments gone. The niggling feeling told me one was ours. What were the damn odds? No one but Slade, Zethan, Castor, or I knew who delivered our product. If we had a traitor, it had to be one of those three. Unless Joey shot off his mouth to someone and words traveled.

Castor inched forward, gun aimed. "Where's Joey?"

Bill cleared his throat. "The freezer's this way."

The freezer.

Joey's company transported pet food from the manufacturer in Blayney to Sydney and across the state and stored product in the freezers out back.

My stomach dropped. I didn't need to follow Bill back to the freezer to know what we were going to find there. Joey had been processed and packaged by whoever he wanted to disappear from.

"After you." Fingers clenched tight on my gun, I followed him, Castor behind me, making a single file line as we crossed the warehouse floor.

Bill wasn't lying when he said the place was all shot up. Dead bodies drenched in blood lay in the aisles face down. Men who'd run for their lives and the cowards shot them in the back. Bullets were sprayed from machine guns, hitting the pallets, chipping metal shelves, cutting up the merchandise and packaging. We side-stepped the bodies, taking care not to get our feet in the mess and leave footprints. At the back of the warehouse, the motor for the freezer hummed, doing its job despite the horror we'd find inside.

"I ... I don't want to go in again." Bill's stutter conveyed his trauma.

But Castor and I weren't stupid enough to enter together when old Bill could lock us in, leave us here to answer to the cops, while he crossed the border to a new life in Queensland.

"Stay here, watch him," I ordered Castor.

My brother was more than happy to oblige.

I tugged at the handle, rolling back the thick, heavy freezer door. Boxes were piled up in neat stacks. Three lay open in the middle of the container. Gun ready, I approached with care, one step at a time. Blood stained the edges of the cardboard labeled for delivery to our distributor.

"Fuck!" I raised my free wrist to my mouth, gagging at the contents.

Severed head and hands alongside a lone packet of Pharaoh. I checked the other two boxes and found more of Joey sliced up and packed into the cardboard. The rest of him hung from meat hooks at the back. Someone wanted to send us a message. Message received. Loud and fucking clear.

Vomit lurched up my throat, and I had to swallow it back and withdraw before I left my DNA inside the freezer.

"Jesus." I wiped my mouth with the back of my wrist.

The recognition in Castor's eyes told me he didn't need details.

I cocked the gun. "Who the hell killed Joey?"

Bill's gaze flicked from the gun to my face and back again. "I ... I don't know. I checked the security footage, and the tape's been stolen along with two shipments."

My finger tightened on the trigger. "The shipment bound for Richmond?"

Bill must have seen something in my eyes, or it may have been my menacing tone, because he backed up and all but jumped out of his skin when he bumped into a stack of boxes. I stalked toward him. I hated playing the heavy. That was Castor's role in the club, and we watched his back while he got it done. But since it was my responsibility to get shipments to and from their destinations, I took the lead on this one. Bill didn't need to get the shit beat out of him. The fear in his eyes told me he'd tell us everything we needed to know. Didn't mean I felt good about it.

Bill raised his hands as if to placate me. "Don't shoot me."

"I tell you what, Bill." I jerked my gun. "I'm going to give you a second chance here, because I know whoever killed Joey left you no other choice but to clear out of town."

Bill's gaze locked on the barrel of my weapon.

I walked him through my plan step by step. "You're going to call the cops and tell them you found a body in the freezer."

"They'll think I did it." Bill's voice hitched a few bars.

I kept my voice steady and firm. "You aren't going to tell him why or how there's a body, just that an employee discovered one." Bill furiously nodded his head. "If any more of my associates find their way here ... well, you don't really need me to elaborate, do you?" I tapped the gun against my leg.

"Yes, I ... I mean, no. No, I don't." Bill patted down the sweat on his brow with a handkerchief. "I'll take care of it."

"See, Bill, you can make the right choice when you put your mind to it."

"Okay." Bill nodded. Smart man.

I left him standing outside the freezer, snatched the lone bag of Pharaoh, and walked out of the warehouse with Castor by my side.

Castor's hand slid from side to side on his chin. "Slade's not going to be happy with this development."

One million in Pharaoh missing. Fuck, no. He'd burn down the clubhouse. With our product in the wrong hands, competitors could test it, work out the formula, replicate it, sell it, and undercut us. Without our signature drug, we were fucked. We had to find the missing shipment and the culprits responsible for stealing it. I had a terrible gut feeling whoever did this intended to destroy us. They'd already declared war on us. Two prime suspects shone on my radar: The Wolves ... or someone far worse ... someone we had bad blood with.

CHAPTER 16

$\mathcal{A}$aliyah

Day 2 at the Shelter

Alaric and Castor returned to the shelter, faces drawn, eyes weary, jaws tight. Something had gone down. Time for me to finish up with Jamie and mosey on up to see what I could extract from them.

First, I emptied the last of my magic into Jamie, breaking up the oxygen-deprived blood in her bruise, helping the body to clear it away and heal the broken blood vessels. The color in her purple skin lightened. All the while, I pretended to hold her hand while we sipped our tea, and she poured out her heart to me about what her fiancé had done to her.

Alaric's gaze flicked to me, ever watchful, narrowing with disapproval as he locked onto what I did with my magic. "I'll call Slade. You take care of her."

Castor followed his brother's line of sight, and his jaw hardened further. He stormed over to me, fire in his step. "Alexa, a word, *now*." He grabbed me by the upper arm, denying me a chance to excuse myself, dragging me into the nearby storage closet, closing the door behind us.

Okay. I crossed my arms. Not even my boss treated me like that when I was tired and almost gave the patient the wrong medication because my eyes were crossed from a triple shift.

Castor's brows came down in a hard line. "What do you think you're doing, Alexa? You can't throw your magic around like that. We don't want to draw attention to ourselves." His hard, deep cadence weakened my knees, and I wanted to do something naughty again just to have him chastise me and maybe put me over his knees for a good spanking.

Then my senses snapped back to reality. Who the fuck did he think he was, telling me what to do? I used my magic all the time on patients. No big deal. Not one person had ever caught on, and I wasn't about to stop now.

"How about you stick to your lane, and I'll stick to mine?" I injected some real sass into my reply. "I don't tell you how to apply your powers."

Maple eyes darkening, he cornered me against the door and my back thumped against it. The fire in his gaze told me he held his cool outside, but on the inside, he boiled. Everywhere his eyes touched, my skin burned, and my body responded, flaring with its own needy and combative heat. The way he rolled his lips over his tongue to moisten them. Hot damn. That kind of move should be criminalized.

Hell, he smelled even better than the night before. The anger made his spice and cinnamon scent flare, and I almost lost control, slid my hands behind his neck, and pulled him down for a kiss. Fuck this mate bond bullshit. I hadn't been able to stop thinking about it after Slade's warning.

I pushed at Castor's chest to encourage him to move back, but he stayed put, as immovable as stone. The little bitch in heat within me wanted to rub up against him, welcoming his proximity. God, the longer I was around these men, the stronger the magnetism of the mate bond. I had to get what I needed and fast before I fell victim and slave to these four gorgeous men bound to me.

"We don't wear our cuts around the shelter and let the women know our identities." He counted on his finger, listing off the rules. "We never use magic on them. Women gossip. We'd have every club come down on us, and we wouldn't have the resources to fight them all off."

Funny, he didn't come across as a rules man. More like one who discovered ways to break them. The reason became apparent when the head of an ibis flashed across his forehead. Thoth, the ibis-headed god. Finally, I knew his avatar identity, and I'd let him know I'd figured it out.

I set my palms on his chest, this time with more force. "Those are your rules, not mine, Jackal. Or is it, avatar of Thoth?"

He snorted, keeping his gaze leveled at mine. "You'll play by our rules soon." His gaze dipped to my lips, and the need in me practically burst. "When you're one of us."

Before I had time to process that horrifying idea and rebut it, he leaned down to kiss me, intense, passionate and brimming with longing. I responded with my own need, leaning up into him, my traitorous damn hands doing what they'd promised moments earlier. My fingers laced through his dark, shoulder-length hair, tugging gently at the curls, making him groan and press against my body harder. His hands finally moved, one rubbing my arm, the other curling around my waist.

If Castor was anything like his god, like I was with mine, he would be an intellectual man, experimental, thirsty for knowledge. Collected and practical, he didn't give me the impression that he lost control easily. The only thing capable of breaking him was our connection and me. And I took full advantage of it. So, help me God, this would be the first and last time we'd ever do this. I only let myself have this little moment to investigate the mate bond, desperate to find an antidote to deploy whenever one of the Jackals came near and activated the intoxicating and irresistible influence between our gods. Next time, I'd be damned ready, and they wouldn't have this sway over me.

His kiss contained all the inquisitiveness I'd anticipated, exploring my mouth, studying it, learning it, every curve, every trace of skin, all the softness. I reciprocated, committing every part of his lips to memory too. The more he kissed me, the more he weakened my resolve, and I slipped into the darkness that was his kiss and the secrets and mysteries it contained.

Hot damn times two. He surprised me, deepening our kiss, parting my lips with his tongue, seeking entry. Our tongues curled and flicked at first, the motion turning desperate, hungry, even demanding. Until I pushed back with my own, showing him his kiss wouldn't silence me, wouldn't break me, wouldn't make me submit to his will. Our tongues dueled each other like our earlier battle of wills, striving for dominance, control, to win the argument. Castor was stubborn and refused to submit. Good, so was I.

His hands slid behind my neck, holding me in place, and a part of me wanted him to hold me there forever, for this to never end. The other side shouted *don't be fooled, he's a Jackal, a murderer*. That latter side of me won in the end, and I pulled away, panting. Reluctantly, he let me go, pressing his lips to my forehead, leaving a burning pattern of his mouth there. I touched my damn lips where they tingled from his kiss.

"You know I'm the club's Enforcer," he whispered. "I'll happily deliver that punishment again if you disobey." Damn him and the sexy way he promised to make good on that threat.

Speaking of the club, time to ask questions. I could hardly breathe, let alone get out my next sentence, but I managed somehow. "Something happen earlier? You and Alaric looked pretty serious."

"Trouble with another club." Castor stroked my hair, then sniffed it. *Sniffed it.* Even the way he did that was sexy. This man was a delicious Arabian prince, and I wanted to taste every part of him.

"I've seen how that plays out." Both in the hospital and in my time serving as a part of the Wolf family when I was younger. It never ended well.

"We'll deal with it." Castor pulled away to look down at me. His gaze zeroed in on my lips again, telling me he didn't want to talk club, he wanted to get me naked and fuck me against the wall.

I ignored that fact ... or rather substituted it with another diversion to distract myself. Damn, he was tall. A good foot on me. Not as tall and bear-like as Slade, or as muscled as Zethan or fit as Alaric. Sexy, nonetheless. If his god was any indication, Castor preferred working out his brain than his body, but he was still well defined, broad, muscular. That was more than okay with me. I'd met my fair share of muscled nitwits in the ER, all brawn and no brain. Though, I was sure Slade and Zethan were smart men, otherwise they wouldn't run a club and women's shelter.

"I need to take my mind off it." The back of Castor's knuckle trailed my jaw along to my ear, communicating what he preferred to be doing.

Nope. Bucket of ice water. Antarctica. Glaciers. Emperor penguins. Emperor penguins were the least sexy bird, right? The way they waddled. The way the men protected their egg from the cold while the females hunted. Oh God, why was I thinking of cute little house husband birds?

I cleared my dry throat. "It's getting close to dinnertime, and the women are hungry." Biggest cold shower ever.

"Good thing I like to cook." Castor withdrew and stroked his blade-sharp jaw. "How about helping me prepare beef bourguignon?"

Double cold shower. Shit. I was trying to get away from him, not run to him. Since when did bikers like to cook anyway? My dad and all his men hadn't been near a stove in their lives. Although, they grilled a mean steak on the barbeque, but that was all I'd give them.

"I'm going to pretend I understood that."

His smile nearly laid waste to all my resistance. "Beef stew."

Why'd he have to say it so sexy? He had my mouth watering, my pants steaming, and my pussy burning for him to kiss it there, to whisper his sexy French words to me while he went down on me.

I put a lid on that bitch with a third cold shower. "What do you need me to do?"

He grabbed a sack of potatoes and passed them to me. Then he collected a handful of carrots, cans of tomatoes, and mushrooms. This place was very well stocked, and with fresh produce, by the look of it.

"And a little secret recipe." He materialized a bottle of red wine and a long loaf of French bread.

I thumped him in the shoulder. "Uh-uh." I waggled a tut-tut finger at him. "No magic, remember?"

He shot me another panty-melting smile and tapped me

lightly on the ass with the bread. "We can bend the rules, sometimes... out of sight."

"Oh, really?" I didn't mean for it to sound so flirty, or for it to grab his attention, accurate and piercing. "I bet you and your god find plenty of ways to get around the rules."

At my unintended challenge, he approached slowly, like a looming lion, cornering me again. "Our little secret, huh?" This time when he kissed me, I swooned, and my legs buckled, and I almost dropped the potatoes on his boot.

Fuck. He was a rule-breaker, all right.

Desperate to cool down, put distance between us, settle the call of the mate bond, I slipped away and moved to the door. I stood there for a moment, collecting myself, squeezing that damn sack of potatoes as if it contained the medication I needed to break the connection between us.

His hand found the small of my back, easing me out the door, not leaving my body until he dropped off the ingredients on the kitchen counter and retreated to gather stewing beef and some herbs.

I got busy finding a chopping board, peeler, and knife, peeling and slicing the carrots into large chunks. "How often do you help out here?"

"Not often." Castor removed a large stewing pot and set it on the stove. Large enough to feed at least ten people. "I've got a reason to come round more often now, don't I?" At his last two words, his maple gaze shot to me, pinning me to the spot, and I almost sliced right through my thumb. I wanted him to visit more too.

Shit, Aaliyah, concentrate. Control that libido!

I went full one-eighty, turning the conversation around, knowing I had limited time to gather intel for my brother before I had to leave this place.

"Heard your boss is under a murder investigation." I didn't mention the club in case of prying ears. My body tensed, hoping the question didn't raise too many red flags. There was no good way to tiptoe around it, and I wanted to know which of the Jackals had a solid alibi.

Castor stopped removing the packaging from the meat and set down his knife. "That's not common knowledge." His narrowed eyes told me I'd stepped in hot water. His magick flung the door closed. "How'd you hear about that?"

Fuck, Aaliyah, think.

"Some woman bragging about being the wife of the president of the Savage Souls." *Quick thinking, Aaliyah.* Luckily, I knew the name of other clubs within the state. I resisted the urge to pat myself on the back for the lie.

"Word's gotten around then?" Castor started to ferociously cut the meat into cubes. "Like I said, women gossip."

So, he didn't like gossipers. Wonder if he considered me one for spreading the rumor? Too bad. I didn't want to like him or his club mates.

"What the cops are doing borders on harassment." He targeted the potatoes with the same ferocity. "Their evidence is circumstantial and falsified. They'll never get a conviction. The judge will overturn the case." He sounded pretty confident about it.

Big words for a biker. But he did work hand in hand with the god of Writing and probably knew the law word for word.

"Well read on law textbooks, huh?" I was no attorney and didn't know the law very well, but from what Danny told me, the police had a solid case against Slade and intended to charge and convict him.

Castor tossed the potatoes into the pot along with the meat. "Bachelor of Law degree from Melbourne University." Impressive. "Six years practicing. Until the judges kept letting off the guilty. And a few clubs taking issues with cases I prosecuted with a senior barrister."

He was a barrister? This man embodied more mysteries than the oceans. "I can't imagine you wearing one of those silly white wigs."

"I rocked that wig." He snatched some of the carrot and tossed it at me.

"I bet you did." *God, shut up, Aaliyah.* It was like the mate bond had taken over, and I had no control of my mouth when I was around him. I had to get the conversation back on track. Determined to beat the link, I took the reins back and assumed charge. "Where were you on the day of the murder?" I mocked a stuffy old judge's voice.

He lowered the knife and raised both palms, feigning innocence. "I was overseas at the time, your honor." He did an even better version of the stuffy voice back to me, and I giggled, surprised by how at ease he put me despite the danger. "Avatar business. Helping out an old friend. Owed him a favor."

Castor winked at me, and my vagina sighed, said fuck it, checked out and went into overdrive. She was sick of fighting with me and wanted his cock buried in her, balls deep. I was on my own now, and no amount of cold water was going to slow her down.

"Do you have a stamped passport and visa papers to corroborate this testimony?" I joked, hoping the ruse would pry him of the information I needed. "What was your business to travel overseas, Mr. Castor?"

"Mr. Redding, your honor," Castor corrected.

Redding. Really? Fitting that his god liked to read, and Castor's last name related to his trade.

"I was gone for a few days rescuing a woman from Hades' Underworld." He said it with such seriousness that I blinked. "The avatar of Hermes can provide me an alibi, your honor."

"Hermes?" I set aside the courtroom play to finish chopping the carrots and set my knife down. "I didn't know the pantheons intermixed."

"Hermes' avatar and I play similar roles," Castor explained. "We exchange information every once in a while. He's a valuable contact."

I bet he was. I wondered if I could contact him somehow and get dirt on the Jackals. Or was he loyal to his old friend and colleague?

I pretended to flirt, pointing the tip of a carrot at Castor. "Can you account for the whereabouts of the rest of your men, Mr. Redding?"

"Zethan was a couple of hundred miles away picking up a woman from a different shelter, your honor." Castor inched closer to collect the carrots, brushing my arm, purposefully running the side of his hand along my wrist. "Slade and Alaric were at the club."

So Zethan and Castor had solid alibis. The police must have thought so too because they still weren't suspects. That didn't totally absolve them. They had to know what happened to my father. The president of a club doesn't kill his rival without the other members knowing. Not when his actions would cause an all-out gang war. That kind of decision went down under a church vote.

The police zeroed in on Slade because of the trace DNA. Alaric as his alibi must have been sketchy and unreliable. My mind went to the next likely suspect. Alaric. The way he stood at attention like a soldier safeguarding his superior told me he had military training. Ambush killing wasn't outside his skillset. I remembered Slade referring to his killer instincts. A hint, perhaps? And I now had another person to question.

So, why didn't it feel right? Why did my mate bond protest and shout that someone else was guilty?

Either way, I'd find out who murdered my father. I just

had no idea how to broach the topic with Alaric when he gave me a guarded vibe. I'd have to befriend him like I had Castor, dig for history, use it against him. A knife as sharp as the one I'd used to cut the vegetables stabbed me in the heart for betraying the men who the mate bond deemed I belonged to. It screamed at me, protesting these men's innocence.

No. That didn't change the fact that my father was murdered. Didn't change the fact that his killer remained at large and possibly belonged to the Jackal's Wrath MC. I had to ignore the lies thrown at me by the mate bond and push on with my mission, not letting my confused feelings get in the way.

I wanted to find something concrete to give my brother the justification he needed for his damned war and the closure I needed to truly put my father to rest. I wanted the Jackals to be guilty. They had to be. There wasn't anyone else. Was there?

Slade recognized the goddess I belonged to the night he came into the ER. Recognized I was his mate. It only made sense the others did, too. Did they also know my real identity? Nothing made sense. Why they brought me to the safehouse after I was attacked when I was the daughter of someone they'd killed. Because I was an avatar and we were destined to be together?

Well, I call bullshit.

Yes, there was an attraction, some inexplicable magnetism that drew me to them, but that didn't erase everything that happened. Attraction boiled down to a base animalistic need driven by electrical impulses and chemical reactions inside the body. It was just hormones, and I didn't believe in mates, fated or otherwise. I believed in evidence and I planned to follow it, but I had a terrible suspicion I wouldn't like where it led.

CHAPTER 17

*A*laric

GUARD DUTY. What I did best. My hawk eyes and ears targeted danger. When I wasn't on official Road Captain duty, Slade posted me here and with a new addition to the shelter, one more important than any woman we'd protected before. I was more than happy to agree. To guard her was an honor not just bestowed upon me from my president and leader. It was an honor to protect the one my hawk and god regarded as their mate.

After a walk around the perimeter, I made a room-by-room check. Everyone had turned in for the night and was tucked into their beds, including Alexa. Hair draped over the side of her mattress like an onyx curtain. The covers clung to her curves like a horizontal hourglass. Darkness cloaked her striking features, hiding them from view. I didn't need the light to see her beauty. She was radiant energy, and I was drawn to her from the moment I saw her in the hospital emergency room.

My mind kept reminding me that we already had a mate, and she'd claimed my heart. But she was gone. Hawks mated for life, and if one of the pair died, they took another mate. Nature, fate, or the gods intended me to claim another. No matter how many times I tried to deny it on the drive back from the hospital, my hawk claimed Alexa as his own, and there was no going back once it made up its mind. Not for Alexa. Not for me, or any one of my brothers.

Castor warned us the cycle would repeat itself until the curse was broken. Yet I longed to be able to choose a partner for myself, not have one dictated to me. Unfortunately, I'd accepted the role as Horus' ambassador and didn't get a say in this any more than Alexa or my brothers had.

Curious about her, what drove her, I decided to use my power again and dig a little deeper. Horus bestowed me with the gift of sight, glimpses of their present and past. Insight into their life's actions, which developed a character profile. Each person appeared as a thread in a giant tapestry. Follow the thread, follow the memories, follow a person's motivations and uncover the truth in their heart.

Several days ago, I'd attempted to delve into her past, only finding murkiness. I'd put being off my game down to the shock of finding the next avatar of Isis. Giving it a second try, I tapped into Horus' magic and searched the astral plane for Alexa, locating her gold amid all the others. The metaphysical connection was strong, thanks to the mated bond of our avatars. I pulled the thread, followed it down from the moment I found her in the parking garage and hit a mental block at the point when she got on the elevator. That was a first, and it better not turn into a regular occurrence.

When I gained the sight, I used it whenever an opportunity presented itself, and sometimes when it didn't. The more I used it, the easier it got. Images came faster and clearer. It let me know which cops to roll and which contacts were telling the truth. Turned me into a damn human lie detector and search engine all in one.

Using it wasn't without risks. Peering into people exposed their darkness and weaknesses, and I couldn't control the things I saw when I looked at someone. Godly power didn't exactly come with a filter or a pause button when you caught something you didn't like. Once I started, I had to ride it out no matter where the visions took me. I thought I'd seen and experienced more than my fair share of scary shit while serving in the military. None of it held a candle to the things people did outside the rules of engagement. It was hard to avoid triggers when you had zero control.

Frustrated by Alexa's block, I tried again and again, each time hitting the same wall. It puzzled me how she blocked me. It bothered me even more that she hid something. I needed to find out what it was. Exhausted, I let go of the bond. Memories of my haunted past rushed to fill the void the magic left behind. I pulled out my flask of whisky to drown them, washing the whole container down in three gulps. That would only hold it at bay for a while. I'd need more to shut them off completely.

While the women slept, I sat down in Zethan's office, pulling out papers from my satchel. Papers I'd been meaning to fill out but had put off for too long. My hands shook as I stared at the title. *Department of Veterans' Affairs Rehabilitation and Compensation Claim.* Reading the title brought back the flash of memory from earlier. Edgy and needing something to bring me back down, I went to Zethan's cabinet, removing his whisky and topping up my empty flask. Whisky burned as it slid down my throat, chasing away the cold brought on by memories. I took a few more sips, swallowing the golden courage to complete the form.

I didn't need the money when I had plenty of my own. The shelter could use it. To buy better beds, furniture, more medical equipment, to get a few guard dogs for when I wasn't around. So, I pushed myself to fill in my details in black ink for them.

Hell, I was lucky to emerge from my service with every faculty of my body intact, with the exception of my eye. Some of my fellow veterans weren't as lucky. The PTSD did us all in. Mine kept me awake or threw me into panic attacks. What little compensation I could claim for that trauma would go to the shelter.

When it came to the section where I had to describe my injuries and how they affected me, my shaking worsened, and I struggled to move the pen on the page. Not even the whisky dampened the horrors carved into my mind. Flashes came on with full force. The whir of the helicopter blades. Rapid beeps of alarms as the damaged chopper spiraled toward the ground. Me burning up in the desert sun without water, bleeding, broken, in pain. Guns cocking and the shouts of enemy soldiers as they apprehended me. I was in the throes of a full-fledged panic attack before I knew what hit me.

"Alaric." Distant calls of my name made me look up. "Alaric, are you okay?" Someone reached for me, fingers brushing my shoulder, making my nerves snap with fear and my body jerk away.

At the touch, a face morphed in front of me. *His face.* Nicotine-stained teeth in poor health. Uneven lips bordering on brown twisting into a predatory smile. Threats I didn't understand until he showed me the knife in his hands.

No. Not again.

I fought against my rope bindings, desperate to get out of

there. My chair rocked, tipping me over to the concrete. Rope snapped as if broken, and I lunged free from my chair. I caught my captor by the neck, choking him, each gasp for air feeding my vendetta.

The distant voice screamed and gurgled as my captor struggled for air. Blood struggled to pump through his veins as I squeezed the life out of him. My arm registered the dense thud of a fist pounding on my flesh.

"Alaric, let go," the voice rasped. "Let go."

No. Rage erupted from the depths of my tormented soul. Enough. I'd had enough. He wouldn't torture me or anyone else ever again. My hands clamped around his throat like a vice, cranking tighter and tighter.

"No more!" My shouts burned my raw throat from all my unanswered pleas for release. "You won't hurt another again."

"Alaric, please." I refused to listen to him beg. To take pity on him as his life drained from his eyes.

"Alaric, get the fuck off her!" Someone rushed me from behind, grabbed hold and tossed me across the room. I hit the wall and then the floor before I realized what happened. What I'd done.

Castor knelt in front of Alexa, doing his best to reassure her. She had one hand on her neck and the other wrapped around her middle as she coughed and gasped for air. The red rings around her neck from my hands would blacken, purple, and morph to yellows and greens. A haunting reminder of what I'd done. I hadn't choked *him*, I'd choked *her*. Fuck, I'd slipped into a PTSD attack and hallucinated. Again.

"I didn't mean to hurt her ... is she okay?" I picked myself up off the floor and staggered toward them. "Please tell me I didn't hurt her."

Horrified at what I'd done, I couldn't bring myself to talk to her, so I kept apologizing at her and Castor. It didn't matter how many times I said it. It would never erase the fear laced with pity I saw in her eyes. Or stop the constant reminders that I'd done the same to Liz. Disgusted with myself, I backed out of the room.

Three words stopped me dead in my tracks. "Alaric, I'm okay." Alexa's jagged whisper ripped my heart to shreds. I caused the pain in her voice. The startled glaze in her eyes. The marks on her skin. She pressed her hand against her throat as she swallowed. "It's okay."

"No, no, it isn't." I held her gaze for a moment that stretched into eternity before walking out of the room and leaving Castor to tend her wounds.

This wasn't the first time I hurt someone I loved, and it wouldn't be the last. I was broken. Beaten. Scarred. She didn't need someone like me dragging her down with their emotional baggage. Alexa, and the goddess she carried inside her, needed someone who could protect them. We lost Liz because of the curse. I wasn't going to be the reason it happened again.

No, it was better for Alexa if I kept my distance. Which was easier said than done when she and the mate bond were so goddamned hard to resist.

Footsteps padded behind me. Alexa. I turned to her.

Castor was close behind her. "Come with me, and I'll get that looked at." He slid his hand into hers, and my heart tore all over again at not being able to hold and comfort her.

"No, it's okay." Alexa crept over to me, brushing hair from her face, drawing my attention to the red rings on her neck.

I crammed my eyes shut, unable to look at them. At what I was capable of. Her fingertips brushed the edge of my scarred arm, and I flinched.

"Don't," I told her, frightened I'd hurt her again.

Castor marched over, and I snapped my eyes open, catching him dragging her back.

Dauntless, she wrenched her arm free and moved closer. "That's happened before, hasn't it?"

"I'm fine," I got out between ragged breaths. She didn't need to know the particulars of my brand of fucked up.

"You don't look fine." She closed the distance between us, backing me up against the wall.

"I said I'm fine." My fight or flight instincts kicked in hard with more flashbacks of his leering, smug face, and I struggled to get them under control. Fighting the instinct to react, snap his neck again, I raised my palms. "I need you to step back."

"I can do that, but I need you to do something for me, okay?" Her harsh rasp scraped along my spine. She inched backward, giving me the space I needed. "I need you to slow your breathing down, Alaric. Can you do that? Slow, even breaths."

Castor hovered close behind her, wary of me losing control again. I was lucky it was him there to drag Alexa away. Slade had beaten the shit out of me when I hurt Liz. He was an act first and ask questions later kind of guy just like his god. I deserved every fist, every bruise.

Dumbfounded, I stared at her. "Why are you helping me when I just hurt you?"

She huffed. "You think I let a patient in an Ice rage hurt themselves and others because they hit me?" She rubbed at her arm. "It's my duty to help them, even when they're not in their right mind."

Not in their right mind. I hadn't been in control when I'd attacked her.

"Are you going to breathe for me or not?" she croaked, switching into nurse mode, giving me immediate comfort.

In that instant, I could tell a lot about her. She didn't back down, didn't give in to her fear, and she never lost her compassion for those in need, even when they couldn't help themselves.

I took my first deep breath for her. Then my next, filling my diaphragm.

"That's good. In through the nose, out through the mouth." She breathed with me, air crackling in her throat, and I found myself lulled into her rhythm. The expansion and shrinking of her reddened neck, the rise and fall of her breasts.

Self-soothing ... I knew the technique. My military therapist encouraged it. It didn't work. Neither did the sessions. Eventually, I stopped going. But to get my discharge paychecks, which I fed to my mom, I had to keep up appearances. Doctors appointments. Take medication. Sign form after form. The damn doctor pumped me full of three different medications that dulled my senses and made me dopey, but didn't stop the onslaught of anxiety. The club and the work we did with the safehouse were all the therapy I needed.

Maybe that was why Alexa became a nurse. Avoidance. You didn't have to focus on fixing your own problems when you were busy fixing everyone else's. I knew about that too. The reason I joined the club in the first place. Except, in the early days, we caused more problems than we fixed. It didn't matter.

"Better?" Her lips curved into a reassuring smile.

"Yeah." My gaze fell back to the tempo of her pulse, the undulation of her chest. The faintest hint of a blush stained her cheeks when she caught the direction of my gaze.

"Shit, sorry." Neck and face burning, I turned away. She thought me a pervert when I stared for relief and because I couldn't meet her gaze. I wasn't like Slade. Didn't take what I wanted when I wanted it. I respected my woman and her body.

"Would you like to talk about it?" Each rasped word made the pain in my chest deepen.

"Not really, no." I rubbed the knots of tension in the back of my neck. "It'll pass. It always does. You should get back to bed."

Following my cue, Castor stepped forward, taking hold of Alexa's arm. But she raised her palm at him, signaling for him to wait. She glanced over her shoulder at him, giving him a reassuring smile.

"Okay, if you're sure." She rubbed at her arms. "The offer stands if you change your mind."

"Sure. Thanks." I moved away, back to Zethan's office.

She wouldn't let me go otherwise. Liz was the same, wanting to comfort me after a nightmare, even when Slade dragged her away to his room to protect her. They'd fight like cat and dog until he won, and she gave in to keep the peace. Something told me Alexa wasn't so easily beaten into submission. Slade's lion to her bear.

It was better this way. Safer. Alexa needed to stay away from me. In the meantime, I'd watch over her, protect her. In the background, I'd fight the mate bond and help Castor find a way to break the spell tying us together, freeing us from the constant ache for our mate. Freeing me of the burden of wanting her so badly when I only brought her pain.

CHAPTER 18

*𝒶*aliyah

SLEEP CAME IN FITS. Whenever I closed my eyes, Alaric's hands wrapped around my neck, choking the life out of me. Up close, his breath reeked of whiskey, the scent assaulting me as heavily as his hand had. His dampener of choice. I'd seen plenty of men and women fall into this trap. I empathized with them and their condition, but the choice to treat the symptoms with alcohol only made things worse.

Just like Alaric's choice to become a Jackal. The violence, criminal activity, and everything about the motorcycle club life prohibited him from healing the scars of whatever gave him the Post Traumatic Stress Disorder. A high-stress environment like a biker club was the last place someone recovering from that condition should be. And I bore the bruises from it, even if they were caused unintentionally.

I rolled onto my side for the hundredth time and pulled the blanket tighter over me as if that would protect me. My throat ached like hell and kept me up most of the night. Bruises from my mugging had healed with surprising speed, leaving me with a faint purple and yellowish complexion. I wondered if it had anything to do with being closer to other avatars.

Zethan put every woman who came through the safehouse at risk when he assigned Alaric to security detail alone. He couldn't trust his own mind, and without treatment, he couldn't be trusted with the safety of other vulnerable people. We were lucky none of the women had witnessed Alaric's panic attack, otherwise they'd be frightened of him and not want him around. I'd heard his strained shouts and went to investigate in Zethan's office, getting trapped against the wall by Alaric.

I had to say something to Zethan as soon as I got my voice back. Alaric was dangerous and a loose cannon. If I could even pin Zethan down. For someone who was supposedly my 'fated mate,' he did a fine job of ignoring and steering clear of me, locking himself in his office. I thought it might have been because I didn't have another set of clothes other than my scrubs and had gotten a little stinky. But Carlie had given me some jeans, t-shirts, and sweaters yesterday to wear around the place. A nice addition to my warm shower. Besides, he should be used to that. Bikers weren't exactly fresh after a long ride cross country.

Birds gave their morning chatter outside in the rugged Australian bushland surrounding the shelter. They weren't going to let me go back to sleep with their calls disguised as sweet and innocent when they were really demanding we get up too. Lesley and her little girl, Danya, were out on the porch, feeding hamburger meat to the magpies and spotting wildlife.

Yesterday, the other women and I sat out with them, drinking hot chocolates. We saw kangaroos hopping around at dusk. *Kangaroos!* I couldn't believe it. I hadn't seen one outside of a zoo. Danya wanted to feed them, but Zethan told us not to approach them as the males might get aggressive.

This place was so tranquil, the perfect environment for these women to heal and disconnect from life and all its problems. I might have used the opportunity to share a little group healing too. Screw Castor's warning. No one was the wiser, and I'd keep it that way.

I wrapped my blanket around my shoulders to stave off the early morning chill and headed down to the kitchen for tea and honey for my throat. Besides the excited murmur of Danya, the shelter was quiet.

If I hadn't experienced it firsthand, I would never have suspected the commotion that happened last night with Alaric. I could have said the same thing about the entire chain of events since my father's murder. I had no clue what I was doing, masquerading around as a nurse with a fake name, infiltrating my father's enemy to honor his legacy.

While things were quiet, I needed to call Danny and tell him where I was, how I ended up here, and what I planned to do. Find irrefutable proof that Slade was the one responsible for my father's death. And no Jackal – no matter how many good deeds they did or how many women they claimed to save – would stop me.

Tea could wait. Alaric had gone outside for his perimeter check, so I snatched up my cell from beneath my pillow and set phase one of my plan to infiltrate the Jackals into motion. Borrowing someone else's phone was out of the question. They'd trace the call, and my cover would be blown. I had to get one of the Jackal's phones or a landline.

Quiet and light on my feet, I made my way through the hall to Zethan's office. I hadn't gotten a good look in there yesterday, playing the innocent, abused nurse while trying to calm Alaric. I slid into Zethan's makeshift office off the kitchen, converted from a utility room. Wire shelves stocked with canned goods and paper products lined one wall, with a utility sink and cleaning supplies on the other. A desk large enough for a laptop and a printer sat in front of the back wall. A cordless phone teetered on the edge of the desktop. My heart raced as I snatched the phone from its charging base with trembling hands and dialed Danny's number from memory.

He answered on the third ring.

"Yeah?" My brother's groggy voice came through the line.

"Hi." I hoped he recognized my voice. It still hurt to talk, and I had to use as few words as possible and make them count.

"Aliyah? Is that you?" He made some rustling noises in the background.

"Yeah." I clutched the cordless phone so tight my hand ached.

A woman moaned. "Baby, what is it?" Not his wife. Fucking asshole!

"Shut up, babe." Judging by the further rustling, he got out of bed and took the personal call. "Why the fuck are you calling me at five-thirty in the fucking morning?"

When the Wolves partied, they never got out of bed before midday.

"I'm in." I glanced over my shoulder, tense as a damn board, terrified someone would hear or catch me in the act. "What do you need?"

"Aliyah, where are you right now?" My brother's voice deepened with concern.

"With the dog pack." I tried to emphasize what I hoped were keywords to clue my brother in to what I meant.

Come on, Danny. I need you to figure this out. You have to.

It seemed my prayers were answered because he said,

"Holy fucking shit, you did it. I knew there was a wolf inside you."

The mention of the animal left me hollow inside. I'd never been a Wolf. Dad let me into the club, despite objections from the men. Never as a fully patched-in member, though. Although, I sure acted like one. He'd hoped I'd expel all that pent-up teenage frustration. But his men never accepted me, always keeping me on the outer fringes, forcing me to engage in more elaborate and dangerous stunts to earn their attention and camaraderie.

"You did good, Aaliyah." I imagined Danny fist-pumping down the hall of whatever skank's place he stayed at for the night. Poor Melissa. His damn wife put up with so much of his shit.

Over his elated voice praising me in the background, I heard the click of a door nearby, and I froze, listening. I didn't know if it was Lesley and Danya or Alaric.

"I want to know everything," Danny went on. "Their movements, their product, when their shipments are coming in."

Boots tread lightly on the wooden floors, and my heart leapt into my throat. Shit, Alaric was coming. I had to wrap up this conversation. I tried to speak, but the words stuck in my throat, and my hands cramped with fright, unable to drop the phone.

"We're going to hit them where it hurts, make them suffer, and then ... then we take them out." Danny went on like an eager child out to build a superior sandcastle when someone had kicked his original one into smithereens. He didn't mention dad or his legacy. Just straight payback.

I struggled my whole life with the eye for an eye club code. Wreak havoc and commit murder in retaliation went against everything I believed in. Well, before they killed my father. First, I wanted to know who was responsible for my father's death, then I'd figure out the next step.

Isis had always taught me not to retaliate with violence. She'd fought her brother, Set, after he murdered her consort and husband, then again to restore her son to the throne, the rightful heir of Egypt. Along the way, she lost her husband to the Underworld, and her son's trust. When an ancient goddess said there were much better ways for vengeance, I listened.

"Yeah, okay. I'll call you when I get back." I tried to end the call, but Danny didn't take the hint, rattling off the things he wanted to do.

Alaric tore open the door and entered. Fuck.

"Okay. Love you too." I hung up and set the phone back in the base.

Alaric looked just as startled by finding me inside Zethan's office. Shame flooded his eyes, and he bent his head and withdrew a few steps. I felt a subtle shift in the energy in the room. An ancient power. He lifted his gaze, his golden eye illuminating, circles of dark gold whirring in them. Magic rippled through the air as he tried to read me.

Alarmed by his intrusion and use of power, I knocked the phone and a stack of papers off the desk onto the floor. My hands trembled as I fumbled to pick everything up, regain my composure, and straighten everything back where it belonged. He took two long steps toward me before stopping himself, returning to the door, keeping space between us. Probably a good thing. I'd been victim to what he did when he lost control. My gut hardened at what he'd do while in full control after discovering my treachery.

"Who were you talking to?" Alaric's voice darkened with suspicion.

I turned to face him, calling up my best calm and guiltless expression in the face of the looming danger several feet away. "My mother." My voice came out sharp and croaked, making my throat burn.

"Your mother?" His voice held more than a hint of disbelief.

Yeah, I wouldn't have fallen for that either. Alaric had a naturally suspicious temperament. I hadn't figured out which god he belonged to yet. Someone important and high up in the pantheon from the strength and energy pouring off him. A god that protected others and watched over them. A shepherd to his flock. Why else would Slade have posted him here?

"She worries." The rasp in my voice made it difficult to use inflection for emphasis. "Especially after Dad died." Not a lie.

I shrugged off his suspicions and headed for the kitchen.

Alaric stopped me at the doorway, reaching out to grab me. His hand crunched into a fist, and he let it fall to his side. "You know you're not supposed to use the phone."

I had to hold my own with him, not let him intimidate me. If I did, I'd feed into his distrustful nature and prompt him to follow me everywhere I went.

"I'm not being stalked by an off-the-hinge narcissistic, asshole boyfriend, am I?" *Okay.* So, I might have thrown the last bit in to warn him from even thinking about trailing me and cramping my style.

"Rules apply to everyone for safety reasons. You're not given partiality and favoritism because you're our ..." He stopped short of the big *mate* word and I was glad for it. The bond tugged at my heart, urging me to move closer to him, to take him in my arms and soothe him the way his scarred soul needed it. To use my gift to heal the wounds in his mind.

Snap out of it, Aaliyah.

Fuck, I was going to have to be more discreet and clever next time I got a message to Danny. Otherwise, I wasn't getting out of here and back to my life. The Jackals found their fated soul mate, and if the indications of our bond were to be believed, they weren't going to let me go so easily. If they uncovered my identity, who knew what they'd do to me.

"I'm hungry." I stared him down, pushing aside the raw sting in my throat. "Can I get breakfast?"

Alaric let me pass. With his imposing physique, he could have stopped me if he wanted to without any trouble. He followed me into the kitchen, and I felt a tingle down my back, the trail of his eyes admiring my body. He left a warm glow everywhere his gaze touched, and the mate bond compelled me to turn around, push him up against the wall and enjoy the heat of his real touch.

Hell no. I didn't want his hands on me again after what happened last night. Being near him frightened me, and not just for that reason. The mate bond between us was strong and unyielding, and I worried I might be the one to lose control this time.

Eyes bloodshot from lack of sleep, Alaric grabbed a bottle of Jack from a cabinet above the fridge and sat down at the table. He spun the lid off with a flick of his thumb and took a long pull straight from the bottle. "What? It's five o'clock somewhere," he said in response to my astonished stare.

"Yeah, five o'clock in the morning." I didn't bother to hide my disgust as I ransacked the cabinets for tea. "You didn't get much sleep either?"

He winced at my use of the word either. "No."

Topic change. "Shit, you've only got instant left." Nurses and doctors went through the instant coffee at the hospital faster than water.

"Beggars can't be choosers." Alaric gave a half-hearted smile. "I'm doing a supply run today. Carlie gave me a list."

I filled up the kettle and flicked it on to boil the water. "So, Zethan runs the safe house, like management, and you take care of the supplies?" I traded his whiskey for coffee while subtly gaining information about their roles in the organization.

"This is Zethan's baby." Alaric poured himself a small finger of whisky into his coffee mug. "He and Carlie set it up two years ago. They've had thirty women, some with children, through the doors this year alone."

Incredible. I never would have picked the Jackals for rescuing abused women. The statistics alone were enough to depress me, and that didn't even cover the entire country.

"He rehomes some of them interstate with money to get started."

That must have cost the club a fortune. Clearly the Jackals were rolling in dough.

Alaric and I went to grab the boiling kettle at the same time. Our fingers brushed and charged with power, amping up the mate bond, and I crushed my fingers into a fist to resist cupping his face. He felt it too, shoving his hands under his armpits. With a coy smile, he gestured with his head for me to get the hot water first.

The bikers I grew up with didn't have many manners. Belching, farting, sticking their hand down their crotch or scratching their plumber's crack. Alaric was different. He waited on me like an old-fashioned gentleman. The way my grandfather did with my grandmother. Opening doors for her, lifting heavy items for her, and offering a hand to climb out of the car. They were so cute even into their eighties. God rest their souls.

As thanks, I poured hot water into Alaric's mug first when he motioned at me. "How can Zethan afford that?"

Alaric stirred his whisky coffee mixture. "He doesn't take a paycheck."

Hot water spilled over onto the counter as I struggled to

reconcile the world I found myself dropped into with my image of the Jackals.

"Shit." I dried it up with a tea towel, then resumed my coffee creation.

I dropped milk into mine and tasted it. God, it really soothed my throat. If only caffeine were a wonder drug to heal my injuries. My powers didn't work that way. I hadn't mastered how to heal myself quickly like I could with others.

Alaric eyed the black coffee with apprehension and rubbed the back of his neck. "Listen, about last night."

The nurse side of me, backed by the damn mate bond, wanted to know his story. "It's okay, really."

"No. It's not." He slid his arm across the counter, taking my hand in his. The move both shocked and excited me. His warm touch made me giddy, and I wanted his hands all over me.

Fuck this mate bond. It ate away at my resolve, and I wasn't going to be able to fight it for much longer. I had to break the spell it had over me. To leave soon, before I became a slave to it.

I couldn't withdraw from his grasp fast enough, folding my arms across my chest to avoid touching the bruise on my neck. "You have flashbacks? It's very common in people suffering from PTSD."

His eyes glazed over as he nodded.

I had to keep him focused on me to avoid him spiraling again. "Dwelling on what happened last night isn't going to help. Let's just put it behind us, okay?"

"Yeah, sure." There was a hint of skepticism in his voice.

In truth, I wasn't as upset with Alaric as I was with the rest of the Jackals. Club members were family, and you took care of your family. You didn't leave them holding on by a thread when you could throw them a lifeline. He needed to be cared for as much as any of the women who came through the safe house. Was it different just because he was a man? Or because he refused the help?

Alaric looked uncomfortable, so I rushed to fill the awkward silence that fell between us. "What do you, Castor, and Slade do?"

He gave me a smile with a cocked eyebrow. "We're not supposed to talk club business." Rules. He liked following them. Definitely a military man.

I glanced around, emphasizing we were the only two awake. "It's five thirty-five in the morning. Lesley and Danya are still outside."

"Are you always this inquisitive first thing in the morning?" He arched a quizzical brow.

I was in danger of crossing the line between casual conversation and inquisition. If I asked too many questions, he might get suspicious.

"Sometimes I believe six impossible things before breakfast," I quoted Alice in Wonderland. "It's been a trying couple of days, and I feel out of sorts." I rubbed at my bruised forehead, regretting it, and wincing. "I just want to get a handle on who's who, you know? Especially if we're supposed to be …" I had to swallow hard to spit out the next bit. "Fated mates."

"Yeah, I guess it's a lot to take in." Alaric seemed to agree with me on the surface. Something in his tone and eyes said otherwise, but he played along. "It was tough for us at first, too. Liz wasn't our regular type. She was twenty years older."

I choked on my coffee and spat it out, making a mess of the counter. They had another mate? Shit, how many mates did they have? "Where is she?" I got out after my coughing died down.

Alaric stiffened, clutching his mug so tightly, it might smash. "She died two years ago." Sore topic. His rejected tone told me not to go there again.

"I'm sorry to hear that." I drowned out the silence with a gulp of coffee.

We both had history, previous relationships, and part of me was cool with that. The side of me fueled by the mate bond wanted to claw out the eyes of any female who dared get near her men. I was not letting that bitch through.

Alaric took a sip of his steaming coffee then glanced at me, like he had something else he needed to get off his chest. "Castor's our Sergeant at Arms and Enforcer. He handles protection for the club on our turf and enforcing the rules."

I wouldn't have picked Castor for an Enforcer. When he mentioned it, I thought he was joking, flirting with and teasing me.

Patterns swirled in Alaric's golden eye, and I blinked, swearing I caught hieroglyphs. "Slade's our President and Zethan's our VP."

I nodded, feigning innocence as I cupped my mug. The characters in his eyes had come and gone too quickly for me to get a handle on them.

"What about you? Mysterious you." My voice came out a little too flirty for my liking.

He smiled like a damn GQ model and leaned in close, real close, just where my mate bond wanted him to be. So close, I noticed the feathered strokes in his gray eye and the veins of gold in his other. Beautiful. Something about the iridescence of his golden eye told me he saw more than he let on, that Alaric peered right into my soul. I shivered, rubbing at my arms, hoping he didn't investigate me and uncover my real identity.

Wary suddenly of his proximity, I flinched, reminded of what he did to me.

Noticing my discomfort, he withdrew. "I'm the Road Captain." He took another sip of his coffee, unbothered by the heat of it. "I handle the logistics of rides, product and protect the club away from home."

"I'm going to pretend I know what that all means and just nod." I had all the information I needed about their roles. Now I needed specifics on the products, inventory, shipments, and deliveries. Information I doubted he'd give me without being a club member. Although, he might confide in me if I became his mate. Nope, I didn't care what Danny thought, I wasn't going all *Mata Hari* and sleeping with any of the Jackals to obtain the information.

I opted for the coffee, thinking out my next move and how I'd achieve it. When I was alone, I had a clear head, my mind made up. The more time I spent with these four Jackals, the harder it was to concentrate on anything else but the desire flowing through my veins like liquid fire. Reality warred with fiction. Everything raised more questions, and it became more difficult to reconcile who they were with what they did. I needed the caffeine almost as much as I needed to get off the emotional rollercoaster I was on. Because something told me I was on a collision course with disaster.

CHAPTER 19

$\mathcal{S}$lade

"A shipment went missing?" I clenched the cell phone tightly, the plastic case creaking against the pressure. "Get Castor to find that truck and get it back." Raging like a storm inside, I threw my cell at the wall. Third one I'd broken this year.

One million dollars down the fucking drain. Money we'd invested in the stolen shipment. We were low on stock, and the rest of our cash poured into other shipments. We wouldn't be able to make that cash back for another two months. Enough time for the thief to have our product analyzed and replicated. Whoever stole our shipment wouldn't be able to completely duplicate the product because we harvested extinct Egyptian plants grown in the Underworld and gardens outside Thoth's library. But that didn't mean an imitation couldn't be chemically replicated. A cheap knock-off manufactured and slid into the market to compete with us.

Thunder rumbled outside in the dark gray clouds hugging the sky like exhaust fumes. The weather matched my goddamn mood. Not an uncommon occurrence when you were the avatar for Set. Wind and rain began to pound on the roof the moment I hung up on Alaric, responding to my magic. Armed with the elements, I could leave a trail of destruction in my wake and level the damn clubhouse in the blink of an eye.

Zethan pinched the bridge of his nose. "Fuck. Who called it in?" He leaned back further in his chair, his legs on my office coffee table.

"Alaric," I growled, snatching up the pieces of my phone, tempted to crush them. This fucking device had been the bearer of bad news all fucking week.

Zethan gave me a look, the one that said, *'don't do it, man,'* and he used his power to resurrect my phone to its original glory.

The Egyptians knew his god, Osiris, as the God of the Underworld and Resurrection. Set, the jealous fuck, had chopped Osiris up into little pieces, scattering his parts across the world. Isis had located them, all but his cock, bringing him back to life with her magic. Don't ask me why she wasn't called the goddess of Resurrection when she did all the work. Ancient Egyptians didn't make a lick of sense to me.

I grunted and stuffed the prick of a phone in my pocket. Second resurrection this year. The first I told Zethan not to worry about it 'cause it was time for an upgrade.

"Is Set running the show right now?" Zethan's boots lifted off my coffee table and stomped on the ground. "Because this feels like something the god of Chaos would do. Stirring shit up, you know?"

The anger simmering inside me threatened to boil over, and that was never a good combination with Set. The god of Chaos wasn't exactly known for linear thought. Rash decisions with a touch of mayhem were his specialty, and I didn't want a repeat of this shitty week with paperwork to lodge insurance claims to rebuild the clubhouse if I burned it down. We needed information on who targeted our product and why. Intel we wouldn't get with Joey and all the other witnesses dead.

"We need to put an end to this shit, Slade." Zethan came to stand beside me, worry darkening his green eyes and creasing his forehead. "Missing shipments are cutting into profits and hurting our—"

"Reputation. Yeah, I know." I didn't need the reminder from my VP. "Whoever it is isn't hitting Tony's warehouse."

Tony manufactured Pharaoh exclusively for us and he'd take the recipe to the grave.

"They wouldn't hit, Tony." Zethan removed his knife and holster, tapping it on his leg. "That's too close to our home base. These fucking cowards are too afraid to get caught and hitting higher up the supply chain."

I pinched the corners of my lips. "I want men posted on it anyway. Meanwhile, we need to visit Tony and get another batch ready ASAP."

Zethan came to stand by my side. "With what cash?"

"We made that fucker a millionaire," I snapped, grabbing the keys from the desk drawer. "The least he can do is a favor for us."

"I'll drive." Zethan shoved out his palm skyward. "We'll get there faster."

"Like hell." I smirked at him. "Nobody handles my baby but me."

"We both know how you drive, and you don't need another charge added to your list." We always argued over every decision, even down to something this small. Our gods never got along, and Set murdered his brother. Zethan and I were brothers in arms and still came to blows.

"Fuck off." I left him there. "You've got as much chance of driving my cage as you have of finding your dick."

Zethan smashed me in the arm with a fist. "Asshole."

The wind and rain picked up the moment we stepped outside. Lightning lashed at the ground like a whip of pure energy flicked by Set himself. Thunderstorms were bad for bikes, but it allowed me to stretch the legs in my old GTO with a new matte black finish. Chaotic and dangerous was how I liked it. After being fucked over three times this week, I was not in the mood to be messed with again. Once I caught the pricks responsible for this, they'd die slowly, painfully, and with every torture method in our books. Torture delivered by me personally. A role I used to play when my dad was president. Rest in peace, Pops.

I unlocked the driver's door, slid behind the wheel and reached over to unlock the passenger side. With Zethan beside me, we took off onto the road, wheels skidding in the rain. At the end of the street, I turned left onto the highway into town to avoid the morning traffic rush.

Our private clubhouse was situated out of town, tucked away where no one could find it. The business clubhouse, where we conducted meetings and trade talks, was located closer to town. A precaution after the Winters Devils burned our first clubhouse down.

A ten-minute drive took us to our destination. I noticed an unmarked cop car pull into the curb outside Tony's place. Fuckers followed me everywhere I went.

Good thing Tony had wire fences and security systems around the yard to keep him safe. At the gate, we pressed the button, and he allowed us inside. He wrapped up his illicit substance manufacturing business before school let out so he could pick up his son. Business hours were the best time to visit him, and this conversation couldn't wait.

I glanced over my shoulder at the cops watching our every move.

Tony greeted us under the porch of his warehouse with a smile and a handshake. He'd stripped off his usual lab coat and safety glasses for the occasion. "Boys! Good to see you. Wanna come in? I've got a pot of coffee."

I clapped him on the shoulder. Tony was our favorite manufacturer. Family man, and treated us like one of his brood. Loyal to the tee. Discreet and concealed his side hustle under the guise of his soap manufacturing business. I didn't associate with slimy junkies who dabbled in their products. Couldn't trust them. Unreliable as hell. We got fucked over when we first started out. Smartened up since then.

"Can't stay, Tony." Rain hit Zethan as we huddled under the porch, sliding down his cut. He'd seen the cops too by his glare in their direction.

Tony's forehead creased. "What brings you here then, boys?"

I waited for the thunderclap overhead. "We've received another massive order from interstate and need another shipment prepared."

Tony didn't need to know the finer details. Telling him would send him into a tailspin and reduce his cooperation to replace the stolen product.

Tony hitched his pants over his beer gut. "Sorry, boys. I'm waiting on a delivery of Arnicum root. Won't be here till Friday. Then two days to manufacture, distill and dry the product. You're looking at a seven-day wait."

Fuck, we couldn't wait that long. My hands curled into

fists, and I almost went off like the lightning flashing overhead.

Zethan took over for me while I struggled to rein in the chaos bubbling. "Can we do anything to speed up the shipment? Organize transport?" While I represented mayhem and destruction, Zethan was the calm to my storm, and I fucking needed him right now.

Tony scratched his chin. "You got a truck with a fridge in it?"

"No."

"Sorry, boys." Tony shrugged his shoulders, and fire shot through my veins. "Let me make some calls and see what else I can do."

Zethan glanced at me, and I knew he sensed the explosion brewing. "Appreciate it." He shook Tony's hand and dragged me away before I did something I regretted.

"Slade," Tony respectfully called out after me, and I saluted with two fingers, because it was all I could do to maintain control.

On my way out of the gates, I called down a lightning bolt, powerful enough to charge the shell of the cop car. To ruin the circuitry, I encouraged it to jump into the engine, and blow the tires out as an added gift. The cops in the vehicle got such a fright that one dropped his coffee in his crotch, and the other mushed a donut on his tie. Fuckers deserved it for tailing and harassing me. Barry, my solicitor, would be hearing about this.

I'd always been a hothead, even as a kid, from punching out bullies, standing up to teachers, and going head to head with gang members. Got me where I was today. But all this bullshit made me lose my grip.

Set and I were one and the same. Black sheep of the family. We loved, but never got along with our parents, siblings, or other gods. The rules dictated by others were not our thing, and we lived by our own. Fire and anger coursed through us to match our talents of chaos and mayhem.

I was an avatar, not an angel, with a rap sheet longer than my arm, and those were the ones the cops knew about. When the time came, I'd be judged, but not by a justice system that we bought and sold like commodities. No, when my time was up, I'd stand before Osiris in the Underworld like everyone else. For now, though, there was no point worrying about the afterlife when I had enough problems to sort out. A curse, a new mate, and a war. Any one of those on their own was enough to keep a man busy. All of them at once? A trifecta of trouble.

"Bring it down a notch, brother." Zethan snatched the keys off me and shoved me out of the way from getting into the driver's seat. "You're not driving when you're like this."

"Fine." I got into the passenger seat.

He was right. I was as erratic as the storm, and dangerous when I got like this. I'd drive like mad and probably blow out the tires of my car, too. Reluctantly, I gave up the keys and let Zethan drive me home, cooling off when my back hit the leather interior. I threw on my seatbelt like a good little boy, not wanting to give the cops more ammo.

Zethan cranked the engine and shifted into reverse. "Tony will make good on his word."

"We can't afford for a competitor to pop up in our absence."

Zethan glanced at me before pulling out into traffic, flipping the cops the bird as we passed them. "Let's get through one problem at a time." Sage advice from my VP and best friend. When I got like this, I couldn't think past my anger.

He was right. I had to take things one at a time. First, find my missing shipment. Second, take out the son of a bitch who stole our product and end this war for good. I had a short list of suspects for this one, but an accusation without concrete proof was how you ended up dead or at war. Third challenge—tackle the trumped-up murder charge. That one wasn't so easy.

My stomach crunched as I scrolled through my phone, checking messages, dreading more bad fucking news. An email from Australia Post caught my attention. Clothes I ordered for my date with Nurse A. were on their way. My mood shifted, and I sat up straighter, smiled, imagining my gorgeous mate in the green dress with gold highlights. My cock hardened at the thought of her curled up behind me on my bike, then seated opposite me at dinner, where I'd take her long leg and massage it under the table. I'd planned everything out. She was going to be mine that night, and I'd claim her, seal the mate bond, and then she wouldn't want to return to her life in Sydney. Thinking about it got me hotter than a car hood in the sun.

"Swing by the shelter," I ordered Zethan. "I want to see my old lady and make sure she's safe and well."

Extra cautious? Fuck yeah. But I had every reason to be. My mother was gunned down before my eyes when I was a kid. My last mate taken from me by a sick fuck who cursed us. I'd not lose this one.

My VP took the next right. "She's not ours yet."

"She will be." I flicked off my phone and looked at him as I stored it away. "Have you spoken to her yet?"

"A little." By a little, he meant probably a hello and running off to hide in his office. Poor bastard blamed himself for what happened. A freak fucking accident that killed our mate.

"Fucking chicken." I flapped my elbows and clucked like one. "You got a beak like Castor's!" I mimicked the long ibis beak with my arm.

Zethan thumped me in the arm. "Asshole."

Through the mate bond, I felt the ache in his soul, his

longing for Nurse A., the torture of not being able to hold her. I felt sorry for my best friend and what had been done to him.

I rested a hand on his shoulder as we pulled into the shelter's parking lot. "Castor's working on it."

"I know." Zethan's gloomy smile broke me. He tossed me the keys and got out of the car.

I pulled out my fresh batch of cigarette supplies. Two nights ago, I'd given Nurse. A my goods, thinking I wouldn't need them. I didn't last a damn day. I lit up a smoke and watched Zethan walk away, his steps heavy and agonizing.

These past two years had been agony without Liz, her absence a dark, bitter hole in me. We all felt her loss, Zethan even more so, the regret and guilt shared between the mate bond. Now we had a new mate in our lives, and it tore him up inside, and I couldn't do a damn thing for him. I felt like an asshole, flaunting it in front of him, buying our mate clothes for a date he'd never get to go on. With the curse looming over Isis and Osiris, Zethan could only look on from afar, or risk Liz 2.0.

I finished my smoke and strolled inside to see my mate. A man had to take what was his. After that shitty call and disappointing meeting, I just wanted a moment of peace, a moment with her to make me forget the destructive storm brewing within me.

"Nurse A.!" I called out, crossing to her, interrupting her mother's meeting with the other women. "Just the woman I came to see."

She didn't even look up at me. "I'm busy." Oh, I'd spank her for dissing me with that sass. I know she'd been talking to the other men. Felt it in the mate bond. I loved it when she played hard to get with me.

Bruised, purple faces of the women surrounding her glanced up at me, and my dick shrunk like a turtle retreating into its shell. I had one rule. Never hurt an innocent woman or child. Not after what happened to my mother. Low dog act. A cunt that fucked me over, though, they were fair game, regardless of sex. I just had to be careful I didn't tip the balance. God's rules. The fucking Egyptians liked to weigh their hearts for equal good and bad deeds. And if I didn't want to lose my title as an avatar, end up with a bullet in my brain, and descend into the pits of hell, I had to play by their rules. The main reason I let Zethan set up this shelter and funneled club funds into it.

Magic crackled in the air and zapped along my skin, making the hairs on my arms stand erect. Nurse A. had applied hers to the women.

"Sorry to break up your conversation." I burst into the circle, grabbed her by the upper arm and hauled her to her feet. "I'll bring her right back, promise."

One of the girl's lips curled into a sultry smile. *Sorry, sugar. Taken.*

"What do you think you're doing?" Nurse A. fought me, and my dick reappeared from its hideout.

"Didn't anyone tell you the rules?" I growled at her. That was Alaric's job to secure everyone.

She wrenched free of me, slapping my hand away, and my dick punched for freedom, gladly accepting her challenge. Her chest was a whole other ball game. The skip of her pulse twanged the mate bond, telling me the way I bossed her around, turned her on. But like an asshole cat, she wouldn't submit to the order of a lousy human. My mate was trouble. Defiant. Willful. Just like her damn goddess. But I'd break her down.

"Your clothes are on their way." I didn't hold back, stroking her shoulder. "Hope you like Versace and Jimmy Choo. Size ten and eight, right? I guessed your size. They'll arrive in two days for our date."

"Date?" Her haughty tone had me hard. I liked it when she fought me. Made the challenge to conquer her that much sweeter. I wanted to work for it too. I didn't do easy pussy. Period. My mate had to be worthy of me. Worthy of a god. "I told you no. I'm going back to Sydney once I'm better."

"Oh, you're coming," I said it nice and slow, so she understood. "You'll beg to get on the back of my bike with me."

She rolled her eyes the way she'd do when I fucked her senseless, and her eyes rolled back in her head. "You might get your way with other women, Mr. Vincent." Fuck me. The way she said my name, like a hot school teacher, turned me on like nothing else. This was *the* woman for me. "But you won't get far with me. And I already have a boyfriend."

Liar. Her accelerated pulse, shooting down the mate bond, said otherwise. "Really? Hope your boyfriend likes to end up second best."

"What do you want, Sl ... Mr. Vincent?" Course correction. I almost chipped a bit of her armor off. I'd keep working on it. We could play this game all night. My god liked mischief and trouble, and so did I!

"Nothing." I shrugged and gave her a killer smile. "Came here to visit you. Had a shit day and wanted something to brighten it."

"You're not getting down my pants, so don't bother trying." No, not until she was ready. But I'd have her wet and begging for it over dinner. Trust me.

I crossed my arms, playing with her. "Well, that's presumptuous. At least we know what's on your mind, don't we?" I winked at her.

"Ugh." She tugged at her hair, her cheeks staining pink. Cute. I got her flustered, chasing her tail. "Your innuendos are infuriating."

"I wasn't implying anything, Nurse A." I smiled again. "That was all you." She opened her mouth and snapped it shut. Game, set, match. One more chunk of her barrier broken. I was so ready for this. I curled an arm over her shoulder and led her away, enjoying teasing her when I got her riled up, hot and bothered. "Come get your old man his lunch."

CHAPTER 20

Aaliyah

THE MATE BOND was driving me crazy. It turned me into a hormonal crushing schoolgirl all over again. All morning, I'd waited for Zethan to arrive, curious to speak with him about the shelter ... and try to corroborate Alaric's story. Zethan showed up with Slade after lunch, features tight, marching straight to his office and slamming the door. I kept wandering past, urging myself to go and talk to him until I chickened out and ran away to talk with Deb.

Then Slade came in and dragged me away from my conversation like he owned me. The man made me want to scratch at my chest to dig out the source of the mate bond and remove it from me. His audacity and arrogance to think I'd make him lunch and go on a date with him. Who did he think he was, throwing around the old man title and promise of designer clothes? Fabio? Walking around in jeans, cut and tight shirt. Abs on display. All six of them. Not three. Six.

Ugh, the man was a perfect combination of masculine brawn with pure authority. He oozed sex. Blond hair slicked back on top of his head with shaved sides. Short, thick beard. Hard angles that matched his hard eyes. His dominance hung heavy in the air, and when he looked at you, or spoke to you, the mate bond told me to obey. But I wasn't like the other women falling at his feet and batting their eyelids. I'd come with a mission. Although, I could play the part to fool him.

And Versace? It wasn't like I'd been saving up for one of their dresses or a pair of Jimmy Choos. I'd give him one thing. The man had impeccable taste. And an uncanny ability to get my dress and shoe size right.

"Lunch?" I withdrew from the arm he hung over my shoulder, spinning to face him.

Dimples played at the corner of his victorious grin. I knew what he was up to … trying to tease me and wear me down until I gave in. Well, he had another thing coming. Two could play his game.

"How about you get your ass in the kitchen and make your mate lunch." I used my stern voice, normally reserved for interns who talked down to nurses. It was razor-sharp and brooked no arguments. Triumphant, I purred inside, hanging to see the Jackal's President play husband.

"I don't cook or clean, Sugar." He didn't even try to lobby me back with one of his flirty comebacks. Disappointing to say the least. As much as I found him annoying, I enjoyed the thrill of our banter. I swear, if he said that was his old lady's job, I was going to hit him.

I tried another angle. "How about you make me lunch, Mr. Vincent, and I'll go on that date with you."

Slade's dark blond brows arched to his hairline. No one had ever challenged him like that. The darkening of his piercing blue eyes told me he rose to the occasion. Slowly, seductively, he leaned in to whisper in a gruff voice. "Are you bribing me, Nurse A.?"

I played his game, moving closer, my breath making the hair above his ears prickle as I whispered back, "No bribe, Mr. Vincent. It's a negotiation. You can throw me on your bike and take me on that date. I'll sit there, blink and stare off into space like your damn blow-up doll."

"I don't have a …" Quick to protest. Definitely something to hide there.

I pressed my fingers to his lips. Big mistake. The link between us rippled with desire. Mine and his. I tore my hand away and tucked it to my side. Tight. Real tight. "I won't give you a thing. Won't eat anything. No conversation. Nothing."

Slade Vincent got whatever he wanted. Not me. Not ever. I had to make it clear we weren't playing on his terms. I'd agree to his damn date only to seek information, but we were doing it my damn way, not his.

He pulled away, his gaze going from my eyes to my lips. "You don't want to know what I did to the last man who bribed me." A cold shiver of both arousal and trepidation chased through me.

"What?" I challenged, lifting my chin and my gaze. "Stole his salami?" It was my turn to wink and walk away into the kitchen. I paused by the entrance, glanced over my shoulder, and tapped my Fitbit watch. "Waiting, Mr. Vincent."

He followed close behind, the heat of his body chasing the cool I exuded.

I sat at the kitchen counter stool. "I like salami and cheese on rye with a little butter."

Slade shot me a look that could kill lesser men. "Woman, I'll teach you not to play with me." His threat sent another shiver vibrating along my mate bond, straight to my pussy. And damn, he smirked, sensing it too.

Fuck. I had to find a way to hide this or control what I

communicated through the bond. Who needed the gods to betray my true motivations when I had a curse that bound me to four men and enabled us all to read from the bond? If they knew my emotions, the way my body reacted to them, would they be able to detect my identity and purpose? I tried not to think about it. Enjoy the small win against Slade while it lasted. I'd enjoy bringing the Jackal's President to his knees.

Enthused, I clasped my hands together, mocking him with my gleeful smile. "Coffee too," I added as he removed the bread from the fridge. "Milk and sugar, please."

Slade's throat rumbled at me as he tossed the loaf, wrapped meat, cheese, and butter on the counter. "You're really making me work for it."

"Don't you know it, Mr. Vincent." I smiled sweetly.

He must *really* want that date to cooperate with me. I'd play along, go on the date with him, slide up behind him, one hand in his hair, the other pressing a knife to his throat, ending him for taking my father from me. I buried that thought in case it sang across the bond and alerted him.

"Oh, Mr. Vincent, you know how to spread butter," I teased as he layered four slices with it.

The mate bond went taut with his need, and my body reciprocated with a deep, growly beg. I ignored that bitch and concentrated on breaking down the man before me.

He jabbed his butter knife at me. "That's not all I'll spread." God, him and his insinuations.

He packed on the salami as if he hinted at the size of his meat, and I hid my smile behind my clasped hands. Lastly, he sliced and added the cheese, then patted down the top piece of bread, set it on a plate, and slid my sandwich first. That little motion told me he didn't just take what he wanted. He looked after his mate's needs. Pleased her. My thighs crashed together, trying not to think about the ways he'd please me.

Delighted at my victory, I tasted his treat, my mouth

watering at the combination of fatty meat, cheese, and butter on the crusty bread. I didn't thank him, because he gave me the impression he took what he wanted without thanks, and I'd reflect that.

"You know how to melt your cheese, Mr. Vincent." The flirt slipped out and I tried to wrangle it back in. Too late. Oh, well. The sandwich was incredible, and he deserved a little praise.

He took a slice of salami from his sandwich and came around to my side of the counter. Meat grazed my lips as he tempted me to draw it into my mouth. Thick, hungry need twisted the mate bond, and I struggled to hold on with him doing this. His revenge for my flirting and bribing him. He wasn't kidding when he threatened me. I'd pay for what I did. He'd torment me through the link, chipping away at my resolve, bit by bit, until he had me where he wanted me. And damn, before I knew it, my lips parted and he slid the salami between them, and I sucked it in nice and slow, like I would his finger. Air hissed between his teeth, and the bond went rigid with desire.

Someone entered the kitchen, but it didn't chase him away, and his hand crept back to reach for his plate.

"You made lunch." The plate scraped against the counter as Castor dragged it away. God, not two of them.

Join in on the fun, my mate bond screamed. *Feed your hungry mate.*

Bitch!

Jealousy pinched at the connection. Castor didn't approve of mine and Slade's vicinity. A bit of competition for the alpha males.

He groaned on purpose as he tucked into Slade's meal. "Oh, God, this is incredible."

Slade's attention snapped to the left. "That was mine, asshole."

Castor smiled. "Not anymore."

Slade stood to his full height and moved behind the counter. "You're the culinary whiz. Make me another."

Lesley and Danya entered the kitchen. "Is lunch ready?"

Castor jabbed a finger at Slade. "Yeah, Uncle Slade's making sandwiches."

"Fuck off." Slade's low growl warned Castor to back off.

Castor patted his grumbling president on the shoulder and left the kitchen with his sandwich.

Clever. I giggled.

"Did you just swear?" Danya hit Slade where it hurt. "You owe money to the swear jar, Uncle Slade."

The Jackal's President towered over her like a giant about to crush her beneath his boot. "Come here, you." He swept her up and tickled her. "You just volunteered to help me."

She giggled and wriggled in his grasp. "No, I didn't."

"Uncle Slade is the boss, and he says you are." A deep longing stretched down the mate bond, and this time, it wasn't for me. He wanted children or missed his own, and my heart softened a little toward him.

"Am not," Danya sassed back.

Slade cuddled her tight. "You'd make an excellent addition to my team."

"What team?"

Uh-oh. Didn't want to know about his recruitment activities. Smiling to myself, I snuck away to the porch with my lunch, to get away from the heat building to an explosive crescendo.

Castor glared through the kitchen window as I sat down. "Kudos on how you handled him back there. I've never seen him make anyone a sandwich."

I blew air on my fingers. "That's because I'm the master."

Castor ate the bit of cheese that slid free. "You only

deserve that title if you can bribe him into wearing women's panties."

I snorted and hit him in the arm, making him chuckle. "You shouldn't encourage me, you know. I'll do it."

"I don't doubt you." Castor's eyes lightened with mischief. "I've never seen anything so impressive. I can't even dupe him with my mind tricks." He waggled a finger at me. "You make Isis proud."

"I only gave what I got." I smiled over my lunch. "I can teach you."

His eyes were like a magnet, and I couldn't look away from them. "Did you just make a date with me, too?"

"No." Shit, I was running out of sandwich to hide behind.

"Your calendar's going to be full soon."

I punched him again. "Stop it."

His maple eyes flashed, eyebrows raising. "So, you're not sticking around to date us all then?"

Yes. I'm yours.

Definitely not. I didn't care what the mate bond said. "You know I can't."

He pressed a hand flat to his thigh, and my eyes went there, noting how thick and long they were. "Slade will probably kidnap you then."

I folded my legs together. "Not funny."

"Why don't you stick around here a little longer?" Castor tapped his thigh with a finger. "Give the mate bond a chance." At least he wasn't as pushy as Slade. Still, he tried in his own way.

I pulled my legs to my chest. "I don't believe in fated mates. In not being able to choose my partner." The mate bond said otherwise. That bitch shouted at me for being a liar.

Castor finished half of his meal. "Four men, one woman. What kind of fuckery is that?"

I laughed again, feeling uneasy. I'd never been with more than one man. Never even experimented in bed. Plenty of cases came through the ER of kinky experimenters. Objects stuck in places they shouldn't. Vaginal cavities locking up with their men stuck inside them from trying strange positions their hips and pelvis just couldn't tolerate. Dicks broken from vigorous lovemaking. Awkward shit happened. It put me off trying anything funny.

The idea of dating four men at once was equally as strange and daunting. Dating my enemies even stranger. Falling for them impossible and not going to happen.

"What do you want from all of this?" Castor's question took me aback. Three of the Jackals, including him, declared me theirs, and I didn't think they'd give me a say. By all accounts, the mate bond dictated their choice, and they'd make me their woman. "Stay or go?"

I picked cheese from my lunch and gave him the truth. "I want to go home. I have a life and a job."

Solemn, he nodded, staring at the wood floor of the porch. "I thought so."

"Is that what you want?" I didn't know why I asked the question or why I even cared.

Castor stared out at the pastures behind the shelter, at the grazing cattle. "I don't want to share. I want what's mine." He rubbed his palms together as if it might shed the curse. "I didn't believe in magic and gods until one saved my life. But I signed on for this. Doesn't mean I accept it."

Isis came to me one day when I went to the beach with Barb and her family. I fell asleep reading a book, and she dropped into my dream. I hadn't been in danger, though. There was certainly no mention of four men that came with the avatar package when I agreed to represent my goddess.

"I'll find the spell to reverse the mate bond one day," he

said it like he didn't have much hope or didn't want to break it.

The idea that Castor sought a way to break the bond gave me hope. I didn't want to be tied to these men any more than they did to me. Slade seemed to accept it and go with it. Alaric followed orders. By Zethan's reaction to me, he didn't want me around, and I felt the same.

Curious to know Castor's story, I asked, "Saved your life?"

Castor kept rubbing his palm. "An MC went after me for prosecuting their VP."

I blinked. He'd gone from one extreme to the other. Solicitor to Enforcer. Complete opposite ends of the spectrum. Ironic in a way, that he became one of the men he prosecuted in legal proceedings.

I hugged my legs. "And you joined the Jackals for protection?"

"No." He laughed, a husky thing that stoked the small flame in my chest into a bonfire. "I smote those bastards."

"Remind me not to get on your bad side." I nudged him in the leg. "What's your story then?" I leaned back, giving him license to lean his arm over the back of the long chair, and the link ushered me to scoot closer, snuggle up to him. "Why'd you quit the law?"

His body language changed, and he rolled his shoulders, removing his arm from behind me, and a little piece of me sighed, wanting him back. Wanting to snuggle into the crook of his arm and chest.

"Disillusionment," he said. "I entered starry-eyed and passionate about the law. Ready to do justice and fight for what's right."

I sensed a dark story coming on and tensed, clutching my legs tighter.

"One too many lost judgments and motions." He cracked his knuckles.

"Criminals walking after screwing over my clients. Judges letting rich criminals off too easy. My clients left in massive debt fighting for justice." He leaned his elbows on his thighs and hung his head. "The justice system is bullshit. It serves corporations and the wealthy and doesn't care about citizens."

He was pretty skeptical. But I guess he worked with criminals of the underworld and those masked as authority figures, corporations, or citizens.

Sometimes the hospital system felt the same. New policies implemented that changed everything: reporting lines, record-keeping procedures, and even who could do what.

"Working in the ER is a little of the same," I admitted. "Politics, procedures, and toeing the line. It gets tiring. I just want to heal. No bullshit."

He turned his knees inward to me, and I found myself doing the same. "Have you ever thought of a different form of healthcare?"

I raised a palm, sensing where this was going. The mate bond confirmed it with a light tug to come to him. "I'm not going to join the Jackals and become your medic."

He pressed a fist into his thigh and raised his elbow. "You know a lot about club life."

Shit. That was the second time I'd given away too much with him. I almost broke under his probing stare. Sweat beaded my forehead as I used everything I had to stop it transferring along our link. He mustn't know who I was or what I intended to do here.

"I've ... read a lot of romance novels and am very intimate with motorcycle club law and operation." Lie. I crushed the guilt down so it didn't spread through the connection.

"Intimate, huh?" Castor took that as an invitation to take my hand and stroke it. I almost passed out from the heat that swept through me. Such a small gesture set me on fire. Aided by the guilt of my real reason for being here. "How much?"

God, not another flirt. More my style, though. With jokes behind his hints.

He waggled his eyebrows at me. "Bet the romantic leads weren't as handsome and complicated as me." He gave me a cheeky smile, and I giggled.

Yes, I beat the mate bond. That bitch was not going to sucker me into falling in love with my enemies.

But if I was real with myself, nothing compared to him and those maple eyes that made me think of melted butter and brown sugar caramelized. Nothing compared to Slade either. Or Alaric. Zethan, too. Four of the most gorgeous, sexy, rugged, and fit men I'd ever seen. Not even my ex-boyfriend compared to the four Jackals bound to me.

Thinking about them all enabled the mate bond to sink its claws into me and trick me into brushing my thumb over the top of Castor's hand. He reciprocated, light, respectful, but I felt the deeper urge throb through the link.

I hadn't been able to escape the memory of him kissing me yesterday. Damn, that man knew how to use his mouth and tongue. It wasn't the mate bond talking, either. From the soft, exploratory crush of his mouth to mine, deepening as he learned the symmetry of my lips, to the tangle of our tongues and the way he pressed me to his body. My lips had tingled all throughout dinner just to remind me, yearning for another kiss before we parted at lights out. He lingered for one too, and I almost let him, coaxed by the pull of the bond, the pulse of his heart echoing in mine. Until the rational side of me pricked that bubble.

These feelings weren't real, though. They were the product of the curse between us, tricking us into the attraction, flooding us with intense desire and need. No, I had to keep a level head, because I'd be damned if these emotions were real. If my feelings went deeper than hate and revenge.

Castor rubbed at his thigh as if it replaced the touch of my hand. "In all seriousness, I've seen you with the women here. You're good with them."

The idea appealed to me. Filling out paperwork consumed half of every shift. Memberships to nurse and medical associations cost money and time to build on my skill set every year. Policy had me a pawn to a major conglomerate hospital that dictated what treatments we used, like chemotherapy for cancer when many other treatments existed. They refused to investigate or consider them if they weren't likely to generate income. I wanted to do more than that.

I set my feet back on the porch and stood up to leave. "I'll think about it."

CHAPTER 21

*Z*ethan

IT HAD TO BE DONE. Avoiding it got me nowhere. Carlie called again. Another woman needed an evacuation to our safehouse for help beyond the services her shelter provided. The woman tried to lay low at the local shelter in town, but her ex tracked her down. Pricks usually did. My sister's shelter did good work, providing a warm bed, clean clothes, a hot meal, and access to legal aid. The Jackals provided papers, identification, and the cash needed to buy a clean slate. A one-stop shop for a fresh start.

The collection point was always the worst part of this venture, but it had to be done. Years of assisting domestic violence and sexual assault victims had hardened me to the realities of it. My crew brought women to my safehouse, where we protected and cared for them until their fucker husbands, boyfriends, or assailants were put away, or we could relocate the victims safely if they couldn't get a conviction.

Dread coiled in my stomach every time my phone went off, and my sister's number flashed on my screen. One more broken and beaten woman to rescue. I thought I'd seen every possible act of violence through the police and my four years as club VP. Nope. Worse. Each one broke my heart at how fucked up this world was, and nothing I did was going to change that.

This instance was different. The woman I had to collect needed urgent medical attention, and Dr. Shriver couldn't get there until later, so I had to transfer her to his waiting room. For that, I needed Alexa to come along and stabilize her for transport. There was just one problem with that. The curse.

Instead of running towards Alexa, I ran away. Slave to the god of the Underworld, I didn't have a choice, and it was better for everyone involved. It didn't matter what Slade or the others said. They weren't the ones under two fucking curses. Liz's death ruined me. Shattered my heart into a million pieces. Some of which were never recovered, thanks to that godforsaken curse. I patched myself up the best that I could, but I'd never be the same. Too many holes, too many pieces of myself were still missing. She was my first love, the love of my life, my destiny, and I destroyed it. Destroyed all of us.

Distance between Alexa and me meant she hadn't experienced any of the side effects of our curse. Something that would be impossible to do in close quarters on the drive over to Carlie's shelter. Still, I couldn't turn my back on someone in need. Not when I had the means to help her.

I cast my gaze across the hall full of abused and sexually assaulted women. This bunch were in pretty bad shape. The dark-skinned bird in bed one had an arm twisted at an awkward angle when she first arrived. Broken in two places before Doc Shriver fixed it. Arabian Nights in bed six had eyes so purple and swollen I feared she had a fractured nose and might need surgery. The Asian woman in the far left was bleeding out her ass.

Alexa had broken the rules and helped these women, filling them with an unusual calm and resolve. I let it slide and kept her secret. Slade would have gone off his tree if he knew.

Alexa's voice in the kitchen drew me in like a siren's song. Light, fluid, and hypnotizing me into her spell. They weren't the only features that called to the primal side of my avatar. The curve of her lips, the swell of her breasts. Inevitably, she was my mate. Destiny fulfilled when the gods created her and made her the avatar of Isis.

She stood at the sink washing dishes while Slade towel dried. Fuck me. I'd never seen my president behind that counter. She worked her magic on him.

I whistled at him. "The things we do for love." *Or the mate bond.*

"Fuck off." Slade tossed the dish drying towel at me and stormed away, probably to go regrow his balls and regain his man card.

I chuckled, watching him leave.

Alexa's cheeks deepened with a rosy pink. Cute. I wanted to make them go pink from another activity between us. Pipe dream.

My chest burned whenever I was close to her. The call of our bond.

Don't lose focus, Zethan. Not now. Not when so many are depending on you. I needed to keep my shit together for the Jackals and the women who came through the safe house. For Abigail, my murdered sister.

"I'm headed out and could really use your help." I rubbed the back of my neck where a slight ache settled in.

Physical effects of the curse were already starting. Aches and pains, fever, stomach cramps, and nausea were the curse's less severe but most common ailments. The connection between our avatars was strong if I felt them already.

Her shirt rode up as she stretched, exposing smooth skin and a toned midriff. My fingers flexed with longing to touch her there. Everywhere. Fuck. My mate was beautiful in spite of the ruffled hair and fading bruising. Staying away from her hurt just as much as the side effects of the curse between our two gods.

"Who's hurt?" Her voice croaked less with each day.

Fuck Alaric for choking her. Slade had to hold me back from kicking his ass. The guy needed to get help and take his damn medicine. But he was terrified to confront his damn demons. Some part of me wondered if Alexa could bring him the peace he'd searched for all these years. I damn well hoped so. He deserved it.

"A woman came into Carlie's shelter this morning." I scratched at my neck to relieve the cramping muscles. "Her husband found her and refuses to leave without his wife. The cops won't do anything. Too low on their priority list. Busy attending to some other bullshit in town."

"Oh, God." Alexa's hand went to her mouth.

"Carlie and her team can't get her to the hospital with him blockading them." I rubbed my throbbing forehead. "And I don't want my sister facing this dick alone when she's pregnant."

"Let's go." Alexa didn't hesitate. Medicine and healing flowed in her blood, like it did through her goddess.

That was easier than expected. The ride to the shelter was not.

"There's a first aid kit in the back seat." I rolled open the back door of my van. There was no way she was riding beside me. We'd never get to the shelter alive. "You can ride back there." I jammed a thumb in the direction of the van's bench seat in the hope she took the hint.

"I'm sure it's well-stocked." Fuck. She climbed into the passenger seat. Any closer, and she risked her life.

Stomach contracting, I climbed in beside her, cranking the engine, letting it warm up. Alexa shifted in her seat, crossing and uncrossing her legs and tugging at the seatbelt strap repeatedly. I cracked the windows to circulate some air and did my best to ignore the pain increasing with each passing mile as we drove away.

"There's some antacids in the first aid kit." I would have told her I had a gastroenterologist tied up in the back of the van if I thought it would get her out of the passenger seat, away from me.

Thank fuck, she unfastened her seatbelt, climbed into the back and started ransacking the first aid kit. She found a packet of Rolaids and cracked them open, chomping on the chalky tablets. "Did they say anything about the woman's injuries?"

"Broken nose, possibly broken ribs, and concussion." I gripped the steering wheel hard enough to meld my hands with it as I recounted the woman's injuries.

"She's lucky she made it to the shelter." Alexa set out multiple rolls of Ace bandages on the seat beside her. "How much further? My stomach is killing me. I think Slade served me some moldy cheese or bread or something."

Fuck, she thought Slade did this.

"A few more minutes." I checked the speedometer and punched the gas pedal.

My stomach eased as she sat in the back, clutching hers. Liz 2.0 rolled closer, and my nerves were fraught. The shelter came into view, and I floored it. Busting to get out of the van,

I pulled into the shelter's parking lot too fast, sending Alexa sprawling.

I shrugged off my cut and left it in the passenger seat. "We're here." It came out harsher than I meant, but the fucker who beat up the victim stalked the parking lot, shouting at Carlie and her workers, who held him back. My sister was not getting involved in this.

Before I killed the engine, Alexa slid the side door open and leapt into action. She tucked the first aid kit under her arm like a running back and hauled ass inside the shelter. The woman must be one hell of a fireball in the emergency room.

I remained outside. Had someone to deal with first. Anger surged within me, and I needed an outlet for the pent-up energy the gods provided. Hands clenched into fists at my side, I marched over to the ex. It could have been ten to one and the odds still wouldn't have been in his favor. Being the avatar for the god of Death had its advantages. Sucking the life out of someone was one of them. I would have snatched the breath from this prick's lungs and dropped him in the parking lot. Witnesses. Three of them.

God knows the police would do jack shit in this case unless the woman made a statement. Eighty percent of the time they were too scared to, leaving the police helpless to pursue criminal action against the partners.

"Brother," Carlie ground out a warning. She never used my real name so the guy couldn't report me to the cops. She knew what I was about to do. I had no shame in it. I'd take pleasure in it. He'd not hit a woman ever again.

"You okay?" I stroked her hair. "Did he hit you?"

"Nah, he's just aggressive and won't back off." Carlie rubbed her stomach.

"Leave it to me." I crossed to the prick making a scene

outside my sister's shelter. "Get the fuck out of here." I shoved him from the side.

Five eleven, blue-collar worker, fit, but the years of downing beers were starting to show. He staggered sideways and regained his footing.

Carlie activated the recording function on her camera. Evidence for when the cops finally showed up to interview the wife. If she gave a statement. I'd be happy to give one too. Happy to testify against this prick.

"You got a problem?" The fuckwit of a husband rolled up the cuff of his long sleeve shirt, exposing the bruised knuckles he'd used to hit his wife.

"I got a problem with you being here." I got up in his face. "Now fuck off. This is private property, and you're trespassing."

"I'm not leaving until I get my wife back." His voice hitched when he caught the tattoos up my neck and along my exposed arm.

"Your wife is not your concern anymore." I dragged in heavy breaths. "Here's what you're gonna do. You're gonna hire a solicitor, draft up divorce papers, leave her the house, and you're gonna fuck off. You got me?"

A hot, red rash spread across his chest, neck, and face.

"Who the fuck you think you are, man?" The guy's body stiffened, and his muscles twitched as if he wanted to take a swing. I was ready and waiting. "She's my wife, and she does what I say. You don't get to tell me what to do."

"You like to prey on women, huh?" I asked in a low menacing voice. "Beat your wife senseless? You know what they do to guys like you in prison, Jacoby? Guys who like to hurt women don't last long in gen pop."

The man's gaze scanned me up and down. "What are you? The muscle?" He laughed my accusation off, trying to save face.

Typical narcissist. Dealt in fantasy, blame, and projection. Nothing was ever his fault. He was perfect to the fucking tee. Plenty of crooks like him out there. Seen the gambit of them all in my five years on the police force. Ditching the force for the Jackals gave me permission to beat the shit out of assholes like this and give them some of their own fucking medicine without suspension and having to deal with commission authorities. Few cockheads like this had been smart enough to walk away and give up. The majority dumb enough to hurt their partners again. But that was the woman's choice to go back. And as much as I hated it, how it triggered me over my sister's death, because she'd done the same thing, there'd come a time where I had to be objective and let go. Otherwise, each one of their stories would destroy me.

I knew exactly the response to get this fucker to take the first swing. "I'm her fucking lover. Bigger dick." I thrust my hips for emphasis. "I last a hell of a lot longer than your thirty seconds. I give it to her good."

The rash on his face completely blanketed his features. He came at me,

swinging with a wild haymaker. Aiming for a one-hit knockout punch. I blocked it and threw a short right jab. It connected. He stumbled back, clutching his bloodied nose. Eyes wild with fury, he returned, moving in with a flurry of body shots. This guy had practice. Probably caused a stir at the local bar and got into drunken fights with patrons.

I kept my defenses tight, elbows tucked in, and deflected most of the blows. They were too light for me to feel any pain. Another bonus of being an avatar. I wore him down, waiting until he punched himself out and went on the offense. Jab, jab, uppercut, finishing with a body shot to the liver. Rage and adrenaline-fueled every shot. I wanted to humiliate him, for him to feel every blow like the ones he'd inflicted on his woman. An overhand right to the head would end it, but that would have been too easy. I dragged it out for maximum pain. By the time I finished, the ex slumped to the ground, right beside his car. Blood dripped from his nose and several cuts on his forehead and cheek.

I crouched beside him, went through his wallet, memorizing the address on his driver's license. I flashed it to Carlie to record on her camera. We'd been through the motions several times before and she knew the drill.

I slapped the groaning prick on the cheek hard enough to rouse him. "I'll be dropping in now and again to see how you're doing, Wayne." I flicked the card at his forehead, and he flinched.

That was Carlie's signal to cut the recording, and she lowered the camera and deactivated it.

I slapped the guy's cheek again. "You go to the cops, or come by here or *your wife* ever again, and you won't be alive to tell the tale." I kicked at him, and he scrambled backward, digging in his pocket for his keys. "Don't forget those divorce papers. I want them signed and delivered here by Friday. Got it?"

"Fuck you." He spat blood and clambered into his car.

This wouldn't be the last I'd see of him. He'd be back with cops or friends. Then I really would deliver the full force of the Underworld.

Carlie's assistants went back inside, and I waited until his car tore out of the parking lot in a screech of tires and burning rubber.

"Thanks, brother." Carlie set a calming hand on my shoulder.

"Any time." We both walked inside, and I took one glance at Alexa, treating the abused woman.

"She's a miracle worker." Carlie gave me another pat on the shoulder.

"You have no idea," I replied, reminded of the woman who used to occupy the same space in my heart.

Heart heavy, I excused myself and left Carlie to lock the front door. In the bathroom, I looked at myself in the mirror. My eyes were a dark shade of green, like seawater. Blood had splattered my face, and I rinsed it clean and wiped it with a paper towel. I combed my fingers through my light hair that went everywhere from hitting the husband.

Memories of Liz flickered through my mind like an old film reel, and I gripped the edge of the bathroom counter. Emotions I struggled with every day stirred. Anger, sorrow, love, bitterness, and betrayal by the gods. They gave us something beautiful, something people only hoped to find in their life, and they took it away. They let her die and left us to suffer without her. I punched the tiled wall and made it crumble. Heavy breaths dragged in and out of my mouth as I struggled to gain control.

The gods like to play their sick games, and kept a new lady in waiting, tossing her into the mix without so much as a warning about what they'd gotten her into. She had no idea what I could do to her, or her to me. What danger she was in. Alaric and I should have never brought her back with us. I flexed my hand in and out of another fist, tempted to break more than the tile.

I'd watched Alexa these past few days. She was a born healer, a nurturer with a calming way about her, and it had nothing to do with her goddess. Isis boosted her natural healing abilities with magic, speeding up the process of mending broken bones, or in Slade's case, stitching someone back together. But she didn't need it. This was her calling, and the gods fucked up when they selected her as a vessel. From what little I'd observed of her, she was smart, tough, gifted, and gorgeous. The whole package, and thanks to the curse weighing down on me, totally out of my fucking league.

I sucked in a long breath before joining my sister in the main hall. Something was wrong, though. Carlie's assistants rushed around, grabbing towels and things from the first aid kit.

"What the fuck's wrong?" I asked, my heart beating wildly.

The answer came a split second later, and I scrubbed my jaw, then squeezed it.

Alexa glanced up at me, aqua gaze dark with worry. "She's bleeding internally, and I can't stop it."

CHAPTER 22

Aaliyah

EVERYTHING SLIPPED out of my control. Her heartbeat slowed down as the body gave in. Bodily functions shut down. Life bled from her, and I couldn't do a damn thing to stop it. I was too late. We'd arrived too late to save her. Limits restricted my powers, and unfortunately, this was one of them. Tears dripped from my cheeks onto the woman's stomach.

"No!" I pressed my hands harder to her abdomen, as if that would pump more potent magic into her and do something to change the decline in her state.

"Stop!" a deep voice commanded from behind me, and the mate bond stood to attention, listening intently.

I didn't listen to him. Didn't need another Jackal to tell me what to do. This was my job. My world. His world existed to protect and defend his club and battered women.

"You can't do anything." The insistence in his voice aimed to discourage me, but I ignored it and kept going.

"Yes, I can," I snapped, forcing more magic into her, exhausting myself.

Carlie's assistants glanced at each other, solemn expressions wearing away at my confidence.

Exhaustion set in as I fought with everything I had.

"Stop!" Zethan's arms hooked beneath my armpits and hauled me to my feet, dragging me away, my feet slipping to get purchase. "There's nothing you can do. She's gone. Carlie, call 911."

"No. No, she's not." I fought him with everything I had, punching and kicking the air, shrieking. No. I had to save her. She still had a chance.

Being around all the battered women at the shelter did something to me. Flipped my switch. Emotions from the past few days were intense. Beaten up on my way home. Rescued by the Jackals and deposited at their shelter. Stories from all the abused women. What they endured for so many years broke my heart. To top it off, I had to defend my heart and mind from an ancient curse that threatened to make me fall in love with my damn enemies. It was enough to break even the strongest of women.

From several feet away, I poured more of my power into the woman, feeling her heartbeat stop and her pulse flatline.

Zethan shook me as if that would spark some sense into me. "Stop, you're hurting yourself."

I didn't care what he said or what he thought. This was my job to save her. The reason he'd brought me here. And I failed.

Zethan's hand clasped my neck tightly. Tight enough for the mate bond to flood with warmth, comfort, and desire. Instantly, I fell still, obeying him. I leaned into his grasp, wanting more. I'd wanted this the moment I set eyes on him. More than any of the others. A deep part of me recognized him as my mate. And the curse had nothing to do with it.

Avatars and gods had everything to do with it. Isis and Osiris were mates. This was my true soulmate, curse be damned.

"She's bound for the Underworld, there's nothing more you can do." His whisper in my ear weakened my resolve to fight.

"What are you talking about?" He clutched me tighter when I tried to spin to face him.

"I've got to take her," he breathed in my ear.

At the hospital, we transported the deceased to the morgue for investigation by the coroner, before the body could be transported to a funeral home for burial. In this case, we'd probably have to call the cops or something because of the extent of her injuries.

I rubbed at my moist cheeks. "Good idea. You gonna call the cops?"

He groaned in my ear. "Carlie will take care of it."

My body froze. This hadn't been their first incident. I wanted to ask how many times this happened, but I lost my voice. Deep cramps started in my stomach again, like my bowels were ready to perform a violent ejection. I wriggled to get away to go to the bathroom.

Shit, Slade, what did you give me?

Zethan pushed away from me, panting, clutching his abdomen.

I pinched my aching sides. "Are you sick too? Did you eat Slade's iffy sandwich?"

"Something like that." He stood straighter, pretending he was better, but I felt the echo of his discomfort along the line. "Listen, I've got to take care of something." Strain tightened his voice. "Wait for me."

"Okay. I need to use the bathroom, anyway." I backed away, bumping into a chair. "Excuse me for a minute."

I never dealt with losing a patient well. It left me helpless to save them and feeling disturbed. I hurried away, stumbling through the crowd of onlookers, down a hall to the bathroom. Chips in the floor tiles told me this building was really old, probably from the sixties. The walls and ceiling needed a good sanding, followed by an application of paint. An ancient hand dryer looked ready to fall off the wall. Unable to breathe, I braced my arms against the sink, staring at the cracks in the faded, cream tiles with a floral pattern. Eventually my heart rate slowed, the air settled in my lungs, and I could stand again.

I didn't like what I saw in the mirror. Yellowing bruises on my cheeks, nose, and neck. Puffy skin around my eyes and lips. Not a sight for sore eyes. God, why was Slade laying the flirting on so thick when I looked like a walking zombie? The mate bond responded with an answer, and I stuffed that bitch back down, not wanting to hear from her.

Keeping occupied, I rinsed my hands, cleaning the blood from them and the back of my arms. Her face had burned into my brain, and I saw her every time I blinked. All the faces of the people I couldn't save haunted me. I went through the motions, grieving for them all over again.

The door flung open and squeaked. Zethan stood in the doorway, clutching a blue spiked flower. He smelled like mud, sand, and something sweet I couldn't place. "Want to go back to the shelter?"

"No." I scraped my shoe along the floor. "I need a minute."

Zethan backed away as if I'd called him a horrible name. "Are you okay?"

"We were too late." I slumped against the bathroom sink counter.

He leaned on the wall by the doorframe. "Don't do well with death?"

"No." I slid my ass along the counter to be closer to him, and he stumbled backward, his back hitting the door, as if I'd ripped out a sword and threatened him with it. "What's wrong?"

He raised his palms. "Just stay there, okay? I don't feel well."

Neither did I. Damn Slade. Last time he made me a sandwich. The man didn't belong behind a kitchen counter. He belonged at the head of a motorcycle club. "Okay."

Zethan twisted the blue flower in his fingers.

"Nice accessory." I smirked. "You gonna put it in your hair, princess?"

"Fuck off." He tossed it on the bench at me. "It's for you."

Confused, I accepted the flower. "You stole a fake flower from the male bathroom?"

His chuckle rumbled through my chest and warmed me all over. "I'm not below stealing what's mine." He wasn't talking about the stupid flower. The mate bond thrummed with his promise. His eyes burned with longing, and the intensity made me look away. He cleared his throat and picked up the flower. "Just smell it. It'll help you remember."

"Did anyone tell you how weird you are?" At my question, he laughed, husky and throaty, and pushed the flower at my nose, forcing me to inhale the sweet, rich flavor.

Memories of a land long gone hit me. People dressed in cotton robes working the land along a long, winding river. Reeds rustling in the wind and the blue flowers rolling with the current. Crocodiles scouting the water for food. Sandstorms blurring the pyramids in the distance. A lavender sky and golden sun dyeing the landscape in the same colors. Ancient Egypt, somewhere. Then one name came to me. Blue Lotus. I twisted the gift from Zethan, smiled and sniffed the flower.

More words echoed in my head. *Welcome to the Underworld, my Queen.*

Shit. I dropped the flower. "What was that?"

"Where I took the deceased woman you treated." His reminder of my failure stung. He picked up the flower and gave it back to me.

I pressed a hand to my head and paced the length of three stalls and two showers. The Underworld. He'd just gone to the freaking afterlife. Nothing surprised me anymore. Gods and magic and all. "You ... you took her to the Underworld? Why? How?"

He rolled up the sleeve of his t-shirt, and a golden hand flashed on his buff upper arm. "It's my job. Avatar of Osiris, King of the Underworld." He pointed to his chest, and my eyes paused on his broad, firm pecs, showing through his ridiculously tight t-shirt. Who wore a shirt that tight anyway? Criminal. Illegal. Delicious. I was so done for.

It took me a few seconds after he let his shirt fall over his arm for me to stop staring. I rubbed at my eyes with the heel of my hands to clear my tears crusting over and to rid myself of the vision of his damn fine body.

My stomach soured again as the mate bond began to sing like little angels mocking me. Isis and Osiris were consorts. Something told me Zethan and I were bound in the same way, and I just couldn't deal with another surprise like the link.

Skin burned on my upper arm. The same spot where Zethan showed me. I hissed, yanking back my clothes, finding the same golden handprint as he had. "They called me *my Queen*. Am I the Queen of the Underworld?"

"Isis was Osiris' queen," he corrected, and my heart sank. "She was never associated with the Underworld. But she can resurrect people."

"Then why do I have this mark?"

"Because you belong to me. To Osiris."

My head spun. I went from mate to queen to necromancer in the space of three seconds. "You're saying I could have resurrected the abused woman? Why didn't my magic work then?"

"She was too far gone when we got here." He looked at the floor, depriving me of those glowing green jewels he called eyes. "I took her to the afterlife. She's happy now. Free."

I rubbed at my aching abdomen. The loss still felt raw and cut me deep. "Fuck. This is a little … too much."

Zethan nodded, sliding his cell out of his pocket to dial a number. The phone rang three times before someone answered on the other end. "Jimmy. Hey, it's Zethan. I've got a body at my sister's shelter. Domestic violence. You think you can investigate it?" He paused and nodded. "Uh-huh. It's …" He reeled off an address. "Thanks, man. Appreciate it." He paused again. "See ya' buddy." He hung up.

Curious, I twisted the flower and asked. "Buddy?"

"Senior detective." Zethan replaced his phone in his pocket.

Someone to destroy evidence and give them the head's up. "On the take?"

Zethan's gaze snapped up to me, assessing and analytical, and suddenly I felt like I looked into the eyes of a cop grilling me. Shit, I'd revealed too much again. He was onto me too. I thought of the first excuse that came to mind.

"What?" I shrugged. "I've watched plenty of thrillers. Good cop, bad cop."

Zethan slumped against the door. "Former colleague."

Surprise had me jump to my feet. "You were a policeman?"

"In another life." Zethan scraped the back of his neck. "He'll look into the deceased's circumstances, and hopefully, he finds enough information to charge the husband with spousal abuse and second-degree murder. The video we took outside the shelter will work against him."

"I hope so too." I tapped my fingers on the counter. "Video?"

"Shit." He smiled, something so fleeting and beautiful, that it gave me the impression he didn't smile much. He *needed* to smile more. His straight teeth, curved lips, made my heart flip and holler. "It's procedure to document everything if a partner arrives to protect the woman, the shelter, and staff."

"We do that at the hospital too." Sometimes nurses or doctors were called as witnesses in abuse cases to support the aggressor's behavior. But I didn't want to talk about the dark stuff.

The last three days, I tried to get close to him to talk to him. He avoided me like the plague, and I wanted intel to corroborate stories, alibis, and see what he would spill. Another part of me wanted to get to know her soul mate.

I inched closer to him of my own accord. No mate bond involved there. "What made you leave the police force?"

Zethan cringed and backed himself into a corner like a frightened animal. "You need to stay away."

"Why?"

"I don't want to hurt you."

My legs carried me back three steps to separate us. Fear gnawed at my gut. Castor's warning rang in my head. *Stay away from Zethan, he's dangerous.* How? Why? He seemed lost, wounded, like he carried the weight of blame for something. The anguish and sorrow of it thrummed along our bond, and it broke my heart.

"You won't, will you?" My words came out stuttered.

He didn't answer, instead choosing to address a previous question. "I left the force because I couldn't take it anymore."

My chest ached to hold and console him thanks to the mate bond. The real me wanted to grab the closest weapon to hit him on the head.

"What happened?" I tried to keep him talking. That was what the training at the hospital said when we got a dangerous patient who threatened us.

"A series of events." Zethan's voice lowered. "I got sick of the injustices. Murderers and rapists going free or receiving sentences that were a joke for their crimes. Apprehended Violence orders doing jack shit to protect wives and girlfriends from an abuser. Children suffering because of druggie or pedophile parents."

Deep-seated pain sang across the mate bond. He didn't intend to kill me. It hadn't even crossed his mind. Hurt, bitterness, and despair bubbled inside him like the setup for a bad fire about to go off and raze everything to the ground. Something deeper ran through his vein of torment, but I couldn't read it.

"Something happened," I said. "Didn't it?"

His gaze flicked up to me quickly then went straight back to the floor. He swallowed hard. "I don't like to talk about it."

"I'm sorry." Instinctively, I moved toward him. "Your pain, it's haunting, dark, and heartbreaking."

Unable to go anywhere but out, he raised his palms. "Stop.

"What's wrong?" I came to my senses again. Shit, I couldn't believe I felt sorry for and wanted to comfort a Jackal.

His eyes slammed shut, and he trembled. "My sister's ex murdered her."

We both had murder in common. Who would have guessed?

"Fuck." I ran a hand through my hair. "I'm so sorry." My heart wanted to bleed my whole story to share the pain, but my mouth clamped shut.

"I ... I couldn't do anything to save her." His hands fisted, and his eyes dulled. "The judge issued an AVO, and he kept stalking her. I warned him to stay away, but he didn't listen."

God, that was awful. My friend Anne had been stalked by an ex, but he didn't come near her after a judge issued an Apprehended Violence Order. She was one of the lucky ones. The deceased, not so much.

I crossed the small bathroom and touched his shoulder. "I'm sorry for your loss, Zethan."

He rolled his arm to shake me off. "I told you not to touch me." Another one with PTSD perhaps. Autism, maybe. Whatever it was, I wasn't sticking around long enough to find out.

The cramps set in again, and I needed to get a drink of water. "Okay, then."

"Let's go." He yanked the door open. "I can't breathe. I need to get out of here."

CHAPTER 23

*S*lade

THE CLOCK TICKED on the dull wall, tempting my patience to crush it with my magic. Nah. Clonk one of the detectives on the back of the fucking head. End this interrogation. Add another charge of murder to my growing list.

Old fluorescents flickered overhead, giving me a fucking headache. Two hours I'd been here, and we were going around in circles. I tapped my finger, waiting for the next question, counting down until I could release the chaos and frustration welling inside of me.

Detective Smith hiked up his pants, grunted, and flicked through his paperwork. Happened when he wore pants one size too big and hoisted to his armpits to sit over a fat gut. "What brand of cigarette do you smoke, Mr. Vincent?"

"We've been through this already," I ground out, sick and fucking tired of the questions. Sick of the accusations. Sick of having my ass hauled in here whenever the cops demanded.

I glared at my lawyer to interject or something.

Finally, the asshole I overpaid four hundred a damn hour objected. "My client quit smoking over thirteen months ago. You swept the clubhouse, the shelter, and his home and found nothing. Not one cigarette butt. Move on. Cease badgering my client, or I'll end this interrogation."

The other detective, Senior Detective Beatie, a Chris Meloni wannabe, leaned the edge of his elbow on the table. "Evidence proves otherwise. Answer the question, Mr. Vincent."

I clasped my fingers together to stop myself from smacking the prick. "Rollies papers, drum tobacco, and bull filters."

My solicitor took the opportunity to point holes in the detective's case. "My client doesn't smoke Winfield Blues as found at the crime scene."

Weak evidence. Circumstantial, Castor called it. I could have bummed a smoke from anyone, and the cops found it and placed it at the scene with Heller's damn body. They'd wanted to put me behind bars for three years. My third rodeo with these particular pricks. Once I got the heat off me, I'd put a bullet in the back of their heads, and send them to the fucking Underworld where no one would find them.

"We have a case of conflicting testimonies here as to Mr. Vincent's whereabouts." Barry Ingram, my solicitor, adopted his vicious tone well known in the courts in the Central West. "No judge will accept this as evidence in a case, and you know it. Your case will fall apart, and you won't get a conviction."

Mr. Vincent. I know of a certain nurse I'd like to call me that right now. Not this fucker.

The bulky detective leaned back, sweat forming on his

forehead, the task of questioning me too much exercise for the lazy prick. "We found gunpowder on your jeans that matches the powder from the shell casings pumped into Alexander Heller's brain."

Oh, did they now? Convenient. Except for the shooting range we owned, I rarely used a gun or bullets unless I really had to. Didn't need to with the power behind me. Snapping necks was more my style. Followed by emptying a cartridge to make it look legit. Couldn't have all the other clubs talking, now could I? But that was Castor's job, not mine.

I leaned back and let the solicitor do the talking. Let him earn his keep.

"You're reaching, detectives." Barry folded his arms over each other. "My client owns a registered shooting range in town and could have contaminated his pants there. This evidence is inconclusive like the rest you're trying to pin on him. Have you got anything conclusive? Otherwise, you're wasting our time, and I'm going to have to wrap this up?"

Both detectives started to sweat now. They knew their case was flimsy and bullshit. Fabricated. The whole damn thing. The only thing real in this case was Heller's dead body.

"Yeah, what next, detectives?" I crossed my hands behind my head. "A fragment of my bike tire at the scene? My cum up Heller's ass? Or …"

"Mr. Vincent." Barry slammed his writing folder shut.

"Smartass," Detective Ingram muttered.

"This is the third time you've hassled my client with fabricated evidence." My solicitor rose from the crappy plastic chairs. "This is harassment, and I'll be lodging a complaint next week."

I pushed my chair in nice and slow, making sure it grated along the floor, pissing off the detectives.

Outside of the Chifley Police Station, I shook Barry's hand. "This is getting beyond a joke, Barry."

"I'll deal with it, Mr. Vincent." Barry clutched his briefcase. "Wrap them in so much red procedural tape, it'll be coming out their ass." I laughed. Outside of professional meetings, the real Barry shone through. Partly why I hired him. And because he had a vicious reputation. "I'll get them off your back."

"Thanks." I clapped him on the shoulder, got on my bike, and cranked the engine to life. It vibrated between my legs, making me imagine Nurse A. in the same spot while I rode her. Thinking about it got me hard. I'd go back to the club, grab a few beers, then head back to the shelter to visit my fine, little mate. Get to know her beyond her sass and resistance to the mate bond.

Back at our public clubhouse, the party was already kicking without me when I rolled up and parked in the garage. AC/DC rock music thudded inside. Jaxx and his old lady made out on the back of his bike. Brix had two groupies straddled on his lap out on the porch. Tank was getting down and dirty with his missus, dancing up on each other in the doorway. I had to push them out of the way to get inside.

Castor, Zethan, and Alaric crowded around the pool table. Nurse A. carried a pool stick in one hand and a beer in her other. Heat scorched the back of my neck. Who the fuck brought her back here? Club rules stated no outsiders unless vetted and approved in church. Nurse A. might be our mate, but the rules applied to her too. We'd all been too busy to investigate her. Whoever broke the rules would be disciplined.

An empty vodka bottle and five shot glasses rested on the table behind them. They'd gotten stuck in the heavy shit. Zethan only drank it when something shitty happened, and he wanted to get wasted. Otherwise, he drank whisky at club parties, and he and Alaric drank us under the table.

Fuming at the asshole that broke protocol, I marched

over to the table. Nurse A. leaning over the table to take her turn distracted me for a second. That ass. Round. Thick. Plenty to dig my fingers into as I pounded her doggy style. Fuck me. What had I come over here for?

Alaric poured me a whisky, but I shook him off, not in the mood yet.

"Another Boulevardier for the lady." Castor handed her some crimson French cocktail.

I snatched it from him, sniffed it, and almost barfed, handing it back to Castor. He was always making cocktails, drinks, or meals we'd never heard of or could pronounce. "Keep her away from this shit, you fancy fuck," I shouted above the thump of music.

"That's mine." Nurse A. reached for it.

I held it away from her grasp. "I don't want you drinking this heavy shit when you're recovering from injuries. You should be on juice or something lighter."

Castor sipped at the drink and arched his eyebrows at her.

Her condition had improved. Reduced swelling opened her left eye. Bruising lost its dark purple color and changed to yellow, making her aqua eyes even brighter. I was glad to see her looking healthier and on the mend. It hurt my heart to see her wounded. The beast inside me wanted to destroy the bastard that did this to her, but Zethan had already taken care of that.

I had more important shit to deal with than a goddamn drink and her sexy, sassy ass. "What the fuck is she doing here? Does no one respect club rules anymore?"

"Nice to see you too, Mr. Vincent." Nurse A. took a long swig of her beer instead. Mesmerized, I watched her throat bob, jealous of the malty liquid sliding down her long, graceful throat. I wanted her to suck my cock and swallow my cum like that. Like she was thirsty and couldn't get enough of me. Something we'd be doing real soon when I took her out back to punish her for entering our club without authorization.

I shook off my growing hard-on, resolved to deal with her later. Then she could call me Mr. Vincent until her pretty little heart was content.

"I brought her here." Zethan's pool stick wobbled as he jabbed it at me to move out of the way and let him make his next shot. "Get the fuck off my case."

Fuck, he was drunk and in one of his moods. Must have lost a woman at the shelter. Whenever that happened, he got pissy and snappy. Didn't give him a pass to break the rules. We'd discuss this in a day or so when he was clearer-headed.

The way Castor shoved a cooled beer in my hand with a *don't ask* expression, told me everything I needed to know. I acknowledged his silent communication with a clink of the neck of my beer to his.

Shit. It was my duty as Zethan's best friend to say something. I set my hand on his shoulder. "I'm sorry, man. For whatever happened."

Zethan glanced up, green eyes bloodshot and narrowed. "We lost her."

Fuck, I was right. Blame lay at the hand of the abuser, period. But Zethan took every death personally as if he'd been the cause. It ripped him apart for days. Reminded him of losing his sister and not being able to save her.

I drew him in for a hug and clap on the back. "There was nothing you could do, man." I rubbed his sweaty hair. "You did your best. You always do."

Behind him, Nurse A. studied me, biting the top of her bottle. My dick wanted to zone in on her lips and teeth, but I was too lost in my best friend's grief.

"We were too late," Zethan sobbed into my shoulder.

Fuck, my VP needed to pull it together. Life and death.

Black and white. No in-between. Of all people, the King of the Underworld should know that. The gods gave us free will and choice. Zethan was not to blame for the woman marrying a cunt that treated her badly. That was on her.

Too many times he went down this dark path, beating himself up when it wasn't his fault. Shit happened to good people all the time. He needed to understand that. I'd not sit around and watch this destroy him again when the club and I needed him.

I led him away from the table to the sofa in the center of the room. "How about you take one of the rooms and sleep this one off?"

"I need to finish my game." He turned to go back to the pool table.

I took the pool cue from him. "I'll finish it for you."

"Okay." Zethan swayed on his feet with his few unsteady steps, crashing face-first into the cushions and passed out.

I crossed to him, lifted his legs off the ground, spinning him onto his back so that he lay on it. He snorted and rolled over, curling his body.

Nurse A. came over, crouching beside the sofa, checking to make sure he breathed. Her long fingers brushed his hair from his eyes. Jealousy hit me with greater force. I wanted her hands on me doing that.

"You shouldn't do that." I dragged her a safe distance away. "Don't get so close. It's not safe."

"He's passed out." She jerked free. "What's he going to do?"

I pulled her flush to my chest, wanting to feel her body crushed to mine. Her warmth radiating into me. The swell of her breasts rubbing against me every time she breathed. Her pelvis grinding into my leg as I swayed us across the floor, slow dancing.

Yeah, great idea, Slade.

When I picked up her hand and set it on my shoulder, then collected her other hand in mine, her pulse went wild.

Oh, yeah. She liked this just as much as I did.

Breath held in, she moved with me, slow, hesitant, and stiff. The woman needed to relax, she was so guarded. I moved one hand to her hip, prodding her to relax, move with me. She gave a little, digging her fingers into me.

"Hey, old lady." After my shitty meeting with the cops, I wanted a bit of mischief and fun, for her to brighten my afternoon. Teasing her was one sure way to get there, and fast. I fingered a loose lock around my finger. "I've been thinking about your ..."

"About taking cooking lessons?" she sassed back.

"What?" I laughed. I liked a woman who made me laugh. "I was talking about your membership. Then you can visit whenever you want to come dance with me ... or on me."

She snorted and hit me in the chest, and my Jackal responded, growling, licking his lips, wanting to mount her. "Why would I want to dance on you?" Oh, the beer loosened her up a bit. Got that stick out of her ass. "You gave me food poisoning, asshole."

Asshole? The only asshole we'd be talking about was hers when I fingered it or when she did the same to me. "Food looked okay to me. I didn't get sick."

She tightened in my grasp, and I wanted to lean down, wipe away the pout with my kiss. "I had stomach cramps after I ate it."

"Nah, that was ..." The rest of my sentence got interrupted by hooting at the pool table.

Alaric swung something long and brown in the air. He laughed and shook it at Castor's face, making him swat it away. Cock on the loose. A clubhouse party was never complete without a prank at Zethan's expense. One eye closed to concentrate, Alaric bent over the billiards table, and used the wooden cock to break the balls.

"Aw, fuck." Zethan's feet flew off the sofa and hit the floor with a thud. Dizzy and drunk, he hunched over and cupped his crotch.

For my friend's sake, I'd intervene, but I was not touching that damn cock. Who knew where that thing had been?

"Give it back, you dickheads!" My shout prompted Alaric to laugh and whack more balls into holes with the phallus. He drank the most out of all of us, partied the hardest, and did outrageous shit. Typical pilot making up for having to take orders from some uptight asshole.

Zethan glared at the pool table with a tight face. He wavered on his feet as he staggered over to the guys and snatched back his cock, pressing the erect wooden piece to his crotch. Golden fingers of magic illuminated his jeans as his cock reattached, transforming back into flesh and veins beneath the denim. Thank god we didn't have to see the real thing.

"Damn fucking cock!" His mouth parted with a relieved sigh, and he flopped back onto the sofa, passing out again.

"What the hell was that about?" Nurse A. asked me.

I cupped the back of her head, lifting her gaze to mine. "You know the Osiris myth?"

"Kind of." Her tone sounded unsure as her gaze flicked to Zethan.

Fuck. Not a fun story for a party. Set always got a laugh, but he was the only one. Prick. Who did that kind of shit to their brother, anyway? Cut off his cock? Come on man!

"You know." I nudged her with my hips as I shuffled her to the left in our slow dance. "Set tricked Osiris into a coffin. Cut up his body and buried the pieces around the world." Wanting to feel more of her, the soft curve of her lower back and her ass, I moved my hand lower. "You should know this story as Isis' avatar."

Miss Prim and Proper readjusted my hand to her back. "*I don't.*"

I shrugged. She could have it her way for now. Later was a whole other story. "Isis tracked every part down besides Osiris' cock, which unfortunately for the dead guy, digested in the gut of a crocodile."

God, why was I talking about Zethan and Osiris' dick when I should be on the subject of mine?

She thumped me in the arm again, and my jackal went wild. He'd give it to her rough. Get her to thump him over and over. "That's nasty."

I'd give her nasty. Whatever she wanted, so long as it wasn't vanilla. This slow dance bullshit was as romantic as I got.

"You asked." I moved her to the left, tipping her back a little, kissing her soft, sexy neck. Her heartbeat went wild beneath my lips, and I loved the effect I had on her.

"Okay," she squeaked, shoving at my chest, trying to get back to her feet. All it did was make my jackal and me more aroused. "Then what happened?"

Really? She wanted to talk about Zethan's dick? Mood killer.

"Isis put her husband back together and resurrected him with her magic." I pulled Nurse A. closer after she'd inched away to draw in air. All this phallus talk and our proximity got her hot and bothered. Hell, it did the same to me. "She fashioned a wooden phallus and attached it to his body, rode that bad boy, got pregnant and gave birth to Horus. Then, Osiris descended into the Underworld."

She didn't stop my hand from wandering south. "Your god is an asshole."

"He's the god of Chaos, Destruction, Mischief, and the

Dessert. It's who he was born to be."

Every pantheon had the good and bad. I happened to fall on the darker spectrum. Best place to be.

Eager to feel the shell of her ear next to my lips, I leaned down to whisper to her, "Zethan earned the same scars as Osiris. Unfortunately for my VP, his cock goes missing occasionally. It gets worse with stress … like today."

She cupped her mouth. "Oh, shit."

"Mine's intact, though." I cupped my package to demonstrate. Large and living. Loud and proud. "No problems in that department."

She snorted once more and hit me again. Cute.

My jackal roared, his desperation for her intensifying.

I lifted one of her arms and spun her around. "Playing pranks with his dick is a rite of passage, and we take full advantage of it."

She leaned her head on my chest, calming my beast, but making my cock harden. "You're a bunch of assholes."

"Yeah." We sure were. Zethan would have done the same if one of our cocks went missing and turned into a wooden phallus when separated from our bodies. We'd gotten him good with some pranks too. Hide the cock was always a classic whenever he passed out. The next morning we'd holler as he hunted for it. "End of story. Now let's talk about our date."

"Slade." She pushed at me to get away, but I held onto her. "Just because I'm dancing with you doesn't mean I'm your old lady."

Time to rile her up. She looked sexy when she was hot and bothered. "Yes, you are, *old lady*." She shivered at the words, and I knew they were true. This was my mate. The gods declared it, and I took what was mine.

"You don't question anything, do you?" Her fingers traced patterns on my arms, lighting a new fire inside me, one that wanted to consume her, burn her with my love. "You just accept the mate bond?"

"The gods know best, Nurse A."

"How? The gods are cursed." She questioned too much, like fucking Castor.

Set was as natural as the chaotic forces on the Earth. Hurricanes, storms, fires, drought, and flood. Unpredictable, unforgiving, and invincible. Unable to be controlled, just like the mate bond.

She liked to be in control. It gave her power and purpose. Under the mate bond, she lost her control, and that scared her. Sometimes a freefall was the best medicine. I lifted her chin to stare into her beautiful eyes and chase away her residual doubt. We were mates whether she liked it or not. She could run and deny it, but eventually she'd give into it. Just like Liz had.

"Fight it all you want, Nurse A." I twirled her again. "But I'll win in the end. I always do." My reply charged up her resistance, and she tensed in my arms. I needed to break down another wall she placed between us. Needed her to stop fighting me and just go with it like the cycles of fucking nature. "Listen, we want you to stay. We want you to join us. Become a member of the Jackals and be our medic."

She stared up at me, those stunning aqua eyes melting me down in a hot, thick puddle of need. "Slade, I c—" I pressed a finger to her lips. She used my name. Not Mr. Vincent. No trace of sass in her voice. Just soft reluctance that hinted at a no. I stopped her right there. No one turned me down. No one. I went with the pros. The name. Her letting me hold her and not resisting. Slowly she came around to the idea. Soon I'd make her mine. She smiled and closed her lips, biting back the no. Fuck, she was beautiful. All mine.

"Don't make a decision just yet," I whispered in her ear. "Think about it and get back to me."

CHAPTER 24

Alaric

We hadn't spoken since I hurt her. I'd avoided her, despite the intense and unrelenting pull of the mate bond. It was better that way. Looked like that was about to change. After Slade let her go to visit the men's room, she slowly approached me, rubbing her hands down her jeans.

"Hey." Alexa jabbed a thumb over her shoulder. "Finally got away from Slade. Thought I'd come over and see how you were." Her voice softened when she said Slade's name. It was a subtle change, but I still envied him over that small nuance.

"I'm fine." I kept my focus on the game with Castor.

"That's good." She picked up her beer and awkwardly drank from it. "Can I play a game with you next?"

"I'm gonna head to my office soon." I scratched at the back of my neck. Slade had warned me as a friend to stay away from her. If it were an order from my president, I'd be breaking the rules right now. Still, I'd stick to his warning. I'd not hurt her again. "Got to plan a ride upstate next week."

She rested a gentle hand on my arm. That one delicate touch was enough to break down all the barriers I'd erected around my heart and mind. "Can I come with you? The music's giving me a headache."

"No." It came out hard, fast, and rougher than I intended. I tried to soften it with, "You'll only distract me."

"Don't bullshit me, Alaric. Slade ordered you not to." It was a statement, not a question, and she sounded more than a little disappointed. "He thinks you'll hurt me."

"It was more of a threat than a promise." I spared a glance in her direction to gauge her mood before turning my attention back to the game.

She sucked down more beer. "Slade doesn't speak for me. We're not damn mates. I can make my own decisions."

I admired her. She could hold her own. Stood up to Slade. Gave him a run for his money. Nurse A. was no pushover. Neither was Liz. But she was softer, elegant, and didn't like confrontation, so often let Slade win the argument to prevent it escalating.

As for the mate's part, Alexa was wrong. I felt the pull of the mate bond. The magnetism between us kicked my flight instinct into high gear. If I wasn't inside the clubhouse with her and Castor, I would have shifted into my bird form and taken to the skies. It was the only place I felt free from the burden of my past.

"See you around, Alexa." I set my cue on the clip along the wall, nodded to Castor, and excused myself.

My keen senses detected her soft footfalls behind me. I spun around to face her. "What are you doing?"

"I need some air."

"You're not coming with me."

"Why not?" Her eyes darkened with anger. "Because Slade won't allow it?"

"Slade has nothing to do with it."

"I just need air. I'm feeling lost and raw." Her heartache at losing the woman at the shelter screamed down the link. The alcohol probably didn't help either. We had five shots before Slade pulled up.

Intent on getting out of the bar, away from everything, Alexa moved to the hall, opening doors, searching for an exit.

Hell, I wasn't in the frame of mind to help her come to terms with everything that happened to her over the last week. Especially not when I almost killed her. The mate bond screeched at me like my hawk telling me to go after her. Console her in my arms. My leg jerked, ready to leave at my command. I warred between the duty to my club and my mate. In the end, she won out. Fuck. Slade was going to kick my ass, but to hell with it. A few quick strides caught me up to her. I grabbed her hand, linking fingers, and dragged her into the third door on the right. My office.

She gulped in air and combed her fingers through her hair. "Thank you. I just couldn't think in there." Our bond wavered with emotion about to break.

When Alexa and Zethan arrived back from Carlie's shelter, they were quiet, withdrawn, heads low, and got stuck into the alcohol. Castor and I knew what that meant and didn't need to ask. They lost a woman they were caring for. It happened about twice a year. It gutted Zethan every time, and we had to be there to pick up the pieces.

A tear streamed down Alexa's cheek, and she dried her face on her sleeve. "I heal people. It's my passion and my gift, but it has limitations. I can't fix myself. No matter how broken I am, and I'm feeling pretty fucking broken at the moment." She choked back her sobs.

Fuck, that was more than I'd bargained for when I

decided to sneak her in here. But it was all I needed to sweep her into my arms. I brushed at the tear threatening to fall. Then I kissed away the other that escaped. Her lips parted and she let out a soft sigh when my mouth connected with her flesh. I wanted to do more, but it didn't feel right to take advantage of this moment when she grieved for the dead woman.

"There's a place we can go," I whispered into her hair, sniffing the fresh citrus scent. "It's quiet, helps me clear my head."

I longed to shed my human form and soar high above the clubhouse, watching out for my brothers below. Shifting with someone in the midst of a breakdown was not a good idea. Alexa had those abilities too—well, at least Liz did. But I doubted Alexa was ready for that, and in all honesty, I wasn't ready to share that part of myself with her either. The lookout would have to do.

She brushed at her forehead. "Can we go?"

"Let me get my bike keys." I crossed to the table where all my maps lay spread out across it.

"This is your office?" She wandered over to my bookshelf, full of old street directories, maps, diagrams, and books, pulling out a volume of old plans of the Bathurst township from the early 1900s until now. Smiling, she flicked through the pages.

Anything with a map in it, I collected and memorized it. I knew every road, every back lane, every highway in the state. Slade called me the walking encyclopedia of plans. It helped that I had the Sky god in my head. He knew the layout of the entire world, but I hadn't memorized that yet. I could access it anytime I wanted to, but I preferred to learn it on my own.

Her fingers trailed along the A3-sized schematics in the center of the table, and she twisted her head, eyes tracking the path I planned to take to escort the delivery of our next shipment of Pharaoh. "You're going to Sydney?"

I squeezed my keys in my palm. "Next week." I never put anything to paper, but the layout of the maps suggested my route.

"That's an odd route." She moved her forefinger along the Great Western Highway. "Why aren't you taking the highway?"

"Got to stay off the main roads." I wasn't studying the map. The curve of her neck, the soft flesh between her shoulder and ear, all I could concentrate on. Where I wanted to kiss next. Filled with longing, I reached out to stroke her, but pulled back, the fading ring of bruises a reminder of what I'd done when I touched her. The point of the keys dug into my flesh. They clattered on the table as I dropped them. I stepped back from her, keeping my distance. She wasn't safe with me, I could hurt her.

"What's wrong?" She watched me expectantly.

"I can't take you," I bit out. "It's not safe."

Our link flared with her defiance. "I don't care what Slade says. You won't hurt me."

She approached me the way one would approach a cornered animal. Slow. Cautious. Hands raised. Her thumb stroked my face. Once. Twice. A third time. I leaned into her, seeking her heat and comfort. Our bond roped around us, drawing us together. Closer. I missed my mate, our friendship, the companionship, and intimacy. I cupped her cheek, drawing her to me, and that was all the permission she needed to fall into my arms. Fuck, she felt incredible. Soft, delicate, and so warm. The urgency singing along our link told me she needed our connection just as much as I did. I tucked her head beneath my chin, and she sought the security of my chest.

My allegiance to the club took issue with what we were

doing. *Fuck Slade.* He couldn't keep me from my mate. I'd do whatever it took to keep her with me. Whatever it took to keep her safe. I'd not hurt her again.

"Come on." I collected her hand and snatched the keys, dragging her out to the garage before my rationale could talk me out of this decision.

I gave her a helmet, put mine on, then threw my leg over the bike. Seated, I held out my hand, giving her balance as she slid on behind me. The warmth of her body snuggled to mine soothed the raging storm in my soul and the demons nipping at the back of my mind. She fit just right up against my back, hands around my waist. Like she was designed for this. I guess she was. The gods had always intended this for her. Intended her for me. For the four of us.

Vibrations rumbled through me as I started the bike. Enjoying her holding me, and not wanting it to end, I let the motor warm up for as long as I could. It roared at me, wanting to be unleashed, to go eighty miles an hour along the road from the clubhouse. After about two minutes, I pulled out of the garage and shouldered onto the road into town. Eighty horsepower thrummed through my veins as I pushed her, making Alexa squeal. At William Street, I jerked the handlebars right, taking the lane up to the mount. The bike flew up the mountain, hugging the curves the way she held onto me.

I never took anyone to the lookout. When the memories of war threatened to swallow me, I went there. Mt. Panorama was my safe place, away from the noise and the violence we all grew accustomed to. Through my service in the military, I'd lost a part of my humanity and I came here to retrieve it. Alexa was the first and only person I shared this place with.

Cars zoomed by, speeding, pretending they were the race cars that came here several times a year to compete in major races. Signs along the racetrack advertised everything from motor oil, and exhaust systems, to beer. Everything a racing enthusiast could want. Rolling hills below were home to the township of Bathurst, the nearby campus of *Charles Sturt University*, wineries, and orchards. Thousands of people below this mountain lived their lives completely unaware that gods disguised as devils walked among them.

An eagle soared overhead, scanning for prey. My hawk squawked at me, wanting to go up there, warn it away. This was his turf.

But I ignored him, killed the engine, and turned to Alexa, shaking her hair as she removed the helmet. I wanted to twine her hair over my fingers, pull it taut, draw her to me, and kiss her. Long, deep, and achingly hard. Just like I'd longed for these past two years without my mate.

"This is where I go when I need to escape." I waited for her to hop off the bike first. Mom, dad, nan, and pop raised me to be a gentleman.

"It's beautiful." She set the helmet on her seat like she was born to do it. "Quiet. Isolated."

"There are better places to dump a body. Trust me." I chuckled, reaching into my pack for my whisky flask.

"Hah! Hah!" She came to me as I dismounted and leaned on my bike. I liked her close to me. She wasn't afraid of me even though she should be. And she certainly didn't hold the other day against me.

I took a swig from the flask and handed it to Alexa. "You seem like you have a lot on your mind. Besides this afternoon."

"The clubhouse." She coughed after a long pull of whiskey and handed me back my flask. "The dance. The invite to join the club." Slade invited her when he stole her away to slow dance. Good. Incentive for her to stay. "This whole fated mate's thing, it's overwhelming."

I circled a finger over the flask's rim, where her lips had been. "Well, this is where I come to work shit out." I tasted her, drinking from the same spot, unable to get enough of her sweet vanilla flavor.

"Does it help?" She accepted the flask and tapped the side of it.

"Sometimes. It's pretty heavy stuff, being a Jackal." I leaned back on my elbows. I didn't want to go into detail and scare her off. Liz didn't approve of the way we lived our life, but she accepted it. "We do a lot of good with the safe house, but is it enough? Does it outweigh all the bad shit we do? It feels like we're meant for more. You're a nurse. You use your abilities to help people. It seems like you have a handle on it."

"Do I?" She laughed. Warm. Honeyed. Heavenly. "I was in the middle of a meltdown five minutes ago."

"You've had a few curve balls thrown your way, especially with the mugg—" I couldn't bring myself to say it. "And the mate bond, but before that, you found the balance, right?" I didn't mean to sound so hopeful, as if my peace of mind was tethered to her saying yes.

"I never put much thought into it." She shrugged and took another swig from the flask. "When you're finishing classes and then working full time in the ER, you don't really have time to think about anything. I've had more time to think since you brought me to the shelter than I have in years."

"And?" I slid the flask from her fingers before she drained it dry. I wouldn't earn any points with Alexa or the guys if I brought her back to the safehouse drunk. God knows Slade would chew my ass off and probably put me on discipline. Worth it for thirty minutes alone with my mate.

"I don't know ..." She twisted to lean her elbows over the bike and stare up at the sky. "I think I still have a lot to figure out. This isn't what I expected. None of you are what I expected."

"What did you expect?" My curiosity piqued and I emptied the flask, capped the lid, and shoved it into the pack.

She widened her hands quickly and then folded them. "Gangsters. Murderers. Thugs."

I chuckled again. "We protect our turf, businesses, and family fiercely. Our women, even fiercer."

Her throaty laugh had my chest purring. "What'd you do to the schmuck who tried to steal my handbag?"

"I know nothing." I poked her in the side. She didn't need to know about that side of us yet. I didn't want to scare her away before she got the chance to really know us. I changed tack. "Does anyone know that you're an avatar?"

I could count the number of people outside the club who knew what we were, with fingers left over. Whenever I went up to scout, I kept a team half a mile back to avoid them witnessing my transformation. We couldn't be too careful. Any of the members could squeal to their old ladies, friends, or another club. Bikers understood guns, money, and women. But when it came to the supernatural, it did their heads in.

"No. I never told a soul." Alexa drummed her fingers on my bike, tempting me to pick up one hand and kiss the tip of her knuckles. "I'm not close enough to tell anyone."

"Not even your family?"

"Sometimes I don't feel like I'm even a part of my family." She sighed. "It's complicated."

"Family is always complicated." I twisted on my side, leaning into her, wanting more of her, her body on mine and her mouth over mine. "You don't get to choose the family you're born into, but you can choose the one you want to belong to. When I was in the military, my unit was my family. Now, the Jackals and their wives are my brothers and sisters."

She nodded. "Who is your god?"

I rolled up my shirt sleeve and pointed at the hieroglyph of a hawk tattooed on my forearm.

"Horus." She sounded matter of fact, as if she took it in her stride like she had my PTSD or my mismatched eyes.

Impatience bloomed in me. I wanted to know everything there was to know about this woman. I didn't want to have to wait to get to know her. This was my mate, and I wanted to claim her. Make her my mate for life and protect this one at all costs, so we never lost another again. I tapped my magic enough to cast a small net around Alexa to see what, if anything, I could pull from her timeline. But like previous attempts, she was a blank slate. How in the gods' names was she doing it? What was she hiding? Whatever it was, I intended to find out.

"We should probably head back." She slid off the bike's seat and stood up. "Slade will probably have a shit fit."

I groaned. Punishment and discipline. Fuck. I'd do it again in a heartbeat if it meant I got more time with her. "Yeah, you're probably right."

"Alaric?" She rested her hand on my arm, leaning in when I turned to face her. "Thank you. For everything." Her fingers traced the tattoo on my arm.

My hawk went wild, fluttering in my chest, pecking at me, desperate to get to his mate. "It's nothing." I shrugged, playing it cool despite the heat flushing my body from head to toe.

"It means something to me." Alexa closed the last few inches that separated us and pressed her lips to mine. The kiss was soft, sweet, and over too quickly for my liking.

Desire burned within me, drowning out the suspicions of her that I had moments before. Horus recognized his mate. As much as it pained me to admit it, so did I. I deepened the kiss, sliding an arm around her waist, dragging her to me. She moaned as I tasted her, explored her, giving her everything I'd wanted to for the last week she'd stayed with us.

Alexa was everything I ever wanted and more than I deserved for what I'd done to her. Staying away from her was going to be difficult. Not being able to be alone with her, torture. I was going to have to face my demons to earn the right and permission from Slade.

CHAPTER 25

Castor

THAT WAS NOT what I expected first thing in the morning. I did a double-take and panned my gaze up and down Alaric. "What the fuck are you wearing?"

His hands protectively shot to cover his groin. Over the lacy pink thong on top of his jeans. "Punishment for taking Alexa out yesterday."

As one of Alexa's four mates, Slade couldn't officially order Alaric to stay away from her, but the President could damn well warn him not to be alone with her. Yet they'd gone into his office. Alone. Where he could have been triggered into another attack. Then they'd taken off for a ride somewhere afterwards before I could check on them.

Slade hit the roof. Sent me out with him, searching for them. Alaric was lucky he got off light. Disobey Slade and get booted from the club or worse ... dead. I'd learned my lesson once. Never made that mistake again. Our President commanded absolute respect and loyalty. Those who didn't meet the cut didn't get the patch.

"Serves you right, asshole." I hit Alaric on the arm, then dumped the cashed-up envelope in my pack.

"Fuck off, snitch." He thumped me back. Not hard. Brotherly. We had a good relationship. Slade and Zethan were best friends even though they fought like cat and dog sometimes. Alaric and I were the last few members patched in and we became close.

I raised two palms and chuckled. "When your president asks where his old lady is, you don't fuck around."

"Yeah, well, taking her to the mount was worth every minute." Alaric plucked his ginormous wedgy out of his ass before throwing his leg over his Chieftain.

Didn't need to see that. Or how they rode up his ass. Burned into my brain like everything else I remembered. For once, I wished I could wipe some memories clear. "Jesus, cover yourself up, would you? You're going to make me crash."

"Stop checking out my ass, then." He lifted onto his foot pegs and wiggled his ass for me.

Fuck, this was going to be the longest ride ever.

Alaric settled his lacy ass back down. "Where are we going?"

We frequently collaborated in our roles. Me as his backup and vice versa. We had an incident once when we got split up and didn't have a route. Ever since, I memorized Alaric's shipment route, and if he got into trouble on a ride, I'd assume his position and lead the club on an alternative route to safety.

"Meeting with a bagman on Alpha Street," I replied. "Organizing a fall guy."

Bagmen were contacts we paid for information. Our payroll cop provided me the name of a perp he wanted to lock up and remove from the community. Someone expendable to take the heat while we moved our product. People with outstanding warrants or extensive rap sheets were our preferred choice. Easier to get our fall guy convicted and off the streets. We hired them for a job, planted shit on them, and called in an anonymous tip to the crime hotline. Opportunity and motive for Marcus and the police to swoop in and nab his bad guy while we made off with our shipment. Win-win. I got one less low-life off the streets. We'd conducted this mutually exclusive arrangement for the last three years. Worked well so far.

"Gorman's Hill?" The Jackal's resident Street Directory confirmed.

"Yep." I slid the key into my Classic. "Follow me?"

"Yeah." Alaric kick-started his Chieftain and let it warm up.

"I can't have you meet our contact like that, though," I shouted, pointing to his underwear.

"I'll stay on the fucking bike, okay."

"One hundred feet, minimum." Christ, I couldn't stop looking at him. I couldn't afford for my contact to think the Jackals were a bunch of pansies.

Alaric flipped me the bird and tore away on his bike. Intent on catching up to him, I settled my helmet on and left in a haze of fumes and dust.

My shoulders were killing me by the time I made it to Alpha Street. I made a mental note to talk to Tank about ordering new handlebars for my bike and rolled into the lane where Marcus waited in his unmarked department-issued silver BMW police sedan. Or I could hit up Alexa for a massage. I went with that one.

Alaric kept a discreet distance, thank fuck. He came as my back-up. New orders after the recent spate of events.

Industrial fumes hung in the air from the railway line

maintenance company a few hundred feet to the west. Trucks came this way to bypass traffic in town. Other vehicles traveled along Russell Street to the private hospital or retirement villages further down. Not one hundred percent secluded, and not my first choice for a meet spot, but options were limited when meeting a dirty cop. At least they weren't having a school athletics day on the oval at Proctor Park by the Macquarie River.

Marcus flashed the headlights of his sedan and signaled the all-clear. We had enough problems without taking unnecessary risks. Better safe than sorry. I scanned the lane before dismounting the bike, collecting his payment envelope and tucking it into my cut as I walked over to the car.

"What's the matter, Robin, you don't trust me anymore?" Marcus struggled to squeeze himself between the seatback and the steering wheel as he climbed out of the driver's seat.

Whenever dealing with a cop or contact, we always used a fake name.

"I haven't survived this long by trusting people. It's nothing personal." I reached into the makeshift pocket between the liner and leather of my vest. "Brought you a little snack."

I tossed the envelope wrapped with rubber bands and stuffed with tens and twenties. Marcus preferred small bills. Spent them easier than hundreds or fifties. Looked more legit and less suspicious. Cashiers slipped twenties into a cash drawer without batting an eye. Banks sometimes checked for watermarks. Not that many of our informants were dumb enough to cash the money.

"You want to count it?" Every time I asked him, he said no.

"You haven't shorted me yet." Marcus took the money out of the envelope and shoved the fat stack of cash into his pocket.

Cops and high roller criminals had a delicate relationship. They wanted our money, and we wanted their resources, namely information. Police sometimes pushed too hard or turned greedy. Overall, it was a hell of a lot easier to pay off the cops than to try to work around them. Bribes were negotiated annually.

Marcus had earned past raises, but he'd slipped lately, and things didn't look good for his upcoming review.

"What'll it be this time, Robin?" Marcus picked at a crusty stain on his tie. "Same as usual?"

"Just a stunt man." Code for a fall guy.

Our last run required a police escort, which ate into our profits. We decided to keep things simple and use stunt men going forward. Some of the cops on the take weren't happy with Slade's decision and the subsequent reduction in bonus pay. I wouldn't put it past one of those assholes to have coordinated a sting as retribution, Marcus among them.

"That's all, huh?" He scrunched the envelope and shoved it in his jacket pocket.

Dirty fucking cops were one of the reasons the perps I tried to convict went free. Evidence going missing. Witnesses not interviewed. Leads not followed up. They could hide behind their badge all they wanted, but it didn't make them any better than the other criminals, myself included. Still, they were a necessary evil.

Marcus had a good heart and wanted to protect his community. But most cops could be bought for the right price. One day he'd ask for it. I'd rather him be motivated by honorable means than criminal.

"You're not getting greedy on me, are you?" I kicked at the ground.

"It's for my kids' college fund."

"You don't have kids."

He shrugged it off. "Can't blame a guy for trying."

Fuck. Sounded like we might have to part ways with Marcus next year. Asshole didn't have a chance in hell of squeezing me for more money. The rate was the rate. No renegotiating. Bottom line. Damned shame. Good help was hard to find.

Money didn't buy loyalty when it came to dirty cops. They could switch sides at any time and screw us over. Greed made people a liability and untrustworthy. A cop championing for what he believed was right was another story altogether. Those were the ones we wanted as contacts.

Years of negotiating with these assholes taught me the signs and what to look for. Marcus had two plays that he could make—threaten to actually do his job and bust our deliveries or turn to the Wolves and hope they paid more. I had one solution: phase Marcus out. Money had a way of ruining everything good in our world.

There was too much shit happening with the club to stand around all day while Marcus dicked around in the hopes of squeezing more money out of the deal.

"Yeah, I can, actually." I made sure I emphasized my point. Dirty fucker. "Just give me a name so we can both get out of here."

Muscles cramped in my forehead and eyes, and I rubbed at them, doing nothing to ease them. I'd been reading until the early hours of the morning, searching for a spell for Zethan. I was exhausted and needed sleep. Wanted my woman cuddled up beside me, warming my cold, lonely bed. Something told me that wouldn't be happening any time soon. Alexa had serious reservations about our lifestyle and the four of us.

"Jake Martin." Marcus fished out a packet of Winfield Blues cigarettes. "They call him The Snake because he's a slippery son of a bitch. He's in the security business, squeezing the local businesses for money in exchange for protection." He lit a cigarette, took a drag and blew out a puff of smoke. "He's got a thing for strippers. Spends his money and his nights over at Maxine's."

Perfect. Maxine's was our strip club in town. I'd get one of our staff to approach him.

"We'll be in touch." I nodded and left.

Marcus wouldn't hear from me again until we made a call with an anonymous tip about Jake pulling a big score. Smoke and mirrors.

With our business concluded, I got on my bike and made the short ride over to Alaric, pulling in beside him. "Want to tag along to the shelter?"

I wanted to drop in at the shelter and see my woman. Wanted to do more than hold her hand. Corner her again for a steamy kiss in the pantry. Run my hands all over her body. My lips burned for hers. Fuck, I hadn't been able to stop thinking about our kiss from a few days ago. She had my dick hard and ready every time I thought of her.

"Like this?" Alaric gestured to his crotch. "Slade will pierce my dick with a pink ribbon if I break my promise again."

I laughed, almost falling sideways off the bike. "You've got to match your lacy thong!"

"Asshole." Alaric shook his head, gave me the bird again, and shot off in a rumble of engine and screech of tires.

Eager to see my woman, I set my helmet on and took off, faster than I should have, but not caring if a cop caught me. Five minutes out from the shelter, a patrolman came out of nowhere, riding my tail. I used my magic to send his radio an alternative call out, and he decelerated, turning off the highway, leaving me alone. One of many benefits of being Thoth's avatar.

At the shelter, I found her in the corner chatting with two of the women whose names I could have learned but didn't care to. Damn, she looked good with her legs molded into those jeans. The way her sweater clung to her chest. When she met my eye, I jerked my head at her and she nodded, excusing herself.

"Hey, there," she greeted me with a sultry smile and clear eyes.

I folded my fingers in hers and led her away into Zethan's vacant office, closing the door behind us.

I brushed a stray hair from her temple. "How are you, my dark sorceress?" A nickname worthy of her goddess. Isis was famous for her knowledge and practice of dark magick like my god. If Alexa stuck around, I'd teach her a thing or two about her gifts. We could teach each other.

She groaned and rubbed her eyebrow. "I've got a decent hangover."

I laughed. "We'll have to break you in and build your tolerance."

"God, no." She rubbed her forehead. "I'm never drinking again."

I backed away to sit atop Zethan's desk and beckoned her over, going for casual with a hint of sexy. I didn't expect her to come. The other day I'd lost control when I'd cornered her. Need had gotten the better of me. It didn't take a genius or the mate bond to understand her wariness and reluctance of our lifestyle. Of us as men. Our character. This time, though, she came without her earlier hesitation. Wearing a smile too. Just for me.

I was no Slade, bold, brutish, and taking what I wanted like a caveman armed with a club. To him, there were no boundaries or lines he couldn't cross. Alexa held reservations, and I wasn't going to push her limits. But I also wasn't going to be shy in asking for what I wanted. I'd use my brain to win her over.

This was my mate, and I couldn't tame the growing need.

Everything about her made me want to lose my head, grab her and kiss her. She tensed a little as I caged her between my legs. Her body buzzed with need and uncertainty, and I wanted to be the one that sated her. I wanted her in my bed, unwilling to share her with everyone else. My arms molded around her waist, making her work her teeth over her lips. Sexy and alluring. My heart struggled to keep a steady beat as I imagined them crashing to mine.

I kept my dick in check, for the moment, anyway, and asked the most pressing question, "You haven't left yet. It's been almost a week. I thought you'd run off after a few days. Does that mean you're staying?" Hope crested in my chest, ready to break like a wave the moment she gave the right answer. The one that would complete us. The doubt between us tore me apart, and she'd destroy me—all of us—if she turned us down.

Her hands landed on my arms, her touch soft and unsure, filling my insides with a pleasant warmth. I fucking loved it when she touched me. It left me weak and unable to resist her. The impulse to care for her, protect her, consumed me. Fever burned inside me as I caged my arms around her, pressing her to my chest, leaving no air between us. The rise and fall of her chest against mine had my dick hardening.

"I want to visit my mom, see how she's doing," she replied. "She worries if I don't call her."

"That's not a no." I lowered my face to hers, our lips an inch apart.

"No." She wiggled her hips against my legs, and I crushed her tighter.

"If I have to wait to see you again," I breathed in her ear, hot, heavy and inviting. "I want a taste to see me through."

Hunger tore through her. Primal. Raw. Knowing I caused this reaction in her set me on fire. I couldn't wait another second and slammed my mouth over hers. She had me so lost in the moment, forgetting about the shit week we'd had. Her body ached for comfort, and I gave it to her. A flurry of emotions took over me. Hope, need, and desperation. I just needed her to see we weren't what she thought we were. Devils disguised as angels.

CHAPTER 26

*A*aliyah

CASTOR'S WORDS went straight to my stomach, awakening a primitive part of me. The part where my mate bond, soul, and goddess resided. My mind warred with my body on how to process everything. Staying in the room with him when my urges weakened my resolve. Scratching at my chest to free myself of all the sensations assaulting me. Lust. Arousal. An irresistible craving I'd never felt before. Yearning for one of the pieces that would complete me.

The way he looked at me earlier, hungry, devouring, and drowning, inched me into his arms. It frightened me that I let myself get swept away by my emotions when I didn't believe in fated mates or the magic tying us together. But I couldn't fight it. Couldn't stop myself from falling.

Each moment with one of them, my tight grip on maintaining a strictly platonic relationship to gather information slipped from my grasp. I didn't know how much longer I could hold off the mate bond's calling. Fate decided for me in that instant, igniting the slow burn I'd been fighting all week, and the brilliance and intensity prompted my withdrawal before it scolded me.

Castor clenched his legs around me tighter, refusing to let me go. Heat from his body was like a wildfire on mine. The deep sound he made from the back of his throat shot a hot pulse of need to my core. He needed me. Wanted me. I'd never had a man ache for me that much, and his longing weakened my will to fight the bond, fight him, because I wanted the same.

"Alexa," he tried my name on his succulent lips. Heck, it might have been fake—my cover—but the sound of it, deep and gravelly, sent a jolt to my system. In this moment, I wanted everything this man was doing to me and more. The heat between my thighs turned into a frantic, urgent drumbeat.

Hot biker shouldn't have been in my vocabulary. The way his leather moved when he turned to look at me, when he caressed my shoulders and arms, made my damn thighs clench. My fingers clamped on his cut, gripping so tightly, I feared I'd fall if I let go.

This man, all four of them ... Jackals ... enemies ... mates ... frightened me more than I knew. Because of the things they made me want and feel. Fighting them and the mate bond was futile. I couldn't stay away from them any more than they could me. He knew it. I knew it. That was why he made the move. My four fated mates wanted to own me, and they didn't know half the trouble that came with that responsibility.

Guilt clawed at my back. No, I shouldn't be doing this. Shouldn't enjoy the company of killers when my father's remained at large. Slade or any one of his men could be responsible for his death. *Stupid woman.* I let the mate bond get between my reason, judgment, and purpose. This, whatever this was, confused desire wrapped up in a magical spell, I didn't need it right now. Stick to the plan. Get more information from the Jackals that would lock up my father's murderer for good.

Using more force this time, I extracted myself from Castor's hold, both physically and emotionally. Hand to my chest, I gasped, trying to recover the breath he'd stolen from me.

"What's wrong?" He tried to caress me, but I stepped away. Not a good idea. His touch weakened me. Dragged me under his spell.

I speared a hand through my hair. "You said just a taste."

"Little tease." He smiled like a damn sexy demon, stroking his bottom lip. His damn lip. Where I'd been moments ago and longed to return. "You're going to leave me high and dry, baby?"

Baby. That one word, the gruff way he whispered it, had me inch closer. I wanted to go back for more. *So much more.* But I knew if I did, there'd be no turning back. No escape for me. I couldn't risk that.

"I need to go." The moment I turned, he caught my wrist, jerking me back.

Firm, possessive arms trapped me. "Stay. I promise I'll be a gentleman." Why did he have to say it like that? Gravelly and full of promise. I wanted to jump him and push him down to the desk and attack him. "For at least the first five minutes."

At his tease and wicked smile, I snorted and shook my head. No, he wouldn't. He couldn't help himself, and neither could I.

Admit defeat, the mate bond screamed at me. *Take him. Take everything he's offering. He's yours.*

I taught that bitch a lesson, jumping up and down on her

like I was a cartoon character stuffing trash in a bin. Satisfied I'd gotten rid of her, at least for the moment, I cleared my throat.

Time to talk business. Extract what I could. "Alaric said he was planning a ride into Sydney next week. Does that mean you'll leave me all alone?" I went for coy and teasing at the same time. Flirting one-oh-one.

Once I got the information I needed, I was out of here. The longer I stuck around, the more dangerous it became … for me falling for them, and them discovering my real allegiance. I'd not end up dead and buried like my father.

Castor's intense eyes harpooned me to the spot. "I don't mix business with pleasure, baby. Don't try your dark sorceress powers on me." He stepped closer, ghosting my cheek with the back of his knuckles.

My eyelids closed and fluttered. *Fuck them!*

"What *do* you want to talk about then?" My tone made it clear I didn't want to play, and he recalled his hand. "Client-lawyer privilege."

His deep rumble left me tingling all over. "You're just as cunning as your goddess."

If only you knew, pal.

He moved back to the desk, crossing his arms, highlighting the planes of his muscles and the light ink decorating it. A snarling Jackal, a bust of Isis, and a quill resting on a book. Everything to do with him and his life.

"Just don't leave tomorrow, okay? I'll need my goodbye kiss." He patted the side of his stubbled face, and my pulse shot into hyperdrive.

Tomorrow. Shit. They were leaving tomorrow. I had to get a message to Danny before then and plan my escape when they weren't around to prevent me from leaving.

My back groaned with relief, longing for my queen-sized bed. The beds in the shelter were too small to stretch out in.

My neck ached from the soft pillows and I wanted to snuggle into my memory foam. The thought filled me with instant loneliness at returning to my cold, empty apartment.

"Does that mean I'll have to get all shot up to get a visit with you?" The fire burning in his eyes promised he'd do it too.

The heat of my blush broke out over my cheeks. "I'll kick your ass if you show up all bloody in my ER."

My imagination ran wild. Bare chest with a smattering of hair on his pecs. Ink across his skin, trailing down his sides. Discovering what else hid beneath his clothing. God, I couldn't control my eyes wandering over the tattoos peeking out from beneath his shirt. They had my *full* attention.

Somehow, I managed to untangle myself from those thoughts.

"How would you like me to show up?" God, he wasn't giving up. "Flowers? Chocolate? Strippergram?"

I snorted at the last one. "You will improve patient well-being if you do the last one."

"Bust some moves." He did a little *Magic Mike* move, and my heart swooned. We both wanted to see more of that.

I leaned to one side, tilting my hip out, and his eyes went down there, lingering for a moment. He licked his lips.

"Come on, baby, give me something here." I'd give him an A for effort. "I know you don't approve of our lifestyle. But can you give us a chance? We're not angels, but we're not demons either."

"Fallen angels?" I threw in.

He smiled, sexy, broad, his eyes curling too. "Something like that."

"Well, tell me what you do, then." I needed to get him to open up. He was a closed book. Mysterious as the gods. Secretive as a man with skeletons. "As an Enforcer?"

He set both palms on the edge of the desk, and yes, my

eyes watched every flex of his muscles. "You don't want to know about that."

"You enforce rules?" I prodded. "Are you like Happy on *Sons of Anarchy*?"

"Something like that." His tone was as taut as his body.

"What?" I threw up my hands. "You don't like being questioned? So, I'm just supposed to pretend you're a fairy tale prince and fall in love with you? Without knowing a thing about you? It doesn't work that way."

These men were dreaming if they thought I'd fall for that crap.

I moved closer. "I swear to my goddess, if you bring up the mate bond, succumbing to it, or whatever, I'll send your bloody body to the local ER!"

"Feisty." Castor smiled, still as much an enigma as ever.

Frustrated, I turned my back on him, ready to walk out. "Bye, Castor."

"It was the only opening the Jackals had." His words stopped me in my tracks. "I don't like what I do when I have to enforce. But I justify it by being able to get justice for the people I failed. My own form of justice. One less criminal on the street harming innocent people."

Shit. I hadn't expected an answer like that. Enforcers were sick bastards who liked to beat the shit out of people. Castor tied it into his former life as a lawyer and the criminals he prosecuted. I smiled at him, showing my appreciation that he shared something with me, no matter how small.

"The gods expect a balance." He pointed to the quill tattoo on his arm. "The goddess Maat weighs her feather against the heart of every man, woman, and child from the Egyptian pantheon when they go to the Underworld."

The story sounded vaguely familiar. I think I'd seen it in a movie. What was it called? *Gods of Egypt.* Mmmm Nikolaj Coster-Waldau. *Come to Mama!*

"For every law we break, we must atone." Castor's finger trailed along his book, and I imagined all the names of sinners in it.

I think I understood where he was going. "So, you run the shelter because you don't want to go to hell?"

"I'm already going to hell, baby." His contrite smile and the pain echoing down our bond encouraged me back to his side, and I placed my hand on his arm and squeezed. "But I don't disobey my god." His other hand came down over mine. Warm. Protective. I sighed at how good it felt.

Something told me his words held a double meaning. Was that why my mates didn't question the bond between us? I caught myself and backed up. I'd called them my mates. Our relationships were shifting, growing closer, and it scared the hell out of me.

"We don't trade in heavy shit, dark sorceress." Castor brought me back into his arms, and I didn't resist. I wanted to pry him open and uncover his secrets. Soothe the seething turmoil inside him. "One of our own died from meth complications a couple of years back, and we got out of the nasty drugs. Our drug has no side effects but an incredible time. We're not here to kill our customers. We want them to have a good time and live a long life."

He leaned his forehead to the side of my face. His steamy breath on my ear sent delighted shivers down my neck. I cupped his face, rubbing his stubble, enjoying the bristling sound it made. He took my other hand in his, lifting it to his perfect lips, kissing my knuckles, then my palm. I trapped the moan wanting to escape.

This small admission told me he wasn't like any of the Wolves. While they took glee in breaking the law and being outlaws, he still respected law and order. The courts had failed him, and he sought his own form of justice with the Jackals. I didn't defend what the club did. Drugs, guns, strip clubs, bars, whatever. But I appreciated that Castor had found a law he belonged to, even if it crossed the lines of societal regulations.

From what I knew of Zethan and Alaric, I didn't think they were like the men from my brother's club or others I'd crossed paths with during my stint with the Wolves. Outlaws, yes. Devils, no. Fallen angels, hell yeah. Jury was out on Slade, though. I'd come across his brand of cocky, flirty destruction before.

I took a mental step back from everything I thought I knew. All this time, I'd pinned the Jackals all as murderers and thugs like my brother and the men he ran with. Knowing this new information about the Jackal's club, their honor code, allowed me to respect them as men. And I never thought I'd consider that, let alone admit it.

Sure, the Jackals caused havoc, killed their enemies and those that crossed them. So did my father. But I still loved and accepted him. Didn't mean I approved of the life he led. For five years, I'd admired him, wanted to be like him, emulated him, trying to fit in where I never belonged. Where it never felt right. I always thought my conscience got the better of me and I stained them with the law-breaker brush. That excuse never sat right, either.

I didn't want to be part of that life and had run headfirst from it. But something always called me back. Christmas or Easter celebrations with the club. Dad's sixtieth birthday road trip. His death. As much as I hate to admit it, motorcycle clubs were in my blood, and I couldn't run from that.

The mate bond hummed to me, telling me I belonged with the Jackals and their club, and I crammed my eyes shut, fearing she was right. I could do so much good with them. With the shelter. Being their medic. I wouldn't have to follow procedure or fill out forms. I'd be free to practice medicine the way I saw fit, just like Castor got his justice through his enforcing.

Shit. I rubbed my forehead. I couldn't believe I considered staying and working with them. Couldn't believe I saw my enemies in a fresh light. This didn't absolve them from my father's murder by any stretch, but it certainly changed my opinion of them. If they killed my father, then they had to have a reason. Something I didn't know about. Perhaps dad deserved it. Perhaps he was a fall guy. Whatever the case, I'd find out why and put this matter to rest for good. I'd not rest until I did.

CHAPTER 27

*S*lade

SHE FOUND MY GIFT. The soft pink bag I left on her bed beside the kitten heels I'd bought. I leaned in the doorway, watching her. Curious, she inspected the bag, removing a bottle green dress with flecks of gold and a pleated skirt. Her elegant fingers traced the chiffon. A card slipped out from the dress and fell onto the bed.

Two women crowded around Nurse A., admiring the thousand-dollar dress. Small fries for me. Money I shouldn't have spent, given we needed every penny to afford the replacement batch of Pharaoh. I'd not stop spoiling my woman because things turned to shit. That wasn't how I rolled. We'd figure it out. We always did.

"Good God, girl," one of the women said. "That's one of the most beautiful things I've ever seen." Gotta love the shifter hearing, enabling me to spy on her conversation from thirty feet away.

"The color suits your skin tone," the other said, brushing the material.

The first one picked up the fallen card and handed it to my mate. "Looks like you have an admirer."

"Or a few." The second nudged Nurse A. "Have you seen the way those gorgeous men look at you? Honey, I've never seen such adoration."

She was right. We loved hard. Adored our mate. Spoiled her. Nurse A. didn't know what she missed out on. How every one of us would satisfy her needs ... and I wasn't just talking sexually. Liz relied on my strength and conviction, Zethan's dedication and passion, Alaric's romantic affections, and Castor's support and humor.

Nurse A. crushed the dress to her stomach and smiled as she read her card.

Put these on and meet me outside at my bike.
Slade

Careful not to tear the dress, she shoved the card and shoes in the bag. "I can't." She bit her lip, and fuck me, if it wasn't the sexiest thing she could do.

"Girl, don't be stupid," the first said, before wandering away with the second.

Yeah, don't be stupid, Nurse A.

The answer '*hell no*' screamed down the mate bond. Her heart shouted back at her, *don't be a fool.* Overwhelmed by her conflicting emotions, I fisted my hand. Tempted, she peeked in the bag, working that sexy bottom lip of hers between her teeth. My dick sprang to life, wanting her to work it between those gorgeous lips of hers.

Yeah, I knew how to tempt a woman. They didn't call my

god the devil of the Egyptian pantheon for nothing. Literally and figuratively.

"Why aren't you dressed for our date, Nurse A.?" My voice caressed her from the doorway where I waited for her.

The mate bond sang with the flavors of honey mixed with cayenne pepper. She had me worked out. I was sugar and spice, but nothing nice.

She lifted the bag and handed them back. "I'm not going on a date with you, Mr. Vincent." Sweet Jesus, the way she said my name. Tonight, I'd have her screaming it, and leave her croaking tomorrow.

Nurse A. wasn't the kind of woman to bow down to my whims, and it made me hot all over, arguing with her. I drove her crazy, but also made her heart beat faster. Mate bond aside, I knew she was the woman for me when she opened her mouth and gave me sass at the hospital. The moment she said my name, all stern, her eyes strict, lips pressed tight. She didn't understand all the crazy new emotions flooding her. Or how fired up Castor and I were to find our new mate. How our bodies felt more alive than they ever had.

Liz had been our mate. True and dependable. But she wasn't intended to stay with us for a lifetime. Nurse A. was that lifetime love. The one we'd marry and take as our old lady. I knew it in my heart the moment I laid eyes on her.

"Yes, you are." My tone was clear; play by my rules, not hers. "Old ladies do as they're told."

She smacked me on the chest, and my insides ignited. I enjoyed it when she touched me, even if it was rough and intended to reject me. This woman had me burning up hotter than the damn sun. Had me working hard to win her over. I loved every fucking minute of it.

Her heart changed her mind with one look at me. She hit the throttle, reversed, and jumped off the bike at my feet.

God, I loved the mate bond. Not much hid from it. Nurse A. couldn't resist the pull we all felt.

She tried a different tactic, appealing to the sensible side of me. "The dress is beautiful, Mr. Vincent, thank you. But it's really expensive and I can't accept it."

I didn't care about the money. I'd buy her a thousand more of these. Whatever she wanted. So long as I got to strip her out of them at the end of the night.

Beneath the strength of the mate bond, there was no room to negotiate. She was coming with me. Tomorrow I might not return. Tony had pulled through on getting the next shipment of Pharaoh ready early, and we had to escort it to our distributor and make sure it got there untouched. I didn't trust our enemy wouldn't make a move and try to kill us. A risk to my club.

Muscles in my jaw flexed. "C'mon, Nurse A. I might die tomorrow. I'd rather die a happy man, knowing you came with me tonight."

She wavered on her decision when I used the happy man line.

"Does that line work to convince your other girlfriends?" Ouch. Prickly and full of sass tonight. I loved every minute of it. This woman was more than a walking wet dream. Shame her tricks didn't work to hide what I read through the bond.

Accepting her challenge, I snatched the shoes and bag, and threw her over my shoulder. "Have it your way." She shrieked, hit, and kicked me, but it felt like a tickle. "Yeah, keep touching me like that. I like it." She stopped immediately. Yeah, I riled her up and fucking got off on it.

I set her down in Zethan's office. He was dropping off a woman to one of his contacts to get her out of the state to a new home before we left for our big ride down to Sydney tomorrow.

"I want more of you." I shoved the bag and heels at her. "To get to know you. Do you want to come or not?"

"We've only known each other for a week." The mate bond and the way she clutched the gift told me she was torn on whether to accept it. "Don't you think this is moving too fast?"

"Relax. I don't want to marry you. I just want to go on a date with you. Spend some time with you. Is that a crime?" She stiffened at the last word. Judgy little thing. She didn't approve of my career. Not that it was any of her business. I was who I was. I didn't hide it, and I sure as shit didn't pretend to be someone I wasn't.

"I don't believe in this fated mate's thing, and I'm not sticking around." Again, the mate bond said otherwise.

"Keep telling yourself that." One kiss from me, and she'd never want to leave.

"Go away."

I crossed my arms, ready to deliver the big guns. "You know, the god of Chaos conjures images of thunder, lightning, and hellfire. Which I'm all for." I flashed her a classic Slade smile. "Love me a good firestorm. But that's not all there is to me."

I had her full attention. Those aqua blues were glued to me.

I leaned down, whispering in her ear, giving it to her straight, "I also sense the chaos inside a person, their storm of conflicting emotions. Curiosity and unease. Desire and hesitation."

Nurse A. could argue until she was blue in the face, but I knew otherwise. I turned my back on her to give her privacy. Checkmate.

Her end of the mate bond made cracking sounds. I broke down one of her walls. Only fifty or so more to go. As the avatar to the god of Chaos, nothing kept me out. She groaned, and I heard her ruffle around in the bag.

"You need to back off," she said. "You come on too strong."

"I don't do slow or soft."

"You will if you want me." That meant she considered it. A win. I'd go with that. Chances were, she'd tried to sneak away tomorrow when we left for our ride, and I had to take this opportunity before I lost it. In case I really didn't return.

I heard her slide on her dress, and I rubbed at my palms, excited to see her in it. My dick ached to bend her over the desk and take her from behind while she wore it.

"Ready." She didn't sound very enthused. The opposite, actually. Ready to get it over with, like sex with a pencil-dicked dude. My hard-on deflated in an instant as I turned around.

Hackles on my Jackal raised at the leopard print dress she'd slipped on. Not the green and gold dress I bought her. Where had it even come from? Anger swarmed in me like a sandstorm. "What the fuck are you wearing?"

She ran her hands over the tight dress, accentuating every curve, making my balls tighten with need. "The dress you bought me."

My Jackal growled savagely, and it vibrated along the mate bond.

"Take it off." I grabbed at the hem assisting her, and she batted me away.

"The other one is too long. It'll get caught in the wheels." Fighting me again. Don't get me wrong, I loved a challenge, but this woman was starting to become a fucking headache.

My Jackal slashed at my chest, growing, protecting its territory. I jerked at her dress again. "Get it off."

She backstepped. "What's your problem, Slade?"

Slade. The name made me pause.

"My problem?" My voice came out a gruff growl. I skimmed my hands under her skirt, along the outside of her thighs, and she trembled, clenching her legs together. "Leopards prey on Jackals. I'm not gonna sit opposite you and look at that hideous dress."

She broke out into laughter, and my Jackal whined. "It's not literal."

This woman made my dick hard, and my head hurt in the space of two seconds. The whole ride over here I had a hard-on, eager to see her in the dress. Now I wanted her out of this offensive one. She released a pissed-off groan and moved away. We'd always have this battle of wills to determine who was the strongest.

Tiring of the aggravation, I let out a slow and deliberate breath. "The more you fight this, the harder I'll try." I brushed her thighs with my nails. Every nerve ending came to life and sang down the mate bond. I quickly pushed her over the edge of reason.

"Shit," she hissed, like her body didn't listen to her head, and she forced me to turn around while she threw on the green dress. With it on, she moved in front of me, indicating she wanted me to zip it up for her. Her submission stirred my cock to life.

My pleasure. Slowly I crept the zipper up, delaying it, kissing each shoulder blade, then the silky flesh between her shoulder and neck, finishing on her left ear. The sigh she let out nearly made me explode in my pants. Fuck me. Her little noises were an incredible turn-on. I imagined what she'd sound like bent over the desk, moaning as I drove into her. My lips switched to her right ear as I jerked the bodice closed. Her heat flared, and I wanted to bend down, bury myself beneath her dress, and please her right here. Not yet. She wasn't one hundred percent ready. Tonight, she would be. At dinner, she'd see another side of me, and I'd remove that stick from her ass.

I shook off my jacket and threw it over her shoulders. "For the ride."

She smiled up at me, warmer, more receptive than she'd been earlier. This one was tough and resilient. She wouldn't let me break down those walls without a battle.

I clasped her hand, rubbing my thumb along her knuckle as I led her out of the office, through the shelter's hall and out the front door.

T-bone was outside having a smoke. "President." He nodded. "Can I have a word?"

I didn't want to leave my woman, but club business took precedence over a date. "Sure." I reluctantly let Nurse A.'s hand go, hoping she didn't refuse it when I returned. "What is it?" I asked when T-bone and I moved aside.

My club brother rubbed at the back of his neck. "I can't make the ride tomorrow."

My back tensed. "Why not?" He was a good rider and we needed him.

He sucked down his cigarette, and I was tempted to bum one from him. "Mindy and the kids have got a stomach bug." Translation: Dad duty.

Fuck. A stomach bug went through the school of my nephew and niece. Wiped out my brother's entire family. Third time this year. Mom would have to bring meals around for them. The bug was the reason I'd got the dinner reservation in the first place. It had been booked for Charlie's anniversary with his wife.

"Family's important." I clapped him on the shoulder. "I'd prefer if you kept clear of the club and don't give it to anyone else."

"I'm sorry to let the club down."

"I'll get Mom to make you some meals and send them around." Stepmom. All I had left of my parents.

"Thanks, Slade." T-bone smiled.

"Have a good night, buddy." I whipped out my phone as he walked away, instructing it to text my mom to make some meals for his family. When the phone finished the text, I moved to my Harley, where my woman waited for me.

"That was really sweet what you did for T-bone." Damn, my old lady was already getting to know the names of my brothers.

I threw a leg over my bike and sat down. "Didn't think I had it in me?"

"No." At least my woman was honest.

I twisted and held out my hand for her.

"Whatever happened to ladies first?" she purred. Teasing would get her everywhere.

"Hell, no." I patted my thigh. "I want to feel you slide on behind me."

Climbing on, she tried not to touch me, and I knew she did it to piss me off. She maintained the distance between us as she settled behind me, her knees modestly pressed to my hips. God, I'd never worked so hard for a woman in my life. All the effort made my dick ache. Determined to beat her at her own game, I leaned back so my spine brushed her chest. Her nipples hardened at the contact, hard as diamonds. Suddenly shy, she froze.

"Closer, Nurse A." I slid my hands beneath her knees and dragged her forward. Stiff nipples brushed my back. Again. Thank fuck I loaned her my jacket, otherwise I would have been deprived of their sweetness. I purposely rubbed my back into them.

"Stop it." She giggled. Finally, a laugh. It was harder to get than an original Harley Davidson.

"Why?" I brushed up against her harder. "Afraid you'll like it? Afraid to let go, Nurse A.?"

She laughed harder, the sound sultry in my ear, awakening my Jackal again. "You're like an animal in heat, rubbing up against me."

"I am in heat." I gave her one final, teasing grin. She thumped my arm, telling me I'd hit her limit. Time to rein it in a notch.

My god and I never liked government or rules imposed on us by the pantheon or the regulators. We made our own and lived by them. The pantheon hated us for it, but we didn't care. Wild and free, that was our motto. I sensed a wildness in Nurse A. too. She just had to be shown how to let loose.

"Arms, Nurse A." My tone switched from light and flirty to harder and commanding. I wanted her wrapped around me, not shy.

"Do you ever say please?" she snipped.

"Nope." And that was the truth.

She gripped my waist, soft and unsure. Like holding me tighter might break down another of her walls.

"C'mon, Nurse A. Don't be shy." I pulled her hand to my stomach, showing her how it should be done. I wanted her arms caged around me. Tight. Her palms flat against the undulation of my stomach. Fingers and nails digging into me.

The gesture was intimate, and I felt her apprehension down the mate bond. Damn. I'd forgotten how good it felt to have my mate at my back. Warmth clinging to me. Chest sculpted to my back, arms, and neck. Something told me she hadn't been held in a long time and she needed the reassurance.

"Safety first." She stretched forward to point to my helmet dangling from my handle.

"Don't need that." I twisted to give her another dimpled smile. "Not when I've got you to heal me."

"Quickest way to get pulled over by the cops." She snorted and shook her head, taking the passenger helmet from behind her and jamming it over her pretty little head.

Fucking cops. They better steer clear of me tonight. After my earlier interview, I wasn't in the damn mood for their bullshit.

I stuck my helmet on and cranked the engine of my Harley. While I let it warm, I set a palm over her thigh, using her to steady me and bring my anger back down. For once, she didn't push me away or fight me. Her breath quickened and her chest grazed me faster. Fuck, my dick hardened like a damn lead weight. This ride was going to be fun. I was one step closer to securing my woman's heart.

CHAPTER 28

*A*aliyah

Holy hell, Slade Vincent was a dangerous man. He took what he wanted when he wanted. And that included taking the corners like he was born to break them and the bike in the process. I thought we'd fall off at least three times and had screamed for each one. My fear only excited him more, and he rode harder, faster, meaner—the way I imagined he'd fuck me. I clenched my legs and arms tighter as he led us to the pits of hell, because that was where I would end up after agreeing to a date with the devil himself.

I stared at the menu, but all the letters turned into hieroglyphics. Isis could have helped me out, but she laughed in the background.

"Crazy, young, and in love," she said, before receding.

Oh, God. No love. Hunger, yes. Arousal, check. Nipples, a hard yes.

I rubbed at my forehead as if that would wipe my mind

clear of the accidental nip brush on Slade's back. The cheeky bastard had only encouraged them to harden when he grazed his hard, ripped back against my chest. Tingles had chased through me, and I had to use all my restraint to hold back my moan. The man was so damn dark, dangerous, and sexy. And I wanted him. All of him.

"Would you like to order, madam?" the waiter asked … I think for the third time. Couldn't be too sure. Still caught up on my nipples' reaction to Slade.

"Er." I scanned the menu for the fifth time, but couldn't concentrate. "I'll have whatever he ordered." I flicked my finger at Slade.

"Excellent." The waiter smiled and retreated.

"Steak and vegetables." Slade grinned. Sexy. Alluring. Irresistible. Those dimples made my heart roll over, part her legs and stick them in the air. "You've got a healthy appetite. I like a woman who's not afraid to eat."

I coughed and took a sip of water to clear my throat. He was laying it on thicker, even after I told him to back off. The man did whatever he wanted. Wild. Free. Ruthless.

Doing everything to avoid those dimples, I studied the private area Slade had booked for dinner. Brick walls gave the restaurant a warehouse feel. Plastic chandeliers warmed the room. Plants in the corner and a rose in the center of the table. Thick, frosted windows blocked out the murmured conversation from the other side of the restaurant. He'd gone all out and spent a bit to get this reservation.

"Nice place," I commented, taking a sip of water from my glass to coat my throat left dry from screaming the whole bike ride. I'd ridden since I was old enough to handle a bike. Thirteen or so. Short and long rides. Ridden by myself and bitch with my ex plenty of times. Never like that. Never again.

Slade buttered his roll sensually, and I imagined my skin

beneath the spread of his blade, taking every glide of that slippery, melted butter. Fuck, I was a goner! "If I had known you were such a screamer, I'd have taken you for a ride sooner."

I spat out my water and fumbled to soak it up with my napkin. Oh, God. Heat coursed through my cheeks and I bent my head to hide it. I didn't want him to see how he affected me. How he melted my insides and made my chest purr at the same time as it twisted with guilt and disgust.

He grinned, leaned in, and quirked a pale brow. "Nurse A.? You dirty little bird." He feigned innocence with a mock hand on his chest. "I meant my bike. What were you thinking?"

He knew how I interpreted that. The mate bond gave me away. Damn bitch! I couldn't hide anything from the Jackals … except the secret I kept close to my heart. Guarded and protected, never to be discovered. I didn't know how I kept that a secret for so long. Maybe it was part of Isis' dark gifts. The ones Castor had spoken of where the goddess had deceived Ra, the King of gods.

Slade just never let up. He leaned back, setting his crusty roll down, my eyes going to the generous slather of butter, imagining him gliding it over my body and licking it off. Fuck, the mate bond was coming on strong tonight, just like him.

Realization hit me in the head like someone had thrown a bread roll at me. The mate link responded differently to each man I was with. Secretive and longing with Castor. Guarded and withdrawn with Zethan. Haunted and sweet with Alaric. Hot and heavy with Slade. Was that what it was like in their hearts? With them as mates? In their beds?

"You don't get out much, do you?" Slade embarked on his assessment of me. "You're all work and professionalism. Play by the rules. Don't date the doctors. Addressing people by their *last name*."

Fuck, he had me on that one. I only used his last name to annoy him because he worked me up so much.

"How long's it been since you've been on a date?" He ignored the beer glass and drank straight from the bottle. He was a no-frills kind of guy, and I liked him like that. Uninhibited. Unrestrained. Unhinged.

I threw up both hands. "Whoa, getting kind of personal." Bad move. Proved his assumptions, which he rubbed in on his next comment.

Slade poured me a glass of red wine, and I had to look away, reminded of the blood flowing from the bullet wounds in my father's back. "Let your hair down, have some fun, Nurse A." His face pinched. "You're so wound up and tight." He wriggled his shoulders. "It's making me tense."

Maybe because I'd been forced to come here by the man who killed my father. The man whose heart I wanted to drive a knife through. The man who drove me wild with lust.

"I have fun." I rolled my shoulders, trying to shake away some of the tension at sitting across from a potential murderer.

"Oh, yeah?" He stared me down with his sensual, piercing indigo eyes. "Rearranging the bandages cupboard?"

Fuck, that was kind of fun, sorting out the different syringe sizes. I liked to do it when the ER quieted down. It helped clear my mind after a busy or testing night. God, he had me pegged. I really was a sad, dateless geek who ... Annoyed, I puffed out my cheeks and leaned back in my chair. I really needed a new hobby, to live a little. I sipped that red like it was going out of fashion to prove him wrong.

"Be serious for once." I threw my napkin down, trying to clear my head and think straight. Out of all of them, he flustered me the most, and I didn't know why. "I want to get to know you. How'd you get the reservation? Pull some strings? Offer to pay them double?"

Slade sighed. "My brother's family also got the stomach bug going around town." He scratched at his pale beard. "I'd reserved the table for his anniversary, but he couldn't make it."

Lord. Slade had a considerate bone in his body. Never would have known it. "Careful, Mr. Vincent. You're showing a sweet side. You don't want to ruin your bad boy reputation."

He leaned forward, sliding his arm beneath the table, setting it on my knee. My heart thundered in my ear. "I'll show you how bad I can be later. After dessert." He accompanied his dark promise with a seductive wink.

That was it. I needed to level up. Go for the alcohol. Ease the tension growing in the pit of my stomach. I snatched my red wine and sipped at it.

Slade gently squeezed my thigh, and I clenched my legs together. "This is my place. One of two up-market dives in this town. Except I don't charge my customers for the private dinning experience. I'm not like those other elitist pricks. Every week the manager takes a lottery of names and picks out one couple every night to get a table in the two private areas. We get hundreds of applications every week."

The place was packed with people waiting outside to get in, telling me it was really popular with the locals. My dad never got into any restaurants. His club owned a few bars and titty clubs.

Impressed with Slade and the Jackals, my mouth fell open. Who would have thought he had a fair bone in his body. The man's attractiveness kept growing by the minute, and I found it harder and harder to hate him. Beneath the charm laid his dark side. Pure destruction and chaos. The side capable of taking lives. I had to hold firm on that and not waver from my goal to avenge my father.

"What?" He took a sip of his *Great Western* beer. "Thought I was just a thug with no business acumen?"

Yeah, I did, actually. The Jackals didn't become one of the most powerful and wealthy clubs from good business practice and family values. They took over territories, swamped their competitors' products and destroyed them. The handbook of Slade's god, Set.

"You continue to surprise me," I admitted, needing another sip of wine.

"Thanks for the compliment." His throat bobbed as he swallowed more beer, and I couldn't look away. He set his bottle down, piercing me with his lethal gaze. "I don't need a business degree to run a successful empire. Richard Branson is my fucking hero. High school dropout. Dyslexic. Driven. A genius." Fan-boying. Adorable. Words I never would have used to describe him. "He started his first business at sixteen, branched out into record stores, eventually bought his own train and airline carrier services and record label. I've listened to all his audiobooks."

The mate bond communicated how Slade saw himself in the billionaire entrepreneur. Now that I thought about it, Slade waved away the menu, and I wondered if he already knew what he wanted to order, or he couldn't read like his hero. I decided to test it.

"I can't quite read what's on the specials board." I squinted to make it look legit. "Can you read it? You're closer."

"I don't read, sweetheart." It came out hard and fast.

"You can't or you won't?"

"Can't," he growled it out as if ashamed.

Aw, Slade Vincent, Jackal's President, had an insecurity he hid behind. Men who talked themselves up this much always did. No biggie to me that he couldn't read. Didn't make him less of a man. One of the nurses at work had Dyslexia and we always helped her out. I just hated the way men like him and my father weren't emotionally available. They buried their vulnerability and weakness because they felt they couldn't be leaders. No one was perfect.

"No shame in it." No wonder he admired Richard Branson. The darkness in his eyes and transferring along the link prompted me to change gears. "What other legit businesses do you have?"

His gorgeous eyes sharpened, and I knew I'd asked the wrong question. "You ask a lot of questions. You know we don't talk club business."

I had to keep the heat off me, while still managing to extract information. Otherwise this whole exercise was pointless.

"Fine." I brushed his hand off my leg and folded my arms, drawing his gaze to my chest. "I'll just be your mate, and we'll talk dirty all the time, then?"

His gaze lifted to meet mine. "No complaints here."

I waited to continue after the waiter delivered our meal. "Seriously, you expect me to be your mate and club medic, but you won't share with me?"

The food smelled incredible. Steak on a bed of grilled vegetables. The meal tasted like mud because I was pissed off. Everything about this man drove me insane with lust and annoyance.

"Why do you make me work so hard, Nurse A.?" Even the way Slade cut up his steak was sexy. The damned rings on his fingers; a skull, rose, jackal, and Harley Davidson caught the light. I imagined his metal trailing along my body. Sliding between my legs. Pushing into me. "I'm busting my balls here."

His jokes were his weapons. They were also his defense. He liked to push my buttons.

Fed up with the back and forth, I jabbed my fork at him. "Why do you make me work so hard to get to know you?" Talking to him was exhausting, trying to get anything intelligent or serious out of him impossible. "I'm trying to build a bond beyond the stupid fated mates one."

Once I got back to the shelter, I'd call my brother and arrange for him to pick me up. I wanted to go home. No more Jackals and mate bond.

Slade pinched at his lined forehead and threw his napkin on the table. "Fuck, I don't need hard work."

"I'm the one with a stick up my ass," I snipped. "You're a pain in the ass."

Hopefully we were leaving. I swallowed some water to unblock the sandy meal stuck in my throat. Then I stood. Chiffon tickled my legs. Damn, this dress was beautiful. Right up my alley. Gold hit the light in all the right places, twinkling amid the sea of green. I looked like a goddess in it. But I couldn't wait to get out of it and away from any reminder of Slade fucking Vincent.

The Jackal's President scrubbed his drawn face. The mate bond hummed with his reluctance to share club business and his desire to grow closer to me. His duty to his club versus his woman. Finally, he gave in to me. "We own lots of commercial rentals, bars, clubs, a few hotels, and two construction companies. One my brother runs."

"Your brother isn't in the club?" I remained standing to make my point.

"Nah, he quit when Dad died of heart disease two years ago." Slade got up, moved behind me, and pulled out my chair for me. His way of saying he didn't want me to go. The closest I'd ever get to him admitting he was sorry and being a difficult ass.

I sat down and let him push me in. Bursts of electricity shot down my arm when he brushed the outside of my shoulder. My breath stopped as he twirled my hair around his fingers. He leaned down to place a rough kiss on my cheek. Heat pooled in my belly and core. Flames licked at the spot where he'd touched. My whole world pitched at the contact, and I shifted my face in his direction. But he was gone before I knew it, returning to his seat, leaving my heart aching for another desperate touch. Something I hadn't expected from him. I expected him to kiss me and conquer me in the same breath.

I took another sip of water to cool myself down. "Was that when you took over the club?"

Slade nodded and lifted his beer to his thick, luscious lips. He had a really sexy mouth. Larger, poutier top lip and thinner bottom lip, and I just wanted to suck on both.

"Thank you for being forthcoming with me." I picked up my fork and continued eating. The flavor returned to the meat and grilled vegetables.

"Christ, Nurse. A." Slade stared at me. "You better be worth it and not a goddamn headache." Speak for himself.

He'd live to regret that statement. Once I was done with him, I'd be more than a goddamn headache. For what he'd taken from me, I'd be his worst fucking nightmare.

CHAPTER 29

*A*aliyah

CONVERSATION IMPROVED THROUGHOUT THE MEAL. Questions were answered and reciprocated. I found out he liked to golf and go to the shooting range on weekends to kick back. One thing we had in common since I used to go golfing with my dad.

Once we hit dessert, things took a romantic change when Slade adjusted the position of his seat next to mine. His left hand wormed its way beneath the table to take residence on my thigh. That touch had me sweltering and sweating in the damn dress. Wine gulped down my throat, but it did nothing to extinguish the raging fire he lit within me. I should have called it a night. But only angels did that. Around him, I lost my damn halo.

He spooned the mud cake with chocolate raspberry sauce and held it out for me with his right hand. "Don't be a pain in the ass, Nurse A. Just eat it and please your old man."

We were already like a bickering married couple going in crazy circles. "You're not going to stop with that, are you?"

"Nope. Not even when it's official." He caught a drip of chocolate raspberry sauce and licked it. Fuck me, it was one of the sexiest things I'd ever seen, and I wanted to lick it from his finger.

I took the spoon as a close second. Sauce dripped down the sides of my mouth, and he wiped that from me too, parting his mouth, licking it slow and sensual. God, I wasn't getting out of here without a damn taste of him.

We went on like that for three more spoonfuls before he caved and stuck his finger in the sauce, lifting it to my lips. Encouraged by the intensity of the mate bond, I licked his finger slowly, hesitantly but turned on as all hell. His finger tasted smoky and salty. Delicious. The next time he fed me, I took his finger into my mouth, and he hissed.

His gaze heated up, and he groaned like a starved man. "Fuck, you do that again, and I'll bend you over the table."

Tempting. I held back, though, struggling to get a handle on my feelings and work through the emotions of the past and the present. Work out why I deserved to be bound to my enemy, the man who took everything from me. With him, with all of my supposed mates, I fought my darkness and lost. Who was I kidding? Slade was damn well right; I couldn't beat this mate bond.

Slade offered me a raspberry and chocolate finger this time, the red and brown swirls an indication of my fate if I continued down this dangerous path. I couldn't stop myself. My head knew it was wrong and argued with my heart. Guilt weighed heavy on me for even welcoming this attention. But I'd been thrown headfirst into the deep end, and the only thing that could save me from drowning was him. In the end, I chose to turn a blind eye and forget everything. Just to let go like he said and have fun while it lasted.

His breath turned choppy as I tasted his finger, teasing. "This is the only gentle you're going to get," he warned, waking my pussy from her slumber. "Enjoy it while it lasts, Nurse A." I had him in such a spin, he could barely spit out the words.

Taking control, I sucked his finger, taking him deeper, making his breath hitch. On the next round, Slade spread chocolate along my lips, and I licked it off. Every nerve went up in a ball of flames.

"Wait for me." I let him do it again. This time he flicked his deviled tongue along my lips. His tongue was rough, like it had hundreds of tiny pads on it designed for pleasure. I moaned at the massage to my mouth.

God, what was I doing? I went from loathing the man to not wanting to be near him, to wanting him close and feeding me. I was fucked up. Twisted. Sick. My father probably rolled over in his grave. But I couldn't deny the call. Couldn't cut ties with him when my heart refused to. This man was sex on fire. The devil dipped in chocolate. Every time he touched me, looked at me, I fell deeper under his mesmerizing spell.

"I bet your pussy is as greedy as you." Slade spooned me a final piece of cake and sauce, and I descended into hell with him, accepting it. The fires of Hades roared around me, burning me, destroying me.

That was all it took to make me break. A loud snap traveled down the mate bond, and he jumped at the opportunity. His mouth crashed down on mine like hail pelting the grass, flattening it. He conquered my damn mouth like he was born to do it, and I was helpless to fight him. With my tongue, I swirled cake into his mouth, and he groaned, tasting me back.

"Fuck, woman, you've bewitched me with your sassy mouth and now your kiss." Our tongues fought for dominance and control, both of us determined to win, neither of us giving in.

There was no turning back now. I'd unleash the frenzied beast inside him. With him, I didn't want to be smart or even careful. The man brought out strange, new, and irresponsible impulsive urges in me. Wild, free, hungry. Hell, dammit, I was letting go.

He lifted me, spun me around, and pushed me to the table in one hard motion. Material on my dress lifted as his hands skimmed along my thighs.

"Fuck, you're so beautiful." He crouched down and left a burning trail of kisses along my flesh. Bold, daring, and fucking hot. "And mine."

Mine. My body and the mate bond shivered with the promise.

"Fuck me." His firm grip spread my legs wider. Fingers roughly grazed my sensitive inner thighs, and I bucked. "The moment I saw that dress, I knew it was for you. It hugs your curves, shows off those pretty breasts. I'm going to bend you over and fuck you in this dress."

I moaned at the threat, inching wider, telling him where I wanted him to go.

"You're so wet." He bit my ass cheek through my underwear hard enough to leave a mark. "You get all hot when you fight with your old man, don't you?"

I made a simpering sound in response to the hot finger he used to push aside my panties and swipe along my pussy. Rough and dominating. Yes. He made me crazy with irritation and hunger.

"You smell incredible." He tore my panties away with a loud snap, and I gasped. His knees kicked my foot out, widening my stance, and I was bare before him.

Something unclipped and clunked as he set it on the table. A gun. Smith and Wesson forty-five caliber pistol with a little flick at the end. Same gun my father carried on his person. By my right hand. Fuck. I clenched and tried to withdraw, but Slade's possessive grasp held me firm.

"It's okay, baby. I won't hurt you." He made a long, pleased hmm sound before he buried his tongue in my pussy.

My back arched, responding to his rough drag and the raspy surface on his tongue. Like a damn cat. Friction built with every glide over my clit. His mouth was just as wild and brutal as he was, and I spread wider, letting him apply every part of it to my aching, burning heat. I bucked as he licked, sucked, and blew on my tiny ball of nerves. My clawed fingers scratched at the tablecloth, fisting what I could, making the dessert plates and glasses rattle. His beard tickled my sensitive flesh, grazing it, giving me even more friction.

"That's it, Nurse A., give me all of you. Don't be shy." His teeth sank into the tender flesh of my burning folds, a command to submit to him completely. I cried out at the harsh sting. He soothed it with a few dark kisses.

My head spun with fear and arousal, and everything slipped from my control. Need and want rolled through me, and I zoned in on his dominant touch and let it take over me entirely. Wanting more, I rocked back against his mouth.

"Oh, God. Right there." That was all I could get out when he suspended me in a world of pleasure I'd never encountered before.

"Yeah?" His harder suck had me gasping for air and dragging the tablecloth away from its place.

The gun dragged along the table as he collected it. Nervous, I clenched again, making his fingers dig into me tight. Bruising tight.

"What about this?" His weapon found its prize. My tight heat. Cool metal doused the fire he injected into me.

Desperate to get it out of me, I yelped and bucked. I'd

seen one too many gunshot wounds and knew what those things were capable of. One shot could tear up my insides.

"It won't go off when I control it." I didn't trust Slade and what he was capable of with other men. But I knew he wouldn't hurt his mate. Magic thrummed inside the pistol, holding back all the mechanisms from springing and firing. That small bit of comfort provided me security that he'd keep his word.

He drove it into me with more force, and I groaned and bent my head on the table. "Keep going!"

"That's it. Fuck my gun." The gun slammed in and out like his cock would. Aggressive and merciless. Encased in my tight heat. "I want to smell you tomorrow while I'm gone. Want your pussy right by my side."

Oh, my God. That was the most erotic and dirty thing anyone had ever said to me. It turned me on like nothing ever had before. Desire to chase my orgasm replaced my concern, and I rammed back into every stroke to take the gun's full length like I would his cock.

"I love the way you fucking taste." His growl thundered along every nerve of my pussy, through my body, lighting me up to the point I might spontaneously combust. "Hot, wet, and dripping all over my face."

His dirty words thrust me up to the ultimate peak. The barrel of his gun zoned in on the right spot, and my body started to convulse. Facial hair scraped along my swollen pussy, and I broke apart. I moaned so damn loud I was certain the patrons heard me outside.

"That's it, Nurse A." He breathed on me. "Come all over me. Louder. Harder." I gave in to him as he commanded. My body shook uncontrollably over his gun and mouth. His tongue didn't slow down until he'd lapped up every last part of my juices, and I twitched as the nerves in my clit turned sensitive.

My moans faded as I came back to myself. I clawed at the table to stay upright, but even that slipped. "Fuck." I couldn't catch my breath or my senses.

His dominant, rough hand moved to my lower back and shoved me back to the table. "Scream for me again, Nurse A."

In one brutal move, his cock was planted inside of me, his thick intrusion stretching me. Slade Vincent didn't do foreplay. He was the arousal. One tall, tanned, delicious ball of it, and he knew it. I scrabbled for purchase on the table, unable to get a grip when he kept hammering into me. Heat built from within, quickly rising into a forge, a volcanic eruption. Electricity coursed through my skin, and I'd never felt so alive or aroused before.

Slade fisted my hair and wrapped it around his fingers. I moaned at the pain stinging my scalp, turned on by the forceful way he pinned me down. "Once you take my cock, you'll never want another."

Cocky much? Terrible at math, too. Think he needed a reminder about a vital factor he'd forgotten. "What about my other three mates?" I panted out.

He leaned down to groan in my ear, and goosebumps erupted across my flesh. "You'll love their cocks, but always come back to mine."

Head spinning, my body buzzed, heart raced, I could barely think straight. He made my senses come alive at each deep and forceful thrust.

"That so?" I grunted as he entered me harder.

"I'll make you come three times, every time, Nurse A." Big talk from Mr. President. As if to prove his point, he strove harder to send me to destination euphoria, pounding into me with a ferocity bordering on savage.

Punishing fingers clasped my jaw, twisting my face toward him, and he licked my cheek and jaw, then dropped his mouth to mine in a dominant, all-consuming kiss. My body quivered as I came for the second time, first time on his cock. I moaned desperately into his mouth, and he drowned it out with one of his own. Dark and dangerous. Forbidden and oh, so wrong.

Fuck, this was thrilling, hot, and terrifying at the same time. I was fucking my enemy, and this went well beyond infiltrating his club. *Disloyal. Traitor. Whore.* The words slammed in my skull. I locked them out, focusing only on the pounding of his cock in my pussy and his grunts in my ear.

Slade slid a finger between my lips, his command silent. Suck it. Hard. Dirty. My tongue found the calloused flesh and took it deep. The motion drove him wild, and he groaned, bucking harder. Not one ounce of mercy existed in this man. I was his. My pussy his. And he made it so. I crashed over his cock a second time, walls in my pussy contracting.

"Fuck, that's so good, Nurse A." His fingers tightened in my hair, and I cried out. "Come on me again." His order sent me straight to the edge.

This was the real Slade Vincent. The one who didn't hold back. Wild, free, and destructive. Hints traveled along the mate bond that his last mate didn't allow this, and he had to restrain himself. And it never did well to contain a storm. With me, he could unleash his tempest and destroy me in the process.

The final crest threatened to flatten me, and there was no stopping it. When he slammed home, I came with such force, the plates and silverware rattled, and the glassware toppled off the table, smashing everywhere in true Slade Vincent destruction. Spent, he collapsed on top of me, breathing heavily. His grip on my hair loosened to let him stroke my face. We lay there, slumped, him over me, his arms and body wrapped around mine.

He wasn't kidding when he said I'd come three times.

When Slade said something, he meant it. The man got his way. Every single time.

Sense slowly reasserted itself as my orgasm ebbed away. Voices in my head got louder. The ones drowned out by the desire flooding my mate bond.

Stupid, idiot, my head screamed. *What did you do?*

I let him into my heart and head. Let him win. What had I been thinking? The fucking link had taken over me. I'd lost my damn mind and fucked Slade Vincent. The man I wanted to destroy. The man I hated for ending my father's life well before his time. Shocked, I froze beneath him, hating myself for what I'd just done. Sleeping with the enemy went too far. Dangerous waters covered in flame floated all around me. I'd go to hell for this, for betraying my father's memory.

Tears wet my cheeks. I pressed a hand to my moist skin. Infiltrating the Jackals meant getting answers and evidence, then getting the fuck out of there and never going back. It didn't mean compromising myself.

I'd also failed to get more intel to my brother about the ride tomorrow. Somehow, I had to find a way to do that after Slade took me back to the shelter.

Sourness and heat flushed my stomach. I'd just crossed a line I'd never be able to erase. This man was my personal apocalypse, and I was going down with him.

CHAPTER 30

Alaric

WE HAD a shipment run scheduled within the hour, and I needed to get my head in the game. Yet the only thing I could think about was my mate. Damn Alexa sank her claws into me with one kiss and I couldn't shake her. Thanks to Slade, I hadn't been able to go near the shelter or see her in days.

Yesterday, Castor expressed her desire to leave today, and that left feelings between us unresolved. I wanted her almost as much as I wanted to know more about her. But every time I tried, I came up empty-handed. I teetered on the edge of obsession. I didn't trust anyone I couldn't read.

A run was exactly the distraction I needed to get my head in the game.

Slade gathered the riders in the garage, all of us overlooking the map spread out on the table where I gave them the rundown one more time. Some clubs preferred to stay off-grid and relied on old maps to get from point A to point B. The Jackals relied on my inner GPS.

Concluding my presentation, I asked, "Are we clear?" and eyed every one of the riders.

Castor, Slim, Jaxx, Rusty, and me. Three riders in front of the shipment. Me leading with Slade and Jaxx. Three at the rear, consisting of Castor, Slim, and Rusty. Plenty of protection. Nothing was getting through us. After one missing shipment, we weren't taking any chances. Everything was triple-checked. Our guys confirmed the containers arrived fully stocked and ready for transport. Slade handpicked the drivers. We planned for everything and anything, eliminating all threats. This shipment would get to the distributor without a problem. Otherwise, we were fucked.

"Yes," a chorus of voices echoed.

Slade glared at me, and I nodded. He moved to the side of his bike, giving us the signal that it was time to go. "Jackal's ride!"

Everyone got on their bikes and called their engines to life.

Our President stood beside his bike, pulled out his gun, sniffed it, licked it, and kissed it. Never seen him do that before. Must have had a real taste for blood today.

When he caught me staring, he said, "Got my woman close to me." I didn't understand that or want to know what that meant.

Slade grabbed his helmet from the seat of his Harley and threw it on, then he rolled his bike outside to start it. Engines rumbled like a chorus of wolves from which the jackal descended. I checked I had everything. Gun, radio, phone, and flask. Everything essential.

Slade waited for me up front to take the lead as I always did. With my magical eye, I scouted for danger, roadblocks, cops, and anything that could jeopardize the run. Engine warm beneath me, I took point for the first five or six miles of the run. The group hit the Western Highway, just out of Bathurst, cruising either side of the truck. Nothing to see here.

After another twenty miles, the guys would pull back until my tail lights disappeared from their line of sight. If there was trouble on the road, I radioed back, and Castor rerouted. Slade and Jaxx would stick close to the truck for protection. Castor, Slim, and Rusty kept watch at the rear.

Passing the airport, I noticed the first cop car and gave the guys a heads up over the radio to keep it under thirty-five. Cop vehicles patrolled the highway for speeding motorists to pull over and write tickets. Revenue raising for the state of New South Wales, and we didn't need to contribute to their deep coffers.

Five miles east, I encountered a second cop car, which pulled in behind me, hovering but not signaling for me to pull over. My body tensed. The pit of my stomach churned. Something was going on. He pulled off before Meadow Flat, where another police van, unmarked but unmistakable with all their radio communication antennas, took over. One cop wasn't reason to panic. Two put me on alert. Three, and it was time to call the lawyer about arraignment proceedings because by then, we were fucked. They were following us. Harassing us. Some prick tipped them off.

I radioed into Slade, yelling into the transmitter over the roar of the engine. "Third cop car since Bathurst. Navy blue. Unmarked."

"We'll call out new directions." The radio went dead. Slade didn't want to risk it. "Castor, initiate detour. I'll radio the truck."

"Roger that," came Castor's reply from the back of the pack.

The guys would bail from the highway and hit the back

roads at Lithgow. I was ahead of them by at least a mile and would have to catch the next exit and double back. As I hooked the radio back on my jacket, two more unmarked cars pulled out of an emergency vehicle access, sped up and met my pace. The PIT maneuver happened in the blink of an eye, too fast for me to do anything about it. Lights flashing, they surrounded me in the overtaking lane, forcing me to pull over to the side of the road.

"Fuck." I shut down my engine and slid off my helmet.

First time for everything. Given the current climate of everything happening to the club, this felt sinister, planned, and well-coordinated.

I hoped Slade got warning before he marched into a trap.

Six cops with guns rushed out of the vehicles before I could get off my bike. One tried to yank me off while I was still straddled. A slew of instructions came at me from every direction.

Hands up.

Walk backward to the sound of my voice.

Down on the ground.

All it took was one wrong move against a cop with an itchy trigger finger, and I was dead. It was easy to make the wrong move with so many people saying different things.

"What are you pulling me over for, sir?" I tried to keep a level voice as I addressed the officer in my face.

"Possession." The dirty cop pulled out a bag of drugs and threw them on my bike. This was far from a routine stop, and they were looking for something other than drugs or an illegal firearm. "An offense under Section Ten of the Drug Misuse and Trafficking Act."

Fuck. My brothers would get worse if they were caught. Life in prison for transporting a narcotic throughout the state of New South Wales.

"Planted evidence," I said, clear and emphasized in case they wore body cameras.

"We all saw Officer Denny remove it from your pack." Another officer went behind me, shoving me forward over my bike, yanking my hands behind my back and cuffing me.

Dirty cop pricks.

"I was out for a casual ride on my bike," I growled as he jerked me to a standing position. "I'm innocent of these charges and request to speak with a solicitor."

He confiscated my cell phone and searched me. The knot in my stomach twisted to the point of pain. Fuck, I was helpless and had no way to warn the others that they were headed into an ambush with the cops behind it.

"Get in the fucking car." The cop shoved me forward, making me walk to his vehicle, pushing my head down, and forcing me inside the backseat.

The cops took me back to the Chifley Police Station in Bathurst and locked me up. A short trip to county lock-up, fifteen minutes. Still, it was more than enough time for me to replay the events that led to fingerprints and a photo session with Bathurst's finest.

"Can you get one from the left? It's my good side." I held the intake card in front of my chest with one hand and gave them the finger with the other.

After processing, the two officers marched me down the hall to where a telephone hung on the wall.

"Make your call," one of the officers grunted at me.

I used my only call on Slade, and it went straight to voicemail. Not a good sign. The harsh beep at the end made my blood ice over.

Still, I left a message just in case. "Slade, Amber's sick. Can you pick her up from school?" Code for an ambush.

The knot in my gut hardened into a sharp rock, and its jagged edges pierced my intestines and organs. I tried to convince myself that my president didn't answer because it was an unknown number, not because they were in trouble. But I knew better. Slade would have picked up because I went missing. No one got left behind. A first for everything.

At the end of my call, the officers dragged me to a holding cell where I waited to see a solicitor or get questioned. Detained and isolated from other prisoners, I waited hours without a word, and certainly no lawyer. Fuckers made me sweat.

Eventually, two more cops came for me and dragged me into an interview room. A cold, gray square with a table, two chairs, and a window behind me.

A detective came into the room. Marcus, the greedy prick Castor met with the other day who hit him up for more money. The one who's entire conversation I overheard, thanks to my hawk-like hearing. He carried a stack of manila folders with papers inside. His chair creaked under his weight as he slumped into it.

Another cop came in to deliver two paper cups of water. I didn't accept them. If the cops had speed on them, who knew what they might have laced the water with.

Marcus set his phone on the table face up, activating the recording function. "Chiefly Police Station interview with Alaric Hawke at 10:20AM on Friday the thirteenth of June, 2021." He paused, his ugly brown eyes flicking to me. Smug and traitorous. He'd given Castor the opportunity to pay him more. Castor's blow-off made this prick flip us. "Do you understand why you're here, Mr. Hawke?"

"Nope." My cuffs jangled as I set my hands on the table. I went for casual with a hint of fucking menacing to show this prick what he'd get for crossing us. Dead, lying face down in the grass somewhere once I got out of this joint.

Marcus went with the ruse and flicked open his top folder. "Illegal possession of narcotics."

I rubbed at the dark ink on my thumb. "What drugs?"

Marcus read from the statement prepared, probably by one of the arresting cops who planted them on me. "Methamphetamine."

The Jackals didn't deal in that heavy shit. We hadn't for three years since Slade's buddy had overdosed. This was a set-up.

"Those drugs were planted on me." I leaned back in my chair. "The search was illegal. No warrant. And I wasn't read my rights."

Outcome: I should have been back out within an hour or two from whenever I was booked. But I hadn't called a fucking solicitor. I hoped Slade and the rest of the crew hadn't been booked and thrown into cells like this.

Another paper turned, and Marcus read from it as if recounting a damn script. "We arrested Jake Martin last night on suspicion of transporting a shipment of narcotics."

Fuck, that was the name of our fall guy. We'd hired him to distract the police when we moved our shipment out this morning. But he knew none of the details about what, where or when. We'd planted some shit on him for the cops to have an excuse to arrest him.

Marcus skipped to more paperwork, and I scanned it. Arrest warrant for Jake Martin. Fuck, they'd set us up. "Mr. Martin said he worked for your club."

Sweat broke out of my brow. I didn't know how we'd get out of this one. "We have no affiliation with him."

"What's the route of your shipment?" Marcus took out a stick of Wrigley's gum and started to chew it. "Where's the map?"

I laughed at the crooked ass cop. "We don't use maps." I memorized everything in case of moments like this. No paper trail to pin to us. I focused on the long game—getting the fuck out of here on bail.

The cops were on the take from someone. All signs pointed to a set-up, and I had a pretty good idea who was responsible. City government officials, perhaps. Another club … all fingers pointing to the Wolves. Unfortunately for me, it wasn't us the police worked for anymore. I knew every dirty cop we ran. There wasn't a familiar face among them when I got printed, my mugshot taken and thrown into a cell.

Another suspect worked into my head during a moment of clarity in the back of the patrol car that brought me in. Alexa. It explained why I couldn't turn up anything on her. Why I'd walked in on her making a secretive phone call in Zethan's office. She'd been privy to my office, my maps, and she knew the date we were leaving. Maybe she worked for the cops. Castor searched for her but found nothing. The cops must have covered her tracks and erased any record of her. With the circumstances we found her in, it never crossed my mind that she could be an informant. And it should have.

If she was a mole, she'd played us like a well-tuned piano, and the betrayal stung more than I expected. Our mate wasn't supposed to deceive us. I'd felt the spark of attraction, the push and pull of our mates. After I caught her making the call, she'd given me a valid excuse, and I'd accepted it. The woman knew how to hold her ground and stick to her story. Smart, strong and had a stubborn streak a mile wide. She was more than just a pretty face and possibilities.

Yeah, like a fucking cunning traitor.

It fucking figured with the curse in play. Except this time, instead of us destroying Isis, Alexa was sent to destroy us. Payback was a bitch. And I brought her home like a stray kitten. If something happened to Slade or the others, I'd never forgive myself. Never leave a man down.

I needed a stiff drink or ten. Hell, an entire fifth sounded more like it, but the bartender was off duty. The only thing on tap in that shithole they called a holding cell was the water in the paper cup in front of me. Like a deep well that I wanted to fall into.

My throat locked up, and my chest tightened. Cold seeped into my body. It worked its way from the tips of my fingers and toes straight down into my bones. Everything felt numb except for my lungs, which burned like I'd been breathing hellfire instead of oxygen. Darkness crept into my peripherals as the anxiety attack took hold.

The demons who made a home inside my head after the war reveled in the horror-filled highlight reel from my time as a POW. The memories of my torture were peppered with images of Alexa and that fucking kiss. My subconscious earned itself an A for effort. Sweat beaded my brow and soaked through my shirt. I was losing ground. My demons were winning. I gripped the edge of the table to anchor myself in reality before I sank even further into the anxiety attack.

I swiped at the paper cup of water Marcus had set down for me. My throat worked hard as I gulped the water down. Slade and the others couldn't afford to follow me down another PTSD-induced spiral of depression. The best way to start was to help myself, and that started with getting my head screwed on straight. If I could manage it.

CHAPTER 31

Aaliyah

THIS WAS MY ONLY CHANCE. With the Jackals gone on a shipment run, I snuck past Brix as he went for a piss break. Armed with my cell phone, handbag, and keys to Zethan's van, I hightailed it without a goodbye to the girls. I didn't want them snitching on me. Phase one of my plan to sneak out was well underway.

Sliding into Zethan's van, I asked all the gods within earshot of my prayers for a miracle and a quiet exhaust. It had been years since I drove a stick shift. There was nothing stealthy about grinding gears or a glass pack muffler. All the bikers I knew liked their vehicles souped-up and loud. I hoped the Jackals were the exception.

It seemed the gods were on my side. The van was automatic, quiet as a mouse, and handled like a dream. I got the vehicle out of the drive before Brix ran out after me. He couldn't leave the women. Not when other club members were sick or tied up with other business.

I overheard Alaric tell Castor they were leaving at 8AM. That gave them a one-hour lead time as I snuck off to Sydney an hour later. Hopefully, I could return Zethan's van somehow. Get it trucked back to Bathurst. I sure as hell wasn't driving it back myself. Slade and Castor made it clear they didn't want me to leave, and a trip back might trap me here indefinitely.

When I approached the Great Western Highway, I debated visiting my mother to let her know I was alive or delivering intel to my brother. I hadn't found a shred of real evidence that connected Slade to my father's murder that couldn't be explained away by a well-paid defense lawyer. Like a cigarette butt. All evidence suggested they were somewhat good guys.

Whatever information the authorities had on Slade, the Jackals weren't dumb enough to hide it in the shelter or the club. There may have been something on Zethan's laptop, but as expected, it was password protected. If I wanted dirt on the Jackals, I wouldn't get it by ransacking their office. I'd have to join the club as Slade offered. Become one of them and learn their secrets. A dangerous game that could get me killed. A game I didn't intend to play, so, bad luck to Danny, because I wasn't getting anything else on them.

Plus, I'd already spent a week away from home. How the fuck would I explain this to Barb? I'd be lucky to keep my damn job after this.

I made the trip to my mother's house in record time. She and dad lived in an upmarket place in Vaucluse, right on the water, bought with money earned through the club.

The only sign of her presence at home was her car parked in the private driveway beyond the spiral iron gate. I jammed my finger on the security system button, jerking my knee and biting my lip as I waited.

"Aaliyah, is that you?" my mom's voice returned moments later. "Where have you been? What happened?" She bombarded me with questions as the gate buzzed and rolled back, allowing me entrance into the property. As the wife of the ex-president of the Savage Wolves MC, she had security up the wazoo.

Tucked beyond the gate sat neat gardens, surrounding a sandstone block home that covered two storeys, with large, bay windows.

Mom came outside, dressed in a silky nightgown and pink, fluffy slippers. Something she would never be caught dead in outside the comfort of her home. Immaculate and ever the glamor-puss, mom always wore her hair styled, makeup pressed on, nails done, body packed into something tight and sexy with pumps that made me wince looking at the height on them. Since my father's death, she kept odd hours, beleaguered by insomnia and a crippling case of anxiety. Despite my protests, she refused to take the medication her doctor prescribed. From her disheveled appearance and dark circles under her eyes, I knew she needed a dose of the medicine only I could provide. It worked for a day or two but not any longer than that, and I couldn't afford the trips down to see her.

On the nights I stayed with her after the funeral, I camouflaged my gift of healing with honey and chamomile tea. Something I couldn't do every day with my weird hours and when I worked and lived over an hour away.

"I'm okay, Mom," I said with a sigh of regret.

She ushered me into the house. "You look like hell. Come inside."

If only she knew how bad I looked a week ago. Thanks to the godly power within me, most of the bruises had faded, except for the stubborn ones below my shirt and jeans. Mom would have a fit if she saw those.

Inside the foyer, I slipped off my work sneakers on the parquet floors. The stately home featured soaring, ornate ceilings, and Hermes wallpaper. My mom had expensive taste, and dad could afford to shell out for it.

I threw Zethan's van keys in the candy dish on the large, round table in the foyer and sniffed at the dark blue irises mom displayed in the vase. The keys hit a pack of cigarettes. *Winfield Blues*. Dad always smoked *Marlboro*. When their old men died, the wives were forced to marry someone in the club and didn't get a say who. The idea that she already saw someone stung deeply.

"Mom, whose are those?" I pointed at the candy dish.

"Hmm?" She glanced back. "Oh, your brother left those here when he brought me home after the funeral."

I should have been relieved that she hadn't moved on from dad. But something about the cigarettes made me stiffen when she said they belonged to Danny. He'd always been a *Champion* man. Fitting. Small dick energy and similar sized ego, my brother needed a brand to make him feel more like a man. Maybe he borrowed the packet from one of the other club members. Doubted it, though. They all smoked *Marlboro* like my dad, or *Peter Jackson*.

Murmurs from the TV in the living room called us down the hall, into the open-plan chef's kitchen and family room.

"Want a cup of tea?" My mom was already at the cupboard, collecting her Royal Doulton china cups and throwing teabags and sugar in them.

"Sure." I leaned on the marble island kitchen counter next to the butler pantry. This place was spacious compared to my squishy little box of an apartment. But I didn't want to take any money from my dad. Blood money. Dirty money.

"Mom, come sit down. Let me finish that." I steered her to the island counter and pulled out her chair.

"What's going on, Aaliyah?" The worry lines around her eyes deepened with her furrowed brow. After everything she'd been through, I hated that I was yet another reason she wore that expression. "I've been worried sick. Left ten messages. Why didn't you call me back? Did something happen?"

"I'm okay. I promise." A white lie to soften the truth.

"Aaliyah." The disappointment in her voice broke my heart. "Why would you lie to me? From Danny, yes. I expect it, but not you."

"I need to talk with you, but I don't want you to worry. Okay?" Unless the Jackals discover the truth about me. I doubted even a mated bond would save me then.

My mother dramatically pressed a hand to her chest as only Amanda Heller could do. "Aaliyah, please, I don't need any more bombs dropped on me, okay?"

It was stupid of me to show up unannounced in the middle of the day to unburden myself when she had enough problems of her own. My mother had been my rock, the one person I could count on for support. In my entire life, I'd only kept one secret from her—being an avatar. Now, it was the one thing I needed her advice on the most. The idea of being fated to four men I barely knew and suspected of destroying my family, terrified me. How the hell did I raise that with her? It might send her to an early grave, too.

I finished pouring hot water into the tea and handed my mom hers, and she led me outside to the Alfresco entertainment area, to sit on the sun chairs. Her sunbathed terrace overlooked the sweeping views of the water below. They'd bought the place before Sydney's real estate prices shot up to ridiculous and exorbitant amounts.

Reclined into the chair, I sipped at my tea, desperately

wanting her to tell me everything would be all right. That I wasn't crazy for letting doubt creep into my mind after watching the Jackals care for and protect the women and children at the safe house. That Slade had an alibi, and one of the women who worked at the safehouse vouched for him the night of my father's death. That I hadn't made a mistake when I decided to infiltrate the Jackals.

God, where did I start?

The conversation about being an avatar was one for another night. Bound to four other men through a mate bond, fated to be their woman, the growing physical attraction between us. Shame burned my cheeks. I slept with the damn Jackal's President for fuck's sake. Something I could barely admit to myself, let alone my mother. What would she think? She'd disown me and never want to see me ever again.

I jiggled my tea bag, which I kept in my cup because I liked it strong. "I'm sorry I didn't call, Mom. I … I was with the Jackals."

My mom's caramel face paled. "What does that mean, Aaliyah? With the Jackals?" She slapped her hand against her seat. "Stop dancing around the truth, right now, and tell me what is going on."

There was no chance of denying it at this point. "Danny came to see me at the hospital and asked for my help again in getting more evidence against Slade Vincent and the Jackals and I…"

"Is that what the two of you were arguing about after the funeral?" She knew the answer. I could see it in her eyes.

"Yes. Initially, I said no." I held up my hand to stave off her questions. "It's a lot, Mom. Just let me get through all of it, and then you can ask me anything you want."

She nodded and sipped her tea while I explained how I ended up in the thick of a rival gang.

"I never planned on playing detective or spying on them

for Danny." I took a sip of my tea to coat my dried throat. "I turned him down at the funeral and when he visited me at the hospital."

Mom rubbed her forehead. "He went to your work? Your father would have his hide if he were still alive. Bless his soul." Sadness crept into her voice, and it broke my heart.

She and dad had been high school sweethearts. He never looked at another woman in her presence, but I'd been privy to his hard partying behind her back. His fair share of women when he went away on business rides.

I nodded gravely. "Slade came into the ER with a stab wound, and I patched him up. A junkie attempted to rob me in my work parking garage two nights later, and the Jackals rescued me. They took me to their safehouse where they help battered women and children." I paused to catch my breath and give her time to answer.

"Safehouse?" My mother's perfectly manicured brows pinched.

"Yeah, who would have thought?" I smiled, remembering how they helped Francesca rent a new house in Western Australia to get far, far away from her abusive ex. Fuck. Why was I smiling thinking about them?

"Why didn't you leave and call a cab, Aaliyah?" My mother's scolding tone made me bristle. "Thank God you got away." She believed what the cops believed: Slade or another member of the Jackals killed my dad. Seeing firsthand how they operated, I had my doubts.

"You're not going back, are you?" My mom's tone pitched. "To infiltrate them for Danny? Oh, God, Aaliyah, you're not an undercover cop, and you're nothing like Danny or your father. I thank God for that every day." My mother's shaking hands set aside her tea on her glass garden table. "The police think the Jackals are responsible for your father's death.

What do you suppose they'll do to you if they find out you're working with your brother?"

Many years ago, I'd tried to be just like my dad.

Mom continued her rant, "What about your nursing career? Are you just going to throw that all away? You help people, Aaliyah, you don't destroy them with addiction or weapons."

Shocked, I slumped in my chair. I'd never heard my mother speak like this before. I always thought she accepted this life. The money and perks it gave her. She never had to work a day and got all the time in the world to raise Danny and me.

Suddenly my tea tasted bitter and strong. I set the cup aside on the table between us. "What does that mean, Mom?" I clasped her hand.

"Stay away from the Jackals and the Wolves." She pulled her hands free of mine. "And that goes for your brother, too."

"Why? What has he done?" My back went rigid as I sat forward, knowing I wouldn't like the answer.

Mom massaged her forehead. "Your father would be rolling in his grave if he knew what his son was up to. The Wolves don't help women like your new *friends* do." She laced the word friends with a little venom.

I felt sick to the stomach. "Did Danny hurt someone?" She left me more confused than I was when I showed up on her doorstep.

"Your brother and I have hardly spoken since the funeral." She pulled her robe tighter over her chest. "He made a decision for the club that the senior members and I do not agree with." She wiped a stray tear from her eyes. "I overlooked a lot of things your father did … the guns, the drugs, the other women, because I loved that man. What Danny is doing is a line even your father wouldn't cross as a father and a husband."

Oh, God. No wonder Danny pushed the issue of the Jackals. Something told me he wanted to start a war between the clubs. My infiltration was his excuse to set that keg bomb alight and sink the Jackals' ship.

Mom gripped my hands again, pulling back some of the strength I'd borrowed from her to tell her my story. "Your brother has gotten himself involved in dark business dealings and he's dragging the club down with him."

"What? How?" Sick to the stomach, I scooted my chair closer to my mother and pulled her into a hug. She was, by far, the strongest woman I knew. Supported everything dad did.

"Before your father died, Danny tried to convince him to expand the club into prostitution and pornography to make more money." Mom closed her eyes and took a deep breath. "Your father was a good man. He wouldn't sanction it. He wouldn't build up the club by forcing a woman onto her back."

Shock thread through every cell in my body, numbing it. The Wolves weren't known for their charity, but my father and the people who rode with him lived by a code. No women, no kids. Danny made a conscious decision to break that code. Exploitation of women was horrendous. Outraged that my brother would sink so low, I squeezed my mom tighter.

"They fought about it for months." Tears flowed in rivers down her cheeks. "Danny threatened to break away and start his own branch of the Wolves."

Shushing her, I brushed her hair. How long had she bore this burden?

Mom dabbed at her cheeks with the tie of her nightgown. "Aaliyah, what am I going to do with him? He doesn't listen to me anymore."

Doubt crept into my mind, and I began to scrutinize

recent conversations with my brother. The real reason behind his interest in the Jackals' comings and goings, the when and where of their shipments. This wasn't about justice or avenging our father. Danny's *so-called* justice was nothing more than another business opportunity. Expansion of the Wolves' territory.

The more I thought about it, the more I questioned other things, too. The evidence against Slade with the cigarette and alibis. Slade told me he quit smoking a while back but had picked up again with recent stresses in the last few months. The woman at the shelter swore black and blue that Slade had been there the night of my father's murder. Fast forward to the day of my attack in the parking lot. What were the odds that mere hours after Danny threatened me and swore off the Wolves protection that I ended up assaulted in the parking garage at work? Suddenly I had the sinking feeling that my brother had something to do with my father's murder.

The cigarettes in my mom's candy dish triggered something in my memory, and if I was right about my suspicions, things were about to get worse for what remained of the Heller family.

Fuck. Had I infiltrated the wrong club? As if answering my question, the queasiness in my stomach heightened. Something wasn't right with all this.

My brother had always been a loose cannon. Tight leashes always worked best for dad to bridle Danny. Unrestrained, he would go wild and feral, like a wolf rejected from its pack. Sending someone to rough me up would be the exact kind of thing he would do. Manipulation, pure and simple. Did he know the Jackals were watching me? It had to be more than a coincidence that they were there to rescue me. Absently, I scratched at my forehead, wondering if it was a fluke. Had it been a chance meeting with Slade two nights earlier? Or were the Jackals somehow tied into this? God, did they owe my brother a favor?

Pity my brother didn't know me as well as he thought he did. I wasn't the same insecure girl who dropped out of the Wolves and went off to college, uncertain if she could make it without her family's money or protection. This past seven years, I'd made something of myself on my own terms. I'd also caught the eye of a goddess and become her vessel. Now, it was high time I acted like an avatar. I had to return to the Jackals and find out what was going on. Tell them who I really was. Ask the hard questions about my father. Warn them in case my brother tried to start shit with them.

War with the Jackals would wipe out the Wolves, and as much as I'd run from them, I'd grown up with a lot of senior members, and they were like family to me. My dad's best friend, Jerry, was my godfather and I called him my uncle. Rev, the club's pastor, was like a father to me.

"Mom, I've got to go." I rubbed at her shoulder.

"Where, honey? Will you be back?" She picked up both the teacups and rose to stand with me.

Dark suspicions crawled around my brain. I couldn't share those misgivings with her when she wasn't ready for the whole gods and fated mate's conversation. Any more than she'd be ready to hear what I alleged her son had been up to. Deep in my heart, I knew that Danny set in motion some dark, sinister plans that likely led to my father's untimely death. The only ones who could answer that were him or the Jackals. I'd not risk my brother going nuts and hurting me if I accused him of that. If he'd arranged for the junkie to attack me, imagine what he'd do to me.

Trust had been broken between Danny and me the day he threatened to remove my protection. As much as I hated to admit it, I was beginning to think I trusted my enemy more than I did my own flesh and blood. Dark days were coming.

"Bye, Mom." I kissed her on the cheek and left her in the Alfresco area.

Outside in the van, the engine rumbled as I turned it over. Everything hit me, and I rubbed at my cheeks, trying to get a handle on everything. The gate rolled closed, and my mother waved from the fence. I waved back at her. Leaning back in the seat, I did the only thing I could do for her and pushed a little energy her way to ease her troubled heart and mind so she could rest.

As I shifted the stick into gear and hit the gas, an arm came around my throat, squeezing me in the crook of an elbow. The sharp bite of a needle hit my flesh, and a burning liquid injected into it. I was out in seconds. Gone. Kidnapped again.

CHAPTER 32

Castor

I KNEW something was wrong the minute Alaric radioed back to us. At the next exit, we turned off, re-routing, and I assumed the lead. Fumbling, I called up my database of knowledge, filtering through the maps, new routes, ones I hadn't studied and memorized.

Alaric had gone AWOL, which was very unlike him. The man followed orders to the letter, no matter how difficult or uncomfortable. In the two years I knew him, he'd never let the club down. Either he bailed, or he'd been intercepted. I sifted through the trail of data available through my god's channels. Emails, text messages, records of phone calls, reports, and other documents. If the cops had gotten Alaric, they kept it off the books. I was blind, and I gripped my hand grips tighter. I never went blind.

Slade had ordered Kill Bill to leave the club, scout out the route, and check Alaric's position. In my rearview mirror, I caught my president taking a call while on his bike. Electricity zapped over his knuckles as he hung up. I braced for bad news.

A call over the radio came through a few seconds later. "Kill Bill found his bike. The cops have got him."

Fuck, he must have been losing his cool if the code fell away. We were high and dry without our eyes in the sky. Blind, just like I was. Without Alaric, he couldn't shift into his hawk and scan for danger or scan the road ahead and behind. It felt like we rode into a trap, one we couldn't escape from, and my back and legs ached from tensing.

I lifted the radio to my mouth. "What do you want to do?"

"Stick to the plan," came the answer, sharp and severe.

Slade wasn't letting one setback ruin this shipment. But he took a major risk by continuing. At any moment, the highway patrol could come after us and arrest us for transporting narcotics. The lawyer in me screamed to call an end to this and turn back and go to the club. Find another way to get the delivery to Sydney.

I kept a handle on the radio and sent him a second message. "That's risky, Prez. I advise against it."

"Stick to the fucking plan." The bite in Slade's words told me he'd not be convinced otherwise. He put us all at risk, including himself. If we were caught, it'd be up to Zethan to assume leadership.

Fine. Soldier on. We kept on riding, and my brain sorted through the maps and images, winding us through tight, patchy roads with potholes and sharp, dangerous corners, getting us further from the police.

"Are you trying to kill us?" Kappy, the truck driver, radioed through to us.

"Sorry," I buzzed him back. "We had interference and had to reroute."

"The truck isn't made for these roads," Kappy snapped. "Get us back where there's pavement."

Asshole. Shut the fuck up and drive. I kept navigating us through the back roads to Sydney, where we spat out somewhere north of our target. Easy. I'd get us home. Half an hour later, I pulled the crew up a quarter of a mile out from our destination. I killed the engine to avoid being detected. No point tearing into there when the cops might be lying in wait.

I dialed Reg, our warehouse contact, and he picked up in three rings. "Yeah."

"Got a delivery ready," I told the man responsible for distributing our product across Sydney. "Party shit. Can you take it?"

"Yeah, yeah, sure. We're waiting." Reg's voice sounded strained and tight, like he had the barrel of a gun tipped at it.

I hung up and turned to shake my head at Slade, who sat on his bike beside me.

"Fuck. Cops?" Red hives broke out on his neck and chest beneath his sweatshirt with the arms cut off.

I scanned all my channels finding nothing. "If it's them, I can't find anything. Radio silence. No paperwork trail."

Color drained from Slade's eyes as he stared into mine. "Do you think they know what we are?"

"Impossible," I replied.

He whistled and yelled, "Jaxx, get your ass over here."

Jaxx clomped up to Slade's bike. "Yeah, Prez?"

"Scout the place out." Slade pointed down the road. "Castor doesn't have a good feeling."

"You got it." Jaxx removed his cut and gun, giving the first to Slade and stuffing the second in the back of his jeans. His boots rapped on the pavement as he departed.

Leather crackled as I crunched my riding gloves. My

stomach didn't let up the whole twenty minutes he was gone. Alaric's disappearance made me fear for the worst.

Jaxx returned with wary eyes and a short smile. "Looks good to me. I checked every car and van. No cops."

"What about the warehouse?" Slade growled impatiently.

"Operation as usual." Jaxx squinted into the sun. "Forklifts are transporting crates of product onto shelves and loading trucks.

Slade dismissed him, and Jaxx returned to his bike at the back of the truck.

My president's narrowed eyes shot to me. "What do you think, Bird Boy?"

My hands fisted. Fuck, enough with the Bird Boy shit. If it weren't for me, we never would have gotten here. "Something feels off."

Electricity crackled over Slade's knuckles again. "I feel it too." He glanced up at the sky. "Where the fuck's Alaric when I need his eyes?"

"He's gone dark." We stayed off the topic in case the feds listened in on our phones.

"Let's pay Reg a visit before we party." Slade got off his bike and moved to the rear to give the orders to Slim, Rusty, and Jaxx to guard the shipment while we went in to investigate closer.

Slade and I moved in unison, entering the warehouse's driveway, avoiding the front reception entrance. Diesel fumes spat out of the forklifts rolling around. Truck engines purred as the drivers waited to leave with deliveries. Reg ran a small freight company in the east district of Sydney. Relations with the club went back fifteen years, to when Slade's father steered the ship.

"Where's Reg?" Slade grunted at one of the workers dressed in a bright yellow safety vest, directing employees where to relocate crates.

"Inside, I think," he called out, refusing to stop, heading away from us.

At Slade's irritated twitch of his head, we entered through the side roller door, going in the back way. Edgy, he scanned the office complex with jerky motions. With Alaric missing, he didn't appear to be in the mood for more bullshit going down.

Alert, I went into the next room to question the receptionist, preferring to know if we walked into trouble. A room full of cops trouble. "Is Reg in?"

She took one look at my cut and bowed her head. "Out … out back." Her hands shook as she pretended to type something. Something was up.

My jacket crackled as I leaned an elbow on the raised shelf of her desk. "Everything okay, sweetheart?"

Her gaze shot up. Fear exploded in her eyes. Her mouth parted but no words came out. Her attention flicked behind me as someone moved.

Fuck. I went to unclip my pistol when another clicked.

"Drop your weapon and hands up." A voice thick with disdain.

I lifted one palm and cleared my holster of the gun, setting it on the desk. The receptionist squeaked and dived under her desk. Slowly, I turned, expecting to face the cops. Shock jolted through my body. Someone else entirely stood behind me, shotgun aimed at my chest. Red and blue patch with a howling wolf.

The Savage Wolves. Just as I suspected.

Before Danny took over, old man Heller and Slade had an agreement in place. Mutual respect over territory. Danny had broken that pact. Time for payback.

Our rival jerked his gun. "This way."

Fuck. Danny Heller was here and waiting for us, ready to put a bullet in our brain and steal our shipment. Where the fuck was Slade? I shouldn't have separated from him. I made the mistake every criminal I prosecuted made.

Guided by the gun at my back, I moved into the adjacent hallway. Another Wolf lay in wait, lunging out from a dark corner where he'd been waiting to ambush us. Slade came up behind him, putting a bullet in his brain. Blood spattered my face and chest. Slade's gun lifted and aimed behind me, taking out the fucker hiding behind the receptionist's desk. The frightened girl behind screamed and ran out the front door.

"Fuck. Heller and his men would have heard that," I snapped.

"Too late," Slade grunted.

When the next Wolf came my way, I grabbed him, putting him in a rear choke hold and cutting off his air supply. The prick dropped to the floor once he passed out. Guns went off and bullets sprayed the walls. Flicks of plaster and wood went everywhere. Two Jackals against a bunch of Wolves.

Slade paused by the wall to listen for movement in the next rooms.

My brothers in arms, my family, and their survival was the mission. That meant destroying anything that threatened us. I was tempted to summon Zethan to deal with them. Deploy his death breath and drag these fuckers to the Underworld for burial. Deal with these Wolf pricks once and for all. They'd interfered for the last time.

"Osiris!" I called out to Zethan's god. "Who goes and who stays?" If anyone could answer who was destined for death, it was the King of the Underworld. The summons brought Zethan into the room in a flicker of golden light. When death called, he used his magical gifts to cross time and space.

He paused to assess the situation. "I think you already know the answer to that."

"Duck!" Slade shouted, all too happy to launch a blade in the direction of someone attempting to sneak up behind me.

The guy gurgled and dropped to the floor.

Golden light swirled around his body as Zethan collected him and transported him to his ultimate resting place. Sayonara, dead little wolf.

More Wolves approached from all angles. One down the hall, one behind us, and one from out of the room. Slade looked down the wrong end of three guns. Chest rumbling with rage, he fired a shot at the guy trying to take him out from the left. Bullets kicked up from all around. Electricity snapped all over Slade's body as he called on his magic and drew the lightning to him. Air around us charged with static electricity, cracking to life in a violent display of light. Metal bullet casings fried to dust as they hit his electrical shield.

Fuck. We never used our powers in front of mortals unless we had no other choice.

Slade moved faster than any human. Pumped full of chaos, he grabbed the nearest Wolf by the collar and belt, hoisting him over his head. With a roar, he tossed him as far as he could. The dude's body speared through a damn wall in an impressive feat. Shards of glass rained down as the overhead lights exploded in their fixtures. Tendrils of smoke snaked out of the air vents and across the room. Slade's avatar, Set, was in agreement with the King of the Underworld. He wanted to put an end to the war once and for all.

Zethan's figure flicked in and out in bursts of gold, his tether to this location weak.

"What's wrong?" I grabbed him by the arm, futilely trying to anchor him here with us. With only the three of us, we needed him.

"Aw, fuck." He gritted his teeth. "I'm being summoned. Something's wrong." In the blink of an eye, he vanished, transported to where the magic took him.

There was no resisting the call of the Underworld magic. Our Vice President conducted Underworld business at night. Something significant must have gone down for him to be called in the middle of the day.

"Where the fuck's he gone?" Slade roared over the gunfire, pinging metal and the whip of bullets biting the wall and concrete.

I pressed up to the wall he used for cover. "He got summoned by the Underworld."

"Fuck." Slade let off a ball of fire that took out one wall, collapsing on several men crouched behind it. Water poured down from the sprinkler system. Fire alarms whooped to alert the workers and the fire department. If he wasn't careful, he'd take us out with them. Fuck, the cops and firefighters would be here soon. We had to end this and get out of here before then.

Worried, I slammed a hand on my president's shoulder. "Slade, rein it in," I shouted over the rush of water.

Slade struggled to bring Set under control, trembling from all the destructive energy flooding his veins. I knew that face. The labored breaths. Flaring nostrils. Tombstones in his fucking eyes. He wanted to unleash more, destroy Danny fucking Heller and the Wolves for their ambush.

The gunfire died down to nothing, and I glanced at Slade. My president's attention snapped to the closest door. So did mine as my hearing picked up the approach of someone. They passed through the damn doorway as if they were God and unafraid of the power my president just unleashed.

The patches on the back of his cut caught my attention. President.

Danny Heller. Prime suspect behind the drug heist and the source of all our problems. He wanted us dead. The feeling was mutual.

Danny clutched someone by the neck. A woman with

long, dark hair and glowing caramel skin. Drugged and barely able to stand.

Breath froze in my chest.

"Nurse A.?" Slade whispered.

He burned with equal passion and destruction, both at odds with each other. By saying her name like that, shocked and terrified he'd lose her, he just signed her death warrant.

CHAPTER 33

*A*aliyah

"WHAT THE FUG'S GOING ON?" I gurgled, my voice thick, tongue even thicker. Shit, I sounded like a patient waking up from surgery.

A heavy weight dragged my mind into the depths of the ocean, and I struggled to think clearly. My muscles refused to cooperate. Haze blanketed my vision, and I blinked, trying to clear it and make out the blurred shapes in front of me. Water dripped down on me, wetting my clothes, and I shivered. Someone held me by the neck, his grip tightening.

"Don't move, Nurse A.," a dark and rough voice warned me. Familiar. Sexy. Dominant. I knew that voice. Where did I know that voice? I searched through the pea soup that was my brain. Vincent someone. No. The name started with S. "I'm gonna get you out of this, okay."

Slade. The name snapped me to more alertness. I blinked

back the fog in my vision. Two men stood in front of me, dressed in denim and leather.

"Slade?" I stuttered. "Where am I? Did you kidnap me?" Fear snapped like cold fingers in my veins. The drug in my system dulled the effect and my movement, preventing me from getting away.

"Shut the fuck up!" The man holding me shook me, his sharp grip tightening to the point of pain. I yelped and jerked, prompting his hand to clamp harder on me, bruising me and making my neck ache.

"You let her go, Heller." Slade's warning held the promise of death.

My body went even number. *Heller?* What the fuck? Danny and the Wolves were rescuing me? A flash of a memory came back. Me in a van. Someone injecting me with a drug. Fuck, the Jackals had kidnapped me. They knew my secret. I didn't say a word, didn't identify my brother in front of them. Self-preservation was my top priority. Getting out of here, my second. Getting the drug out of my system, my third.

"Here's what's gonna happen." Danny pressed the cold butt of a gun to my temple and I moaned. Nope. Not a rescue. I was a hostage. "You hand over that shipment outside, and you get your whore back."

Whore? No. What the fuck was he talking about? The drug weighed my mind down and I couldn't think straight.

"Here's how it's gonna go down, Heller." Slade stepped forward. "You don't tell us to do shit. You declared war, and you're not leaving here alive."

Danny's cold laugh thundered through my body. The safety of his gun clicked. I whimpered as it dug into my temple. Why was he doing this?

Slade started to growl. Savage. Wild. Merciless.

Slowly the haze lifted, allowing me the realization that my brother used me in some sort of exchange.

Smoke filled the air, acrid and carrying the scent of burned hair and skin. Slade charged up his power. I felt his terrifying rage hurtle down the mate bond and braced for impact. The world crashed down around me, crumbling into bits of drywall, lumber, and insulation. Danny cried out and let me go as it smashed him on the head. Startled, I dropped to the floor, barely getting free of the wall falling on my brother. Water from the sprinklers doused everything, and I crawled on my hands and knees through soggy carpet, blood, and plaster dust.

"Alexa." Castor grabbed me and lifted me into his arms. The mate bond flexed with his concern at nearly losing me. In that moment, I knew the extent of how much these men truly wanted to care for and protect me. The power of it shook me, and I didn't fight him to let me go. I threw my arms around his neck to be closer to that complete devotion.

A gun went off, and my brother cried out. His body slumped to the ground with a heavy thud. Oh, God, Slade had shot him.

Gunfire returned at what I assumed was the Wolves' retaliation for their injured or dead president. Sirens wailed in the distance. The authorities were on their way. Both clubs had to admit defeat and get their men out of here before they were arrested for weapons possession and attempted murder. But neither showed any signs of slowing down. Fire roared, and I felt its heat lick at me as Slade's magic consumed everything in sight.

"Fuck," the Jackal's President cursed, and the raw sting of a bullet pinched down the mate bond. He'd been shot.

Isis opened up to me. "Heal him." She always told me those who were destined for the Underworld and those whose time hadn't come yet. That meant she called me to heal Slade's wound.

"Let me go." I fought Castor for freedom.

"A little help, Bird Boy," Slade growled. He was alive. Bleeding but okay. My relief rippled through our link.

"Wait here." A dark shell of magic encased me as Castor set me down behind a conference table and left to help Slade.

Bodies thudded on the ground, and men shrieked and gasped as bullets tore into them. I winced at each one, wondering how many lives were taken. Isis stayed silent. Adrenaline flushed more of the drug from my system and cleared my vision. Frightened, I crawled along the gray carpet, my muscles groaning with complaint and twitching as the drug eased its hold on me.

Bullets whizzed past me from both sides. Slade and Castor took cover behind a wall while the Wolves emptied their guns. When they reloaded, the Jackals sprayed them. Water from the sprinklers blanketed the dust before it made a cloud.

I came to a stop at the horror before me. Blood pooled around my brother's limp body. His breaths labored as he struggled to get air into his punctured lung. I saw the condition in my mind's eye. My gift always showed me where and how to heal it. I had to stop the bleeding and repair his lung tissue before he died. My troubles began with the death of a loved one, and they weren't going to end with the death of another. Not when I had the ability to prevent it. My mom wouldn't survive another death in her family.

"Danny," I sobbed into my hand.

I had to save him if I could. With Danny's head cradled in my lap, I swept the wet hair matted from his forehead. With one hand pressed against his neck to monitor his pulse and the other covering the ash in his scalp, I opened myself to Isis and used the magic she gave me to heal my brother. Wet carpet soaked through my jeans and carried away the blood dripping from my brother's chest in a red-tinted current. My eyes burned, my throat raw from the smoke-filled air as much as the raw sobs that racked my body.

To anyone else, I looked like a woman shaken from the violence happening around her, terrified for her safety as she clung to save an injured man. Not to Castor. My mate. I saw it in his eyes when I caught him staring at me. Wide, laden with confusion, shock, and horror. The mate bond tightened with his bewilderment. He slipped through my weakened defenses and rooted around my emotions along the link long enough to pick up on everything. My feelings for him, the rest of the Jackals and my family, but I broke the connection before he sensed how I planned to act on them.

Shit. He knew what I did. I healed my brother and sealed my fate in one desperate act. Saving my brother, a man who authorized my kidnapping, if not orchestrated this attack on the Jackals, a man I began to suspect was capable of far worse than the violence I just witnessed, wasn't going to win Castor over. Still, despite Danny's faults, and there were many, he was my brother. I loved him, and my mother would never survive losing him so soon after my father's death.

Ever since I arrived at the Jackal's shelter, I winged it, even when surrounded by a bunch of strangers who were my enemies, yet unknowingly claimed to be their mate. I wasn't given a choice then, and I hadn't been given one now. I had to obey the order of my goddess.

Castor had been suspicious of me almost from the beginning. He hid behind the excuse of my goddess' cunning prowess in tricking the god King, when all along it had been me that acted in cunning and self-defense. In that one moment, Castor's trust, or what little he offered, was broken and I doubted there was any way to mend it. His hurt at my deceit snapped the bond between us, breaking it forever, and I cried out at the pain ripping at my heart.

Realization dawned on me. This man was destined to be my mate no matter how much I fought it. It was the will of the gods, cursed or not. With our bond in ruins, I didn't know where we stood now or if there was any hope between us. And I didn't know why I cared when I was free. Confused by my feelings, I cradled my brother, pouring more magic into healing his wound.

Danny stirred in my arms, drawing my attention to him. "Aliyah?" His dazed eyes swept across his torso. "What happened?" He lifted his shirt, finding a pink scar where the bullet had entered him. Mouth parted, he traced it with a bloodied finger, tipping his gaze to me. "What did you do to me?"

"You weren't bound for the Underworld." That was all I'd tell him.

"You ... you ... healed me." His expression shifted from confusion to bewilderment, jumping straight into a cunning smile. "You're a Wolf after all."

I still hadn't forgotten that he'd called me the Jackal's whore. Or that someone, probably his men, drugged me and dragged me here. Just like I suspected they were responsible for the junkie who attacked me. The reason I was thrown into the den of vipers known as the Jackals.

Slade's thrashing anger traveled down the bond into me, setting my veins on fire, my chest alight. "Did you have me beaten, knowing the Jackals would collect me?"

"I did what I had to." He sneered and sat up.

"You bastard!" I slapped his face and pushed away from him.

It didn't matter what I was or what my purpose was. The only thing that mattered was what I could do for Danny Heller and his plans for the Wolves. My moral compass had never led me astray before, but this time following the order of my goddess had gone terribly wrong. Why had Isis ordered me to save him? My attention lifted to Slade clutching his bleeding arm and Castor limping on a gashed thigh. My insides iced over. Or had Isis meant them? My mates? Fuck, had I saved the wrong man?

Danny braced himself on my shoulder, pushed himself to his feet, and stumbled toward the Jackals. He'd worked it out. Two Jackals against dozens of Wolves. All of them still standing. Slade and Castor fighting at half strength after suffering a gunshot wound and stab in the leg. Danny knew they wouldn't hurt me. Not after he experienced what I could do. He knew that I was valuable to them. But they were more valuable to him dead. Gun drawn, Danny staggered forward, ready to end this.

No. I dug my nails into his calf, clawing at his denim clad leg. He lowered his gun and tried to shake me off, but I wasn't letting go. Fire scraped down my arms as he dragged across the floor covered with bits of broken glass. Blood trickled from my wounds down my arm and sides. I had to stop him. Biting back my pain, I grabbed a shard and jabbed him in his leg, just behind the knee, where it would slow him down and bring him crashing down.

Falling beside me, he howled. "You bitch!" He pistol-whipped me in the cheek and flung me back. "You want to stay here? With them? You chose them over your own family? You picked the wrong side, little sister."

Danny raised his gun and aimed it at me. Panic streamed down the mate bond, and Slade turned his attention on my brother. A bullet missed him and nicked the carpet.

"Traitorous whore!" Danny raised his gun and aimed at Slade. "See if you can heal this, bitch."

I leapt to my feet, praying to Isis for strength and speed as I crash-tackled my brother to the ground, hoping to dislodge the pistol from his grasp. Danny pulled the trigger, and the bullet penetrated my abdomen. Pain spread like wildfire as the shot made impact. I welcomed it. It was no more than I deserved for my role in what happened to the Jackals.

My brain kicked into high gear, throwing out medical statistics, triage tactics, and treatment plans, but all my medical training was useless. For the first time, I was helpless to save someone's life and it was my own.

"Looks like I evened the score. Nobody gets the lying traitorous whore." Danny laughed as he attempted to escape through the busted front door.

Slade roared and emptied three shells into my brother's back. Danny jerked with each hit. Somehow, he managed to stay upright as he hit the door and shoved it open. Justin, a younger prospect, waited outside and dragged my brother away.

"Nurse A." Slade cradled my head. "Baby." He stroked the side of my face with bloodied fingers. "No. Not again."

"Set, do something," Slade ground out.

I groaned as his magic inched the bullet out of me. "No. It'll cause more bleeding. Take me to a hospital, please."

Something told me I wouldn't last the ride over to the hospital. Danny's bullet got me right in the bowels. Perforation of this organ usually didn't end well. Contents from my gut would leak food into my blood, and I'd develop peritonitis and sepsis.

Gunfire ceased and a voice shouted for a ceasefire.

"Aaliyah?" Jerry said from some feet away. "Aaliyah, baby?"

"Her name's Alexa, asshole." Slade shoved my uncle away.

"Uncle Jerry?" I reached for him, wanting to hold his hand. If this was going to be my last moment, I wanted it to be with a man I loved as family.

"What are you talking about, Slade?" Jerry snapped. "Her name's Aaliyah Heller. Daughter of Alexander Heller."

Lightning sizzled on Slade's hands. I grabbed them to calm him down. The last thing I wanted was for him to kill Jerry. "Please, no."

"You're a Wolf?" Slade's incensed tone floated to the back of my mind, along with the stinging betrayal ringing down the mate bond.

Voices argued about me. Random words. Hospital. Safety. Flee. It all faded away.

I should have read the fine print when I became an avatar. My gifts weren't as powerful when it came to healing my injuries. I probably would have tackled Slade instead of taking a bullet for him, knowing the limitations of my magic. Probably. Actions spoke louder than words, though. Danny manipulated and used my father's death against me. Thrown me to certain death amid the camp of my enemy. Kidnapped me and used me as a pawn to try and distract the Jackals. Dirty mutt needed to be put down. I hoped Slade's bullets did their job. Because saving Slade was worth it. They all were. The Jackals were better men than Danny and what was left of the Wolves.

I begged Isis for help. She couldn't let me die with unfinished business or without telling the two men hovering over me that I was sorry. Men that I now believed were innocent of any wrongdoing. Black spots danced in the corners of my eyes, and my brother's words rang in my ears as I slipped into unconsciousness. I hoped I served you well goddess, because this was goodbye for me.

CHAPTER 34

*S*lade

FUCKING AALIYAH HELLER was our mate. Daughter of the dead Wolves president. Sister to that cunt Danny Heller who ambushed us and sabotaged our shipment of Pharaoh. Traitor. Deceitful. Wolf.

A wave of emotion sent me to my knees as I watched Doc Shriver do his work to remove the last bullet from my mate's gut in the surgery at his practice. Seeing her bleeding, skin paling, lips going blue, it tore me up inside. I relived Liz's death all over again. Torture, hell, and pain.

But as Doc Shriver stitched her stomach up, the torrent of wrath welled up again, and I clenched my fists, holding it back, preventing a damn explosion. Aaliyah lied to us. Faked her name. Come under false pretenses. Let her brother's goon beat her up so we'd collect her and take her under our fucking wing. The woman was a lying witch. Mate no longer. Enemy number one now that dumb fuck Danny declared war with the club. His sister nothing more to me than a fucking snake in the grass who slithered into my club to infiltrate us. Snakes were dealt with by cutting their fucking heads off!

If we weren't bound together, I would have left the bitch to die at the warehouse. Set had intervened on her behalf and ordered me to take her back to the club with us. Pissed as hell, I summoned Zethan to take the traitor to Doc Shriver for urgent surgery to remove the bullet wound. The doc was finishing up when Castor and I returned home five hours later. Fresh from finding Reg alive and safely storing our drug shipment at another warehouse deeper in town.

"I hate to say I told you—" Alaric started on me.

Set's powers fired up like a furnace ready to melt everything in sight.

"Then don't. Just fucking don't." I leveled Alaric with a menacing glare.

After my solicitor, Barry, got Alaric out on bail, my Road Captain told me everything. The phone call Aaliyah made, which he suspected was to the cops. Now we knew better. It was to her dog of a brother. Alaric admitted his mistake of showing her his maps at the club. Information we believed she'd passed onto the Wolves. Once I sorted out the other shit, I'd find him a fitting punishment. Fuck, what was he and Zethan thinking bringing her to the club? The four of us went mad over our mate and lost sight of everything that mattered.

Alaric leaned against the door frame with his arms crossed over his chest, examining the surgery through the window of Doc Shriver's practice. "So, what the fuck are we supposed to do with her now?"

"Throw her to the Wolves." I kicked my boot against the skirting board of the heritage house the doc called his practice.

You will keep her, Set boomed in my head, so loudly it quaked from my head to my feet, and I stumbled into the wall.

"Slade?" Alaric caught me by the elbow.

You will need her in the months to come, my god's voice lowered but still thundered, and I rocked from the impact. *For the war. For victory.*

I didn't want her anywhere near me, my club or the four men I called my closest brothers. Didn't want to suffer the constant ache in my heart of having her close, knowing she could never truly be my mate after what she did.

But the war between the Jackals and Wolves was coming. I'd pumped four bullets into Danny Heller's back. Time would tell if he made it out alive. Doubted it. Either way, the rest of the club would seek revenge for the death of another president. I was tired of this bullshit. The only one who deserved to die was Heller's son. Danny wanted our territory, our business, and our prized recipe. I'd die before he got his filthy fingers on what belonged to me. I was certain he was the one who pulled the trigger on his father and president. A traitor like his damn sister.

What about your mate? Set asked with a hint of amusement. This was a game to the god of Chaos and Mischief. The gods didn't care whether their servants lived or died so long as another was there to pick up the pieces.

Fuck my mate.

The sister of the Wolves' President held no leverage for us. Danny Heller made it clear how he felt about her. He used her as a pawn to infiltrate us and steal our goddamn product. Called her a traitorous whore because she saved my life. Hit her in the fucking face with his weapon. Shot her, for fuck's sake. The mate bond sent a violent rumble through my chest at his actions. The asshole was dead for more reasons than one.

Fuck, Slade, get your head in the game. She isn't your mate anymore. You don't do traitors. I palmed my tired eyes. God, I'd had my dick and gun in her. I wanted to wash all traces of her from my body and weapon.

"We're keeping her here," I ground out.

Alaric's hand snapped away from my elbow. "What?"

"Directive from upstairs, don't argue." I wasn't in the mood to fight this.

Despite the anger threatening to break free—the power wanting to destroy the world with all my pain, and the pain carried by my god—I couldn't shake the emotions I detected on the mate bond before she fell unconscious. Confusion mixed with hate and desire. Broken tethers to her family, and confliction over where her allegiance belonged.

I couldn't breathe, couldn't think. Fear crippled me, and I worried I'd lose her even after everything. The woman almost cost me my life. Yet, she'd acted on instinct to save me when her brother attempted to shoot me. Fuck me. I fell in love with her all over again at that moment. Despite my instincts and better judgment warning me to stay away, I didn't think I'd have the strength to. The look in her aqua eyes, the loss reflected in the depth of them, told me she'd miss me if she died. The woman sent me spiraling into an abyss of torment from my past.

"Slade?" Zethan's voice called me back from the brink of despair. "Doc Shriver said she'll recover fine."

Thank fuck, my love-sick Jackal said.

Fuck no, the dark recess of hell within me groaned. The side of me that wished she hadn't pulled through and had succumbed to the disloyal fate she deserved.

I scrubbed at my face. If she died, we'd be back to square one. The cycle of fated mates would start all over again. One mate dying had been hard enough. A second would destroy us. Maybe we were destined to be tortured like this over and over by the gods. A sick game of revenge. Fuck, I was pretty frigging tired of this shit.

All I could muster was a weak nod.

"When is she going to wake up and be able to talk?" Fucking Alaric already planned to grill her. So did I. We'd both find out her plans and what the Wolves next move was.

"Few hours." Zethan scratched his stubbled jaw.

Few hours, my ass. She wouldn't be up for talking for a day or two. Time we couldn't afford to lose with the threat hanging over us.

My wrath snaked around my chest, a sharp pronged lash wanting to strike him in the heart for leaving us at a crucial damn time. "Where the fuck did you go? Leaving us in the middle of a shit storm back there?"

Zethan came up to me and set a hand on my shoulder. Comfort bled into me, and my tense torso relaxed. "Sorry, brother. Fucking Colt got himself into some bullshit with Hades and I had to rescue his ass."

Hades? Coltan Raine worked hand in hand with Zethan as Anubis' avatar to oversee operations in the Underworld. By day, Colt ran the Egyptian mafia, an organization we'd cut ties with. Mistakes on both parts cost us big time. We'd narrowly avoided war with him, but had settled it, agreed to go our separate ways. Colt didn't want to go up against the four of us, not when he'd lose.

My hands trembled, reminding me I needed a hit of nicotine. I removed my rollie paper and rolled a cigarette. "What the hell is Colt doing messing around with the Greek pantheon?"

I lit up my smoke and sucked it down deep, lighting up as the warmth chased away the chill that had sunk into my body. A haze of smoke filled the small room outside the backyard operating theatre. The doc would go nuts if he caught me smoking in his place. Like I gave a shit, though.

"Who fucking knows?" Zethan scratched his head. "The Underworld power drew me there because Hades was destroying Colt's soul."

That shit was fucked up. "Can you do that?"

Zethan shrugged. "Never tried." He could do some pretty cool shit with his death breath, choke hold, and heart-attack-inducing blows. "I'll test it on Heller next time." His grim smile broke my heart into pieces all over again. My best friend suffered the most out of all of us, and I wanted to break that cycle, end his hell.

Zethan's gaze dropped to my bloodied, bandaged arm. "You gonna get the doc to look at that?"

"When he gets to it," I grunted, taking another draw of my cigarette and blowing out a thick plume.

My phone buzzed in my pocket, and I slipped it out to answer. "Yeah?"

Castor's voice funneled down the line. "Prez, you need to come down."

My Enforcer had taken three Wolves back to the clubhouse to interrogate them. Two wounded and bleeding out, and the man concerned over Aaliyah.

"Did they squeal?" I inhaled the smoke deep.

"Even better." Castor hung up, and I shoved my cell back into my pocket.

CHAPTER 35

Slade

"I'll be back," I told Alaric and Zethan. "Watch her." They both nodded.

A ten-minute trip took me to our clubhouse. The stairs to the basement creaked as I descended them. Blood, sweat, and fear saturated the air. Three men were bound to chairs. Two bloodied from gunshot wounds. The third had come willingly, more concerned for Aaliyah than himself. He identified himself as Jerry, Aaliyah's uncle and old man Heller's best friend. Castor hadn't laid a finger on him by the lack of blood or bruises.

I greeted Castor with a nod as he wiped blood from his hands onto a rag. "What did you call me down here for?"

Castor glanced over at Jerry and jutted up his chin. "Tell him what you told me, old man."

Jerry sighed. He was too old for this shit. About sixty, graying hair, dark brown eyes, and a face lined with many years of good and hard times. A burden too heavy to bear weighed his shoulders down. "This isn't how Alexander wanted things."

No shit. Heller and I had been on good terms before his death. Respect and cooperation went a long way with me. Someone iced the old man in the back and set me up for it. That someone I now believed was his dog of a son or his lying witch of a daughter.

"Fucking snitch!" the Wolf to his left shouted.

Castor moved to him like lightning, smashing him in the cheek. "Shut the fuck up!"

"Go on." I gave Jerry an irritated flick of my fingers.

"Alexander respected you as a leader," Jerry went on. "He never backed the shit Danny proposed. They argued about it for months before my president's death."

Interesting choice of words. Jerry didn't recognize Danny as his true president. Discord rumbled among the Wolves. It wouldn't be long until someone challenged the young pup.

"Alexander would have died of a broken heart at the shit his son's pulled." Pain cracked in his voice. "It's like he never existed. Everything he stood for wiped out when Danny took over."

By the minute, I became more convinced that Danny was behind everything. Smoked his dad to assume leadership. Set up his sister to take the fall. Started a war with us to expand his club and boost his pin-sized ego.

I held one elbow in my palm and leaned my chin on my other fist. "You think Danny iced the old man?"

Jerry shook his head and hung it. "I don't know anymore. Danny is capable of anything. I knew Alexander for forty years, and his son is certainly not a chip off the old chopping block."

If that was true, then we had to be ready for any retaliation.

"What do you want?" I asked. "Why are you telling me all this?"

Jerry stared me right in the eyes. "Because I want to defect."

***

When Doc Shriver gave us the okay, I had the men transport Aaliyah to the cell below our clubhouse. They set up a mattress for her in the cage, with medical supplies like an IV line, supplying antibiotics, fluids, and painkillers. Zethan, Castor, Alaric, and I were not to go down to see her, so I had a roster of other club members to deliver her meals and water.

I made this trip to get answers. My boots echoed the determined thump of my heart.

At my arrival, her eyes lightened with relief, and she wiggled to sit up and winced at the sting. Bandages circled her torso. Drip lines hanging from her wrists squirmed from her movement.

"Slade, you're okay!" Solace and reassurance streamed through the mate bond. Flames burned the entrance wound where she'd taken a bullet for me. The medication didn't dull all her pain.

I bit my cheek to bury the torment of it. She was the last person I wanted to be relieved for me. The last person I wanted to pity or comfort. I blocked the connection between us temporarily to prevent it weakening me.

"Was your intention to infiltrate and spy on us?" I kept it strictly business. No flirting. Nothing sexual. I had my club and men to think about and couldn't afford for my personal feelings to get in the way. Feelings influenced by the curse.

Feelings not belonging to me. Feelings I should never have acted on. I felt sick to my stomach for sinking my dick into this woman.

Regret and grief hammered me through the mate bond, despite me turning it down. It stung me, and I wavered on the edge of going to her, holding her, comforting her. This woman was very powerful to have that effect. Maybe more powerful than Liz.

I clenched my fists, blocking the assault of the mate bond. I wasn't giving in to it. "Don't pull that shit on me."

Her gaze hardened, like ice, cold and unbreakable. "You think I'm making up what comes through the link?"

"You lied to us," I growled. "You pretended to be someone you weren't. Why should I believe a word you say or an emotion you fake?"

"Everything conveyed through the mate bond is real." She winced at the pain of barking back at me.

My jackal scratched at my chest, begging me to go to her. I took a step toward her and stopped myself.

"The sentiment behind it ..." She hunched over, pinching her abdomen, sucking down deep breaths to relieve the burn in her body. I used all my self-control to remain rooted to the spot. "The fated mates curse thing, that's the only unreal thing about this situation. We wouldn't feel a thing if it wasn't for the magick."

Agreed. I wanted to be free of this fucking curse and her.

"What kind of woman lets her brother beat her up and send her here?"

Flames licked at the ice in her eyes, melting it. "I refused my brother's order. I don't belong to the Wolves. Haven't in almost seven years. I'm sure as hell not crazy or stupid enough to walk into the den of my enemy. You made that choice for me."

"Why didn't you admit who you were then?"

"You killed my father!" Spittle flew with every word. "You started this shit with Danny."

"Did I?"

"What's that supposed to mean?" Her eyes moistened, and my resolve softened. "I just want to know who killed my father. To put that man behind bars."

"I think I have a good idea who smoked your dad." I scratched at my beard. "When I find out, that man *will be* dead."

She rubbed at her arms. "Okay."

"Until then, you're staying here until we decide what to do with you."

"Locked up?" Her tone lifted an octave. "You can't keep me prisoner."

The wrath inside me returned, tearing at my insides, begging for release. "You don't get a say in this."

"Fuck, Slade." She slumped back on her pillows. "How long are you going to keep me here?"

As long as it took to win the war. A reckoning was coming, and there would be hell to pay. But I would not let the Wolves use Aaliyah as bait against us. She was our weakness, our kryptonite, and I'd not let myself or my men fall prey to that again. We needed our wits about us if we were to win. Danny Heller had just challenged four living gods and the most powerful motorcycle club in Australia. He had balls, I'd give him that. But he didn't have a chance in fucking hell.

As for Aaliyah, she was off-limits to us. We would not fall for her charms or be victim to the disaster the gods had laid at our doorstep. This woman was our penance. Our curse. Our mate. The mate bond could burn in hell. Soon, Castor would find the spell to break the tie between us, and then we'd have no limitations, nothing to use against us. The shriek of pain in my heart said otherwise, but I ignored that fucker, left the room, and the woman I let into my heart behind.

Enjoyed this novel? **Leave me a review on Amazon or Goodreads and let me know what you thought. Or send me an email at skylerandraauthor@gmail.com**

Keep reading **for an exclusive preview of the CAPTIVE OF THE GODS or grab it here.**

EXCLUSIVE PREVIEW OF CAPTIVE
OF THE GODS

Aaliyah - Chapter 4

I collapsed on the cot, emotionally spent from Slade's interrogation and being pushed over the edge with the phone call. If I wasn't injured, I'd have gone another round with Slade and still had energy for a third. He might be able to overpower me with strength but not will, and I had that in spades.

Darkness settled over the room as the sunlight waned. The wind hadn't eased up and whistled at the window jambs. Cold draped the room and I sank deeper under my blankets, my body starting to shiver. These wouldn't do and I would freeze down here.

My throat had dried from all the conversation and crying, and I leaned to the side to retrieve my bottle of water. Pain gripped my wound and I whimpered. Whatever post-op pain meds I was given had started to wear off. I glanced up at the drip connected to me, wondering if I should up the dosage. Without knowing what they put in there, I didn't touch it. I could do more harm than good. Frustrated, I finished the rest of my water and tossed the empty plastic bottle on the floor.

My accommodations lacked an adjoining bathroom. At some point I would need to use the facilities but I was still dehydrated from the blood loss, and my body retained what little water I supplied it. Did the Jackals expect me to piss on the floor?

Falling asleep wasn't a problem since I was exhausted. Staying asleep, on the other hand, proved damn near impossible with the constant throb in my abdomen. Normally, I slept on my side, curled up, hugging a pillow, but with the location of my injury, I was forced to lay on my back. Constant shifting failed to provide comfort.

Eyes closed, I prayed to the gods for grace and mercy. Isis answered by blessing me with a rush of healing energy. Warmth spread over my body, easing the pain, and soothing my mind.

Thank the goddess, I thought to myself, finally drifting off into a nightmare-plagued sleep.

The events of my injury replayed over in my dreams. In one, a demon chased me, capturing me, letting Danny shoot me. In another, Slade held me in front of my brother, and the bullets tore into me. In the third, I couldn't bear the pain of losing Slade, and I threw myself in front of him, taking the hit and protecting my Alpha. I woke with a start at the last one, covered in sweat.

Night bathed the room and silence clung to the late hour. Chilled to the bone yet shivering as my body fought infection, I clutched my blanket tighter. Dr. Shriver, the Jackal's medic, removed the bullet and patched me up. Roughly, might I add. The guy was a general practitioner not a surgeon, his wound care in need of some improvement, but he was the best I had on offer.

Something moved on the edge of the bed, and I gasped.

"It's just me." Castor's hand found my calf and squeezed.

Feeling vulnerable, I pulled the blanket over my chest, my body tensing. There could only be two reasons he visited my cell in the middle of the night. And in the dark. Slade had changed his mind and ordered me a grisly death, or he permitted his men to abuse me for their pleasure. I'd not let the Jackals do that. My mind went into overdrive with ways to defend myself and my muscles primed with what little strength I had.

"What ... what are you doing?" I stammered, reaching out across the mate bond for his emotion, finding a murkiness with a dull pulse of desire.

"Don't worry. I'm just here to deliver dinner and let you freshen up." Reassurance streamed down the mate bond. A single blast, no more. Castor shut himself off to me ever since the ambush. The harsh snap, like he'd broken his connection to our link, echoed in my mind whenever I looked at him. We were back to the old mystery.

Judging by the duller sensations coming from my other avatar mates, they'd done something similar. Although, I got more feeling from them, especially Slade, who lost hold on his emotions easily, sensations streaming through from him.

My eyes adjusted to the dimness, making out Castor's broad shape at the end of my cot. A candle flickered to life at my side, and I flinched then blinked, squinting until my eyes adjusted. The cell door hung wide open. Two more blankets rested at my feet, supporting two books. A tray rested on his lap, hosting two bottles of water, a plate of bacon and eggs, and a small bowl with a hand towel. The crispy, salty scent of bacon made my stomach rumble. Dinner. Better than the canned crap they'd previously provided. The hollow ache in my stomach suggested it had been a day or two since eating.

"I've blocked the mate bond with a little help from my magick." Castor sat on the edge of the bed, as handsome as ever. "Can't let you play mind tricks on me."

Darker, dominant and mysterious. Long, inky hair pulled back, scented with a wax that blended with his aftershave, an irresistible spice and cinnamon combination that lit up my senses. The pale light turned his maple eyes a deep, rich amber, almost supernatural in their vividness like a wolf shifter from a movie. He wished. Unlucky bastard got a lame-ass ibis shifter from his god.

Thank fuck he didn't want to rape me. For a moment there, I thought I'd have to use some moves to disarm him, then choke him with the IV line. Relief washed through my tight, sore body and I slumped into the pillow.

Goddess, he thought me a sly, clever manipulator who played him to gain the Jackal's secrets. Guilty as charged. Loyal, strong, independent, caring, honest, described my true identity. Anybody would change their behavior to survive this fucked-up situation. Anyone. And I dared him to prove me wrong.

I picked at the fuzz balls on my blanket unable to meet his gaze, demanding answers. "Castor, I know it looks bad. I was thrown into an impossible situation and did what I thought was best. That's not who I am."

He nodded, absorbing every word, contemplating them, the faintest hint of his analysis pumping through our link.

"I've laid everything bare now. No secrets or lies." My voice came out hoarse and strangled. "Maybe we can clean the slate and start again? Get to know each other?"

"I'll take that onboard." His grip on the tray tightened. No commitment. No indication of how he felt. Closed off to me. Blocked by a wall of steel warded with magick.

"Okay." I guess that was the best I could hope for from him.

His dark pink lips curled upward, chasing away the chill in my bones. "Is that how you'd make your escape? Knock me out with the IV line? No attempt at magick?" At least we hadn't lost the natural playfulness we had between us. "I'm disappointed in your cunning, dark sorceress."

Oh, goddess. The nickname and flirting. His deep, dark

voice, reaching cold places inside of me in desperate need of his fire. Syrupy warmth soaked into my muscles and made me giddy and soft. The spark was still there between us, even brighter despite him dialing back our connection.

My mind quickly recovered and returned to his question about how I'd escape. How the fuck did he know that? I thought emotion was transmitted along the mate bond, not thought or intentions. Fuck, I had to shield my thoughts like he did. Some things had to remain private between the five of us.

I changed the topic quickly. "What time is it?" I adjusted my back and wiped sweat from my forehead with the back of my hand.

"A little after seven." Castor passed the tray to me by shifting it across the blanket. Tempting, but another bodily function needed addressing.

"I ... ugh ... have to use the bathroom first." In the hospital, I wouldn't have batted an eyelid about a patient with a bedpan or taking them for their business, but with him, I suddenly went shy. And I'd never been shy with him.

"Umm." Castor's gaze flicked from me to the empty space in the cell opposite the cot and back again. At least he had the decency to look embarrassed. "The holding cells aren't really set up for long-term use."

I knew too well what went on within these walls. Beatings, interrogations, torture, and murder. Shivers ripped through me, and I clutched my blanket tighter. "Cells? As in plural?"

"We've had instances arise where we needed more than one." Castor shrugged my question off and set the tray he carried on the space beside him. "Jerry, Sonny and Tex are next door."

Uncle Jerry. I flung off my thin blanket and draped my

legs over the side of the cot. Dizziness hit and I sympathized with all surgery patients.

"Easy." Castor stopped me, catching me with both hands on my upper arms. Comforting warmth seeped into me, making me relax. The mate bond flared with a low, burning need. Mine. I detected a faint flicker of his reciprocal response. "Don't exert yourself."

"Is Jerry okay?" I didn't know the other two well. Met them a few times at Christmas and other holiday events.

"He's faring better than the other two." I closed my eyes at Castor's response. Translation—he'd beaten them to extract information.

Uneasiness gripped me and I groped for Castor's wrist, catching it, squeezing. "Did you hurt him?"

Strong as an ox at sixty years of age … like my father would have been if he had lived … Jerry was getting on. Palms burning, I let go of Castor, horrified that he'd hurt my uncle by name, but not by relation. He was family and we'd depended on each other. Jerry had been there for every Christmas, birthday and anniversary. A man I had the highest regard for and utmost love. The thought of Castor harming Jerry left me with an unbearable chest ache.

"I didn't need to." Castor dabbed at my forehead with the wet cloth. "He gave me everything I needed willingly. He also offered to defect."

Jerry was loyal as they came. For him to do that, things must be seriously bad in the Wolves.

"What?" I sighed. Fucking sighed from each gentle dab cooling my skin. "Jerry's the vice president."

"Not anymore." Castor cleaned all the sweat from my face and neck, leaving me burning for a completely different reason. "He was demoted and replaced for not supporting your brother's new politics."

Fuck. Danny had no loyalty or respect whatsoever. He

sounded more and more like a damn dictator with every fresh piece of information to my ears.

"I'll take you up to the bathroom, Aaliyah." Castor leaned into me, stoking the low burning fire between us, filling my senses with his overwhelming scent. "But first, I need you to promise me you aren't going to try to run."

I snorted. Like this? Haphazardly patched up by an unqualified doctor, aching, exhausted, weak and dizzy. News flash... I wouldn't get very far. About as far as some of the elderly patients got when they snuck out of their rooms to sneak a sweet treat because the hospital food tasted like shit. Two hundred feet max before I passed out.

"I'm a little disappointed that the avatar of knowledge and science doesn't know more about surgery, medicine and healing from gunshot wounds." It came out flirty and teasing. *Oh, well.* Too late to recall it now. "Because if you did, you'd know I'm not really feeling up to a marathon right now."

Through the mate bond, I sent him an image of me punching his arm, because I couldn't do it for real without hurting myself.

"I'm serious, dark sorceress." His voice thickened from my nickname. "Promise me you won't magick me and gangrene my dick."

Yeah, 'cause I was up for that too. I searched for my magick, but everything was dark, distant, and unable to grasp.

"Thanks for the tip. Didn't know I had that ability." I smiled, and he cursed under his breath. I lifted my hand in front of my chest, the absence of my magick troubling. "I can't feel her in the darkness."

"It's because the cell's warded." Castor scanned the ceiling then the iron bars and sigils glimmered, responding to his magick. "I had to stop you from getting out and hurting us."

I snorted at his joke, even though that troubled me.

"Probably won't be up for any gangrene attacks or smiting for a few days."

Be smart Aaliyah, my mind warned.

I know, I shouldn't have joked with him, not in such dire circumstances. But he brought it out in me, lightened and cleared my mind, giving me clarity. I didn't want to think about consequences with him. Couldn't a girl get a moment's peace? Away from my brother, my father's murder, my uncertain future, and the threat of the Jackals.

Castor's eyes darkened and his eyebrows scaled his forehead. He wanted me to promise him. Word to the avatar of Thoth was a sacred vow he valued above all else.

I let out an exasperated sigh because my bladder reached critical status and I wasn't up for playing games. "Castor, I promise I won't try to run or use magick on you." Goddess, he made me feel like a schoolgirl promising not to hit Mandy for stealing my *Play Doh*. "Now can you let me out before my bacon goes cold and my bladder bursts and I have to lie in my piss?" Flattering. But I had to get my point across and fast.

Castor seemed to have the most compassion and empathy toward my situation. He held the key, literally and figuratively to my freedom. All I had to do was convince him to let me out and let me go home.

"That's better." He stood up, closed the distance between us and lifted me into his arms. A dull heat banked between us. I'd missed being close to him, in his arms, his body pressed to mine. My lips tingled with the memory of his curious, exploratory and assertive kisses. But his next words killed all feeling in my body. "I'm on high alert with you, dark sorceress. One move and I will hurt you."

ABOUT THE AUTHOR

Never say never. That's Skyler's attitude, and she fills her heroines and heroes with that same philosophy. Skyler is an Aussie who loves traveling and her goal is to one day visit every country in the world. When she's not writing, she's snuggling with a good book and her furbabies. At heart she's a gaming nerd, Pilates and martial arts enthusiast.

SKYLER'S OTHER BOOKS

Are you curious to read the other novels by me?

MYTHOLOGY UNIVERSE (GODS)

OPERATION CUPID
Completed reverse harem mythology romance

1. Battlefield Love
2. Quicksilver Love
3. Awakened Love
3.5 Stupid Cupid - a Valentine's short story

OPERATION HADES
Completed fated mates romance

1. Lady of the Underworld
2. Lord of the Underworld
3. Rulers of the Underworld
4. Return to the Underworld

OPERATION ISIS - Jackal's Wrath MC
Reverse harem paranormal motorcycle club romance with shifters

0.5 Prophecy of the Gods - prequel exclusive to newsletter subscribers
1. Curse of the Gods

2. Captive of the Gods
3. Legacy of the Gods
4. Wrath of the Gods - coming 2022

BLOOD DEBT KINGPIN (Operation Anubis) Paranormal mafia arranged marriage romance.

0.5 Falling for the Mafia (prequel) - coming 2022
1. Married to the Mafia - coming 2022

More gods series planned! Stay tuned.

GUILD UNIVERSE - PARANORMAL ROMANCE

NIGHTFIRE ACADEMY (Guild of Shadows series) Adult paranormal academy reverse harem romance

1. Darkfire
2. Wildfire
3. Crossfire
3.5 Hearthfire - available by signing up to my newsletter http://eepurl.com/dCOqkb
4. Hellfire

GUILD OF SHADOWS Box Set (Books 1 - 4)

GUILD OF GUARDIANS
Paranormal reverse harem romance with m/m

0.5 Witch Hunt (prequel novella)
1. Life's a Witch
2. Hindsight's a Witch
3. Witch Please
4. Karma's a Witch

5. Son of a Witch - coming 2022

Fairytale Retellings:

WINTER QUEEN series (part of the Haven Realm Universe)
Heart of Frost - a Snow Queen retelling with snow leopards

DARK REFLECTIONS series (part of the Haven Realm Universe)
Born into Darkness - a Snow White retelling with panthers

STANDALONES

Charmed- an Aladdin retelling
Claimed- a Little Mermaid retelling

FALLEN STARLIGHTS - Shared World series
   Orion (Galaxy Huntress) Fallen Starlights series

STALKY STALK LINKS

Become a darkling and join my readers group Skyler's Den of Darkness for exclusive content, latest news, and giveaways.

Sign up to my newsletter here https://skylerandra.com/index.php/newslettersignup/

Stalk me on the Gram: skylerandraauthor

Give my Facebook Page a like https://www.facebook.com/Skyler-Andra-Author-324882698294312

Join my Street Team https://forms.gle/eqjhuSb7EJ42X7o67

Watch my videos on Tiktok skylerandraauthor

Check out my Youtube vids, including book trailers and me reading chapters or sample audiobook chapters: https://www.youtube.com/channel/UC-MQvzm8R8MQEWVX2xd4v2g

Follow me on Amazon for notifications on my latest releases https://www.amazon.com/Skyler-Andra/e/B00JQTFBRI

Follow me on Goodreads: https://www.goodreads.com/author/show/8170388.Skyler_Andra

Follow me on Bookbub: https://www.bookbub.com/profile/skyler-andra

Want to get free books? Join my ARC team and leave a review within 12 days to stay on the team and keep up to date with Advanced Reviewer Copies

https://docs.google.com/forms/d/1woqywzG41qzpaXxA4ul02QWSmNYtDs83wzDcAO--TgY/prefill

You're a true stalker if you're following me on all ;)